Also by Carrie Merrill

The Angel Blade Series
Angel Blade
Daemon
Archangel
Harbingers

Also by Carrie Merrill
The Key, the Outlaw, and the Treasure

Harbingers

Carrie Merrill

SOUL FIRE
PRESS

an imprint of
Christopher Matthews Publishing

Boston, Massachusetts

Harbingers

Editor: Jeremy Soldevilla
Cover design: Neil Noah

ISBN 978-1-945146-53-4
ebook ISBN 978-1-945146-54-1

Published by
Soul Fire Press

an imprint of
CHRISTOPHER MATTHEWS PUBLISHING

http://christopher matthewspub.com
Boston

Printed in the United States of America

To my parents, who probably thought their kids
were the embodiment of the Horsemen of the Apocalypse.

Acknowledgments

The entire *Angel Blade* series has been a work of passion and endurance. It turned out to be a roller-coaster of emotions and thoroughly enjoyable to write. I fell in love with the characters and the world. And it turns out that so many others did as well. But it wouldn't be that way without the people that helped make it what it was.

First and foremost, my family has helped me so much. My parents have helped mold and shape my writing and gave me the push to get it published. I thank my siblings for reading my works and giving me the feedback I needed.

Beta readers are invaluable, and I thank those that have helped this series get to this point.

This series would not be possible without my publisher, Jeremy Soldevilla. He believed in *Angel Blade* from the start and gave me the ability to bring it to the readers. It was made even more amazing with the cover art of Neil Noah.

And thanks to my fur-babies who were there for me when I got discouraged.

In the Beginning . . .

Harbingers is the fourth installment of the *Angel Blade* series, the dark story of Nikka Connors, who was dying of cancer until she became a seraph, a powerful being able to exorcise and destroy demons. After she saved Jason from possession by the demon Abaddon, he fought at her side against the demon horde that had infiltrated the government and planned a massive EMP explosion to disrupt life throughout the world. Nikka thought she had lost Gideon, her mentor and her first love, but instead learned that he now had the power of his alter-demon, Pazuzu, and led the forces of Hell toward an apocalyptic future.

After a fierce battle with Pazuzu, cherubim took Nikka from the earth, leaving Jason and Gideon alone to wander a desolate world in search for her with one final scrap of knowledge about her: that she was pregnant when she died. They found Amy and her son Dylan, who led them to the protected outpost of Garnet Falls, Oregon. Here, they discovered that Nikka had been sheltered and safe . . . and was now eight months pregnant without a memory of her previous life.

Now angels and demons alike searched for Nikka, hoping to learn the truth behind her pregnancy. When she is taken by the archangel Samael, who reveals he is the architect of her creation as the seraph, she learns that the forces of heaven and hell want her baby for the power it holds.

Angels and demons descend on her during her escape from Samael. With Amy, Jason, and Gideon at her aid, they seek shelter in a mausoleum where she gives birth to her baby and, in the process, dies of blood loss while Jason and Gideon keep the armies at bay. But Nikka returns just as Lucifer enters the fight, taking Jason captive. She must leave with Amy and Gideon and her baby in order to protect them and teleports them all away from the cemetery.

Part Eight

"Abashed the devil stood and felt how awful goodness is and saw
Virtue in her shape how lovely: and pined his loss."

— John Milton, *Paradise Lost*

CHAPTER 1
NIKKA

T he cry in the night rattled inside Nikka's chest and made her bolt upright from the comfort of the pillow. Darkness filled every corner of the room, and she held her breath. The sound came again, rhythmic and persistent, a noise much closer than the crashing tides outside the window. The sound of a baby's cry.

She stood from the bed and padded across the room until her fingers brushed the edges of the crib. The crying softened as soon as she touched his small chest and picked him up.

"Shhh."

The baby arched his head back to gaze at her through the dark as she held him close to her chest, shifting her hips back and forth until his whimpering eased.

"It's okay, Adam."

The child turned his eyes up to her, and, for only a second, Nikka saw the flash of orange-red, like hot coals in a furnace, burning behind his tiny pupils. Every time that happened, it made the breath catch in her throat. But the light blinked out and she gazed at his face as he calmed down, his lips curling toward her scent and searching for sustenance. At almost six months old, he fed for longer periods of time but also slept more. That still didn't make the dark of a moonless night easy to maneuver when there were no lights to turn on anymore.

After she settled into the chair beside the crib and the baby relaxed against her breast to feed, she rested her head back and listened to the rushing of the tide along the beach. The salty sea air drifted through the open window, and she closed her eyes.

The stiffness in her neck awoke her, and when she opened her eyes, the early morning light shone through the east-facing window. Adam had fallen asleep in her arms at some point. She stood, clutching him to her chest and then nestled him down into the crib. Without the weight of the baby, she now stood and arched her sore neck, her locks of blonde hair falling over her shoulders and down her back. Her shoulders tensed for a moment when the hair brushed against her back, the sensation still foreign after nearly two years with no hair and then suddenly a full head. She pulled it back into a tie since it always drifted into her eyes when the trade winds blew across the beach.

When she stepped out onto the deck, the humidity in the heavy morning air sank into her lungs despite the breeze, heralding another hot day on the coast of Belize.

"You're up early," Amy's voice said from the corner of the deck. Nikka's heart jumped into her throat.

Nikka settled onto the wooden bench beside her and stared out toward the coming sunrise as the ocean stretched out into a deepening blue slate on the horizon. She didn't want to stare, but the circles under Amy's eyes seemed darker this morning.

"Didn't sleep again?" Nikka said.

Amy shook her head. "Damn howler monkeys," she said with a fake smile. "They're getting closer every week."

Nikka nodded, not that she agreed with her. The monkeys were a loud nuisance and had only started to make their chatter heard in the last couple of months, probably because of no human interference in their jungle anymore. Soon they would be descending toward the village when they realized that no man would harass them. But the howlers weren't the real problem, and Nikka knew it, even if Amy didn't want to talk about it anymore.

Amy tucked her feet up on the chair under her and hugged her arms around her knees. This made her shorts look even looser on her than they probably were, but they were still too large for her ever-thinning physique.

Nikka leaned closer to her and placed her arm around Amy's shoulders, pulling her closer. "I understand."

Amy's small frame shuddered against her with the first tears that she had shed all week. "I just keep hoping that something will change. That we can find a way to go back."

"We will."

"We can't. Not while everyone is still looking for us. I still see Dylan's face when I close my eyes."

It grew harder to breathe as Nikka thought about that last night before they showed up in the jungles of Central America. The demons descended on them from one side, the angels on another. She had just given birth to Adam, and both Heaven and Hell wanted him for their own purpose. Something had transformed her that night, brought her back from the brink of death. Again. And now she felt the full-fledged archangel power flowing through her veins after she awoke. She had been able to keep them safe.

But not all of them.

Gideon had been wounded, and she was able to get to him, with Amy holding Adam. The power that she held had protected them long enough to hold their enemies at bay. Nikka understood Amy's sorrow. She recognized the sickening pull of closing her eyes because that was when she would see Jason. Over and over again, she replayed those last few moments before she had to leave him, with him in Belphagor's grasp and Lucifer at his back. He begged her to leave, to escape with the people she had with her and to leave him behind. And that's what she did.

Amy had stayed with her, had protected Adam that night. And doing so meant she had to go with them or remain behind and die at the hands of the demons. But that also meant that she had to leave her son behind in Garnet Falls, one of the last strongholds of humankind. Her only solace was that Dylan was with a community of caring people and soldiers that would take care of him in her absence.

But that did little to comfort her on mornings like this.

"We'll find a way," Nikka said and rested her head against Amy's.

"No, you can't. The moment you use your power, they will know. They will find us."

She wasn't wrong. Her power was a beacon to both the angels and the demons. The moment she used it, they would be swarmed. Samael still searched for her, and she could sense him sniffing around in her dreams at night. The angels wanted to kill Adam for what he was: a half-demon, half-seraph hybrid with unknown potential. And Lucifer wanted him for that same reason.

If they were going to return to find Dylan, they would have to do it on their own without any angel or demon power. And Belize was a hell of a long way from Garnet Falls, Oregon.

Amy leaned away from her, wiping the back of her hand against her cheeks and forcing a smile. "I'll be okay. Just a rough morning, that's all."

"You don't have to be okay, though."

She shook her head. "No. Really. I'll be fine. Now," she said and stood. "It's my turn for some laundry duty." She rubbed her damp hands on the front of her loose shorts and then stepped into the house without another word.

Nikka watched her leave, and she knew that Amy tried so hard to be stoic. She had to force herself to be the same way, because if she thought too much about leaving Jason behind in Lucifer's clutches, then her heart just might rupture.

As soon as the morning light broke over the surface of the water, Nikka returned to the house and decided that Amy wasn't doing the washing all by herself today. She gathered the things that she could and padded through the house toward the front door. The high arched roofs with their bronze-lined ceiling fans that hadn't worked in over a year rose over her like a chapel. The marble floors remained cool on her feet and would stay that way during the day, despite the heat and humidity.

She carried a bag of Adam's clothes, blankets, and cloth diapers through the vast main room and to the high-arching atrium. Every time she moved through here, she pictured the beautiful decadence that it once probably held. When the electricity had worked, she imagined that it looked like a beach-side palace complete with long swimming pools that now held only stagnant water. This entire neighborhood had once been a haven for the wealthy, and now it was a ghost town, except for Nikka, her son, and her two companions.

The atrium opened out to the granite and quartz walkway that wound to a central spring where Amy readied to wash the clothes for the day. She stepped her sandaled feet across the walk, gazing at the wide lawn of overgrown shrubs and palm trees, and she caught sight of the house next door. Its windows remained shuttered and dark, as usual for this time in the morning. They would not likely begin to show signs of life until Gideon decided to awaken when it got hot enough.

By the time she had arrived at the spring, Amy was already on her knees next to a metal basin of water and agitated the clothes with her hands until she had created enough suds.

"Hey," Amy said. "I said it was my day. You don't need to do any laundry today."

Nikka kneeled beside her with her bag of clothes. "I don't care what you said. Adam's still asleep, and I'm restless."

"Okay, fine."

The clothes spilled out over the stones as Nikka gathered another basin to add the rinse water. She poured bucket after bucket of the cold water into the basin. While she loaded the eighth bucket, her eyes drifted back up to Gideon's door.

"Did he stay by the fire long last night?" Amy asked.

Nikka averted her gaze and felt her cheeks grow hot. "Who? Gideon?"

"No. Bob from down the street," Amy said with a wink. "Of course, Gideon."

"I guess for a little while," she said and sat back on her heels while she accepted a handful of soapy clothes from Amy and rinsed them.

Her thoughts drifted back to the fire from the previous night. Every night had become a routine. With the large back yard behind the house where Nikka and Amy stayed, the extensive stone walkways stretched out to pools and fountains that surrounded a central fire pit designed for hosting parties. There, they were able to cook food and sit around the warmth of a fire as a group every night. Amy had recently been excusing herself earlier and earlier, leaving her and Gideon alone.

And, yes. Gideon stayed longer last night. But he played with Adam most of the time, and that was the best part. Gideon doted on him, and she wanted to allow him as much involvement as he could with him. After all, Adam was his child.

But she just wasn't quite ready for anything more than that. And so far, Gideon had never asked for more. He gave Nikka her own space, the most comfortable home in the area, and he stayed next door. For a while, Amy had her own place too, but her anxiety had caused enough trouble that Nikka insisted that she stay with her, saying that nobody needs to live in a seven-bedroom, three bath home with bronze fixtures and marble flooring all alone.

She worked on rinsing the soap out of the clothes, but Amy's eyes flashed toward her. "What?" she finally said.

"Oh, come on. I see the way he looks at you. He's like a puppy dog."

"It's not like that with us anymore. Not after . . . everything," Nikka said and looked away from her, losing her smile as she thought about the events that transpired to bring them here.

"I know," she said. "I think he just hopes that it will someday."

Nikka shook her head. She didn't want to talk about him anymore. She pulled the clothes from the rinse basin and wrung as much water as she could, sighing. "Ugh, I miss my mom's Maytag."

Amy laughed. "Don't get me started."

She wrung out one of her T-shirts and saw the thread-bare edges. "I also miss Old Navy. They had the best shirts."

"I miss hot water," Amy said. "And reality shows."

Nikka groaned. "Reality TV? You mean, like *Survivor*? Sister, you live it every day. You don't need to watch it."

"And dating apps. Can't really meet a nice guy these days," Amy said with a wide smile, and Nikka laughed.

"Too true," Nikka said and lifted the damp clothes into her arms. She stood, turning toward the make-shift clothesline they had erected months ago to dry the freshly washed clothes. Her eyes drifted toward Gideon's house again, and that's when she saw him.

He stood in the morning light, the orange dawn gold against the skin of his bare chest. His loose shorts hung low around his hips as he squinted into the light as though he had just awakened. The muscled curve of his chest that angled down to his mocha skin and toned stomach made the breath catch in her throat for only a second. His hazel eyes turned toward her, and he smiled, as though he had waited to see her after an endless night.

8

Chapter 2

Gideon

Every time Gideon looked at her, the flutters stirred. At first, they would just be little shivers that started deep in his chest, then they grew until his mouth was too dry to talk. And this morning was no different. She glanced at him, too, if only for a moment, and then she turned away and ducked back through the front door of the house.

The scent of the blooming trees danced across the threshold of the door where he stood, wondering if Nikka was going to come back out. There was no use just standing there, just like a stalker, as she would say to him. No. He was determined to do something different today, something that she would not expect.

Gideon stepped back into his quiet house, found a suitable T-shirt and slipped it over his head. He departed through his front door and down the steps toward the spring where Amy finished the last of the washing.

"Good morning," he said to her and dropped down to one knee beside the rinse basin.

Amy's green eyes turned up toward him, squinting into the flashes of sunlight that blinked through the leaves of the tree above them. "You're up earlier than usual."

His hands plunged into the cold water and stirred the remaining clothes around until the suds had dissipated. "There is much to do today."

"Oh, really?" she said and stood, her hands on the edge of the wash bin. She strained to lift the edge to dump the water, but her fingers slipped.

"Wait," he said and touched her hand. "You will hurt yourself."

She released the bin and stepped back as he crouched and lifted the edge of the basin with such little effort. The water spilled over the rim and dumped into the rocks along the spring. He then stooped and lifted the clothes out of the rinse bin and did the same to that water.

"You know," she said, "it really was supposed to be my day to do the laundry. How can it ever be just my turn if you guys keep helping me?"

The fabric twisted in his hands, and the water dripped around his feet. "That is what friends are meant to do." He smiled at her, the clothes hanging damp in his hands.

"She's back there," Amy said.

The flutters began in his chest again. "What do you mean?" That felt like the right thing to say. Best not to seem too eager.

Amy ticked her head back around the side of the house. "Nikka is back there, hanging up some clothes to dry. Looks like those need to be hung up too." Her eyes flashed down to the wet things in his hands.

It was not often that he understood the subtle hints that she tried to give him, but today was different. Or maybe she was not so subtle.

Her sandaled toe kicked at the rocks that lined the spring. "I've still got some stuff do to out here, so you probably should go back there and hang them up yourself."

His fingers tightened around a damp shirt as the flutters intensified. "Very well." He stepped around her as her eyes burned on him the entire time. One more glance back at her made his hands shake. Although she smiled at him, he saw the dark circles around her eyes, a sign of yet another sleepless night for her.

The floral fragrances of the trees drifted through the air, making his head light and dizzy as he stepped around the house and to the expansive back lawn dotted with trees. It was a perfect place to tie the heavy-duty ropes between the trees and create the clotheslines they had needed. The palm trees swayed in the gentle breeze, making the clothes dance along the lines.

And there she stood, her arms placing a white blanket on the rope, the skin of her arms and legs touched with the golden shade of six months in the Caribbean sun. White lines had formed over the tops of her feet where her sandals had protected her fair skin. The muscles in her calves contracted as she stood on her tip-toes to stretch the blanket further across the line, and her legs rose up to her khaki shorts. Long blonde hair cascaded down her back in platinum strands, something that he never got used to seeing.

He had not realized that he stopped to watch her, but then the chirp of a loud bird caught his attention, and he averted his gaze. Gideon stepped toward the line, and as soon as a twig crunched under his foot, she turned back to see him.

"Oh," she said with a gasp and turned back to the line. "You scared me."

"I did not mean to," he said, his fingers tight enough around the bundle in his hands that his knuckles had gone white. The desperation in his voice must have been too thick as she looked at him, her eyebrow raised.

"Not like scared," she said. "Just startled. That's all."

He nodded and smiled, but the flutters in his chest had begun to make him feel sick. For a moment, he was sure that she would just walk away and leave him. Had she not wanted him there beside her today? Her demeanor spoke volumes, as though she did not care that he stood there.

Nikka placed more onto the line and then glanced at him again. "You just going to hold them all day?"

Gideon squeezed his fingers around damp clothes. "No." He stepped up to the line and started to drape them one by one over the rope.

The moisture had vanished from his lips as he thought about the one thing he wanted to ask her today, the thing that would be unexpected and different. In over two millennia, he had never been so flustered to speak to another person as he was when he was around her. As much as he tried, the words just wouldn't come.

She finished draping the last of the blankets in her hands and stretched it out over the line. The breeze drifted through the edges of it, rippling out to tickle against her torso as she finished with it.

That was her last one. She would finish with it and then she would leave, and his chance gone with her.

Just as she turned to walk back to the house, he spun around to face her. "Nikka, wait."

She stopped and looked at him, but he glanced down to the grass at his feet.

"I wanted to ask you something," he said. *It should not be this difficult.*

"Okay."

"Uh . . .," he stammered for a moment. "I was just wondering if you would come fishing with me today. We have not had fresh fish in a while, and I could use some help."

She smiled, her blue eyes catching the sun and he witnessed the faintest hint of violet in her iris. "Sure. Why not."

The weight of the morning lifted off his shoulders. He released a breath. "Excellent."

"I'll just let Amy know. She can watch the baby," Nikka said and turned away from him.

There. It was done. Of course, he did not need help fishing. It was a trade that he had learned over two thousand years ago and he knew every way to catch the most fish. But they had been here for almost six months now, and he still had never gotten a chance to really talk to her alone. She said yes, and they could spend some time together, like back in the days when it was just the two of them, him teaching and training her. And then he had fallen in love with her. That was the end of things being normal. In his entire lifetime he had never loved anything as much as he loved her, but then he had held the baby in his arms for the first time. A thing that Nikka had created, despite everything that he had done. All the years prior to now had been meaningless compared to the moments he had with Nikka and the baby.

And maybe someday she would feel the same about him again, but memories and history were difficult things to change.

Chapter 3
Gideon

Gideon's heart pounded against his ribs when they walked away from the house, leaving Adam in Amy's arms for the morning. They strode from the walled neighborhood and out to the empty streets that wound down to the village. Much of the vegetation had begun to grow over the road without regular maintenance and care. The beach was not far, and the docks where Gideon kept the moored boat was just down from the village.

Nikka shielded the sun from her eyes as they walked down the dock to the boat, a small dinghy that the two of them could guide out onto the water. With the growing heat, she pulled her T-shirt over her head, revealing the blue bikini top that she wore.

Gideon tried not to stare, but he had never seen her wear anything like that. She and Amy had wandered through the empty village when they first arrived here, searching the tourist shops for anything useful. Naturally, they must have found some things that they had wanted. Nobody else would ever use them, like a blue bikini. He turned his eyes to the boat instead and stepped down into it, holding his hand out to help her in.

"Thanks," she said and grasped his hand, which made his tongue go dry again, but he still dared not to look at her.

"So, what is all this?" she said and sat on the bench opposite him as he lifted the oars and untied the mooring.

He looked up at her, his brow wrinkled. "Well, these are the oars—"

"No," she said, her elbows now resting on her knees. "That's not what I mean. Why are we really out here?"

The quivers started in his chest, and he leaned back in the seat as he dipped the oars in the water and pulled back, guiding the boat away from the dock. He wanted to look away from her, but she held him in her stare. "Fishing."

"Gideon, I swear, I will jump from this boat and swim back to the shore."

"All right," he said and tried to smile. He pulled the oars again as they glided out to the brilliant turquoise water of the bay. "I just wanted to spend some time with you. Just you."

"So, you want to know where we stand."

"I am not sure what that means."

She smiled and looked out to the water as the ocean breeze drifted a lock of hair across her eyes. "I forget. Metaphors are lost on you. It means you want to know if things are okay with us."

He nodded and continued to pull the oars. The boat dipped over the small crests of the tide that pulled in and out of shore. "Yes. But I really do want to fish as well."

Nikka laughed, and her blue eyes met his. As soon as she looked at him with the gentle curve of the lines around her eyes, he knew that she had relaxed. The agitation in his chest eased.

"Okay," she said. "You know, I've never fished in the ocean before. My grandpa taught me to fish in the river, though, so there's that."

"Perfect. That is a good start."

When he had guided them far enough from the shoreline and to an alcove, he dropped the anchor over the side and then lifted the seat box to delve into the fishing equipment. The thin threads of the net spilled over his hands as he pulled everything from the box and arranged them on the bottom of the boat.

"First, we need to find the right line," he said, his fingers sifting through the things strewn about the boat. She leaned in closer to him, looking over the things he described. The closer she got, the more he could smell the faintest hint of lavender in her hair, something that had hung about her since she had become part archangel. He forced himself to concentrate on the things he was telling her, but his ears heard nothing while he took in her scent, the fragrance of home and peace and contentment. She continued to nod at the instructions he gave her, even though he barely knew what he had just said.

Her fingers delved into the net next to his hand, and she lifted it. She pulled away from him long enough for him to clear his head, bringing him back to his present situation. Yes, the net. Fishing.

"Okay, now what?" she said, untangling the net as it draped over her bare legs.

He instructed her on the intricacies of casting the net, and within minutes, they both began using it, her hands wielding it just as he had told her. The minutes turned into an hour as she smiled with the haul they brought in, although it was not what he would normally be able to catch. It did not matter. Not when she was here to enjoy the day with him.

After the last drag of the net, they pulled it up and a fish caught in the net flicked its tail hard enough to jerk the line in Nikka's hands. A spray of water coated her face, and she gasped as she closed her eyes, laughing. The salt water dripped from her face as she tried to wipe it away only to have another spray hit her as the fish whipped its tail again.

Gideon smiled and pulled the remainder of the net in, letting a small laugh escape his throat as he watched her. Nikka's eyes opened when she saw him. With a wide smile, she stooped down and caught a handful of water from the edge of the boat. He saw it coming, but it was too late, and the splash of water shot from the palm of her hand and into his face. When she leaned down to do it again, he leaned over the side of the boat and took two handfuls of water, lifting them at her. A scream-laugh erupted from her throat, and he found himself in the full depths of a water fight with her.

For the first time in the last hour, he no longer felt the shaking in his arms or that his mouth was too dry to speak.

The next launch of water from her hands was a big one, and in his attempt to dodge out of the way, the boat leaned against the incoming tide. Before he could catch his balance, the wave slapped the boat again, and he was in the water. Another splash just after him told him that she had fallen in as well.

The muscles in his chest seized for a moment before he broke the surface of the water. He had not meant for her to fall in, and what if she had injured herself? He pushed himself to the surface and gasped for a breath as he glanced around for her. The boat pitched beside him, empty except for their haul. His hand grasped the edge of the boat and looked out at the blue waters that rippled around him.

Then bubbles brimmed to the surface, and she emerged. He held his breath, ready to help her in any way that he could, but her eyes widened, and she laughed.

"You did that on purpose," she said, slapping the water in front of him so that the spray would momentarily blind him.

"By God and this Earth, I swear I did not," he said, wiping the water from his eyes. His hand still clutched the side of the boat, and he almost held out his other hand to help her back in, but she kicked away and swam into the tide.

"This feels so good," she said and dunked the back of her head into the water, pulling the hair away from her face. "It's been way too hot lately."

"So, you are okay?" he said, squinting into the sunlight that sparkled over the water.

"Oh yeah. I need a swim."

She curled under the surface and swam into the calm waters of the alcove. The boat stayed anchored as he swam with her, minutes drifting into an hour. They dove under the waves together, skimming just above the coral and the rock that teemed with schools of colorful fish.

And for only a second when they were down there, she took his hand. Maybe it was to steady herself against a wave, but he hoped that it was something else.

The daylight moved further across the sky, and it was time to climb back into the boat again. Nikka lay across the front seat as he rowed back to the dock. The walk through the village was quiet as they carried the buckets of various fish and shrimp back to the house, but those nervous flutters stayed away this time.

As the house came into view, Nikka slowed her pace. "Hey," she said and caught his attention. "Thanks. I needed that today."

He smiled. "Of course. You know, give an archangel a fish, you feed her for a day. Teach her to fish, and she feeds herself for a lifetime."

She laughed, the curve of her mouth soft. "You know, you're funny when you try. I've always loved that about you."

His mouth went dry again. The smile must have slipped from his lips.

The laugh lines disappeared from around her eyes as well. "I think we're okay." She looked down at the dirt road under her feet. "It takes time to heal. And I'll be there someday, I promise. You love Adam, I see that, and you're so good with him."

Of course, he loved Adam, but maybe she did not see what had tormented him for the last six months, and even longer before they came here. Every day he remembered what had happened, what he did to her. Every day he wondered if she could ever forgive him if she could ever love him again. Would she ever see that he still loved her too?

"We are okay," he said back to her and then turned away, carrying their dinner to the house.

Chapter 4
Nikka

---

*T*he fire crackled, sending pinpoint sparks ascending into the darkening night. The fish and shrimp tasted great, but after the day's events and too much sunshine, Nikka was tired. Adam was bright-eyed, giggling as he watched her smile at him from where he lay back against her thighs. No matter how fatigued she was, his smiles always made things better.

Gideon settled into the long beach chair next to her, the firelight orange against his skin. "May I?" he said and nodded his head to Adam.

Nikka smiled at him. "Of course." She handed the baby to him and watched his eyes soften as the child looked at him. Gideon nestled him into the crook of his elbow, stood and walked around. Adam gazed at everything with interest. They wandered in and out of the firelight as Gideon spoke to him in hushed tones, pointing at the leaves on the trees and the fruit that hung in the branches, to the rocks around the perimeter of the lawn and the bats that squeaked overhead.

Every time she watched him interact with his child, she saw the soul within Gideon glow with a faint light just above the surface of his skin. Amy would never be able to see it, not with her human eyes. Sometimes it shimmered, and at other times it was just a soft, steady white light just like it was tonight. Gideon probably never noticed, and she hadn't told him that she could see it. But it was there, just like it was out on the water today. Whenever he got nervous to speak to her, there it was. That was when it undulated and sometimes turned different colors of blue or purple. It didn't matter what color it was, though. He was learning to use it well, even if he didn't realize it.

And because of that light, there was no sign of Pazuzu. He stayed locked away where Gideon wanted him.

She rested her head back against the beach chair and stretched her legs out as a burst of sparks popped within the fire pit. The fatigue drifted around her, and her eyes threatened to close for the night.

"He's really good with him," Amy said from the chair next to her.

Nikka turned her head to look at her, seeing the circles even darker under her eyes.

"Dylan's father was nothing like that," she said and glanced down at her fingers where she picked at her nails. "After he was born, he just left. Haven't heard from him since the week after Dylan was born. He didn't really want kids. It was sort of an accident."

"I'm sorry," Nikka said.

Amy smirked. "Don't be sorry. That was the best thing he could have done. Dylan and I made it on our own. It's just, every once in a while, it would have been nice if someone would have cared. And then I met Gideon and Jason."

There it was. His name, the one that Nikka hadn't spoken since the day they appeared in Central America. The sound of it made her throat tighten.

"They showed up, and they actually cared. Dylan loved him, called Jason a superhero." She smiled and looked back to the fire.

Tears flooded Nikka's eyes, making the firelight dance in waves. When she wiped the tears from her eyes, she found Gideon standing beside her with the baby in his arms.

"Is everything all right?" he said, handing Adam into her arms.

She forced a smile and wiped the back of her hand across the moisture on her cheek. "Yeah. Just tired, that's all." With the baby settled against her, she stood from the chair and slid around Gideon's side. "I think I'm going to call it night."

The pressure of Gideon's eyes stayed on her back, but she couldn't deal with both of them right now. After Amy had mentioned his name, it brought the weight of everything crashing down on her shoulders, and if she stayed, she would only cry until she couldn't stop. She slipped into her bedroom and closed the door.

Adam must have been tired because he didn't fuss after she placed him in his crib. Thankfully, he chewed on his fist for a few minutes before falling asleep, which allowed her to lay back in bed and gaze out over the open bay window. The sound of the crashing waves pounding on the shore had a way of calming her nerves on nights like this, but the tears continued to fall to the pillow under her head. The moonless night didn't allow much light into the room, leaving her bed plunged into darkness as she lay there alone and thinking about Jason.

It's okay. You'll be okay.

She heard him say it, the words repeating every night just before she fell asleep. They were the last things Jason had ever said to her as he had encouraged her to take the chance and go. It was the only way to save the rest of them. But that didn't take away the sting of seeing him there at Belphagor's hands and Lucifer beside him.

She had left him behind at the mercy of Hell's army.

It's okay.

As much as she wanted to know what happened to him, any use of her power would be too dangerous. Sure. At any moment she could just ignite her archangel power and whisk them all back to Oregon. To the last place where she saw Jason. To Garnet Falls, where Amy's son waited for her. But the instant she did that, angels and demons would descend upon them. In Belize they were safe, their own little Witness Protection Program. It had been six months since they had seen a demon or even another person for that matter.

And it would be stupid to risk it all just to alleviate their grief.

She closed her eyes and let the tears fall, seeing his beautiful face in her memories. Those blue eyes and the lanky blonde hair. His goatee that accented the dimples when he smiled. She never wanted to forget.

A ribbon of cold, moist air tickled against the skin of her neck, almost a relief from the oppressive heat and humidity of the night. She thought it was just a short breeze through the window.

And then it tightened around her neck.

Nikka's eyes opened as something threaded around her throat. At first, she only saw darkness, and then the ribbon tightened, closing off the air from her lungs. Two red fiery eyes stared down at her from an abyss of black that hovered over her body. The beast pulled her toward itself as its face materialized through the dark, its teeth like rows of sharpened, fragmented glass. Her fingers clutched at the tentacle around her neck, gasping for air that wouldn't come.

The creature's mouth gaped wide in an angry grimace, its eyes boring down on her. The tentacle pulled her up, and her head lifted from the pillow. A frosty chill settled over her body as she rose from the bed, levitating toward the beast that hovered above her. More of its arms threaded around her and entwined her limbs. The beast's breath drifted down across her chest in a sickening aroma of rot and death. Her fingers clutched with a frantic trembling, and her brain grew dizzy.

"Yes," the beast said, its voice reverberating against the walls. "Use your power. Destroy me."

Her lips parted in a desperate gasp. The chill that came from the creature surrounded her from where she now hovered above the bed.

"I will gut your boy," it said with a growl. "And you will never be able to stop me. You belong at my side, and I will find you."

The heat first started in her chest, behind the tattoo that the angel had given her so long ago. With every second that she couldn't breathe, the heat warped and shuddered. The creature knew how to manipulate it and pull it from her. She tried to gasp for air again when her eyelids shot open, and a violet light filled her pupils.

"That's it." The beast pulled her closer. "Show me what you're made of."

Her fingers pulled at the tentacle around her throat, and her fingers found just enough purchase to leave a gap. It was enough to suck in a breath, and enough to speak to the monster above her.

"Never," she said and blinked out the violet light in her eyes.

Nikka bolted upright in bed, stifling the scream that had burned within her chest. Cold sweat trickled down her temples and soaked through her thin T-shirt. The space around her was dark, but it was no longer the inky black void that hid the most terrible of evils.

Lucifer.

The Devil himself had come to her. Again.

It wasn't every night, but it was often enough that it began to fray at her nerves. If Gideon knew about the persistent visions, he would panic and try to do something stupid. For now, it was her secret. Lucifer could try his best to scare her, but she had the advantage of camouflage in the jungle of Belize. He continued to plague her dreams because he didn't know where they were. After the first few tries, she recognized it for what it was: the Devil's best attempt to get her to reveal her location.

But that didn't make them any less disturbing. Every time she awoke from the vision, she could feel the lingering chill in the air, no matter how hot the night was. The sickening prickles on her skin from where he would touch her made her want to jump into the ocean and wash clean.

She took in a deep breath and stood from the bed, no longer able to sleep with the jitters of the vision still hanging in her mind. The raw tightness still wrapped around her throat and she wasn't sure whether it was the memory of the thing tightening on her neck or from a scream in her sleep. Her nervous fingers stiffened as she opened her door and peered down the hall to Amy's room. If she had screamed, she hoped that her housemate hadn't heard it. She didn't want to explain to her that she still had nightmares about the things that had happened six months ago.

No candle or flashlight emitted from under her door, but she heard the muffled sounds of Amy in her room. She thought it was only the noise of restless sleep, but she listened closer and heard the faint tones of crying. Nikka bit her lip. As much as she wanted to console Amy, she had done it before in the middle of the night and only made things worse. Amy didn't want help from her, just like Nikka didn't want to share her nightmares. She shut the door and quieted the sounds from Amy's room.

Something else needed to occupy her thoughts. The top drawer of the dresser pulled open quiet enough not to wake up the baby. She lit the candles that she kept stored there, the yellow light chasing away the remaining shadows that dwelled in the corners of the room. The tools and paper were still in the drawer, right where she had left them.

There were some things of the old world that she tried to hold onto, and to find such things even in the villages of Belize was a surprise to her. It had been one of her first scouts into the abandoned tourist docks where she found them: paper, graphite, drawing pencils. And not just the kind you find at your local grocery store. These were the quality artist-level things, and the same brand she had learned to use. Each time she had gone back, she filled her backpack with more pads of paper and pencils until she had taken all that was left.

And it was nights like this when she needed them most.

She nestled against the wall at the foot of Adam's bed and rested the pad against her knees as she opened it. Pages of her drawings still looked back at her. Faces of the past, each drawn to the best of her memory. Her mom and dad. Her best friend from high school. The nurse that cared for her at the hospital. Andy Wolfe and Megan Cavanaugh, the FBI agents that had died to help her. Only pencil drawings, because she had no photos to remember them. That world had disappeared when the lights went out, the world where every mundane memory was kept on a mobile phone or a laptop, and now none of those things worked anymore.

She opened the tablet to a blank page, and her hand grasped the pencil. As though they moved on autopilot, her fingers glided over the page. At first, it was just the outline of a face, a figure. Her years of practice from childhood took control, bringing in the detail through the simple line drawings and circles. The candlelight danced over the paper, letting her see enough of the drawing to keep going.

It was the only way to remember, the only way to ward off the darkness.

CHAPTER 5
NIKKA

A lthough Nikka had been awake for hours by the time the sun rose, she couldn't rest. Not until her hands were done. And with the rising sun, Amy and even Gideon would come looking for her if she stayed in her room.

She collected her things into a backpack, encircled a sleepy Adam into a wrap that kept him close to her chest and headed out the door.

On mornings like this, the air was cool and pleasant with the light breeze that came off the water. She strolled to the beach and kicked off her sandals.

Adam cooed and clicked his tongue as she spread out a blanket on the white sand and sat down.

"Look at you," she said and gazed into his big eyes that now looked at her. "Are you happy to be out of there for a while?"

He smiled at her as she lifted him out of the wrap and placed him down on the blanket. His chubby legs kicked with the freedom of the open air.

"Yeah, me too." She withdrew her paper and pencils and started back where she had left off.

The morning light allowed her to see the lines better, the curves that needed shading and the edges that should be smoother. The picture came together, just as she had remembered it.

It was as though she could feel the cool mountain air around her again as she looked at the page. There he stood, Jason with his long legs and broad shoulders, leaning back against the wall of the cabin, his head tilted slightly to the left, and only the hint of a smile on his face. The flannel shirt hung around his torso just right, and his jeans ruffled around the clunky black boots he liked to wear. Those days in his grandfather's cabin were perfect, as short-lived as they were.

Perfect. That was how she chose to remember him.

"You're up early," Gideon's voice sounded behind her, startling her and sending the tip of her pencil off the lines in the background of her picture.

She clutched the pencil tight and glanced back at him as he trudged his bare feet through the sand. "Yeah. Couldn't sleep."

"Were you fussy last night?" he said as he looked at Adam and kneeled to tickle his belly. The baby giggled, his eyes growing wide and curious as he looked at Gideon.

Nikka nodded, but she could never tell him the truth about last night. "Why are you awake? You're never up this early. Isn't it against your code of ethics lately?"

He smiled at her. "Just unable to sleep well last night."

"Must be contagious."

His brow furrowed. "Amy was awake too?"

"Heard her crying again last night, and I think she went out shooting again yesterday. The guns were all stacked in the garage yesterday morning. She's not coping so well."

"And are you coping?" he said, his eyes flashing down to the drawing in her lap.

Her cheeks flushed. Back when she would practice drawing her comic book art, she never felt embarrassed to show them to anybody, but these pictures where like her own diary. Not the forms of superheroes. These sketches were people she had known and loved. She hadn't expected Gideon to come find her or to see them.

"I think so," she said, but her voice dropped, and she looked away from him.

"It is very good. I have never seen you draw before." He sidled closer to her, his finger touching the page. "This is not how I remember him, though. He was always swearing at me or working on the truck. Always seemed to be dirty."

He nudged her, and it eased the tension in her brow. She smiled and gazed at the picture. "I remember that too."

"You loved him."

This was not the conversation she wanted to have with Gideon this morning. "I still do."

"I understand," he said and pulled away from her, his eyes drifting over the horizon. For a moment he became quiet, and his spine stiffened. Then he leaned over the baby, which made Adam coo again. "May I walk with him?"

"Of course."

As Gideon stood with the baby in his arms, she looked up at him. "You know, you don't always have to ask me to spend time with him."

"I do, and I will, as long as you care for him." He turned away from her and wandered over the sand, toward the shoreline where the water lapped at his feet.

She watched them step along the water's edge, Gideon's strong shoulders holding the baby up in the air until he giggled. A broad smile slipped across Gideon's lips as he played with his son.

I can't keep doing this alone, she thought. Every night she had the dreams, they became more difficult to manage. They had been out here for six months already, and heaven knows how much longer they will have.

She glanced down at the drawing, Jason's face just starting to become defined with the graphite lines. No more, not today. She folded the pad closed and clutched it to her chest.

The fire crackled with aggressive light as Gideon stoked it with the poker and then settled back down on his beach chair beside Nikka, who lay across a blanket with Adam at her side. Amy sat on the other side of the fire, her green eyes staring into the light.

The baby began to quiet down, his head turned as he stared at his mother in the light of the fire. She tickled her fingers across his cheek, humming a song that she remembered from her childhood.

"Did you have enough to eat?" Gideon asked Amy, who remained quiet from where she sat.

"Yeah, I'm fine," she said but didn't look at him.

Nikka had watched her pick through the fruit and some of the tomatoes that she had cut from the garden just that morning. Sure, there wasn't any fresh fish today, but it was something, and it was good. Amy had probably eaten only a few bites, as usual.

Adam's eyes drifted closed as she touched his cheek. She gathered him into her arms and moved to stand when Gideon got to his feet.

"May I put him to bed?" he said.

It was something he had never asked before. Usually, at night he lingered with her at the fire until she put the baby to bed and then he went to his own place. Maybe tonight he had enough courage to ask more of her.

"Sure," she said and handed the baby to him. He held the child close to his chest, Adam's head tucked just under his chin, as he walked back to the house.

When he had disappeared into the back door, Amy spoke. "He would jump in front of a train for you. If we still had trains, I mean."

Nikka turned to look at her. "I know."

"And he would do anything for that kid."

"I know."

"Then maybe you should let him know that. I've seen his suffering for a long time, way back before we found you."

Nikka glanced back to the darkened doorway where Gideon had just disappeared with the baby.

"Go," Amy said, and Nikka turned to face her again, at the dark circles under her eyes. "Don't worry about me. I'll take care of the fire."

Nikka smiled and stood, the fire casting her shadow long across the lawn. She stepped toward the door and entered the quiet of the house. Candlelight flickered through the doorway of her bedroom, where she heard Gideon's whispers as he spoke to Adam. A swell of quivering nerves perked in her stomach.

"I love you," he said. "And I love your mother. Forever and ever."

She peered around the doorway and watched him as he continued to whisper, leaning over the edge of the crib. The moment he saw her, he stood straighter, and he stopped speaking, his lips tight and his gaze dropped to the corner of the room.

"Sorry to interrupt," she said, stepping around to the edge of the crib. "I was just checking to see if you needed help with him."

"He seems to have fallen asleep already," he said and took a few steps away from the crib.

Nikka glanced down at the baby, his eyes closed and breathing evenly in slumber. She leaned over the edge and touched his face, but he didn't stir. "Looks like you did a great job. You didn't need me after all."

"We always need you," he muttered.

She straightened, the nerves tickling in her gut. But as she moved to turn, she bumped into him. He must have stood so close behind her, quiet and listening.

"Sorry," he said and tried to step away. Nikka reacted before she could have a second thought about it. She turned and grasped his wrist before he could pull away from her. His muscles went rigid at first, but she wasn't about to let him go because his nerves got to him. She pulled him closer and wrapped his arm around her torso.

It only took a second, and he embraced her with both arms, as though he had been starving for years and she finally brought the hope of nourishment. He rested his head against her shoulder as he held her from behind, melting against her. Nikka closed her eyes, her fingers holding onto the bonds of his arms. And for the first moment, since she had lost him to Pazuzu, she felt safe with him. He had held her like this only one other time, and that was the night in the old monastery when he first said that he loved her. That had been the most difficult thing he had ever done in his millennia of walking the earth.

His breath quickened against the skin of her shoulder. She turned in his grasp, and he loosened his arms, ready to step away again. Her hands found the curve of his jaw in the dim candlelight of the room, and she kissed him, and it was as gentle as the first time he had ever kissed her. He closed his eyes, but she could still feel his apprehension, even though his lips moved in time with hers.

Then he stiffened and pulled back, his hands against her shoulders like she was a thing to avoid. When she opened her eyes, she saw the grimace on his face.

"I cannot do this," he said. "I must go."

He stepped back from her and moved to the door, but she caught his wrist. "Wait. Please don't go." She wasn't sure at first why she wanted to stop him. Perhaps it had been the memory of the nightmare or being alone at night in the jungles of Belize long before the nightmares had started.

But she knew that wasn't the only reason.

"I must leave now." He turned his face away from her as though it was too painful to look.

"Why?"

"Because," he said and turned to face her, his face drawn in pain. "If I do not leave now, I will not be able to later."

Her grip on his wrist tightened. "I don't want you to go, now or later."

If he left right now, she was sure that she would just shatter into a million pieces and never want to come out of the house again. But his hazel eyes looked at her for a moment, reading the desperation in her face.

When he turned back to her, it was quick and unexpected. He rushed up to her, taking her face in his hands and kissing her hard enough to take her breath away.

Six months she had been with him in this place, and he had been almost afraid to look at her or even talk to her, and she remembered why. There was a lot to forgive, but she also understood it, and she had forgiven him the moment she restored his soul and gave him Redemption. The way he held her now and moved with her toward the bed was firm but careful, no longer the inexperienced novice like he was on the first night they had ever spent together. But he didn't dominate her either, although she had worried about that when he took her in his arms.

The candlelight burned out as they found each other, but in that dark, for only a moment, his pupils flashed red. With the weight of him on top of her, he turned away and closed his eyes, fighting to control the impulse that Pazuzu carried in his soul. She placed her fingers on his face and turned him to look down at her.

"It's okay," she whispered to him. "Don't fear it."

He opened his eyes, the pupils still burning red. As she looked at him, she allowed just enough of her control slip and let the violet light illuminate within her eyes. Breathless, she pulled him down to kiss her again, matching the power that he tried so desperately to control.

And when the whirlwind of it all had settled, he fell asleep next to her. She held his arm that draped over her bare torso as though this moment would dissipate into just another dream. He was real and here with her now, not something that could vanish once she blinked her eyes. She rested her head against his shoulder, and he shifted in his sleep to cradle her against his chest. Her fingers touched the bare skin of his torso, and she found the raised scar along his ribs, the wound the angels had inflicted on him just before she was able to create their escape. He had fought hard that night and nearly lost his life for her and the baby. And, just as Amy had suggested, he would do it again if he had to.

Perhaps with him here, the dark visions would stay away, for she had her own demon to ward them off.

CHAPTER 6
AMY

Nobody had seen Amy slip the knife into the waistband of her shorts. Nikka had cut up the fruit and vegetables for dinner and just left it lying there, forgotten. At first, Amy wasn't sure why she did it, but as the night grew darker and quieter, she had some idea how she could use it. As soon as Nikka followed Gideon into the house, it would be a while before she would see them again.

The trembling first started in her hands and then worked up into her spine like it usually did when she thought about the distance between Belize and Garnet Falls. Her feet walked without much guidance from her brain, numb and transfixed, as she moved out of the yard and toward the beach. The streets had dipped into such darkness with the night that she had difficulty making out the horizon. A grumbling, aching hole had started in her stomach, something that gnawed at her ever since they had arrived here, and now it gaped open so far that she could feel herself falling into it.

She stumbled across the sand and dropped to her knees as the tears flowed down her cheeks. The swish of the crashing waves drowned out most of the weeping sounds that came from her throat. Her fingers found the handle of the knife, and she pulled it free from her waistband as she sat back on her heels.

"Why can't you hear me, God?" she cried out into the night, her eyes searching the blanket of stars overhead. Her fingers tightened around the knife, knuckles white. The blade's edge touched the tender flesh of her inner wrist as her hand trembled.

Just one slice, quick and clean. That's all it would take and then her pain would be over. Nikka and Gideon would be better off without her. She was only in their way.

She held her breath and felt the pressure of the razor-sharp blade against her skin. A thin ribbon of crimson dripped from the closest edge.

One cut and she could finally have peace.

So why would her hand not move? She only held it in place, the knife shaking against her skin.

Then her fingers opened, and the knife dropped into the sand at her knees. Her shoulders slumped with the sobs that caught in her throat. Even this she couldn't do. She couldn't find her son. She couldn't escape the jungle. And now she couldn't slip away into the dark and end it.

Why can't I just do it?

Because you're weak.

I'm too weak to fade away.

It doesn't have to be this way.

There's no way out if I can't even do this.

The little voice in her thoughts stayed quiet, feeding her no more useful information. Her fingers searched in the sand for the knife, but this time she knew she couldn't put it on her wrist again. She didn't have the fortitude to follow through anymore. The old and trusted way would have to do.

She lifted the edge of her shirt and exposed her abdomen, at the patch of repeating horizontal lines along her skin. Each line represented the anguish that she could never speak. The blade touched her skin below the previous line, the one she had made last night, and she pressed it into her flesh. The bite of the knife in her skin sharpened her thoughts and pulled the sting of the tears from her eyes. One cut wouldn't do, not tonight. The blade dropped another centimeter lower and sliced into the skin again in an even parallel to the line above it.

The only thing that makes it feel better, she thought.

There is always another option.

I've tried, more than once. This is my only release.

Not the only one. I can always show you the way.

How can you help me when God won't even answer me?

God doesn't care. Only I can bring you peace. You only have to say yes.

And what peace can you bring?

Clarity. Strength. And I can help you find your boy.

Her thoughts played dangerous games with her tonight, almost as though she could hear them whispering in her ear. But it was just a trick sound among the waves that echoed along the sand or the swaying of the palm trees in the wind that had picked up along the shoreline. She glanced back up to the stars, but the twinkling lights above blinked in and out from the thickening clouds that drifted in from the ocean. The wind picked up a spray from the incoming tide, and it coated the bare skin of her arms.

My boy is gone.

You don't know that. Tell me what you want, and I can help you.

She swallowed the lump that had formed in her throat, tasting the sea spray that had landed on her lips. There was only one thing she wanted in this half-life that she had left.

I want to leave this place and find Dylan. I need to know that he's safe.

I will give you that knowledge. You only need to let me in, and I will help you.

The seductive thoughts pulled at her insides, making the gaping hole in her gut widen with each second that she imagined if it were true. If she could know the fate of her own child. If she could leave here at the snap of her fingers, just like Nikka could with her archangel powers. She imagined what it would feel like to be there in an instant with her son. What if she gave in to that thinking and rested back into the sand, imagining that she was lying beside Dylan and singing him a bedtime song?

Yes. I want it.

Your wish is granted.

The cold entered her body in a powerful jet, leaving a stabbing pain in the back of her head. She gasped as it took hold of her chest, sucking the air from her lungs in a great vacuum. She thought that she had been shot or that the knife had somehow made its way into her heart, the pain was so great. Any visible light around her dimmed, plunging her into a cavity of sorrow and fear, a place much worse than the one she had left behind.

And only too late did she realize that she no longer had control of her body as she rose to her feet and walked back through the village and toward the house. That little voice in her thoughts had taken over, and now she was only a passenger, hearing all of its twitching and grotesque thoughts that took root inside her brain.

CHAPTER 7

NIKKA

T hings last night had commenced on autopilot, not planned in any way. But it also felt right.

When Nikka opened her eyes, the morning sunlight flowed through the windows. It had been so long since she had slept in this late. At first, she thought that everything that had happened was only a dream, one that she had replayed in so many different ways. But then she turned her head, and he was there. His hazel eyes watched her from where his head rested on the pillow like he had been watching her for hours. Even through the increasing warmth of the coming day, she could feel his body heat under the thin sheet that covered her.

She blinked her eyes clear a few times and reached her hand across the narrow space between them, touching his bare shoulder. This was real. He was here and embodied the Gideon that she had always remembered.

He smiled. "Are you okay?"

That question held more weight than just her status at the moment. "Yeah, I'm good. No, I'm better than that."

For only a second last night in the dark of the room, she had seen his eyes change. That had threatened to cause a cascade of terrifying memories that wanted to freeze her body and leave her in a shaking heap of anxiety. But she didn't let it overcome her. She held her power close to her heart, seeing only through the eyes of an archangel, and she connected with him for the first time since she had known him.

There was no need for him to fight the urge of the demon because her power recognized and harnessed it into control. It obeyed her now, moving in rhythm with the frequency of her own power, as though they had only been separated in time and space until that moment. The demon would never again control Gideon without his consent.

His fingers curled around her hand at his shoulder, and he leaned in closer toward her. Just as his lips were about to brush hers, the willowy cry of a baby sounded from across the room.

He stopped, his gazed drifted to the edge of the crib. Nikka let out a sigh. Of course, this would happen right now.

"Sorry," she whispered and lifted up on her elbows.

Gideon moved faster than she did, though, and was up on his hands and knees over her, straddling her over the sheet. "Stay right there," he said with a smile and leaned over to kiss her. "I have not had the chance to care for him in the morning. If I may . . ."

"Be my guest," she said and watched a wide smile form on his lips. He jumped from the bed with far too much energy after the activities of last night. She propped herself on her elbows and watched him lean over the edge of the crib, knowing full well that Adam wanted to be fed and there was nothing Gideon could do about that. But she watched him anyway, the way he picked up the baby with such care and caution. Despite Gideon's best attempt at soothing him, Adam continued to cry until his face was red. It wouldn't be long before his eyes would start to glow.

Gideon flashed her a concerned glance as he held the baby, rocking him back and forth. "I am not sure what to do at this point."

She smiled. "It's okay. Most people don't have the equipment for the job."

His brow furrowed. "I do not understand."

With her two index fingers, she pointed to her chest that remained concealed under the sheet. "He's hungry."

For maybe the first time ever, she saw Gideon blush. "I see." He walked around the edge of the bed and held out the crying baby to her.

He must have never seen a woman breastfeed before, or he had always turned away. But this time, he watched with fascination. Adam had gone quiet as he fed, his eyes half-closed. Gideon settled back onto the bed beside her.

"Truly a miracle in so many ways," he said. His hand reached out to touch the baby's foot, caressing the ends of his little toes.

"A miracle, yes, until you have to change his diaper," Nikka said with a smile.

"Gladly," he said and rested his head back on the pillow.

Gideon seemed just as interested in learning how to hold Adam after feeding and help to relieve the air in his stomach. This allowed Nikka time to be able to wash up and dress, which was something that usually took so long every morning when she had to do all of this herself. And if Gideon wanted to be with Adam all day, that was no problem. She could use some time with her hands free for once.

They had lost track of time by the time they finally wandered out to the dining area and kitchen. Gideon had gathered enough fruit last night that there was still some left on the granite countertops. They both ate their fill for breakfast, and Nikka sat back in her chair on the open deck as she watched Gideon hold Adam on his knee. The child giggled and cooed at the faces his father made.

A singular thought drifted through her mind as she gazed out over the unsettled clouds that had gathered and blotted out the sun. A morning storm grew on the horizon and a breeze picked up along the beach.

"Where's Amy?" she said and glanced around the edges of the property fence. If a storm was coming, they needed to take shelter inside. They had learned from the last time when a typhoon blew over the coast and nearly broke every window in the house and downed a tree on the front lawn.

Gideon glanced up, and his eyes scanned beyond the fence to the beach. "I have not seen her this morning."

Nikka stood from her chair and padded back into the house. Amy had seemed so quiet last night, and then the two of them had just left her beside the fire. What if she had decided to go for a walk? Or what if she had done something worse?

The prickles of her hair along her forearm made her uneasy as she walked back through the house and to the door to Amy's room. She rapped on the door and listened.

"Amy?" she said and leaned in to listen, but no sound came from the other side.

She opened the door enough to peer inside and released a nervous breath when she saw Amy lying on the bed, her back to the door and her red hair cascading over the pillows. Her breathing was slow and even.

Nikka closed the door as she tried to calm the quivering nerves that had begun to vibrate in her chest. Nothing to worry about. If a storm blew in, they were all safe inside the house. Everything would be okay.

On the days when the weather was too stormy to be outside, Nikka often found herself bored. But today was different. Gideon had never played card games before, and with a full deck in the pantry, Nikka began the poker tutorial with him. As soon as Adam was sleepy enough to go down for his morning nap, she and Gideon had the cards splayed across the dining room table. Despite the rumbling thunder and rain pelting the windows, they continued their game with him stealing a touch to her forearm or a quick kiss. At first, she thought he was just trying to cheat at the game, but then she realized he just couldn't stop himself. After the fifth time, she just laughed and made him sit down.

"No cheating," she said with a smile. She sat back in her chair, her leg curled up under her.

"But I just cannot learn any other way," he said, his eyebrow cocked. "My teacher is far too distracting."

"You don't even know distracting," she said with a glint in her eye.

A heavy gust of wind pounded against the side of the house, pulling their attention away from each other. The wind grew, rattling the windows in the panes just like the typhoon from those many months ago. Nikka's nerves quivered again. The beach chairs on the deck then swept across the front lawn, crashing into the fence. Gideon stood and watched the palm trees bend in the unexpected gust.

"I need to close the vent on the greenhouse," he said and glanced back to her.

"Now?" Nikka said and rose from her chair. "That wind must be at least a hundred miles an hour."

"If I do not, we will lose all of it," he said.

In these desperate times, she knew it was true. That garden plot inside the greenhouse in the back yard had been their only source of fresh food except for the fruit trees. With such awful winds, they were likely to lose most of the fruit. Losing the garden could be devastating.

"Be careful," she said.

"I will." He turned toward the door and pulled it open. The wind rushed into the house, scattering the playing cards all over the room. Nikka hurried to the door to force it closed as soon as he ran out onto the deck. The moment the door was closed, she moved through the dining area and into the main room, watching him through the windows as he ran through the rain and wind. His T-shirt was soaked through and the edges whipped in the gust.

She lost sight of him as he moved to the back of the property. The only way to see if he was successful was to try and get sight of him in her bedroom. She moved down the hall but slowed her pace. The door to Amy's room gaped open. Nikka stepped up to the threshold and pushed the door open further, only to see Amy's empty bed.

When had she gotten up? Did she leave the house through the back door? This was the worst time for her to be gone.

"Amy?" she called out to her.

The sound of Adam's cry echoed down the hallway, and Nikka perked her head toward her own bedroom. The pounding winds shook the rafters and whistled through the small spaces in the roof, creating an eerie howl that settled into the corners of every room. She stepped toward the bedroom and around the door but stopped. Amy stood beside the crib, her wavy red hair falling across her shoulders and her back toward the door.

The nerves in her chest settled when she saw her, relief that she hadn't gone out carelessly into the storm. She must have heard Adam crying, awakened by the sound of the storm.

Nikka let out a breath. "Thank heavens. I thought you had left."

Amy's didn't turn or acknowledge her, but she only stood at the edge of the crib, looking down at the baby.

"Amy," Nikka said, the tightness starting in her chest again, as she stepped toward the crib. "Are you all right? I'm sorry I left you all alone last night."

"I'm not alone," Amy said. But her voice sounded odd, a deep rumbling growl just under her throat.

Nikka stopped, the nerves raging deep in her core. Something was terribly wrong.

At that moment, the temperature in the room plummeted, and Nikka's breath escaped in a short fog of white from her lips. Amy leaned over the edge of the crib and scooped Adam into her arms, and that was when Nikka knew she was a second too late. Amy turned around with the baby held close to her chest. The smell of rotting meat drifted from her gaping mouth. Her once-green eyes were now a sea of black oil that oozed and dripped from the corner of her left eye. Her cracking lips curled back against yellowed teeth.

For the first time since she had known of the existence of demons, Nikka could no longer see the writhing insectoid beasts within the possessed humans. That was a gift that only a seraph had. The warning that came with the demon's presence had left when she became an archangel as well. She was left here in the room with limited options as she faced a demon inside her friend.

A demon that now knew their location.

"Amy," she said, trying to keep her voice from shaking. "You can fight it."

"She can't hear you anymore," she said, the growling behind her voice now louder. "She accepted me, and now she's mine."

Nikka watched the creature's arms as they held Adam in a twisted embrace. The demon had her child, and she had no way of stopping it unless she unleashed her power.

"Give me my son," Nikka said and planted her feet.

"And why would I do that?" The demon cocked its head to the side and smiled at her, black ooze dripping from the edge of its mouth. "Amy has told me many interesting things. I know who you are. I know that this boy is my Father's kin and he wants him. Oh, does he ever want you both." The demon's body quivered with delight as it spoke.

"You won't get out of here alive," Nikka said. Her fingers curled into fists. "Now, give me my son."

"Let's see who is the fastest, shall we? Let's see who gets to Father first," the demon said with a snarl. As soon as it spoke the words, the creature turned and leaped through the large bay window. The glass showered down as it jumped out into the rainstorm.

Air rushed from Nikka's lungs, but she raced forward, jumping through the shattered window and landing on the wet ground. The rain pelted her with a gust of wind that threatened to sweep her off her feet. Her eyes stayed focused on the slick of Amy's red hair as the beast ran across the grounds and broke through the back fence. The demon ran so fast that it began to gain ground away from Nikka.

Her heart thundered against her ribs as she sprinted after the creature, the picture of her son in its arms fueling her anger. Then she saw Gideon at the far end of the lawn, and he stood as soon as he caught sight of her. She shouted to him for help but didn't slow down enough to see if he followed.

The demon increased its distance, and it threatened to lose her as she bounded through the fallen fence and into the thick of trees toward the jungle. If she lost the demon in there, she might never find them again.

The air burned in her lungs. Rain dripped down her face and clouded her vision. Her feet pounded against the muddy ground as she kept Amy's form in her sights. The edge of the jungle loomed, and her son was about to plunge into the unknown. The demon was ready to lose Nikka.

She had no choice.

As soon as the thought blasted through her brain, the air charged around her. The energy of the trees, the rain, and even the jungle before her rushed into her body at her own bidding. It welled, swift and strong, into the center of her being, amplifying as she called on the power of the earth. The energy filled her body, and she felt her eyes change. The violet light emitted from her pupils as the power rushed down her arms. She held her palms out before her and planted her feet as the force erupted from her hands.

The power glowed in ribbons of violet light as it shot out as fast as lightning, striking Amy in the back just before she dove into the edge of the jungle. Her body arched backwards as her legs stiffened and she fell back. The baby cried when she toppled against the low shrubs and rain poured down on them.

As the aftershocks of her power jostled through her veins, Nikka ran to Adam and scooped him into her arms. Even through the rain that poured down her face, hot tears streamed against her cheeks.

Gideon rushed to her side and crouched beside her. She met his face, and he had grown pale. He had just seen everything that happened.

"I had to do it," Nikka said as she cried, Adam, screaming in her ear above the roar of the storm.

He nodded his head. "I know." His eyes fell on Amy's still body as he watched her slow breathing. Her eyes remained closed as though she had fallen asleep at the edge of the jungle. Then he gazed up to the rims of the trees around them, searching for anything that could watch them from the leaves.

"We do not have much time," he said. "That demon only left her body. It knows where we are. It is only a matter of time before he brings reinforcements." He leaned down and collected Amy's body, holding her against his chest as he looked back at Nikka. "And it will be much sooner before the angels arrive. We have to go. Now."

CHAPTER 8

NIKKA

---

*T*he rain and the winds dissipated almost as soon as Nikka had forced the demon out of Amy's body. But that was all that she could do. She was no longer a seraph; she didn't have an angel blade to kill the demon. It abandoned Amy's body as soon as Nikka had struck it and now it could travel through the ether and inform any of the others of their location.

That demon was the least of their concerns, though. The angels would have felt the ripple effect of her using her power.

She ran close behind Gideon as they hurried back to the house. Amy groaned in Gideon's arms. Nikka held Adam close to her chest as he cried.

Gideon rushed through the fallen fence of the lawn and to the garage. He pulled open the large door, revealing the silent Jeep that had sat in wait for them like a caged beast.

"Collect what you can in the next few minutes," he said as he moved to the back door and opened it, laying Amy across the seat.

Nikka ran into the house, her heart thudding against her ribs. Each step made Adam cry even louder, but they didn't have time to stop and soothe him. Every second counted against her knowing that an angel or a demon could descend on them at any moment, an angel that would try and kill her son for being what he was.

She rounded the corner into the kitchen and to the back bedroom where she lay Adam on the bed as she rushed to shove the things she could into her backpack. Clothes for the baby. A shirt. A bottle and a blanket. She zipped the bag closed, gathered the baby into her arms and hurried back into the main room.

Gideon stood in the kitchen, filling a box with canned food and bottles of water, their "bug out" bags strapped over his shoulders. He gave her a quick but worried glance as he lifted the full box and moved back out into the garage. Nikka followed him, but as she stopped at the door, she looked back at the place that had been her home and protection for the last six months. This was it, the last time she would ever see it. She had always known she would leave it like this, though. Departing in a panic, hoping they would make it away safely.

She turned away and stepped up into the Jeep, tossing the backpack to the floor as she shut the door.

Gideon slid into the driver's seat and shoved the keys into the ignition. Before he turned the key, he shot a look at her that weighed heavy in her throat. Genuine fear settled into the lines around his eyes, his pupils large with a subtle hint of ember in the dark.

"Pray for it to start," he said.

Nikka held her breath and his fingers clasped around the silver key. He turned it, and the engine made a rolling grumble, but it didn't fire. A frustrated groan escaped his throat as he turned it again.

The baby continued to cry in her arms, and she held him close, his small body shuddering through her T-shirt. The rain had soaked through his clothes when the demon had taken him out into the storm. The engine rumbled, and the starter clicked, again and again, every sound hammering at her nerves. She closed her eyes as she wrapped Adam in her arms, trying to use her own body heat to warm him for now. The starter continued to click.

Please, God, she thought. *Please help us.*

The mark on her chest and along her arms tingled and zapped just under her skin, sending rivers of warmth into her veins. Her power forced itself to the surface, and she opened her eyes against its strength. Her fingers shook as it took control of her limbs. Her hand reached to the dashboard in front of her, and she looked at the plain black vinyl that stretched across the width of the vehicle. The violet pinpoints of light shone in her eyes as she touched the dashboard. The moment she made contact, the electrical circuits spring to life, all travelling back to the core of the battery. The power surged from her fingers and into the battery, firing it and sending the engine into a sudden rumble.

Gideon sat back and looked at the gauges on the dashboard light up with the roar of the engine. The violet light faded from Nikka's eyes, and she glanced at him.

"That is some excellent praying," he said and forced the gearshift down. The tires spun and the vehicle launched from the garage and onto the roads leading from the village.

The Jeep lurched as he swerved around fallen trees and abandoned vehicles, a mine field left behind by the electromagnetic pulse that started the end of the world. Even the depths of Central America didn't escape the effect of it.

As the engine roared, Nikka wrapped Adam in a dry blanket and rocked him in her arms until he had quieted, but his eyes remained open and watchful as though he knew what was happening.

"Is he all right?" Gideon said, his eyes darting to them as he drove along the gravel road that wound into the jungle.

"He's fine," Nikka said and glanced back to the seat where Amy still lay. Her chest moved up and down as though she were only asleep. Nikka had seen this happen before when Samael forced her to learn how to remove an angel or a demon from a human body. It could leave the human dazed for hours, but otherwise unscathed.

"Will she awaken soon?" he asked.

"Maybe," she said and watched her head tilt back and forth with the movements of the vehicle.

Nikka turned back to Gideon and to the grip he had on the steering wheel. His knuckles had blanched, and every muscle and tendon in his neck bulged. She wanted to tell him that everything would be okay, that they had made it out of the house, but she knew that it wasn't true. She had seen what an angel could do. Samael had left an indelible imprint on her, something that she would never forget. Angels were cold and calculating, and if one found them, it wouldn't hesitate to kill them.

"Are you okay?" she said, still watching the grip he had on the wheel. She couldn't forget that he went out into that storm by himself, lured out there by the demon to get her and the baby alone.

"For now, yes, but I will be much better when we are far away from here."

The overhanging palms and trees covered in vines that lined the road closed in along the narrow path, pulling the daylight away from them. They had traveled this route when they first arrived in Belize. They had been lost and had wandered for days until they had found this Jeep abandoned on the side of the road. Covered in camouflage green and stocked with guns and tanks of gasoline, they had surmised that it had been a military vehicle. No other human was around to stop them, so they took it, and it had served them well. Now the road back didn't feel as hopeful as it had before. This route would lead back to a highway that traveled out of Belize, through Guatemala and into Mexico. But was that the best option to escape into hiding?

The dark jungle surrounded them, creating shadows in the low-lying brush and vines that had overgrown onto the road. Nikka's eyes darted through the trees as an uneasy sensation crawled up her spine and tingled against the tattoos on her arms.

A sudden flash of white light filled the heavy vegetation around them, chasing away any darkness that had hovered under the trees. Gideon slammed his foot on the brake and shielded his eyes from the light. Nikka shut her eyes and braced herself against the dashboard as the vehicle screeched to a halt in the gravel. The light hovered in that space of the jungle for a moment, like a camera flash that lingered too long.

The sigil mark on her chest burned, and Nikka knew what was out there, waiting in the road, before she even opened her eyes. The light dimmed into shades of purple until the dark of the forest settled around them again. She opened her eyes and gazed out the windshield to see a figure standing several meters down the road. Hues of violet light emanated from around the man that stood in the shadows.

She had seen those colors of black and violet before, surrounding Samael when he showed his true nature. But this wasn't Samael who stood on the road now. As she clutched Adam to her chest, her muscles tensed against the burning in her tattoos.

The man lifted his head, and his eyes settled on them, violet points of light set in his dark pupils. His face was handsome like he had just walked off the cover of a men's health magazine. And just like Samael had told her, being possessed by an angel made the human rich with beauty and vitality, the opposite of what a demon would do. This man stood there, his shoulders and arms strong under a dark button-down shirt and jeans. His dark brown hair had mussed a little in the wind, and light that had surrounded him settled before them on the road. She would have thought him beautiful if he hadn't been sent to kill her.

"Come out and face me," he shouted to them, his voice powerful enough to make the trees shudder around them.

Gideon's hand shot to the door handle, but Nikka grasped his forearm. "Stop," she said. He looked at her, and the lines of worry around his eyes deepened. A subtle glow of red grew in his pupils, and the sudden chill in the car told her that the demon had awakened. "Don't go out there."

She handed the baby to him, and he reluctantly accepted him. "I need you to keep Adam safe," she said. Her throat had gone dry. The last thing she wanted to do was to go out and face an angry angel, but she couldn't sit back and let Gideon do it either. And if the angel killed her, she knew that Gideon would do everything he could to protect his son.

"Do not go," he said, his eyes pleading with her as he held the baby to his chest.

"We don't have a choice." She glanced back through the window, to the man that stood in the road. She swallowed hard, her hands trembling, and then she turned back to face Gideon. "If it looks like he is about to win, I need you to drive away as fast as you can."

"No—" he said, but she shook her head.

"I need you to promise me that you will save Adam."

"Nikka—"

"Promise me," she said, her eyes boring into him.

Gideon shook his head and gritted his teeth, but he couldn't say anything more to convince her. "I promise."

The look in his eyes made her want to cry, but she forced the feeling deep into her chest behind the sigil that burned in her skin. She leaned across the seat and kissed him before he could say anything more. Then she kissed the top of the baby's head before she glanced back out the window at the angel watching them.

She grasped the door handle and stepped out of the vehicle. The air had quieted, too still as she walked out onto the road before the Jeep and faced the angel that had called her out. Her knees trembled with each step as she neared him. The energy that surrounded him crackled and zinged around her like electricity. The angel stood tall, his eyes burned into her as she stepped closer to him.

Her fingers clenched into fists, at first to get the feeling back into them, but then the power reverberated along her arms. The mark on her chest zapped with a thousand stings, lighting the tattoos along her arms into points of violet light.

I won't be afraid.

The trembling in her knees abated with each step she took. Every inch closer to the angel let her see him more clearly. His powerful stance. The way he cocked his head to one side. The look of disdain in his eyes.

I won't be bullied.

This angel was sent to kill her son. There was no way she was going to let this happen while there was something she could do about it.

Chapter 9

Nikka

---

*T*he angel stared Nikka down, the violet light still burning in his pupils, and the whites of his eyes had gone black. His jaw tightened as he watched her approach, her fists now clenched at her sides. Each step she took threatened to weaken her knees, but she pulled the energy deep into her core, and this steadied her legs.

"You know why I have come," the angel said.

"I do," she said, trying to keep her voice from shaking. "And I won't let you have him."

"It really is not your choice." He raised his hand, and purple light swirled around his arm, collecting into an orb in the palm of his hand. The energy of it sizzled in the air above her as he drew in the power. It took all her concentration to keep her power from drifting toward him.

He readied his own energy to strike at her, so now was the time for her to act. She opened the flow of life force through the bottoms of her feet, pulling in anything she could gather from the surrounding jungle. The forest teemed with life and power, and it gave itself freely to her as she asked it. The energy flowed into her core, bringing the tattoos to life along her arms. Sparkles of violet light erupted along her limbs and ended with the mark in the center of her chest. The light shone through her eyes just as it did in the angel before her. She held her hand out and let the light collect in her palm, readying her defense.

The angel finally smiled, but there was no kindness in his cold eyes. "I see Samael has taught you a little something."

The name of the angel that she hated left a bitter taste in her mouth. "He taught me enough."

"We shall see."

He shifted, leaving only a trail of light around him, moving faster than anything she had ever seen. The motion left a dizzying effect on her eyes. Before she could react, his power struck her in the chest, sending her careening back against a tree. The air rushed from her lungs, and she collapsed to the ground, her chest seizing in a violent cough. He moved again, this time standing only feet from her.

"You were just Samael's plaything," he said. "A toy not to be taken seriously."

She tried to catch her breath when she saw the light grow in his palm again. The soil under her hands and knees where she pressed to the ground warmed to her touch, giving its life force to her. As he released another volley of his energy at her, she forced herself upright and held her palms out before her, letting her power surround her in a shield. The angel's face went slack as he saw his own energy fail against hers and he lost his balance, tripping backwards.

This gave Nikka the chance to jump to her feet and pull more of her power into her arms. The energy flowed into her fingers, and she released it in a series of shots toward him as he staggered back.

The first blast zinged past his shoulder, and then he dodged the next two. His hands reached behind his back, and Nikka felt the breath stop in her throat as she watched him pull two swords from behind him. The blades emerged from invisible sheaths and erupted into purple flames that curled around to the end of the swords. And they were like no other weapon she had ever seen: half-circle cutlasses etched in black symbols, the blades curving in wide arcs that slid from against his shoulders.

The angel twisted and fended off the last of her shots with his new weapons. He steadied his feet and brought the swords to his sides, the purple fire licking around the hilts and illuminating his face from the ground up. A sneer formed on his lips.

Oh no. He was far more powerful than she had expected.

She pulled in more energy as fast as she could, but the angel moved in a blur of light again, and that was when the stinging pain shot through her side. The light shifted past her at the same moment she sensed a warm fluid trickling from her ribs. She glanced down to see a fresh slice through the side of her shirt that had begun to soak red with blood. The wound was shallow enough not to be mortal, but it was a symbol of what he could do to her without trying. Her hand clutched at the wound, and she spun around to face him. He now stood a few feet from her, the blade in his right hand slick with her blood.

"I won't you let you take him," she said, hoping that she could stall him long enough to pull more power in her core. And maybe she could distract enough for Gideon to get away.

"Oh, I am not here just for him," the angel said and stepped toward her. "You will be coming with me too."

She stumbled away from him, the blood trickling down her side. The power faltered in her hands, ebbing away with her lost concentration as the warm blood oozed down to her hip. She tripped and fell back into the road as the angel stood above her, his half-circle swords lighting the space around them in a brilliant glow of neon purple.

"You were not meant to be here. You and that demon have created the anti-Christ, and I will stop the three of you before you can end the world."

The words stung like poison. The light around him intensified, and she squinted as she looked at him. His angry face glared down at her as he brought his swords to the sky. His violet-white light enveloped her, and the heat of it burned against her skin, making the tattoos sizzle down to her bones. The heat built until she could no longer bear it. She clenched her teeth against the pain, ready to scream.

A flash of red light like a band of fire curled through the air above her, and the hot white light disappeared in an instant. The pain in her tattoos subsided, and she righted herself fast enough to see the end of Gideon's fire-whip lash around the angel's neck. Gideon stood behind him, the fire whip in his hand and his eyes glowing red with anger as he yanked back on the lash. The angel dropped the swords and grasped at the cord on his neck, drawing the violet fire out of the blades as soon as they left his hands. Gideon tugged on the whip again, and the angel screeched as he staggered back.

Nikka pulled the energy from the ground where she crouched in a sudden rush of power. It might be her only chance to save them all, and she had to do it now. She forced the energy into her core as fast as she could and then released it all at once toward the angel, focusing it into the center of his chest. Energy that strong could only do one thing, and it was one of the few things that Samael had taught her.

The power struck him, and the angel froze, his arms going rigid at his sides. His mouth opened in a scream that shuddered against the tops of the palms that hung over the road. The violet light in his eyes intensified for only a moment before it went out and the angel collapsed to the ground, still and silent.

The jungle grew quiet, but Nikka's ears still rang, and the wound at her side throbbed. Although she had tried to suppress it, the trembling in her hands now returned, and she was positive she wouldn't be able to stand. She looked up at Gideon, who clenched his fists and the whip that had lashed around the angel's neck now vanished. The orange-red glow in his eyes lingered as he turned his gaze toward her. He bit his lip, closed his eyes, and turned away from her.

"I could not leave you," he said, the tendons in his arms tight with controlled anger.

She nodded only because her voice had abandoned her at that moment. The energy of her power still hovered around her, but she could feel something else there too. Something that still lingered around the trees and drifted among the palm fronds. She glanced down at the body of the angel that lay on the ground only a few feet from her. Right now, that body was just a man, unconscious and unaware of the powerful struggle that had just taken place. The body was devoid of the angelic soul that had powered him, but it now dwelled like a spirit among the trees, watching and waiting for its moment to fill the body again.

There wouldn't be much time, and she had never done it before, but she tried to recall everything that Samael had done to her on one particular day. It was the day that had scared her the most when she was in his possession.

She moved to her hands and knees and crawled to the man that lay on the ground. She had seen that when she hit him with the energy that she had built up in her hands the power had forced the angel from the body, if only for a few minutes, but it still moved around them like a disembodied spirit searching for its host. A plan had danced around her head, and she hoped that she didn't do it wrong because it could backfire in the most horrific way.

Her trembling hands touched his shirt, and she tore it open along the button line, revealing his bare chest. She traced a finger along his sternum, each movement leaving behind a black mark. The memory of the sigil that Samael had placed on her came back as she created the mark on the man's body. Every line and curve was there, at least to the best of her recollection. As soon as she had completed it, she placed her palm on the sigil and closed her eyes.

Samael had taught her how to do this as well, and for now, she was grateful. The power that flowed in her limbs reached out to the environment and searched for that spirit that hung around the trees, staring down at them with malice and judgement. The angel twisted and slipped from her energy grasp, but it had very little power against her in its current form. She finally traced its outline, and her power clutched at it, drawing it closer to her. The spirit moved through her, and it touched her soul. For a moment, she felt the warmth of sunshine and the smell of her grandmother's cookies as it moved into her soul. Every happy memory that she ever had danced in her thoughts as she shared space with an angel. As much as she wanted to embrace those feelings, they were only false emotions brought by a spirit that could destroy her. She forced the angel through her and channeled it into the body of the man under her grasp.

The sigil under her palms glowed with violet light and heated at her touch as she forced the angel back into the body. The last of it slipped out of her fingers, and she fell back away from him as the man gasped and coughed. Nikka scrambled out of his way as he turned to his side, dazed and coughing.

Gideon crouched beside her and helped her up as the angel stumbled to his feet and staggered until he caught his balance.

"What have you done?" Gideon whispered to her as they watched the angel turn his gaze down to the mark on his chest.

The angel breathed through his clenched teeth, his fingers grasping at the edges of his open shirt. "Impossible," he said and then shouted into the air.

Nikka stepped away from Gideon and moved before the angel, the fear leaving her body as she watched him.

"I told you that Samael had taught me enough," she said.

The angel looked up at her, the strain evident in his face as he fought against his invisible bonds.

"A binding sigil," she said, pointing to the mark on his chest. "You're bound to me, and you must enforce my will."

"The others will not stand for this," he said and stood straighter, finally relaxing against the restraint.

"It doesn't matter because I order you to protect my family and me, all of us."

The angel glanced at Gideon. "I will die before I protect a foul demon. Or his worthless offspring."

"And yet, you *will* protect them, and you won't harm yourself." Nikka crossed her arms over her chest, even though the action sent ripples of pain from the wound at her side.

He turned his eyes back toward her, the edges softening as he gazed at her face. "Then we must be going now because my brothers are on their way. It will not be long now."

"Okay," she said and smiled. "I won't let any harm come to you either."

"Very well." He released the edges of his shirt and stood straighter. The angel stood almost a foot taller than she did, so it was no wonder that he had appeared so daunting before.

"If we're going to be working together, I need to know what to call you?"

His brow furrowed as he looked at her.

"Your name," she said.

His shoulders straightened as though he was ready to take on a great mantle. "I am called Jadriel."

"All right, Jadriel," she said. "Get in the truck. We've got a long way to go."

CHAPTER 10

GIDEON

G ideon watched the angel struggle with the binding sigil, although the man never moved much. It did not take much to see that he fought to get his limbs to move the way he wanted them to, but he could only stand there and speak to the half-human half-archangel that had trapped him. If he had the ability to break his bonds, Gideon could tell that Jadriel wanted to snap them all like dry bones and scatter them in the wind.

But Nikka faced him without fear, holding all her confidence in the sigil.

Gideon turned away from them and climbed into the driver's seat of the vehicle, glancing back to Amy, who sat up with Adam in her arms, just where he had left her.

Her wide eyes looked at him and then darted to the angel that moved around the Jeep, opening the door to get in the back seat with her.

"Everything will be okay," Gideon whispered to her before the rear door opened.

"Okay," she said and rocked the baby against her chest.

Nikka stepped into the vehicle and eyed Jadriel as he rested back against the seat, his eyes narrowed and staring straight forward. Gideon started the engine and put it into gear. Just before he pressed the gas pedal, he looked in the rear-view mirror and saw the angel glaring at him. For the first time since he had met Nikka, he hoped that she did not overestimate the extent of her powers.

The truck shot forward through the rough trail that wound under cover of the jungle. Nikka turned back and looked at Amy, whose eyes had not yet narrowed.

"Are you okay?" she asked.

Amy nodded. "I will be."

"I'm sorry, but I had to do it," Nikka said, clasping Amy's trembling arm that held her baby.

"I know, and I'm glad. That thing had me, made me do everything against my will. I couldn't stop it."

"You were possessed by one of his kind?" Jadriel said and shot her a glance from where he sat, ticking his head toward Gideon.

"Not one of his kind," Amy interjected, her words pointed and loud. "A monster." She turned away from the angel and looked at Nikka again. "It came to me last night. I thought it was just my imagination at first. It spoke to me, made me promises. The next thing I knew, it was inside me like a parasite."

"I'm sorry. I should have been there to protect you."

"It's not your fault," Amy said. "You can't be there all the time. I know that."

"And you removed the demon yourself?" Jadriel said, looking at Nikka.

She nodded. "Yes."

"Then it knows where you are as well."

"I'm aware of that," Nikka said. "What about the angels? Can you tell where they are?"

Jadriel looked away from her and stared forward again. "I can hear them from time to time."

"And? Are they still coming?"

His jaw tightened. "Their voices are growing fainter. They were waiting for me. I was the scout, sent to find you and then inform."

Gideon saw the smile form on Nikka's lips at the corner of his glance.

"You weren't supposed to engage, were you? So, you broke ranks, went rogue and did your own thing."

Perhaps it would be best if she did not taunt the angel, but Gideon smiled as he watched the angel's eyes narrow in the mirror.

"I was not supposed to engage. You are correct."

"And now they can't pinpoint us, right?" Nikka said.

"Also correct," he said through clenched teeth.

"Good. I want you to tell me when you can sense them."

He sighed and turned away, feigning interest in the vegetation outside of his own window. "Fine."

"What about Samael?" Nikka asked.

Gideon glanced back to the mirror and saw the tendons in Jadriel's neck soften as the angel looked at her again.

"What about him?" Jadriel said.

"Is he one of your brothers waiting to hear back from you?"

"No. He has been banished from Heaven."

Nikka's eyebrows raised in surprise. "Banished? I thought he was a Watcher? One of the guardians."

"He was, and then he betrayed us." Jadriel's voice raised, the words moving quickly over his tongue. "He created you behind our backs. He broke the rules and turned you into an archangel, something only God is allowed to do. And because of him, the gears of the Armageddon have been set in motion. The anti-Christ has been born. He was caught in his attempt to overthrow the powers of Heaven, and now he has been banished."

Gideon wanted to slam on the brakes and reach back to throttle the angel for the way he spoke to Nikka, but he just tightened his grip on the steering wheel and kept his eyes on the road. Nikka leaned back against the dashboard, her eyes never wavering from Jadriel's angry face.

"Banished where?" she said. Even though she tried to hide it, Gideon sensed the worry in her voice.

"To Earth. His redemption has been stripped from him."

For only a second, Gideon took his eyes off the road and looked at Nikka. Her face had gone pale, and she failed to say anything in response to the angel. It was not like her to just be silent to someone like Jadriel.

"What is it?" Gideon asked as he looked at her. "Something is wrong."

Her eyes flashed toward him. "Samael. I think he's been searching for me."

This revelation shot through him, and his heart rate increased. He forced himself to look at the road even though he wanted to stop and find out more from her.

"How do you know this?" Gideon asked.

"I've been having dreams . . . visions. I thought I was seeing demons, maybe Lucifer. But now I'm starting to think it was Sam. He believes that he can still win if he has access to my power."

"You mean the angel that took me?" Amy said, her voice shaking. "The one tried to make you put a spirit inside me? The one that attacked us in the mall?"

Nikka sat up and leaned back over the edge of the seat, grasping onto Amy's hand. "It's okay. He won't find us."

"But he has before. He took me right out of my house, away from my son," she said, tears now forming in her eyes. "That guy is as crazy as a bag of snakes."

"He doesn't know where we are," Nikka said, her voice steady as she leaned over the seat.

"You are an innocent in all of this," Jadriel said, giving her a side glance. "For that, I am sorry. You do not deserve the fate to be bestowed upon the others."

"Fate?" Amy said.

"Hey," Nikka got up on her knees and moved right into Jadriel's line of sight. Gideon prepared his foot to hit the brake in case things got worse. "Stop scaring her. Now everybody just calm down." She leaned back on her heels and held her arms out for the baby. Amy let him go and rested back against the seat. "We are doing fine. Jad is going to help keep us informed, like our own personal angel radar. You okay if I call you Jad?"

The angel raised an eyebrow and rolled his eyes, indicating that he could not possibly care less.

"Great. See? We will find somewhere else to shelter. In the meantime, just try to get some rest. Okay?" she said and gave Amy a look that Gideon had seen many mothers give to their own children.

Amy said nothing more, but Gideon knew that the concern had not passed, even as she lay her head back and gazed out the side window. Nikka finally turned around and held the sleeping baby in her arms. When she let out a deep sigh, he glanced at her and knew that even she did not believe everything was going to be all right.

Gideon drove as the passengers remained quiet for most of the way. He eventually found the road that took them to the highway. For hours they stayed on that road, travelling the still and abandoned way out of Belize and into Guatemala. It had been many decades since he had traveled the highways of Central America, but even the last time he was here there were armed guards at stations along the borders. Now, in the aftermath of the EMP, the stations were abandoned. They had come across far fewer signs of human life in this part of the world than he had during his trek through the western United States with Jason.

The sun had travelled across the sky by the time they had reached the Mexican-Guatemala border. No guards had interfered in their crossing here as well, but the night sky had come faster than Gideon expected, or his day of driving had begun to weigh on his body. They had to find a place to stop and seek shelter for the evening and at least regroup. His legs had begun to ache from sitting at the wheel for most of the day.

Nikka must have sensed it too as she sat up and watched out the windows, eyeing the passing abandoned villages for any signs of life or activity. The baby started fussing in her arms as he slowed the vehicle to look for shelter options.

"How about that?" she said and pointed to a structure at the top of an oncoming hill. As he neared the narrow dirt road that veered off the main highway, Gideon gazed up at the building and saw the silhouette of a cross atop the highest point of the structure. A church.

"It looks as good as anything," he said and turned the truck up the road. The headlights shone against the orange-red adobe façade of the building, its arched windows dark. Weeds had overgrown around the front walk, and vines stretched across the door as though nobody had entered the premises in a long time. Gideon stopped the vehicle and killed the engine.

"Where are we?" Amy asked as she lifted her head, her voice rough with the short sleep she had been able to get.

"Somewhere in Mexico," Nikka said. "At least it's a roof over our heads for the night."

Gideon stepped out of the Jeep and walked across the dirt path to the front door. He peeled back the overgrowth of vines and pulled the heavy wood door open. The hinges squealed in protest as they gave way and opened up to him. The dark, heavy air that drifted out of the building smelled like mildew and dust as it breathed out into the humid air around him. He stepped across the threshold and let his eyes adjust enough to see the twilight in the night sky shining through the north end of the roof. A portion of it had collapsed, leaving the altar and sacristy covered in fallen timbers.

Dozens of eyes peered at him through the shadows and along the windows, and as he moved down the aisle between the pews, he could see the frescoes of painted faces along the walls. The paint had chipped away long ago, but not before leaving the oil-paint eyes behind to look out into the darkness at those who would trespass onto the church grounds. The wood benches remained untouched save for a layer of dust.

The collapsed roof. The paintings of the saints that peeled off the walls. Crosses and statues that lay in fragments on the dais. All of this reminded him of the condemned monastery where he had once made his home, where he had first brought Nikka and taught her about this world. He had taken shelter in a chapel much like this one in the bottom floor of the monastery, and that was where he prayed to God that Nikka would not destroy him. He had just revealed his demon nature for the first time to her, and it had also been the first time he kissed her. This place held onto its spirit long after the roof had fallen if only to remind him where he came from.

"Is it okay?" Nikka's voice said from behind him. She had startled him out of his thoughts, and he turned to see her standing at the threshold, her form outlined by the fading twilight.

"It will do for tonight," he said, turning away from the altar of broken crosses.

CHAPTER 11

NIKKA

Nikka glanced back to where Adam lay, in his makeshift bed of folded blankets in the cleanest corner of the chapel. He finally settled down to sleep. The events of the day had even rattled him, and he must have sensed that something was off. He had no idea.

The others gathered around the fire that Gideon had built at the collapsed end of the church. At least there was something warm here, something normal like they had in the evenings in Belize. If that could be considered normal. The heat of the fire danced across her skin as she stepped up to Gideon and sat beside him. Amy lifted her eyes from where she sat on the nearest pew.

"He's asleep, finally," she said as he placed an arm around her shoulders. She rested against him, but relaxation would never settle over her.

"Good," he said. She followed his stiff gaze to Jadriel, who stood half-in and half-out of the chapel as he gazed out over the darkening jungle to the south. The firelight flickered over his tall shape and sent wiggling shadows across his face.

"Everything okay?" she whispered to Gideon but kept her gaze on the angel.

"I hope so." Gideon squeezed her closer to him.

"Hey, Jad," Nikka said and felt Gideon stiffen next to her. The angel's jaw tightened, but he didn't look back at her. "Any vibes out there? You hear anything from the other side?"

He sighed. "No."

The angel was angry; she understood that. When Samael had put the binding sigil on her, she had felt trapped and helpless. Binding an angel was the only thing she could think of at the time. Although guilt had weighed on her since she had done it, binding him had kept her and the others alive for now.

She moved to stand up, and Gideon resisted at first, but she nodded to him that she would be okay. Nikka got to her feet and stepped over the pile of bricks to stand next to Jadriel.

"I'm sorry that I had to do this to you," she said to him. He flashed a glance at her from the corner of his eye. "I will release you when I can. I promise."

"The promise of a half-angel abomination and a demon's whore," he said through clenched teeth.

The muscles tightened along her spine, and she balled her hands into fists. "That's not fair. You have no idea what is going on here."

He turned to face her, his eyes narrowed. "No. You do not."

"Then why don't you tell me if you think you know so much."

"You have started the Apocalypse." He said and moved closer to her. From the corner of her eye, she saw Gideon stand, but Nikka held out her hand to stop him. "For thousands of years the cycle of human habitation in this world has run according to plan, and then you came along. You have begun the tide of war that will decide the fate of the Earth."

"What war?" she asked.

His jaw tightened again as though he fought to hold back what he needed to say.

"I order you to tell me everything," she said.

Jadriel's shoulders fell, defeated. It would do him no good to fight the binding sigil. "The war of Armageddon, the final battle to claim rights to Earth."

"Rights? You mean this is like a property dispute for you guys?"

"Yes," Gideon said. "In a manner of speaking."

"What does that mean?"

"In the beginning, God created Heaven and Earth and separated light from dark," Gideon said and stepped toward them. "He created everything on the Earth, and it was all for us. We were the ones that were there from the beginning with him."

"All of us, the Beings of Light," Jadriel added and looked back at Gideon as though he remembered a time when there were no enemies. "There was no contention. No war. The Earth was our home." The angel turned away from him and looked back out into the night. "And then everything changed. God wanted more. We were no longer enough for him."

"God created man," Gideon said.

"We were suddenly not important enough for him. All of his time was devoted to his newest creature. We were no longer welcome on the Earth, and he ordered us to withdraw, giving this place to you." His eyes flashed down to her, but anger no longer resided there. "And then it divided us because some of us understood why he created you, with all your flaws and limitations. Others would forever hate you." He turned his eyes toward Gideon.

Nikka finally understood what years in Bible school as a child never could teach her. "You were all the same until you began to fight about us."

"Yes," Gideon said. "Lucifer rose up, the first of us to say something about God's new creation, and then he was cast out of Heaven. The rest of his followers were then cast out with him. They lost their innate redemption that had been given to them since the beginning of time."

"The rest of us who stayed loyal took on the role of protector," Jadriel said. "For eons, the Watchers have kept you safe, bringing forth the seraph when needed to keep the balance. Your kind," he said as he pointed to Gideon, "have tried countless times to reclaim this world and we have always stopped you."

Nikka felt her stomach churning. All of this began to settle heavy on her thoughts. "Until now."

"Until now," Jadriel repeated, his voice dropping.

"The EMP, it disrupted the balance," she said as the thoughts raced through her brain. "It caused the first catastrophe that could end human life as we know it."

"It caused the first open gateway that let Lucifer's followers have free reign over this world," Jadriel said.

Something else nagged at her, and it had been causing friction in her brain ever since Jad first said it. "You called my son the anti-Christ. How is that possible?"

"He is destined to be the deceiver, Lucifer's tool in the final battle."

She shook her head. "That's not possible."

"Is it? He is equal parts human, demon, seraph, and archangel. There has never been anything like him before, and Lucifer knows it. He will have power over angels and demons alike. The only one with more power is God."

Nausea welled in her throat, and she had to swallow it back. "No, he won't—"

"And who will stop it? You?" he said, his voice mocking.

"That is enough," Gideon said, the warning evident in his words.

Nikka looked up at the angel. "Yes, I will." Although her hands trembled, she stiffened her arms and stood straighter. "I was chosen as a seraph to keep the balance. I can restore it."

A derisive laugh escaped his throat. "You were never supposed to be the seraph."

"And yet, you blame me," she said, feeling stronger as she spoke to him. "Samael did this to me. He set the order of things in motion. I saw him with the demon Belphagor. He played you the entire time."

"You lie. He would never fraternize with a demon," Jadriel said.

"You know it's true. He was one of your own and betrayed you. He created me, this hybrid of angel and seraph or whatever you want to call me. But he did this to me."

Jadriel moved closer to her, and she felt his breath on her skin. "Remember: you were still given a choice, and you chose this."

His words stung. It was absolutely true. That day in the hospital, when Gideon met her for the first time, he had given her the option of dying or becoming a seraph. The angel knew very well what he had said to her.

She loosened her fist. "Yes I did, and I will live with that choice. And now I choose to use it to my dying breath. I will stop this, and I will save my son. Lucifer will not have him."

Jadriel backed up, his eyes softening and he dropped his voice. "That may not be your choice to make."

Her sandaled foot stepped across the uneven bricks as she moved into his line of sight. "Then I need your help." She grasped his hand, and he didn't pull away. "Teach me what I need to know. Teach me the sigils to help stop this, to make me stronger. Samael left me this way, and I only learned a few things from him. But you can show me what I need to know." She squeezed his hand. "Do this for me, and I will release you."

His eyes shot up to face her. "If you release me, I will kill you."

She smiled. "Well, at least you're honest about it. If you teach me the right way, I won't let that happen."

CHAPTER 12
NIKKA

The hard floor pressed into Nikka's hip where she lay next to Gideon, his body heat keeping her warm since the fire had gone out. This part of Mexico was a little cooler and less humid than their place in Belize, and she would never have thought that she would be that "cold" girl that always drove her nuts. The one that took her boyfriend's jacket. But here she was, moving in closer to Gideon for warmth. Maybe it was the cooler air that awoke her or the sounds of bats flying around outside the chapel, but she opened her eyes to the dark night that surrounded her.

Her hand reached out through the dark and felt the edges of the blanket bed where Adam lay sleeping. His small chest moved evenly under her touch as soon as she found him. The baby had slept longer than usual, which wasn't a surprise given the excitement of the day that had upset their lives. But now he lay sound asleep next to her, as did Gideon.

She sat up and slid out from under Gideon's arm. The ache of every bone that had pressed against the hard floor now punished her as she stood. Her eyes adjusted in the dark, and she glanced at Amy's quiet form under a blanket in the far corner of the room. After yesterday, she didn't trust that it would be just Amy over there, and she padded across the floor to get a better look at her. But she lay quiet, peaceful in sleep. No sign of demon activity there.

As she stood straighter from her crouch to inspect Amy, the uneasy feeling settled in her gut. There was no reason for it, at least not from what she could tell. Everyone was here; even the angel had fallen asleep across the pew near her as though he was no longer disgusted to be in the same room as Gideon. So what was it?

She glanced across the room, to the quiet chapel lit only by slivers of moonlight that poured in through the arched windows and the collapsed section of the northeast corner. The frescoes' faces along the wall watched her in the dark, and that was unnerving in itself. She turned away from the chipped paint to gaze out the window.

And then a shadow moved, but it was too late.

The darkness swarmed in her peripheral vision, and hands grasped her from behind. Strong arms wrapped around her torso, pinning her arms to her side and a hand moved over her mouth. She tried to scream, but it came out stifled and almost silent as the form pulled her further into the darkest recesses of the church and through the breach in the corner. No matter how hard she tried to find her footing, the man who held her had lifted her high enough that she could only kick at him.

The cooler evening air hit her as she opened her eyes and tried to scream again, but the man dragged her further away from Gideon and her baby. The arms around her held her so tight that she could barely take in a breath. The dizzying stars swirled across her eyes as she felt the last of her oxygen pull away from her lungs.

Another figure moved through the dark in front of her, and before she could see its face, something fell over her head. A hood. It plunged her into the abyss as the man who held her forced her to something flat and hard. Then it moved. The bed of a truck. He shifted around her, quick and agile, holding back her arms and pressing a knee into her back. Whoever this was knew about her strength and kept her arms back enough to anticipate if she could use her powers. In this position, it would be almost impossible to get anything strong enough to knock him down.

With his hand clamped around her mouth through the hood, she tried to scream again, but nothing came out. The engine of the truck started, and it moved, jostling them both, but each bump sent his knee even more painfully against her spine. The vehicle moved over the terrain, the tires rolling over weeds and not a road. One second. Two seconds. Every moment that ticked by pulled her further away from her family.

Three seconds.

Through the threads of the hood on her face, she saw a blinding white light, and the weight against her spine vanished. At that same time, arms wrapped around her again, but it was something different. As soon as she could breathe, she pulled the hood from her head and saw the white light surround her. Something pulled her body free as though she were on a carnival ride that jerked her to the side at the same time as the truck came to a halt and rolled. Dust surrounded her until she realized that someone held her close in a protective embrace, pulling her clear of the rolling vehicle just before it skidded across the long grass.

She took in a much-needed breath and glanced up to the figure that held her, and she nearly choked. Jadriel still had his arms around her, holding her against his torso as his neck arched back to watch the truck roll. Her knuckles had gone white where she clutched at his arms. Even though he now had her and her feet touched the ground, his grip never loosened as he looked back at the truck.

"Are you okay?" he asked.

Any words stuck in her throat, so she only nodded her head. She glanced back at the settling dust of the truck that now lay on its side, and that was when she saw movement through the dark.

Jadriel turned back to her, his eyes wide and wild. "I protect you. That's what you said."

A form stepped around the truck, undazed by the accident or the angel standing there holding her. At first, she couldn't make out the features of the man that moved toward them, but as he stepped closer to them in the moonlight, she felt any oxygen left in her lungs vanish.

The dim light fell on his blonde hair that hung loosely just below his ears. The blonde goatee hadn't changed in six months, but his visage had grown dark, haunted. He stopped, his shoulders squared as he looked at her from the dark circles under his eyes.

Jadriel's pupils raged into a bright violet light, and he held up his hand to the man that stood before them, his fingers outstretched and ready to hit him with angel fire.

"No, stop," Nikka said as soon as she saw that the angel was ready to strike him down. "Don't hurt him."

The angel hesitated but kept his stance, his tattoos glowing purple and ready to channel whatever energy he needed to protect his charge.

Nikka wriggled free of Jadriel's grasp and stepped between them. Her eyes searched the shadows that fell across the man's face, not convinced that she should trust her own eyes.

"Is it really you?" she said, unable to stop the shaking in her voice.

He almost winced as she spoke to him, and he stepped back with her approach. "Don't . . . ," he said as she got closer.

The flutters moved in her gut and rose into her chest. "Jason? What happened to you?" She looked at the bruises on his bare arms under the sleeves of the black T-shirt he wore. He lowered his head but kept his eyes focused on her.

"Nikka," Jadriel's voice spoke to her. "Please do not get any closer to him."

She stopped as she watched him. His face turned into a pained grimace as his fists clenched tight at his sides. Although it looked as though he had lost twenty pounds, the muscles still bulged in his arms.

"What happened to you?" she asked him again.

He lunged at her and clasped his hands around her neck. The motion startled her, and she fought the urge to jump back and strike him with her power, but his hands didn't clamp down with force enough to strangle her. Jadriel moved toward them, but she held her hand up to stop him. Jason was only inches from her as he drew her close to his face. Something around his neck made a clink sound, and for a moment she could make out a metal collar just above the hem of his shirt.

Her fingers held onto his wrists with his hands around her neck, hoping that he would stay steady as he held her close. His eyes bored into her, a mix of rage and fear. The fingers around her neck tightened as he leaned in to her ear.

"Don't let me hurt you," he whispered. The voice carried desperation, not anger or hate. For only a second, the fingers of his right hand twitched and shifted something firm and cold against the palm of her hand. Then his grip firmed around her neck again.

His hands tightened enough to cut off her air. Her fingers clutched around his wrists and tried to pull him away, but he stared her down as he held onto her. The thing he had placed into her palm bit against her flesh. The panic forced her to collect whatever energy she could through her bare feet and send it into her hand. She released his wrist and pressed her palm against his chest, pushing a collection of energy through her body. The power struck him in the torso, and he released his grip as he flew across the ground, landing near the back of the overturned truck. The air rushed into her lungs, and she coughed against the spasm that now clutched her throat.

Jason scrambled to his feet, ready to lunge at her again when she held another collection of energy in her hand prepared to throw at him.

"Stop," she cried out to him, feeling hot tears fill her eyes. Jadriel almost bounced on his heels, ready to strike if she would only let him. "Why are you doing this?" Her hand still gripped against the thing he had given her, but she didn't dare lose sight of him and glance at it.

Another shadow moved through the dark and stepped up behind Jason. The form tossed an arm over Jason's shoulder as though it was an old friend. His face appeared in the moonlight, and the ground nearly fell out from under her feet. She recognized the man's face, angular and handsome, with a streak of red-dyed hair that fell over his eyes from under the long black mane of hair on his head. Dark-rimmed eyes stared at her with a hint of mockery.

"Belphagor," she said, the spasm in her throat trying to steal her air again.

"Long time, no see," he said with a smile as he hung over Jason's shoulder like his best drinking buddy. Jason only stood there with Belphagor at his side. The last time she had seen them both, the demon had a knife at Jason's throat and the Devil at his side.

"Well, hello, brother," Belphagor said with a glint of red light appearing in his pupils as he glanced at Jadriel.

"You appear to have gained in rank since I last saw you," Jadriel said.

Jad wasn't mistaken. Nikka had seen it herself, Belphagor going from a simple drone to a lieutenant right before her eyes. Now he had Jason at his beckoning, like a trained pit bull. The demon hung over Jason, but she knew there was nothing friendly about it. Belphagor held him in his place, controlling him.

Jason shifted to moved closer, but the demon tapped him on the shoulder. "Uh-uh. No good here. We've done what we came to do. Looks like she won't be coming with us this time." The demon shot another glance at the angel who had now moved to Nikka's side.

What had they come to do, other than torment her with Jason so close within her reach?

Before she had thought it, the sound behind her answered the question for her. The echoed report of gunshots rang out into the night. Nikka glanced back to the church that stood in the distance on the hill. The truck had driven her far enough away, but she could still see the building in the distance, especially now that the orange-red glow of fire erupted from the roof. Her mouth went dry, and her knees shook as she looked at the sight. Her baby was still there. Gideon. Amy. They were asleep in the abandoned church.

She glanced back to Jason and Belphagor. The demon smiled at her with the glint of red light in his pupils. But Jason only leaned back against the demon, his eyes staring at her in defeated agony.

They had done what they set out to do. Indeed.

Jason was the only one that could have gone into that church, being on hallowed ground. No demon could have entered there. He pulled her away, thinning the ranks and protection around her baby. Jadriel was bound to her, and he also left the sanctity of the chapel to save her, further reducing their ranks.

And leaving Adam vulnerable.

Tears fell from her eyes as she looked at Jason one last time before she turned and sprinted back to the burning chapel. Even as she ran from him, she knew he would be gone as soon as she turned away.

CHAPTER 13

NIKKA

---

ikka neared the hilltop. The heat of the dry timber of the roof exploding from the fire rushed over her. Jadriel moved swiftly, in a blur of light and sound, and appeared at the burning threshold seconds before she arrived. At the sight of the angel, a myriad of shapes and shadows receded into the surrounding trees, their red and black eyes moving and drifting in and out of the dark. Beyond the crackling of the timber and smell of the char, the scent of decay surrounded the church. A horde of creatures vanished into the night before she could reach the end of the road and see the inferno that had enveloped the church.

Through the flowing tears, she saw two shapes on the ground just outside the front steps, their silhouettes framed by the burning building. Amy crouched over Gideon, who lay on the ground and bleeding from a wound in his shoulder. Jadriel had run past them, toward the last of the shadows that disappeared with the roar of motorcycle engines.

Nikka rushed to Gideon's side and blinked her eyes clear enough to see him. The wound in his shoulder flowed so fast that it soaked the ground under him in an ever-growing pool of crimson. A mortal wound in his mortal body. He shuddered in pain and distress as Amy leaned over him, the heels of her palms putting pressure on his wound to little avail.

"We didn't hear them until it was too late," Amy cried as she looked down at him. "They burned it to flush us out. They shot him and took the baby."

Sweat had beaded on Gideon's forehead. He grimaced as she pressed harder on him, but blood welled through her fingers. The pallor in his skin grew with each second.

Nikka moved her hands to take over Amy's job, but she couldn't stop the shaking that had started in her body. With every beat of his heart, she could feel Gideon slipping away from under her touch.

"They took him," Gideon said, his voice weak and trembling. "I could not stop them."

She pressed down harder, and Gideon cried out in pain. As sorry as she was, she couldn't let up.

Panic shot through her as blood flowed over her fingers. "Jad," she shouted into the dark, crying out his name. The angel was the only one who could do something about this. She knew it worked; she was living proof of it.

Jadriel appeared in the orange glow of the fire, his eyes wide and his chest heaving from running.

"Help him, please," she cried as she looked up at him. He stood over them, his towering figure imposing in the bonfire behind him.

The angel cringed as he fought against Nikka's binding sigil. The muscles rippled in his jaw, and the cords in his neck bulged. He finally dropped to his knees, his eyes glaring at her.

"Save a demon?" he said with a hiss.

"He is not a demon anymore. He's been redeemed. He has paid his penance, now save his mortal life," she said. "Please, Jadriel."

He took in a slow breath and reached his hand out to touch hers. He lifted her away from Gideon's bleeding wound, the blood dripping from her fingertips. Gideon cried out through a clenched jaw as the angel placed a single palm over the wound and closed his eyes. Violet light shimmered within the tattoos along his arms, a glow that moved down through his veins and into his hand. The light shone from under his palm. The light intensified and Gideon gritted his teeth in pain, pulsing the threads of violet into the vessels throughout his body.

The light vanished, and Gideon gasped as Jadriel lifted his hand from his chest. The flow of blood had stopped, leaving behind a gaping hole in Gideon's shirt but the flesh below it remained intact. The pale visage around his eyes faded, leaving Gideon's skin smooth and untainted.

The angel stood, glaring down at Nikka. But she looked up at him with a smile and tears still running down her cheeks. "Thank you," she said before he turned away from her.

Gideon stood, his hands reaching to the wound and feeling for any further pain. Nikka wrapped her arms around him, and he embraced her as she cried into his neck. Trembling shuddered down her neck. Every second of the last moments crashed onto her shoulders. The demons taking Adam. Jason out in the desert with Belphagor at his side. The wound in Gideon's chest. All of it fell in a blanket of shuddering anger that could only come out of her in wracked tears. Gideon's arms held her tight against his chest until a quiver grew in his arms. She clenched her fists onto the back of his shirt, but he pulled her away from him.

And she saw the growing ember of red in his eyes.

His forearms bulged, and his teeth clenched just before he shouted into the air with an inhuman growl. The ground under her quaked with his rage. Pazuzu boiled just beneath the surface of his skin, the demon fighting against its bonds. Gideon scrambled to his feet and backed away from her, his fingers formed into rigid claws.

Jadriel stepped beside Nikka and pulled her behind him, his arm held out across her torso in a protective stance. The angel only saw the demon rising, but he didn't know Gideon like she did. He had fought too hard to keep control of Pazuzu, and he wouldn't let him out now. She placed a hand on Jadriel's wrist and stepped around him despite the concerning look he gave her.

"Gideon," she said and took a single step closer to him, but he backed away from her, his eyes blazing now.

Those two ember-red lights looked up at Jadriel. "It is time to break the seals."

"No," the angel said.

"They have my son," Gideon shouted above the sound of the bonfire beside him, his voice split into the sound of a human and a beast. "This is what we have been waiting for since Lucifer fell. This is the end of days."

"If they are released—"

"This is why the Harbingers were placed there." Gideon stepped closer to Jadriel, his shoulders wide as he stood before the angel, two powers of Heaven and Hell. "This is the moment they have been waiting for."

Jadriel stood firm despite the demon only inches from him now. "I cannot open the seals."

"No. But she can," Gideon said, his red eyes flashing to Nikka.

All eyes now turned to her. The burning church roared behind her, and the roof collapsed, sending a shower of embers into the air around her, but she didn't turn to face it. An angel and a demon looked at her with all the expectations of something that she didn't understand.

"I can do what?" Nikka said, her voice weaker than she had wanted. She didn't like not knowing what they talked about.

"Release the Harbingers," Gideon said. The red glow in his eyes faded to only a glimmer of red, and the muscles in his shoulders softened. "Only the one with the powers of Heaven and Earth can break the seals. That means either you or our son."

"And who are the Harbingers?" She wasn't sure she wanted to know.

"Four angels set aside for the final judgement," Jadriel said and sighed, exhausted. "They have the ability to end the Apocalypse, they can stop Lucifer. You have the power to release them, but you will also have to defeat them before they will enact their powers. They are agents of neither Heaven nor Hell."

The air around her grew thin, and her ears rang. Four angels. Another group of insane creatures bent on destruction, or whatever it is that they do. The sound of the bonfire grew distant, and her legs weakened. She bent over, her hands on her knees, as she took in a deep breath.

Lucifer had her son now, and she realized that Jadriel had been right when he said that Adam's fate was not necessarily her choice. She had to do something because sitting around wasn't going to help. If she had to face four crazy angels to save him, then there would be no use in waiting to decide.

She swallowed the lump that had formed in her throat and stood straighter, trying to hold back the trembling that had started in her hands. "Okay. I'll do it."

The object still burned in the palm of her hand ever since Jason pressed it there. Gideon turned away from her, and she gazed down at it in the light of the blazing church behind her. The face of a Las Vegas poker chip shone in the light, a calling card sent from Jason. A beacon to the place where the demons took her son.

Part Nine

"Abandon all hope, ye who enter here."
—Dante's Inferno

CHAPTER 14

JASON

When demons moved through physical space, it always made him dizzy and nauseous. He had seen angels move this way as well. It must be something that they can all do, the quick rush from one place to another. Teleportation. They had no need for vehicles unless they were transporting more than they could carry, and he was definitely enough for them to carry.

Belphagor had locked the chain around his collar like a dog and yanked on it as they entered into the grand threshold of the building that had been turned into the largest nest he had ever witnessed.

Night fell over the remains of the great city, but fires and torches lit the entrance of the nest where drones inhabiting the bodies of men and women stood in wait. Belphagor sauntered through the threshold, the chain in his hand leading his favorite pet through the doors and into the sweltering space of the former grand casino and hotel.

Jason cringed away from the groping hands of the demons that always antagonized him when Belphagor led him through the horde. The smell of decay that emanated from the building made him gag at first, but it somehow managed to lessen the longer he stayed in there.

Thousands of demons had gathered in this place in the last several months, crowding around the corridors and lingering in the great atrium. Just like groupies with rock stars, Lucifer's presence brought the horde ever closer.

The chain tugged, and he walked faster, the dark of the entrance closing in on him. Torch light glowed in the distance as they emerged into the atrium of what was once an enormous and gaudy hotel but now had been turned into a demon nest. Black oily eyes turned toward him in every face that watched as they paraded through the atrium. The entourage behind Belphagor moved in closer, and now Jason heard the baby crying in a demon's arms.

The sound gripped at his chest, painful and burning. The demon holding the child stepped beside Belphagor and laughed, drones reaching their claws to touch the child as the demon walked through the horde. The torn cries coming from the baby grew more distant now that the demon carried him further ahead into the darkened corridors. Belphagor must have sensed his agitation because he yanked on the chain. Jason choked against the pull of the collar and dragged his steps closer with the demon that had him leashed.

The corridor plunged into a wide bank of useless elevator shafts. With no electricity, they hadn't worked in over a year, but the stairwell provided ample opportunity to ascend to the penthouse at the top of the hotel. They moved onto the stairs, and the closed-in space mixed with the summer heat should have made the air stifling, but the chill coming from hundreds of demons left the air as cold as the depths of a cave. The closer they rose to the penthouse, the greater the chill. The thing that resided up there made each breath from Jason's lips turn into puffs of white frost.

And each step toward the top of the hotel left his chest hollow as he thought about the fate of the baby in the hands of that beast.

As they emerged onto the top floor landing, the demons stepped aside to allow Belphagor through with his chained seraph and the demon that carried the baby. The others would not be entering the penthouse today, as much as they wanted to. Only the victorious were allowed in there.

The double doors opened, and they moved inside. Every time Belphagor dragged him into this place, his legs weakened, and his stomach turned. The presence that resided here lived in direct opposition to the power inside of him, and his true nature fought against it even at the cellular level. The moment he crossed the threshold, the evil inside twisted its willowy arms around his soul.

Belphagor yanked on the chain again, making Jason trip forward until he stumbled and fell to his knees. When he tried to get up, the demon shoved him down with his boot, pressing his face against the cold granite floor. The room remained dark except for the moonlight that came through the panoramic windows that looked over the dead city. He didn't need to look up to feel the evil move along the glass, admiring the view that he had created.

"It is done," Belphagor said, removing his boot from Jason's back.

Slow, deliberate footsteps clicked against the granite, the sound of expensive shoes even in the Apocalypse. As the evil grew closer, Jason shivered and swallowed back nausea that welled in his gut.

The baby's crying had subsided as the creature moved toward them. Jason glanced up from his position on the floor as the beast reached for the child and drew him from the demon's grasp. Lucifer smiled at the baby, his mouth framed by a thin goatee and his long black hair pulled back into a ponytail. The gray suit he wore today looked like something he would have found at the most expensive shop on the Strip, or what was left of it at least.

"My kindred," he said to the baby and raised it into the air as he looked at him. The child's crying eased, and his small eyes focused on the beast that held him. Through the dimly lit room, Jason could see the small points of a red glow begin in the baby's eyes.

"You look like your father," Lucifer said and then pulled the baby close to him as though he had loved him since the day he was born. "And his mother? Where is she?"

"We were unable to acquire her," Belphagor said and shifted his stance.

Lucifer turned to face him, his black eyebrow cocked in his angular and handsome face. "And why is that?"

The demon cleared his throat. "There were some unexpected complications."

"Complications," Lucifer spoke, his voice even and calm.

"There was an angel with her," Belphagor interjected. "A protector. But we were able to separate her from the baby long enough to get him."

Lucifer nodded, his gaze drifting back to the baby in his arms. "So your little experiment was a success, however."

Belphagor glanced down to Jason. "Yes. It worked perfectly, and I believe that it will succeed in bringing her back here, especially now that she knows we have the baby."

"Well, I hope it does, for your sake. You have one more chance." Lucifer looked up at Belphagor. His eyes swam with a light of black and blue and red that filled the entire orb. "I will have her here, or I will take your head." He walked back toward the panel of windows as the baby made cooing sounds in his arms. "Now, get him back to the angel. I suspect your drug is wearing off."

Jason didn't need to see the shadow of fear settle over Belphagor's face to know that he was worried. He felt the tug on the chain and rose to his feet, more than happy to depart this dreadful room. Being in Lucifer's presence for more than a few minutes made him too sick to think or even breathe. The demon hurried his pace to get out of there, pulling Jason with him back into the stairwell.

"This is your fault," Belphagor said with a guttural growl that hid behind every word. "You had her in your grasp."

They moved down, floor after floor, as the demon moved faster to get back down to the catacombs below the hotel. When Jason didn't provide him with an answer, he pulled the chain with such force that he choked and fell into the wall at the bottom floor landing. The demon rushed around as he pulled the slack from the chain and shoved his forearm into Jason's throat, pinning him to the wall.

"The only reason you're still alive is that He wants to keep experimenting," he said, pointing back up to the evil that lived in the penthouse. "If it were up to me, you would have been flayed and left to be a breeder, or I would have put your head on a spike."

Jason grasped at the demon's wrist, trying to catch a breath, but he was far too weakened to fight him. There was so little power in his tattoos anymore that they never sparkled or gave him the smallest surge of energy to fight. Just as the demons had designed it.

The demon pressed harder into his throat. "I will bring her to him, and there's nothing you can do to stop it." Belphagor's angry face twisted into a sardonic smile. "I would bet that when he finally has her, he will make her kill you. That I would pay to watch."

The demon pulled away, and Jason dropped to the ground, coughing and gasping for a breath. Belphagor stood over him and laughed as he pulled on the chain again. "Come on. Let's get this over with."

He stumbled to get to his feet when the chain tightened and pulled the collar through the doors of the catacombs. The air was not only cold here, but damp and it carried the sounds of crying and weeping. The demons had designed this place to imprison the humans they collected, using them for various purposes. Of course, the catacombs held the people that weren't utilized for possession. As much as he wanted to push the knowledge aside, this place kept the collection of humans they used for breeding. A place to reproduce more bodies for possession.

Jason kept his gaze on the ground when he walked through here. People moved to the barred doors of their prisons as he passed, hoping for news of the outside world. He couldn't look at their faces, hopeless and desperate for a way to end their suffering. He had failed them in so many ways, and some of them knew it. Sometimes, he heard their whisperings as he walked by, with the name of seraph on their lips.

He couldn't save them. The demons had built their prison well, in so many respects, and they had discovered a way to keep him locked inside of it, helpless and powerless. And they hadn't learned it on their own, which was the worst part of it.

They neared "The Clinic," as the demons called it, but it was nothing more than a medical experimentation and torture chamber. Battery-powered lights hung around the room, giving the space a cold and fluorescent glow as Belphagor pulled Jason inside. Others were in there waiting for them, and hands pulled Jason deeper into the room and shoved him onto a gurney locked in the center of the large space. They moved fast to fasten the straps around his arms and legs, although he didn't fight them like he used to. There wasn't a benefit to struggling, he had learned. What was going to happen would happen regardless of his fight.

The door opened again and two demons accompanied by a third man entered the room. The same entourage that always came to administer the treatment. As familiar as this always was, Jason still felt the acid taste of hate build in his mouth when he saw him.

The man approached the gurney, his pale and short blonde hair like a halo above his head. Piercing blue eyes looked down at him from his perfect face.

"You saw her tonight," Samael spoke, the angel's voice almost a whisper and meant only for Jason. "You touched her. I can smell the faintest hint of her essence on your fingers."

Jason gritted his teeth. Everything he knew about this maniacal angel he had learned from Gideon when they were both searching for Nikka after she had gone missing. This was the creature that had taken her and tried to kill him when he had intervened to get her back. He was obsessed with Nikka far beyond anything that the devil could even create.

"Come on," Belphagor said, his voice breaking the silence in the room. "I don't have all night."

For a moment, the angel just stared down at him with those cold and soulless eyes. Then, he looked away and withdrew a syringe from a tray set up next to the gurney. He looked at the dark fluid in the clear vial as he held it up to the light.

"Do these seem to be working in the field?" he asked as he gazed at the syringe.

"They do now," Belphagor said, "as long as we use the blood of a general. He kept breaking through the others. And drone blood didn't seem to last more than an hour. At least these will keep him contained for about four or five hours."

"Have you ever asked Lucifer for a donation?" Samael said and glanced back to the demon who rested his back against the wall.

Belphagor let out a snort. "Are you kidding? Hell no. It would probably kill the seraph anyway."

Samael turned his icy eyes down to Jason. "Probably." Then his voice dropped low enough that only Jason could hear him as he leaned down, bringing the tip of the needle closer to the vein in his arm. "But then again, maybe not. We will never know unless we try."

The needle pierced his skin, and Jason clenched his teeth. The demon blood entered his veins, creating a trail of burning pain that coursed into his bloodstream. With each beat of his heart, it spread the venom into every organ, every cell until it strangled out his own will. Any shimmer of seraph power dimmed with the injection, leaving his brain in a fog and his thoughts incohesive.

The straps loosened around his arms and legs and he stumbled off the gurney as hands moved him to his feet. The next several minutes were a blur until he blinked his eyes and saw himself lying on the floor of his own cell, private and secluded in the deepest and darkest corner of the catacombs.

In that solitude and darkness, with the heavy influence of the demon blood in his veins, he lay on his back and only thought of her. He had touched her, felt her skin under his fingertips for the first time in months. Even though he had betrayed her, he recalled that glimmer of hope in her eyes when she first saw him.

At least she knew he was alive, even if she now wished he was dead.

CHAPTER 15

NIKKA

Nikka sat in the front seat of the Jeep, the door gaping open and her knees drawn to her chest as she watched Jadriel and Gideon argue about the next best thing to do. But when Gideon had mentioned the breaking of seals, she wanted to turn away and run.

The last time she had heard of the seals, she was in a run-down old church in the middle-of-nowhere-Nevada and speaking to a strange old priest. He had told her that she would be present when the seals were broken, that she was a weapon to fight against Lucifer. At the time, she thought it was just the ramblings of an old man, but everything he had said back then had come true. He knew about Wormwood, the military designation of the EMP that destroyed the electrical grid. He knew that Apocalypse was inevitable.

And now, here she was, staring at an angel and demon as they fought over her role in breaking the seals.

She pulled her knees in tighter, hoping to close the hole in her spirit where her baby should reside, where she kept her most treasured feelings about Jason and Gideon. She rested her forehead on her knees and then there was only silence.

"I will take you now," Jadriel said.

Nikka looked up at him as he stood outside the vehicle with Gideon at his side.

"We're going alone?" she said and shot a glance to Gideon.

"Only you and I can go there, nobody else," Jadriel said, extending his hand for her to take.

The nervous fluttering started in her chest. Her mouth went dry, and she bit her lip to try and stop the shaking that started in her spine. Whenever that started, it only triggered a chain reaction of fear and self-doubt. She needed to get it under control now, or it would never stop.

Gideon stepped between her and the angel, his hands resting on her shoulders. "I know it is hard. I would give anything to go in your place, but I cannot."

"I need to tell you something," she said. "Jason was there with Belphagor."

His brows knit together. "What? How is this possible?"

"I think he's their prisoner. They're using him," she glanced to the ground. "That's how they got to Adam."

The hands on her shoulders tightened, and he took in a slow breath. "He did this?"

"He gave me this," she said and showed him the poker chip. "I think he's trying to tell me where they're taking Adam."

Gideon took the chip from her and turned it over and over.

"He had no choice. But now we know where they're going."

"Las Vegas," he muttered.

"As much as I don't want to go back there, it's where we have to go after I do this."

She shuddered, and Gideon looked back up at her. She looked up at him and felt the quiver of tears begin in her eyes. "What if I can't do it? What if I can't get Adam back?"

He leaned in and placed his lips against her forehead. His hands moved to her face, and he lifted her chin to look at him. "You will, for you are one of the archangels. He will teach you your power, more than I ever could. And releasing the Harbingers is the only thing we have left."

"I know," she said and sniffed back her tears. But it didn't matter how many times he said it. The last thing she wanted to do was meet another angry angel. And definitely not four of them.

"He will bring you back to me," Gideon said and shot a pointed glance back to Jadriel.

The angel nodded in agreement.

"And I'll keep Gideon safe while you're gone." Amy's voice sounded behind them. Gideon stepped aside enough that Nikka saw her standing there with one of her assault rifles from the Jeep on her hip. Nikka smiled and stood from the vehicle.

She wiped the tears from her cheeks with the back of her hand and faced Jadriel. "All right. Let's do this. Where do we go?"

"We must be alone," Jadriel said. "And we need running water."

"We passed a river not too far back," Amy said, ticking her head back down the road where they had come the night before.

"Okay," Nikka said. "I'll drive. You just tell me what to do next."

* * *

She pulled the vehicle over as soon as she saw the first bend in the river. Palm trees hung over the bank with a thick layer of vines and brush. The engine rumbled to a stop, but she couldn't move from the driver's seat as she gazed over the smooth ripples on the surface of the water.

"So," she said after a few seconds of silence. The angel didn't move but only looked out over the river with her. "What do I do? Just drink it and wait?"

"You must go into the water," he said, his voice low and even. She had seen an angel get upset and rage before, but she had never sensed fear in one. Not like she did now in Jadriel. That didn't help the increasing buzz of flutters in her chest.

Into the water. Her fingers clenched around the fabric of the long pants she wore and her toes curled inside the thick-soled boots. Thankfully, she had the sense to change into something that might protect her a little bit if she had to trudge down the thorny embankment and into the water. She stepped from the vehicle and loosened the fists that she had made. The angel moved with her to the edge of the bank and let her step first into the water. The river lapped at her boot, and she looked back at him.

"All the way," he said, nodding to the deeper center of the river.

The first hints of dawn left sparkles of orange and pink over the surface of the water, but it kept the depths of it a murky black. The water soaked through her trousers, chilling against her skin. It made her gasp as she moved deeper until it rose to her hips.

Jadriel moved into the water with her. "That is deep enough."

The cool of the water made her shiver, but the goosebumps on her arm also rose in reaction to the nervous buzz that continued in her chest. The warm desert air did nothing to drive away the chill.

"What now?" Nikka asked and turned back to him.

He stepped beside her, the water running between them in swirls of black. "I will now take you there."

"I don't get it." Her lips quivered, and she clasped her shaking hands to her chest.

"They are imprisoned on another plain, beyond the veil of what we see on this Earth." His hand opened out over the surface of the water. "Water is a doorway between worlds. The other option is I strangle you until you enter the other realm with only a single breath to bring you back."

She swallowed the lump that had formed in her throat. "Uh, no thanks. Let's try the river thing first."

"Very well," he said.

The angel stepped closer, standing only inches in front of her. He was so close now that she smelled the familiar scent of lavender that all angels carried. His hands rose up until they settled on her shoulders.

"You must listen carefully now," he said. "You will only have a few minutes. When you first open your eyes, there will be a tunnel. Go as far as you can, no matter how dark it is."

"Wait," she said, the cold of the water now making her shiver and her teeth chatter. "Aren't you going with me?"

"I can show you the way, but only you can enter," he said. "You are a being between worlds, part human, part angel. No other would be allowed."

This was not what she had expected.

"When you get to the end, you will see the Great Seal, and when you see it, you will know what to do."

"What does that mean?" A surge of anxiety bubbled up into her chest. "How will I know?"

"You must believe," he said. Just as he spoke, a surge of violet light erupted in his pupils. The hands on her shoulders tightened into a sudden and painful grip. Before she could push away from him, he shoved her off balance, and she lost her footing on the uneven river floor. The angel pushed her under the surface of the water.

The sudden cold that flooded over her face made her want to gasp. She tried to turn and kick at him but she had no leverage in the water, and his hands were like vice grips. No room to move or twist away from him. She tried to scream, but it only came out as a muffled rush of bubbles. In the undulating surface of the water, two points of violet light hovered in the dark water. She forced her arm to her side, to catch the river floor and gain some ground, but he held her too tight.

The dizzying effect of water and no oxygen starved her brain. The reflexive gasp happened and her lungs filled with water. Nothing left for her body to use. Those two points of violet light faded into the black with the ringing in her ears.

* * *

Her eyes flew open, and she stood in a tunnel, darkness around her and only the faintest light in the distance. Rough-hewn bricks lined the walls of the corridor and plunged into further darkness. She glanced back to the dim glow behind her and saw the rippling surface of water covering the exit like a portal.

That damn angel just drowned her.

You will only have a few minutes.

There was no time to be angry. She turned away from the water and faced the darkest end of the tunnel. Though her clothes and hair were dry where she stood, she still felt the chill of cold river water against her skin. Water is a doorway between worlds; that's what Jadriel said. Everything around her detailed that she stood in a dark tunnel, but the rippling water still stroked her arms even though she couldn't see it. She was slowly dying under the surface of the water, and she had precious little time to find the Great Seal.

She broke into a sprint through the dark. The light of the portal soon faded, leaving her with nothing but inky blackness all around her. The disorientation of it made her footsteps falter. Her hands reached out before her, hoping that she would feel it if something blocked her way or that the tunnel turned.

One minute.

Nothing but darkness and the air thinned around her. Or was that just in her brain, a construct to tell her that she was dying in the water?

Two minutes.

Every step became a struggle. Her fingers searched ahead of her, and her mind reeled in desperation. What if this was just an endless black hole and she was like Alice falling forever as she tried to chase the White Rabbit?

Her feet pounded harder, faster, and she pumped her arms to keep her momentum forward, but her muscles weakened and burned the further she went. Her chest clenched and her lungs ached with each boot fall. To hell if something was in her way. Her arms no longer searched. It was too much effort to keep them up anymore. Then her next step found no ground, and she slipped into the blackest void.

The earth hit her back with a thud, knocking more air out of her compromised lungs. She opened her eyes to a room with no corners, but the darkness had vanished. The same stone lined the rounded walls of this place. She glanced up at the ceiling, expecting to see the long dark hole that had dropped her here but it was only a ceiling of the same stone. Uneven, crude blocks of stone lined the floor and sloped upward in the center of the room.

She pushed herself to her feet and stepped back to see that she had landed on a wide, flat stone with a mound and impression in the center of it. Surrounding the stone were four circles with chiseled markings set within them. Enochian. The same language as her tattoos.

Four circles. Four angels. These must be the seals.

And the mound in the center must be the Great Seal. She stepped closer and examined the impression in the middle of the mound. An imprinted hand.

You will know what to do.

She raised her hand and gazed at her palm as she flexed her fingers. This seal would undoubtedly do something the moment she placed her hand on the print. Once she did this, there would be no going back. This was the only way left to fight Lucifer and get her son back. Whoever these angels were, she had to face them if she was ever going to see Adam again.

She stepped to the mound and extended her hand to the print. Her lungs ached for air again. Her time was running low. Her palm made contact with the stone.

For a moment, she only stood there, glancing around the room without corners. The lack of oxygen made her ears ring louder.

A ghostly green light erupted from under her hand, cold and bright. She tried to pull away, but her hand had fused with the stone. The ground under her feet shuddered. She fell to her knees and glanced up at the stone walls around her that shook. Chunks of masonry fell around her with each swell in the quakes. The green light bled through the cracks in the stone, inching toward each of the four seals surrounding the mound. The sigil within each seal took on the green glow and filled the room with bright light. With a loud crack that echoed around her, each seal snapped, sending out a green mist that rose from the ground below the room.

Nikka pulled at her hand again as the mist spilled out onto the floor. The mound released her, and she fell back. She scrambled to the furthest part of the room and away from the mist that moved across the floor.

The room quaked again, shuddering with each belch of green mist that poured from the four seals.

"Now's a good time to help me, Jad," she called out into the furthest reaches of the room. Maybe he could hear her, from somewhere outside this desperate room.

The light that glowed from under the mound now grew in intensity, casting a sickly green hue across her skin. A crack split across the ceiling and rained down more stone around her.

"Jad," she shouted as the mist rolled toward her.

The water slipped away from her face as the angel pulled her to the surface. She rose with a choking scream, her feet struggling to find the river ground. The angel wrapped his arms around her until she had steadied herself. She coughed and spilled more water from her lungs.

The last memory before coming to the surface still clung to her thoughts, and she glanced down at the dark water around her. The faintest hint of green light still lingered deep in the water, much further down than the floor of the river bed.

She struggled in his grasp to escape the light that shimmered from deep in the earth. Jadriel backed away with her in his arms, his steady gaze staying on the light below the water.

"You did it," he said, pulling her with him to the river bank.

"They're coming," she said, frantic and trying to pull away from him. The sensation of the cold green mist still tickled across her skin.

"Not yet," he said, his voice even and calm. "They have been released into this world. They will now seek to possess bodies, and then they will unleash their powers."

"And what powers do they have?"

"Pestilence. War. Famine and Death," he said, his eyes still searching the waters for the fading green light.

She shivered in his arms as the realization hit her. "Four angels. You mean I just released the Four Horsemen of the Apocalypse."

CHAPTER 16

NIKKA

---

*T*he ride back to the burned-out church dragged on for what seemed like hours. The chill of the river still clung to Nikka's bones despite the warmth of the morning sun. Shivers danced over her skin as she hugged herself and let Jadriel drive. The cold wouldn't leave her, and she knew it wasn't only from the damp. Something dreadful had followed her out of the water and into this world, and the consequences of it hung behind her like a shadow.

She hadn't said anything more to him since she rushed out of the water. He had known that he was sending her to release the Four Horsemen when he pushed her into the river. Maybe he was too soulless to understand the impact it would have on her—on the world—but that wasn't the only thing that bothered her. Gideon knew, and yet he didn't tell her what was going to happen.

The vehicle came to a stop, and she saw Amy and Gideon stand from their place in the shade of a palm tree. He shifted as he craned to see into the Jeep, undoubtedly to know if she was all right.

She opened her door, feeling the warmth of the Mexican sunlight as it touched the bare skin of her shoulders. Her damp hair fell across her back and wet the thin gray tank top that covered her.

Gideon approached her, his arm reaching toward her, but she stepped back and out of his reach.

"Did you know?" she said, her teeth still chattering, as she looked at him.

"Why are you wet?" Amy spoke and neared her.

Gideon averted his gaze, his shoulders curling inward.

"Answer me. Did you know what was going to happen?"

"Nikka," Amy said, trying to get her attention. "What happened?"

She shot a glance toward Amy. "He drowned me."

"What?" Amy said, and her eyes fell on the angel that stood beside the vehicle. She put an arm around Nikka. Her body heat radiated into her core, easing the chills that had settled along her back.

"It was the only way," Gideon said. "I am sorry. I should have said—"

"The Four Horsemen," Nikka said, the words difficult to say because it was so unbelievable. "I released the Four Horsemen of the Apocalypse. Yes. You should have told me."

Amy's face drained of all color, and she stepped back, her glance shooting at each of them. "Are you serious?"

Gideon didn't look at her. The whites of his eyes had gone red with irritating tears and torment, something that he had dealt with alone since she left with Jadriel. He was probably right to have not told her. Maybe she wouldn't have gone, and it was the only thing they had left to get their child back. Gideon suffered too.

She reached her hand to his face, her cold fingers finding comfort in the warmth of his skin. She lifted his chin to look at her. When she met his eyes, she said, "It's done now. The seals are broken."

"They will come for you," he said. "And there is nothing I can do. I have no power against them."

"But I do," Jadriel said and moved from his place against the vehicle. "I can teach you how to use your powers as an archangel."

She glanced back to the angel. He didn't have to offer his help, but the angel did it without coercion. "So, what? Do I just hang around here waiting for them to show up?" Nikka asked.

"No," Gideon said. "We keep moving north. We know where Lucifer is likely keeping Adam. We go until we cannot go further."

"You mean go to Las Vegas." The thought of returning there made a stone settle in her gut. The last time she was there, she almost died. Well, maybe she did die. She wasn't sure these days. Something terrible had happened, and every time she remembered it, she couldn't look at Gideon.

Pazuzu had tortured her there. The pain of it still hung at the edges of her memory, bleeding and raw as though it had happened yesterday. Thankfully, she had gone almost nine months without a single memory of it. But it all had come rushing back as soon as Samael had lifted the memory block that he had put in her mind. Every horrible detail of that night was still there, and so was Gideon's/Pazuzu's smiling and wicked face.

Of course, it would have to be Las Vegas. That place was destined to be the final hold-out of the devil himself, and Jason was there with him. But she would endure anything to get her son back.

"All right," she said, trying to hold back the dizzying effect of her memories. "Let's go then."

With the meager supplies that didn't get burned in the church, they climbed into the Jeep and started along the road that would lead them through Mexico. The landscape changed from subtropical palms and green hills that bled into mountains to dry and isolated desert. The heat of scorching sun beat down on a bleached road that showed signs of abandonment. Weeds had sprouted along the seams and stretched from the edges of the road as they tried to take over where mankind left it. Any small town or village along the way provided an opportunity to stop and look for any signs of humanity. But everything had gone quiet in the last year.

They approached the outskirts of a town as the sun reached to the far borders of the west. Time to stop. Time to rest. The gas gauge had dropped close to the "E" mark, and it would be a perfect moment just to kill the engine and get out for the night.

They stepped out of the vehicle in front of the gaping gates to a palatial but abandoned estate. Vineyards had once lined the landscape stretching out for acres on the inside of the fences, but they had since withered and died. A drive curled around the vineyards to the main house with its darkened windows. When they had searched the main floor, Gideon decided it was empty and safe enough to stay in, at least for the night.

Nikka wandered through the open door of the estate. With the oncoming twilight, shadows glided through the windows. Jagged edges of glass glinted like broken teeth at the edges of the parlor windows. Sand collected in skiffs from the western breezes that drifted through the shattered windows. The smooth layer of sand revealed no other footprints, an abandoned building long-lost to civilization. Her boot broke through the drifts of sand, and she stopped in the central room before a grand staircase.

Empty. Lost to time, like the old ruins of the Mayan culture that had once spread across this land. Now, this civilization was gone as well.

She gazed over the darkening corners of the room. The others had ascended the stairs to find places to settle for the night. They had left her alone, watching the light fade until the empty estate was swallowed in the dark. She finally turned away from the windows and ascended the stairs.

The staircase opened to a broad landing and a corridor that extended the length of the home. As she entered onto the landing, she saw Gideon waiting at the nearest door. She walked toward him, but he stepped back and held the door open for her. As she stepped to the threshold, she saw a large bed, the linens still intact.

"For you," he said with a tired smile. "The windows are not broken, and the bed is clean."

She stepped inside, but he didn't follow her. Instead, he hung back in the shadows until she turned to him.

"I don't want to stay in here alone," she said and clutched at the edge of his shirt before he could back away from her.

"How can you want to be with me?" he muttered, his voice shaking as he looked away from her. "After all this?"

Her brow furrowed and he tried to pull away from her. "Gideon, stop it."

His grip tightened around her hand to free himself from her. "I could not protect our son. I could not protect you."

She stepped in close to him and wrapped her arm around the back of his neck, pressing her forehead against his. He finally stilled as she moved in close to him. "Don't do this. It isn't your fault, you know. I can't do this without you."

Through the dark, she felt his breath against her skin. His arms slipped around her hips, tentative at first, and then he pulled her closer.

"I need you with me," she said.

He moved his head against hers in a nod before he kissed her. In the dark of that abandoned place, they just held each other as they drifted to sleep on the bed, the quiet of the desert around them.

CHAPTER 17
NIKKA

"Wake up," Jadriel's voice spoke through the dark. His hand touched Nikka's shoulder and jostled her. She thought it was the last images of a dream, but he stood over her when she opened her eyes.

"What time is it?" she said, her voice hoarse.

"Early." He shook her again. "I must show you something before the others awaken."

She blinked her eyes clear and shifted on the bed, slipping her arm away from Gideon's torso. He didn't move or even stir when the angel spoke. When she finally got to her feet and steadied herself, she could see the faint light on the eastern horizon as dawn approached. Jadriel stepped out of the room and into the dark of the empty corridor.

What could be so important?

With a yawn, she followed him, her joints stiffer than usual. That was something she could blame on the angel. Sore muscles and bones after nearly drowning her in the river. Another near-death experience had left her drained. Perhaps that was why it took so long to recover this time. She moved into the grand atrium and followed him outside. The desert air had cooled overnight, a product of the low humidity as compared to the jungle of Belize. She glanced around the edge of the dead vineyard and turned to face him. The colors of the coming morning lit upon his face.

"Okay, I'm up," she said. "What's this about?"

"I will teach you, and today will be the first lesson." He stepped closer to her and wrapped his fingers around her wrist, turning her palm upward. His index finger touched her palm, and she winced with the familiar singe of pain as he drew a sigil over her skin. The flesh of her palm blackened, just as it had when Samael gave her the marks. As soon as he had finished, the sigil remained on her skin for only a moment and then vanished.

But the mark never truly disappeared. The power of it bled into her hand, coursing into her veins and inching up her arm until it had settled in her forearm, at the end of the line of marks that Samael had given her. As it moved, she gritted her teeth against the pain, feeling it increase her power by that much more. She glanced down at her arm when the mark appeared, settling in to stay.

"You now have the power of the Angel's Blade." With a faint smile on his lips, he stepped back from her and reached behind his back with both hands, just as he had when he had challenged her in the jungle. His hands found the curved hilts of the swords attached to his back, pulling the half-moon blades from the hidden scabbard. Violet fire caught along the saber edges as he held them out before him.

The moment she saw them, her heart jumped inside her ribs. Was it possible, to feel the sword in her hand again? Was it only a matter of a sigil and an angel spell?

The angel nodded to her, a signal to do the same. She reached behind her, a motion that had become so familiar before her marks had been removed. The fingers of her right hand reached just past her ear, and for a moment she stopped. If she felt nothing back there, she was sure that her heart would shatter. She held her breath and reached just a few more inches.

And she touched the firm edge of something behind her back. Her fingers wrapped around a handle, firm and familiar. Her grip tightened, and she withdrew a blade, the edge long and glinting with silver in a whorl of violet fire that erupted down the length of it as she held it before her. A katana, the weight of it exactly like the one she had grown to love.

The breath rushed from her lungs and her face hurt with the smile she held. The fire of the blade danced around her fingers where she held it, swaying it back and forth as she familiarized herself with its heft and glide.

"Why is it different than yours?" she said, the smile never leaving her face.

"It is the blade that is best for you, as these are best for me," he said. "Your weapon cannot kill a demon, nor can it kill an angel, but it can make them leave their hosts with one slice. It does not take much, but only the seraph can kill a demon."

"So can anything kill an angel?" she said, the violet fire-light glowing neon purple against her skin.

"An Executioner." His eyes grew dark. "They are called by the Guardians, and only in the direst of circumstances. The only other one who has killed an angel was Lucifer."

"Whoa," she said. "Really? How did he manage that?"

"He had power that was second only to God. It was his abuse of that power that resulted in his fall."

"So, who are the Guardians?"

He re-sheathed his weapons, diminishing the purple light between them. She followed his lead and placed the sword behind her again, but cringed at the small twinge of defeat when it left her hand.

"Guardians are the archangels who protect the gates of Heaven. They rarely meddle in human affairs, that's left up to the Watchers."

"A lot of good they do," she said with a roll of her eyes.

"They do," Jadriel said, the hurt evident in his eyes.

"Don't look at me like that. Samael was a Watcher, and look what happened. He screwed everything up. He's the reason the world is dying."

Jadriel looked to the ground. "It is true. He violated the trust that had been given to him. He should never have been allowed to create . . . ." He stopped before he said anything else.

"Go ahead, say it. He shouldn't have been allowed to create me. I'm an abomination, you said it yourself when you met me."

"Yes, well," he said after he cleared his throat, "the Watcher's work is essential to keeping the balance here. As you can plainly see, when it is not followed properly, the balance is lost."

"So that's why we're here," she said and shifted her stance, opening her shoulders. "I let out the Four Horsemen, and I need you to help me defeat them."

He nodded. "Of course." Jadriel moved toward her again, reaching for her wrist and placing his index finger to her palm again, but she stopped him.

"I meant what I said. When I have learned what I can and am able to defeat them and get my son back, I will free you."

"I believe you," Jadriel said. His gaze flashed up to her again, and she saw the faintest hint of violet light in the pupils of his eyes. "It is not often that I have mingled with humankind, but I know that you have been able to bear what you have for a reason."

"Can I ask you something? It might be a little personal."

"Very well."

His index finger still hovered over her palm. "Are you a Guardian?"

He smiled, his eyes softening and making his face even more handsome in the morning light. "I am."

"So you're like some sort of security guard for Heaven."

"In a manner of speaking, yes."

The biggest question burned in her throat, hesitant to emerge, but the implication made her stomach do somersaults. "So, have you seen God?"

He shot her a warning glance and tried to back away, but she grasped his hand and stopped him.

"What?" she said, holding onto him with desperation. "What is the big secret about him?"

"I cannot," he stammered. "We cannot speak of it, and no binding sigil in Heaven or Earth can break that command."

"But why?" she pleaded. "Why won't he come down here and help us stop all this death? Lucifer is winning, and he doesn't seem to care."

Jadriel shook his head. "It is not my place to speak on such matters."

Nikka released his hand and turned her gaze to the ground. "Fine. I'll just do this myself, without his help."

"Someday," he said and approached her again. "You will understand the meaning of all of it. Until then, you are the one that has been chosen to lead the charge. Do you accept this?"

She looked up at him, but she felt the exhaustion fill every cell in her body. "Yes. Of course, I do."

"Then we will continue," he said as he grasped her wrist and his index finger traced another mark in her palm.

As the morning light brightened on the eastern horizon, he placed sigil after sigil on her body, explaining each one and teaching her how to channel the power through the marks. The tattoos lined her arms, legs, and torso once again, just as they had when she was a seraph. The last few appeared along her neck and into her hair line, undoubtedly decorating her scalp. With the new marks, he taught her the fighting skills that she could use in addition to the power within the sigils. Speed, endurance, defense, and anticipation. The knowledge provided by the marks flowed into her thoughts as though they had always been there, just forgotten.

Jadriel moved with her in each stance, helping her place her hands and feet as she used the individual sigils. He stood behind her, his large hands beside hers as she positioned for the next move.

The dawn light fell across the face of the estate, and she caught sight of Gideon. He stood on the front porch, watching her. She smiled at him, but his brow had deep furrows, and his eyes narrowed as he watched the angel move with her. Wearing just a tank top left her arms bare, revealing the new tattoos that now etched across her skin and up her neck. She lost her smile as she looked at him, unable to tell if he was angry or just exhausted. Nikka turned away from him and focused on Jadriel's instructions.

Chapter 18
Gideon

The heat of the desert beat down onto the vehicle as they drove the long stretches of abandoned highways. Gideon rested his head back against the seat and eyed Jadriel, who now took over the duties of driving. The endless hours on the road made his head hurt, and they had last stopped about an hour ago to empty another of the dozen gas cans into the tank. Every town and village they had passed was desolate, except for a few wandering dogs that picked at the scraps of whatever they could find. They had rummaged through some of the homes and businesses to find some packaged food, enough to keep their stomachs from complaining, and siphoned gas from a few of the abandoned cars.

Each place they passed reminded him how lost the world was now. They had not seen a single person in the days since they had left Belize. Perhaps there was nobody left.

He tilted his head to look at Nikka, who sat across the back seat from him. She had pressed herself into the corner between the seat and the door, the wind from the open window tossing strands of her hair across her face as she gazed down at the colored cloth in her hand. Her fingers moved along the crocheted stitching at the edge. He recognized it as one of Adam's blankets, and then he saw the hint of tears swimming in her eyes.

His hand reached to hers and clasped around her fingers. She glanced up at him, and he saw a tear fall down her cheek. He wanted to say something, anything to make her feel better, but he knew there was nothing that could do such a thing. How could he console her when he still felt the rage of it in his own heart? He was supposed to protect the child; he held Adam in his arms when the drones attacked and tore him away. He had failed Nikka in so many ways.

"I am sorry," he said to her. It was the only thing he could think to say.

"It's not your fault," she said and clutched the blanket in her fist.

"Maybe I could have fought harder—"

"No," she interrupted him. "I said it wasn't your fault. They almost killed you, they would have if Jad hadn't been around to heal you. I couldn't lose both of you in one day."

Even though she tried to console him, it did not feel any different. The weight of it held onto his fresh, young soul, the one that she had given to him.

Nikka held the blanket to her face, and a faint smile spread across her lips. "It still smells like him."

She glanced up at him again and held out the blanket. He smelled the baby's familiar scent on it as well, but it only turned his stomach into a rock of anger.

"What will they do to him?" she finally said, her voice dropping.

This was the thing that he had dreaded to talk about with her. None of the scenarios were pleasant in the end.

"You can be assured that they will not hurt him." And this was the truth. Everything that he had ever known about his former life and associates was centered on the idea that someday they will find their anti-Christ and fight their way back into Heaven. "He will be cared for better than any other creature around him. They will want him alive and well and conditioned to their cause."

The tears shimmered in her eyes again. Gideon squeezed her hand, but he knew that it would not be enough to help.

"He will be in Lucifer's hands."

"But he's just a baby," Nikka said. "We can get him back before he's done any of that to him."

"Time and age mean nothing to Lucifer," Gideon said. "He has the ability to manipulate any of it."

The tears escaped her eyes. "What does that mean?"

"It means that you are doing exactly what you need to do," he said, sliding in closer to her. "You summoned the Harbingers. They are the one shot we have left to stop all of that from happening."

He pulled her in and held her, her slender frame shaking in his grasp. At times like this, she felt so human, nothing like the archangel that she had become or the seraph he once trained. Even with the fresh black tattoos on her arms and neck, she was sometimes the frightened and defeated girl that he had found in the hospital so long ago.

"Hey, guys," Amy's voice caught their attention.

Gideon glanced to where she sat in the front passenger seat. Her green eyes looked back to them. "Heads up. There's a big city ahead."

Nikka pulled away from him enough to glance through the windshield. He followed her gaze and saw the rising outline of a cityscape on the horizon. The roads they had taken wound through so many little towns that a city was an unusual site. The weather-battered highway signs alerted them to their location.

"Looks like Tampico," Amy said as the vehicle slowed.

Nobody had to say anything for Gideon to feel the flutters of anxiety build in his gut. There was a reason they tried to avoid large urban centers: that was where demons congregated and built their nests. It was the hard truth that he had learned in his travels with Jason in the early days of the Apocalypse. And this looked to be the biggest city any of them had seen since Nikka had removed them to Belize.

"What should I do?" Jadriel said, his hands clutching the steering wheel.

"Just keep to the main road," Gideon spoke. Of any of them, he and Amy had the most experience with unwanted demon attention in a city. Nikka had spent most of the early days since the EMP in the protection of Garnet Falls and had not seen what a demon hive could do. And Jadriel was just fresh to all of this.

They entered the city limits, and just like every other city he had seen in the world, this place was dead and deserted. Cars littered the roads where they had stopped the minute the EMP detonated, killing any electrical circuit. Jadriel maneuvered around the cars as they all watched out the windows for any signs of human or demon. Time had left the road sun-bleached, and weeds had sprouted from the edges of sidewalks and the cracks in the pavement.

The city had once been large and with significant influence from the United States. He recognized an occasional chain restaurant or grocery store, but they were now dilapidated with broken windows and gaping doors. Such emptiness sent a shiver down his spine as he watched a breeze pick up debris and litter from the parking lot and blow it across the road along with a couple of tumbleweeds. Empty and dead, just like everything else.

Jadriel drove steady down the four-lane road that speared through the center of the city. The salty sea air drifted into the windows and Gideon heard the crashing waves of the beach to the east. His eyes darted to the spaces between buildings, behind cars and in the open lots for any signs of life.

The city opened to large cathedrals and temples dotted along the roadside preceding the shopping district. The discarded traffic thinned enough for Jadriel to drive faster until he came to the intersecting highway that veered north. The abandoned cars thickened enough here that he could not drive through without diverting onto the sidewalks. He slowed the Jeep and drove the wheels onto the edge of the walk. Just as the rear tires bumped up onto the walk, Amy stiffened as she watched out her side window.

"I think I just saw someone," she said.

Gideon's eyes darted along her line of sight. "Demons?"

"I don't think so. I think it was a kid."

The angel drove slower, and they peered between the shops that lined the road. A figure then sprinted down an alleyway and shot left behind the next store.

"Stop," Amy called out to Jadriel, and her hand moved to the door handle before anyone could stop her. She bolted from the car.

"Amy, wait," Nikka called after her.

Gideon kept his eyes on the alley as he bolted from the car and moved after Amy. She ran around the shop and turned down the next block. The muscles in his arms tightened, ready to call forth the fire that now simmered in his core. He would never let a drone party descend on him unprepared ever again. Nikka continued to call after Amy as she followed her.

Then he saw what Amy had noticed from the car. A boy, no older than twelve with a shock of black hair, ran from the alley and across the street.

"Hey, stop," Amy called to him. The kid looked back at her, his brow furrowing as he looked at them. His foot caught the edge of the curb, and he tumbled onto the sidewalk.

She caught up to him before he could get to his feet. The kid scrambled back from her, his gaze darting between the three people that now stepped toward him.

"It's okay," Amy said and crouched down to see him at eye level.

Gideon surveyed the boy's face, searching for any sign of possession but he could not sense anything. It did not mean that there was nothing, only that it was not a drone. But the higher-level demons tended to stray away from younger vessels in favor of those with more advantage.

"Hey, we're not going to hurt you," Nikka said as she approached him. "Do you speak English?"

The boy nodded as he scampered back until he pressed against the wall of a building and looked up at them. "I speak English fine." His words flowed well with his Mexican accent.

"Good," Nikka said. "We're not going to hurt you. We're just passing through."

"You are human?" he said, his eyebrow cocked. "No *demonio*?"

"So, you've seen them too," Amy said. "No. We are not demons, but we fight them."

Gideon stood back as they questioned the boy. He glanced around at the other stores and cars for any other signs of life.

"We can help you," Amy said and extended her hand.

The boy stood up on his own, refusing Amy's hand, and dusted off his jeans and T-shirt. "I do not need help. We are doing just fine here."

"We?" Gideon said, and his eyes looked back at the kid. "Are there others with you?"

The boy's shoulders fell, and he leaned back against the wall again. It was a secret he was probably supposed to keep. "Yes."

Amy folded her arms across her chest. "And are there demons still around here too? *Demonio*?"

"Sometimes," he said. "They come around here in cars like yours. They are the only ones that have cars, that is why I run from you."

Nikka glanced back to the car that Jadriel now pulled next to the curb and stopped. She looked back at the boy. "Well, we came prepared. I'm Nikka. This is Amy, Gideon, and Jad." She held out her hand to the kid, who now eyed the black tattoos on her arms.

He took her hand. "Miguel."

A motion came from the door of the building where they stood, and Gideon went rigid, his arms tight as he eyed the door.

"*Esta todo bien*, Miguel?" a woman's voice called out through the door. She rounded the threshold and came to a sudden stop when she saw the group standing around the kid. Her eyes grew wide and her face pale as she rushed to his side. Her black hair, tied back into a ponytail, fell down her back as she grasped his arm and pulled him closer to her.

"*Bien, bien*," he said and grasped her hand that had locked onto his arm. "It's okay. Carmen, they are good people."

Her gaze shifted to each of them as the kid pulled her hands away from him. He glanced back to them. "This is my sister Carmen." He introduced the others to her, but she kept her distance. He turned back to her. "They are not like the monsters."

"We thought he needed help," Amy said.

"You are Americans?" she finally spoke as she looked at each of them.

Nikka smiled. "Yeah, sort of." She gave Jadriel a quick look. "We are trying to get back into the U.S."

"How did you get a car? None of the cars around here work after what happened in the sky."

"Just found it," Nikka said.

That was the absolute truth, too. Gideon kept his eye on the woman, not yet convinced that she would not run or try to attack at any moment. The longer they stayed out in the open like this, the easier it would be for a demon horde to get the drop on them. These two were obviously human, but they did not appear to need their help, and he had to do something to get them back onto the road.

"We can see that you are not in any danger. We will not bother you any longer," Gideon said, reaching for Nikka's hand. He hoped that she would get the quiet message that they needed to keep moving. He backed away with her hand in his.

"Wait," Carmen said.

Nikka stopped, and he knew that he had lost her attention at that moment.

"There are others with us," Carmen said. "Some of them do need help. Do any of you have medical training?"

Between him and Jadriel, they had enough ability to treat some things. In his millennia on earth, he had learned enough to be a proficient field medic when the time came. There was not a wound that he had not flushed, disinfected and closed in many a seraph and that included Nikka.

"Some," Gideon said. "What is it that you need?"

Miguel looked at his sister and urged her to say what she needed to say. Carmen stepped toward them, and Gideon saw the sack of supplies that she had carried in her hand. She had just come out of a deserted pharmacy clutching spools of medical tape and packages of gauze.

"Many of our numbers have taken ill recently," she said. "Could any of you help us?"

"How many of you are there?" Nikka asked.

"About one hundred, maybe more." Her shoulders straightened. "We have food and water that you can have for your journey."

Gideon had not seen a human collective that large since Garnet Falls. So many people gathered together this long since the demons had taken over meant that they had sufficient defenses and preparation. Nikka looked back at him and then to Jadriel.

"We can't just leave them like this," she said.

She did not have to say it for him to know what she was thinking. Of course, she would want to help them; that was why she had been a perfect seraph. She never backed down when someone needed her.

Nikka turned back to face them. "Take us there."

CHAPTER 19
NIKKA

---

*J*adriel drove the Jeep beyond a full parking lot and into the empty passenger drop-off lane of an airport as he followed the directions that Miguel gave him. Even here, weeds proliferated in the cracks of the pavement and a fine layer of dust had settled over each of the abandoned cars that littered the lots. He stopped under the awning that stretched across the lane. A pair of sliding glass doors permanently gaped open, inviting them to the large open atrium with its empty ticketing booths.

Nikka stepped out of the vehicle and Carmen led them through the entrance. "Miguel and I came here about six months ago. By that time, so many people had already arrived."

"You've been safe here? No attacks?" Amy asked as she stepped beside Carmen.

The woman shook her head. "Not since we came here. We saw much more on the outskirts of town."

"Tell us about those that are sick," Gideon said from where he walked beside Nikka.

"It started a few days ago. Fevers, vomiting. Bleeding from the eyes and mouth. I have never seen anything like it," Carmen said.

Nikka shot Gideon a glance. This didn't sound like anything demonic, but there were so many things that came out of the hell portal the night that she defeated Abaddon. This could be something new. The only way to be sure was to see for herself.

Men, women, and children stood in the furthest corners and walls of the airport, their individual spaces set up in makeshift forts of blankets and boxes. Wary eyes watched them from afar. Mothers held their children close, and Nikka understood this. For all they knew, these new people could be demons introduced into their midst. And a demon in a settlement of humans could wreak havoc. In this new world, they couldn't afford to trust anyone.

They followed Carmen through the remnants of the security checkpoint and into the main floor of the terminal. She pushed through another heavy door with a key pad that had long been shattered, and they followed her down the stairs. The daylight that had shone through the many windows of the upper terminals disappeared as they plunged into the underground levels of the airport. An occasional small window peeked into the corridor, giving dim light as they followed her. Each footfall echoed in the long and empty hallway.

Two men emerged from a door down the hall and stopped when they looked at her. They shouted something in Spanish to her, and she responded just as quick, but whatever she had said didn't ease them. They looked at the newcomers with suspicion as they neared the door.

"We keep them down here, the sick ones," Carmen said. "They were making everyone else nervous."

Carmen stopped beside the door and leaned against the wall as Miguel walked up beside her and gazed through a large lead-glass window that shone into the room. Nikka moved to the glass, feeling the eyes of the two other men boring into her. They backed away from her group and said something else to Carmen that made the woman agitated. She spoke so fast to them now, her hands moving and pointing, until the men stopped speaking back to her. The larger of the two men, the hair on his head thinning save for the thick mustache on his upper lip, folded his arms across his chest.

"Sorry about that," she said as she turned to look through the window with Nikka. "They have been through a lot, and they don't trust anybody."

Nikka didn't pay much attention to the exchange as she investigated the dimly lit room. A dozen or more people lay on the ground in makeshift beds of folded blankets arranged in rows. Two women and another man stood among them, tending to any needs. Some of the patients lay still, probably sleeping but Nikka couldn't tell for sure. Others talked to the people that stood around them, asking for water or another blanket. She scanned each of the patients' faces, some of them mottled with flushed cheeks. Speckles of blood had stained pillow cases or other linens where the people rested their heads.

She turned to Gideon, who stood next to her, his form rigid as he looked through the window. "What is this?" she whispered.

"I do not know," he said.

"Demons?"

He shook his head. "I have never seen demons do this. But I have seen similar things during my days in Africa. Hemorrhagic fevers."

"Wait a sec," she said and glanced back through the window. "I remember learning about that in Biology. Hemorrhagic fever, that's like Ebola and weird viruses like that. What the hell is something like that doing here and why now?"

Deep furrows formed between his eyebrows and then his fingers wrapped around her arm. He pulled her back from the window and away from the group. Carmen's eyes followed them, but she tried to focus on Gideon. His eyes narrowed, the way they always did when a terrible thought rattled around in his head.

"This should not be happening," he said, keeping his voice low.

"I know, so why is it?"

His eyes darted around to every shadowy edge in the corridor as he thought. "She said it has only been a few days."

"Yeah." Nikka nodded but still didn't follow his concern.

His hazel eyes looked up at her, the muscles along his jaw rippling as he clenched his teeth. Whatever it was, it didn't look pleasant.

"A fresh disease, something that should not be here," he said, his words slow and careful, as though he wanted her to understand the underlying meaning.

The cogs of realization settled in her brain as he spoke. She glanced back to the window and the patients that lay beyond it. Blood trickled from a man's ear, a fresh stream that pooled on the pillow where he rested his head. The man, with his tuft of pepper gray hair on his head mussed in all directions, rolled to his side and pushed himself to his feet. A dribble of fresh blood fell from his lips as he staggered to his feet, his eyes facing toward the window. The sclera of his eyes had gone red with hemorrhage, but he stared unblinking at them.

"A disease that shouldn't exist in this part of the world," she muttered to herself and met the man's eyes through the glass. *So this is how it starts . . .*

A woman stepped through the rows of other patients and placed a hand on the man's arm. Nikka could tell that she encouraged him to lie down, but he only stared forward with blood trickling down his chin. Another patient pushed to her feet and stood on wobbling legs, staring forward as well. Then another and another.

"The Angel of Pestilence is here," Gideon whispered.

Pestilence. The first Horseman. *Of course*, she thought as she glanced at each of the people now standing, their bodies riddled with whatever virus had downed them, courtesy of a celestial being. Nikka approached the glass once again, her eyes falling on the first patient who stood to watch her. The woman that had approached him now stepped around to face him. Nikka couldn't hear what she said, but the man paid her no attention, at least not at first.

And then his eyes turned down to her, his jaw slack. His lips peeled back from his teeth, and in a quick motion, his hands grasped around the woman's shoulders and pulled her in close. With lightning speed, his teeth clamped down on her neck, and she screamed, the sound carrying through the glass.

Amy gasped, her hands moving to her mouth and she jumped back from the glass. Carmen gaped in horror and grabbed Miguel. Together they moved back as well. Jadriel stood his ground as he eyed the man who now ripped out a chunk of the woman's neck and still had it in his mouth, chewing. Blood spurted in quick bursts from her throat as he held her. The other two men that had been helping in the room ran to assist her, but the others that now stood descended on them like ravenous hyenas.

The two men beside Carmen cried out and reached for the door, ready to run inside, but she stopped them.

The first patient dropped the bleeding woman at his feet, and his eyes turned back to the glass, still unblinking. Fresh blood coated the front of his shirt from the woman he had attacked, but he didn't seem to notice any of it. He watched them through the window, and his head tilted to the side. Then his body came to life, and he sprang toward the window as he screeched with the sound of a vicious animal. His hands pounded against the glass, leaving bloodied prints everywhere he touched. The sound from his throat penetrated the corridor, a terrible and broken screech. He shifted across the window, throwing his body at it as he tried to get at them. And then he turned to look at the door.

The men beside Carmen froze but came to life as the patient's hands moved to the door knob. The man on the other side tugged at the handle, and the guard held fast to it.

"Lock it," Amy shouted to them.

"There is no lock," Carmen said and pulled Miguel in close to her.

The door pulled open in a sudden jolt, but the man holding the handle in the corridor planted his feet and yanked it closed again. The patient worked at the door again, and it wouldn't be long before he tore it open.

"We need to get out of here," Nikka called out to the others, drawing Amy further away from the window.

The door pulled open again, and every time it did the screeching sounds of the patients echoed into the corridor. Carmen grasped her brother's hand, and they bolted down the hallway. Amy moved with them when the man holding the door cried out for the final time. The door jerked open, and the man's grasp on the handle slipped. His planted feet held him still, and the sudden motion dropped him to the ground. The patient stepped into the threshold and gazed down at him for only a second before he leaped onto him, jaws sinking into the soft flesh of his neck. The man screamed as he reached out toward Nikka, but it was too late. Blood flowed from his carotid artery and pooled around him as the patient continued to chew on his tendons and muscle.

Gideon's hand grasped around Nikka's, and he pulled her down the corridor at a swift run with Jadriel at their heels. The screeching and wailing of the sick room carried down toward them. The clink of shattering glass caught her attention and Nikka glanced back. Just before they ran into the stairwell, eight figures in tattered and bloodied clothes sprinted toward them.

Nikka slipped into the stairwell with Gideon still holding onto her hand. They emerged onto the upper floor. Gideon shoved the door closed and pressed his back into it. Jadriel moved his weight into the door as well when the first strike came from inside the stairwell. The door jumped, and Nikka watched as Gideon's feet slid a few inches.

"Run," he said, his eyes wide as another force hit from behind him.

"I'm not going anywhere," she said. "If this is Pestilence, I have to stop it, you said so yourself."

His feet slid again. The striking on the door came faster, more desperate.

Jadriel looked back at her. "These things are only a manifestation of Pestilence. You have to find the angel itself."

"How do I do that?"

The next strike let the door gape open several inches, and a bloodied hand reached through the gap. Gideon couldn't hold it much longer.

"It is somewhere nearby, in human form," Jadriel said, his teeth clenching together as he tried to hold the door.

Nikka jumped back as the last strike shoved the door open too far and the first of the patients came through. Gideon lost his footing and tumbled forward. The man didn't take long to react before his eyes focused on Gideon and he lunged at him.

The moment she saw the cold, dead look in the man's eyes, she knew what was coming next. Her hand reflexively reached behind her, and she grasped the hilt of her sword. The blade pulled free, erupting into violet flames. The tattoos on her arms and neck glistened in violet light as she stepped toward him and swung the sword. The blade caught the man's neck and cut clean through. His head rolled off his left shoulder and landed with a sickening thud. The body shuddered and spasmed before it collapsed to the ground in a bloody, oozing mess.

She grasped Gideon's hand and pulled him to his feet just as the door gave way and the wave of sick people flowed into the space. They moved quickly when their hemorrhaged eyes fell on Nikka. She turned, and with Gideon and Jadriel at her side, she ran through the terminal. The sound of pounding footsteps, screeching and grunting came from behind them, and every second that ticked by drew them closer.

They rounded the corner toward the security checkpoint and saw the large gathering of people that had collected in the atrium. Carmen, Miguel, and Amy rushed into the crowd ahead of them, shouting for everyone to run. Alarmed faces turned toward them, and then the screaming started. They undoubtedly saw the things sprinting behind Nikka.

Chapter 20

Nikka

Nikka leaped over the long counter that blocked part of the security gate, and Gideon and Jadriel stayed close behind her. The crowd that had gathered outside the gate spoke in hushed tones until eyes fell upon the sick ones running, blood streaking down their clothes and the horrible screeching and wailing sounds that came from their throats. As soon as someone screamed, the people scattered in all directions. Men and women grabbed onto their children and bolted, some going upstairs, others running toward the open doors that led outside the airport.

The biters ran through the security gate, some ducking under the counter and sliding into the atrium. They sprinted to the open door, blocking any access to the outside. They moved like a herd of wild animals determined to take down the prey.

Nikka glanced back to see the first biter take down a woman who tried to run for the next terminal. His teeth sank into the soft flesh of her leg, and the screams echoed down the hallway, her arms reaching out to everyone that ran away from her. The other biters kept going, grabbing at anyone that lagged. They moved with a determined speed as the others behind them continued toward the crowd. That's when she saw the faces of the first victims, the first three people that the biters took down in the sick room. They now moved with the others, gaping wounds in their flesh that no longer pulsed but oozed with thick and clotted blood. There was no way they could still be alive after that amount of blood loss. Nikka saw it herself, and yet they now moved as though they had succumbed to the sickness.

She turned to face the people ahead of her. Everyone panicked and scattered all over the airport now. Amy glanced back to her from where she ran and then to the biters that followed, some now rising to their feet again after taking down some of their numbers. Carmen ran beside her, and Miguel tried to look back, but she pulled at his arm.

"Are there any doors that lock around here?" Nikka called out to Carmen.

The woman looked at her and then glanced ahead of them. Some of the crowd had slipped through rooms alongside the main corridor, only to have them shoved open and the biters attack. But Carmen pointed down the hall and Nikka followed her line of sight. The baggage claim, with the long panels of belts and open space, had a heavy door straight ahead.

"Okay," Nikka said and nodded to the others. "Go."

She turned on her heels and drew her sword again as she faced the oncoming swarm of biters. They had multiplied significantly since she last looked back at them, now doubled with those they had bitten and had acquired into their horde.

Gideon stopped and grabbed her arm, pulling her back toward the door. "What are you doing? Come on."

"Just go," she said and flashed an urgent glance at him, yanking her arm free of his grasp. "I'll be right behind you."

Jadriel stopped as well. "Then I will stay with you."

The angel had his half-circle swords in hand, and she could probably use his help. As much as she wanted him to protect the others, she had to consider that she needed him at her side. "Fine," she said.

Gideon's brow furrowed as he stepped back from her. The sound of the coming horde roared toward them.

"It's okay," she said and nodded to him. "Look after Amy, okay."

He nodded and then turned, but she knew it took everything for him to leave her there. She turned back to face the coming horde, some of them splitting off to follow them and others continuing after the rest of the frightened crowd. Red, hemorrhaged eyes stared them down without blinking. So many more had turned since the original eight only minutes ago. A single bite could create one of these things in seconds. A blood-thirsty monster with the speed of a cheetah on crack. And now a dozen of them ran toward her and Jadriel.

The angel swung his half-circle sabers that burst into violet flames just like her own sword. Archangels, side by side.

"I hope you have a plan," he said, his feet shifting his weight as he readied himself to fight the horde.

"We'll see," she said as she gripped the hilt of her katana. "Just follow my lead and head for the luggage belts. We've just got to give everybody enough time to get through the door."

He glanced to their right and to the long and still black rubber tracks that wound out of the luggage bay, into the claim area and then back into the bay again. The screeching sounds of the sick grew to a deafening level as the horde blocked their escape into the main terminal. The luggage bay was the only way out now.

When she heard the final click of the luggage claim door behind her, Nikka bolted to the right, and Jadriel stayed with her. She leaped onto the black track and dashed over the rise between the tracks that wound around the luggage bay. The horde rushed after them and away from the door. She jumped from the first rise, over the bay of silent monitors that once displayed baggage claim information, and onto the track on the other side. Jadriel landed next to her.

Her heart pounded in her ears. This had to work, and the angel needed to stay with her. She didn't have time to see if he still followed, otherwise he would be on his own.

A hand shot out at her from behind the monitor, grabbing her arm before she could go any further. It's cold bloodied fingers tightened with such force that she cried out. The biters could move fast, even over the mounds, and there was more right behind this one. She turned, and the biter held tight to her arm. It pulled through the monitors, and as soon as it locked eyes with her, it wailed through the bits of human flesh still caught in its teeth. Jadriel's sword flashed between them and the blade sliced through its wrist. The biter didn't flinch though but crawled after her. The hand clamped around her arm loosened, and she pulled it away, tossing it back at the biter on the ground.

She turned back to Jadriel, and he gave her a quick nod. That would have to be good enough for a thanks right now. They ran down the track together. Ahead of them, she saw the gap in the wall where the track disappeared into the luggage bay.

"Are we going there?" Jadriel said.

"Yeah," she said as she re-sheathed her sword. "And be ready to do some cutting."

She pulled her elbows in and sprinted as fast as she could toward the gap. The track disappeared through a curtain of clear vinyl strips that partially obscured the space beyond the baggage claim. She ducked into the space with the angel close behind her. They plunged into a dark area, lit only by the openings in the track and from a door down a long corridor.

A dark form filled the gap and a biter dove through, although its uncoordinated body became tangled in the vinyl curtain. Another came behind him, but the narrow opening created the bottleneck that Nikka had hoped for. She pulled her sword again, the violet light illuminating the area around them, and swung it down fast. The blade severed through the biter's neck, and he fell where he had crawled at the opening. Jadriel followed her lead and beheaded the next two that tried to crawl through. They hacked at each limb or head that pushed into the space until it was blocked with a pile of twitching bodies.

"A diversion," Jadriel said with a smile.

"And while the rest of them keep trying to get through here," she said, "we'll slip out the other way."

She ticked her head to the second opening in the track further down the corridor. Luckily, the biters were as thoughtless as she had hoped. She didn't want to think what would happen if the creatures had actually gone through both gaps.

With her sword re-sheathed, she led him down the track that wound through the back area of the luggage bay until they had approached the gap back into the baggage claim. She peered through the vinyl curtain and to the growing horde that accumulated at the first gap. The baggage claim security door was only ten feet from her at this point.

"Keep quiet and follow me," she whispered to Jadriel and pulled aside the center strips of vinyl as she crawled through the gap.

She emerged onto the track beyond the curtain and stepped down from the belt as she kept her eye on the horde beyond the short wall between the tracks. She moved to the door where the others had escaped, and she knocked with two quick raps.

The click of a deadbolt echoed throughout the baggage claim space and the screeching of the biters silenced for a moment. They listened around them, ears tuning toward the source of the sound. Just as the door opened, Nikka heard the quick shuffle and then the pounding of feet coming back toward them.

She first saw Gideon's face when the door opened and then his hand grabbed her arm, pulling her through the door. Jadriel plunged through and yanked the door closed just as a body crashed against the door.

Nikka plunged into a dark room lit only by a single flashlight in Miguel's hand. The white LED beam illuminated under his chin, casting shadows above his nose and eyebrows. He watched the door with wide eyes and the light trembled in his hand with every strike against the exit. The screeching of the sick on the other side bled through the seams in the door, echoing through the spacious room that opened into the luggage staging area. But the deadbolt held the heavy steel doors together.

Body after body slammed against the door. Gideon pulled Nikka away from it and further toward the crowd that huddled in the darkness. His hand still clamped against her forearm.

"Are you okay?" Gideon said, his eyes flashing toward her.

"Of course." At least no bites from the sick, but she still worked to catch her breath.

"Tell me before you do something like that again," he said and pulled her closer. That was just like him to tell her what to do, just like the days when they lived in the monastery, and he feared for her every time she was out of his sight. Rightly so. She had a tendency to get caught in difficult situations when she went out on her own.

Another bang against the door and the latch shuddered, cracking the frame and raining down a volley of drywall.

Amy sidled up to her. "Got any more ideas?" The shaking in her voice and tremble in her gaze made the hair stand up on Nikka's forearms, and it grew worse with every screech that echoed through the room.

A desperate and heart-stopping scream came through the door as the frame jostled again. The sound was enough to make everyone jump. Gideon pulled Nikka back, and they clambered together with the group, every person pressed back against the furthest wall. Carmen held onto her brother, and the flashlight trembled, the beam pointing at the door. Figures moved on the other side, their dark forms visible as only a slip of black through the golden sunlight that shone under the door. Soft cries sounded in the dark of the room as people clung to each other, hoping that the door held.

The exit jostled again as body after body pounded at it, desperate to get at the survivors in the room. Miguel trembled enough that the light slipped from his hand and rolled away from his feet.

Nikka bent to grasp it just as Carmen leaned in. Their hands clasped the handle simultaneously, Nikka's finger's brushing against hers.

And at that moment, the tattoos along her arms flickered with a singular light that shimmered for only a second. The buzz of adrenaline shot through her veins, a sensation that she had not felt since she was a seraph. Her fingers released the light as soon as she felt it and she straightened, the muscles in her spine and shoulders flexing as her eyes met Carmen's. In the dark, she could barely make out her features except where the flashlight shone from her hand. Even in the shadows, she saw that the woman froze, and her eyes went cold.

Nikka knew what it was when she saw that look. The sigils on her arms had warned her, just like they used to when a demon was nearby. And now that she was an archangel, her power had changed.

She could detect angels.

This was no coincidence. The angel had lured them here, sucked them into this nightmare that it had created. It knew who she was: the one that had awakened and freed it.

Nikka braced herself. Her arms shot toward Carmen, and she grasped the woman's shirt, pulling her close.

"It's you," she said through clenched teeth. "You did this."

"I don't know what you're talking about," Carmen said, her eyes welling with tears as her fingers tried to pull Nikka away from her.

"Nikka, stop," Amy shouted to her.

"You infected all these people," Nikka said, her grip tightening on her shirt.

"You've gone mad," Carmen said as she tried to pull away again. She turned toward the others, tears streaming down her face. "The woman is loco."

Miguel bolted away from the group, but Jadriel lashed out his arm and caught the boy before he could get any closer. He called out to her, speaking a stream of Spanish that Nikka couldn't understand.

The screeching at the door intensified, but the slamming had stopped. They must have sensed that something inside the room had changed.

"You did it because I let you out." Nikka cringed, but her grip remained strong. As Carmen tried to pull away again, she turned on her heels and pulled her through the dark and away from the crowd that now watched them in terror. She pulled her toward the door, closer to the sounds of the biters on the other side.

"What are you doing?" Carmen screamed, her feet now kicking at Nikka, but her feet skidded across the floor as Nikka pulled her with all her strength.

It had to work. Nikka had no other alternative. Tears streamed from Carmen's eyes. Why did the angel not reveal itself? She couldn't be wrong. The sigils on her arms would never betray her.

Nikka's fingers turned the deadbolt of the door, and her trembling hand found the handle in the dark despite Carmen's struggles in her grasp. She yanked the door open, and the bright light of the outer room burst into the dark space. The dozen biters had multiplied into more than fifty now, and they stood out there, crouched and ready to pounce when the door opened. Their hemorrhaged eyes all turned to the door in silent unison.

And then Nikka shoved Carmen into the fray of the sick. Miguel's screams from the dark tortured her ears, and Nikka tried to drown out the sound. This was the only way, and the angel would have to show them the truth. With all the power of her own angel strength,

Nikka forced Carmen into the room, and she fell into the horde of biters that stood outside the room.

She fell back against two men, their clothes soaked in blood from the fresh bite marks on their chests and arms. The biters all watched her fall, and they froze as though they awaited the signal to leap into action.

Then Carmen caught her footing and steadied herself in a low crouch. She turned around to face Nikka, her back rigid. The woman's shoulders stiffened, and her fingers tightened into fists. The dark of her pupils vanished into a bright green neon light and ribbons of green electricity erupted from the edges of her knuckles.

Nikka's judgement hadn't failed her. She now stood face-to-face with the Angel of Pestilence. And it was pissed.

CHAPTER 21

NIKKA

ikka's tattoos shimmered into violet light and the light pierced through her eyes. For the first time, she saw the gossamer undulation of the angel just below Carmen's skin, the edges of it carrying the same green light that now shone through the woman's eyes. The horde of biters remained in place, unmoving and quiet as they watched Carmen in anticipation, awaiting their orders from the master. She controlled them, and she probably had since the beginning.

"Time to play," Carmen said, her English smooth and flawless, no longer the foreign tongue of the woman the angel inhabited.

Her hand shot forward, the green electricity beaming toward Nikka. Before she could turn, the energy grasped at her from where she stood at the threshold of the door. It forced her from her feet, and the angel pulled her into the open space, throwing her across the room. She crashed into the bay of windows that separated baggage claim from the terminal, sending a shower of glass down on her. The impact knocked the air from her lungs, and the sizzle of electricity still jumped in her muscles.

In the seconds it took for her vision to return, she heard the footsteps approach her. Nikka shoved away from the ground and tried to steady herself on wobbly knees, the glass crunching under her feet with every step. Pestilence moved through the horde of biters that parted the way for her like the Red Sea for Moses. The green light still shone in her eyes and the electricity now coursed up her arms.

"You are no match for me," she said, her hand rising and the electricity shooting toward Nikka again. The light raced toward her, and Nikka dodged as it zinged past her, just catching the edge of her arm and leaving a burn across her flesh. She rolled over the broken glass and cringed at the lacerations that formed on her bare arms.

"I know you," Pestilence said, the horde all watching her from behind and still unmoving. "You are the abomination created by Samael. You do not belong here among the Divine."

As Nikka moved to get to her feet again, the angel opened both palms toward her. The green light rushed toward her, but this time she had enough concentration to activate the sigils on her body. She held up her forearms in a cross, and her own power formed a shield of violet light. The angel's power ricocheted off her shield and ebbed back toward her, knocking her to the ground. The bitch must not have expected an Abomination to hold so much power. Nikka grinned and let the shield down.

Nikka hurried to her feet and watched Pestilence fall. The horde looked at the angel, waiting for any further orders from their master. Nikka's own power surged through her veins, fueled by every tattoo on her body. She focused on the woman, who now pushed herself up to her feet, ready to turn and face Nikka.

She couldn't wait; it had to be now before the angel could expect it. Nikka sprinted toward her and leaped, her power carrying her into the air above Pestilence. The violet light filled her hands, and she directed all her energy toward the angel. The light struck Pestilence before she could see Nikka, sending the woman back into the horde of biters.

Nikka landed in the center of the room in a crouch, her fingers steadying her form against the cold tiles. The angel didn't stay down for long, though. She pushed through the biters and her eyes locked onto Nikka.

Another burst of green light shot from her hand, but Nikka pulled up her shield again. Pestilence ran toward her, the power from her arm still directed toward her. If she moved, Nikka could lose her concentration, and her shield would drop. But the angel came closer, and it would only be a second or two before she was on her.

She pulled an orb of violet energy into her palm and rounded back before she threw it toward the angel. Pestilence dodged it, but it was enough of a distraction that it interrupted her power. Nikka rolled out of the way as the angel bore down on her. The angel turned, ready to strike again, but Nikka channeled her power through her core and held both hands out to aim everything she had at the angel.

Pestilence must have sensed it because she twisted at the last moment before the energy struck her. Samael had been strong, after all, he was an archangel and a Watcher. But a Horseman had power like she had never seen, and Nikka was running out of options. It kept coming at her, stronger and stronger each time. Before Nikka could dodge away, the angel shot out a strong burst of her power and it caught Nikka in the chest. The electrical surge seized at her muscles as it wrapped around her body and lifted her into the air. It twisted around her chest in a flash of green light, stealing the air from her lungs.

The angel stood her ground, the power emanating from her hand as she held Nikka in the air. Nikka tried to raise her arms, to fight back, but the power gripped at every muscle and only made her twitch.

"Stop this," Gideon shouted as he emerged from the darkness of the room, his eyes blazing demon-red and the muscles in his arms bulging under his T-shirt.

Pestilence shot a glare at him, but her power never faltered. Its grip still held Nikka frozen.

Gideon's arms opened to his sides, and he glowered at the angel. The cords of red fire appeared in his hands and whipped about in serpentine strips around his feet, ready to strike at the angel.

But there was nothing Gideon could do; Nikka knew that the moment she broke the seals. This was her fight, and only hers. The angel would never let him interfere.

The angel's other hand shot open toward him, and another burst of green electrical light stunned him. The ribbons of electricity enveloped him, and he cried out as he fell to his knees, every muscle in his body rigid.

"You have no power here, demon," she said, her voice steady and calm. The energy pulsed from Carmen's hand toward Gideon, each surge making him seize and gasp in pain.

The fire whips vanished from his hands and his back arched. The angel threw more and more power at him as only an angel could against a demon. Nikka saw not only anger but hate in the angel's eyes as she tortured him.

Pestilence was prepared to kill him, and she would do it without remorse. Nikka watched Gideon twitch and seize under the power of the green light, and every moment of his suffering made her tattoos burn and spark. That power grew under Nikka's skin, through her core and channeled from the center of the earth, just as Jadriel had taught her. She was part archangel, part human. Connected to the earth, unlike any other creature. The power of it obeyed her will as she pulled it into her limbs.

Her muscles came to life and forced away the electricity that zapped at her, controlling her movements. The energy surged through her soul, and her eyes burned bright violet. Pestilence could no longer hold her and Nikka dropped to the ground. When she hit the floor, Nikka rolled until she pressed her feet into the ground and forced herself to her feet. The angel could only stare with wide violet eyes and a clenched jaw at Nikka's shimmering purple tattoos.

As Pestilence stood dumbfounded, Nikka struck her with all the force of the earth in a beam of violet light. The power landed in the center of her chest, throwing her to the ground. Nikka rushed at her while she was still down and pounced on her, straddling her with the angel writhing under her grasp.

Nikka's power still flowed like fire in her veins, the strongest she had ever felt it. The soul of the earth zapped into her nerves, dancing about her brain as she looked down on Pestilence with fierce violet pupils. The faint green light of the angel flowed just under the human's skin, and she could see it like spotting fish just below the surface of the water. The power whispered into her ear, filling her mind with possibilities and secrets that she would never have known otherwise.

What it asked her to do was impossible, even Jadriel had said so. But it urged her, pleading for this one thing.

She placed her hand on the woman's chest, her fingers splayed just as she used to before pulling a demon from a person. The angel's eyes grew wide, and she screamed, writhing and fighting underneath Nikka's weight.

Nikka's fingers illuminated in violet light and sunk into the woman's chest as though there was no substance. She brushed against the gossamer being inside of her, it's warmth curling around her fingers like cotton candy, not like the thick and slimy insectoid thing that demons were made of. She grasped at it, and it slipped as easy as silk from its hold on the human.

"Stop. I yield to you," Pestilence shouted, her eyes wide and bulging toward Nikka. "Please, do not do this."

Nikka halted for a moment, feeling the body of the angel within her grasp. The woman looked at her, pleading and shaking under her weight.

"Please," she said, her lip shaking and the green glow still hovering in her eyes. "I beg you."

Nikka watched a tear fall from the corner of the woman's eye. In that instant, she loosened her grip on the spirit inside the woman and pulled her fingers away from her chest. Pestilence let her head rest back, and Nikka felt her body go limp under her weight. The horde of biters all collapsed in unison and the power that held Gideon released him. He fell forward with a gasp and coughed as the muscles in his chest began to work again. Quick breaths escaped from Carmen's lips.

"You truly are Nephilim," she whispered to Nikka.

Her brow furrowed. "What do you mean?"

"A creature of both heaven and earth, blessed by both. Only God could have given you the power that you wield now."

Nikka swallowed against her dry throat. "Samael did this to me. You said it yourself."

"He brought you to this world," she said, a faint smile forming on her lips. "But he could never give you this kind of power."

Nikka lifted off her, but the angel lay on the ground, her eyes watching Nikka move. The angel's words fell like lead weights onto her shoulders. This creature was right: Samael created her from the beginning. But something else had happened to her since then, the night she gave birth to Adam. Even though she couldn't remember anything until she awoke with an archangel's power, Amy had told her everything that she saw that night. Nikka had died, and something else brought her back.

Carmen lifted up onto her elbows and looked at Nikka. "You have defeated me," she said and reached her hand out to her. "And I will give you what I owe."

Nikka glanced up at the door to see Jadriel step into the light. His eyes met her, and he nodded. This was what she had broken the seals for, and she had to accept it.

She reached her hand down to the angel. Pestilence grasped her hand. At first, the warmth of the angel's hand surprised her, but she let the angel curl her fingers around the bottom of her palm. A green light glowed at the angel's palm, and the heat of it swelled into Nikka's hand. The light burned brighter, and Nikka could see the bones in silhouette through her flesh, surrounded by the green glow. The light coursed into her veins, pulsing with each beat of her heart until it settled into her chest. The angel turned her hand and exposed the inside of Nikka's forearm. As the light faded in her palm, a new tattoo formed under her skin. The symmetric sigil curved in a loop like an optical illusion.

The angel released her hand, and she stood. Nikka backed away from her as she examined the new mark.

"My time here is done," Pestilence said, her eyes flashed toward the people that slowly made their way from the room.

Nikka glanced around them, to the dozens of the dead that had fallen to the ground without the animation of the angel. "And what about all of them? You killed them all just to come here and find me."

"No," she said and shook her head. "It was my job, regardless of you. This was how it was always meant to be. The end of the world is near, and I am the first of many. Those that survive my power will be met by my siblings. Defeat them, and they will give you their power as well."

"But how do I use it to stop Lucifer, to get my son back?" Nikka asked.

The angel smiled. "You will know when the time comes."

Before Nikka could say anything else, the woman's head fell back, and her eyes opened wide. The green gossamer light of the

Harbingers erupted from her chest and dissipated into the air above them. The woman gasped and fell to the ground in trembling silence, her eyes wide with the knowledge that an angel had just abandoned her.

Chapter 22

Jason

*J*ason held his stance, his legs limber over the balls of his feet as he dodged to the side. The other guy's fist swung past his ear, and this gave Jason only a moment to land a strike to his exposed ribs. When his knuckles found the bare flesh, he felt the rib give way under his fist. His opponent cried out through clenched teeth and doubled over. Within the cheering of the crowd, a hundred black and blood-thirsty eyes watching them, Jason spun on his heel and kicked his knee upward into the man's face. He fell back, landing hard on the floor as blood gushed from his nose.

The sounds of the drones shouting and growling grew to a deafening pitch, but Jason wouldn't look at them. This was only sport to them, humans fighting humans, and it would never be fair. He had no choice, not when Belphagor ordered him to do it after injecting him with enough demon blood to inhibit his seraph powers. So he never wanted to give them the satisfaction of looking at them and acknowledging that they had used him. He gazed down at his hands, shaking and speckled with blood, most of which wasn't his own.

Belphagor stepped through the dispersing crowd that laughed and shouted above the music that raged through the speakers. He locked the chain back onto Jason's collar and then placed a heavy hand on his shoulder.

"That's how you do that," the demon said, his mouth parted in a wide and self-satisfied smile. "You'll make me rich if you keep it up. And then maybe I'll move you to some nicer digs up in the hotel."

The last thing he wanted was to be closer to any more of the higher-ranking demons. At least in his solitary cell in the catacombs, he didn't have to be bothered by anyone until Belphagor came calling for things like this. Or when he wanted to go on a raid to find more humans to collect.

The demon turned away from him, and the chain went tight when Jason didn't move but only stared at the bruises forming on his knuckles.

"Hey," Belphagor said. "We don't have all day. Don't make me drag you."

He tugged on the chain again, and Jason moved in step behind him. There was no use fighting the chain, not surrounded by all these demons and his veins surging with enough demon blood to make him sick to his stomach. He had nothing left in his reserve to fight Belphagor tonight.

The demon led him through the crowd, some touching Jason's arms and shoulders as he passed them with victorious smiles on their faces. Belphagor wasn't the only one who had benefited on the wager he had made. The fallen seraph, now owned by the devil himself, and made to entertain the masses.

His knuckles throbbed, and he flexed his fingers as he kept his head down. Walking through the crowd like this never felt like the victory that they made it out to be, especially when the chain tugged at his neck if he fell behind. The groping hands brushed past him, but he was beyond flinching at the touch of a demon anymore.

And then a hand grasped his, shoving something into his palm. The crowd around him fell in closer, the familiar stench of decay heavy, but the figure to his right held firm. Whoever it was had warm flesh, not like the cold and rotting feel of a body possessed. For a moment, Jason lifted his eyes to see the person who stood there, head down and face shaded by the comfort of a hoodie. Nikka was the only person he knew who loved to wear a hoodie over anything else. The pace of his heart quickened as the person pressed in close while the drones around them tried to reach toward him.

The hooded figure leaned closer. "You have only one chance at this." A woman's voice, but it wasn't Nikka, and he felt the hope begin to slip away from him. Then, the person released his hand and faded back into the crowd just as the chain tugged at his collar again.

Despite the drones that surrounded him, his fingers flexed around the object that still lingered in his hand. Belphagor led him through the crowd and toward the door that opened into the catacombs. While the fingers reached for him, he curled his hand against the hem of his jeans and deposited the object behind the waist band, solid against his torso and hidden below the edge of his T-shirt. His pace quickened in case Belphagor noticed that he had slowed and plunged through the door and away from the gawking crowd of drones.

The demon continued through the darkened hallways and toward his usual cell, the isolated room in the furthest corner of the catacombs. He unlocked the door and turned to work on removing the chain tethered to the iron collar.

"You're unusually quiet tonight," Belphagor said and opened the lock. "Where's the typical cursing and spitting?"

Jason refused to look at him but only stared toward the open door and the dark room where he had spent so many nights. Just act normal, like nothing else is different. The object pressed against the flesh of his torso and he hoped that the demon hadn't seen anything.

Belphagor sneered. "Yeah, well, a little demon blood in you and you've just gone mute. I guess that happens when you beat the shit out of someone."

The demon let the chain loose and then gazed down when something caught his eye. The adrenaline still coursed through Jason's veins and having a stranger stop him made it even stronger. But now the demon looked down, and maybe he saw whatever the stranger had given him.

Belphagor grasped his hand and held his knuckles up to the dim light in the corridor, revealing the bleeding splits and bruises. "I bet that hurts. Too bad we don't have any ice to put on that. It's going to hurt like a bitch in the morning."

Hopefully, that was all the demon had noticed, but Jason still held his breath and looked straight ahead. The demon sneered and released his hand. He shoved Jason into the room, and the click of the lock echoed in the barren space.

But Jason didn't let his breath out yet. The sound of the demon's footsteps continued down the hall, growing faint until they were silent. Despite the pain that throbbed in his hands, he lifted his shirt and withdrew the mystery object from his waistband. A crumpled white envelope folded in half. He turned it over and back again, but there was nothing written on it. The object inside shifted but remained firm in his grasp. He tore at the end of the envelope and then dumped the thing into his open palm.

In the faint light, he saw a syringe wrapped in another piece of paper. His trembling fingers pulled open the paper, revealing a glowing blue fluid that swirled inside the barrel of the capped syringe. The light reflected against his flesh, casting a ghostly glow around him. The paper unfurled in his fingers, revealing writing under the light.

Inject me, and then get out as fast as you can. Come to the promenade in front of the Bellagio fountain. I will not wait forever.

He crumpled the paper in his hand and turned his eyes back to the glowing syringe. How was it possible that someone could enter the demon hive undetected? With something like this, it could only be a higher power, maybe an angel. He only hoped that he could trust whoever it was, but he had no choice at this point. It was either inject and see what happens or die as a slave to the drones.

The blue light swirled inside the syringe as he drew it closer to his gaze. He pulled the cap free and saw the glint of the sharp needle in the blue light.

His heart now pounded against his sore ribs. This could be the end of everything, all culminated at the tip of the needle. Something had to free him; it might as well be this.

He bent his left elbow and clenched his fingers into a fist. The needle drew closer to the crook of his arm, to the cords that pulsed over his bulging bicep. The blue light of the mystery fluid cast the needle into a shadow that descended toward his flesh, illuminating the multiple needle marks and old bruises where hundreds of doses of demon blood had entered his body. The tip touched the skin just over the muscle.

Just perforate the vein and inject. And then run like hell.

His hand shook, and the needle danced over his skin. *Just do it already.*

He bit down on his lip and clenched his teeth. The needle plunged into the vein, and he didn't hesitate to inject. The blue liquid flowed into the vessel, leaving ribbons of blue light that pulsated up his arm. Each beat of his heart pushed the stuff into his muscles, through his organs, into his brain. The trail of it left a searing pain like liquid ice wherever it moved, and he fell to his knees as he tried to hold back the scream that caught in his throat. Any noise from this room would bring the demons, and not just the drones. After all, he was a VIP prisoner. The light burrowed into his skull, burning his eyes until the pupils illuminated into dots of blue light.

The scream tore at his lungs, but he balled his fingers into fists and pressed them into the cement as he opened his eyes. The room had gone bright with ethereal blue light, and as he gazed down to his arms, he realized the light had come from the tattoos that had reappeared on his arms. The seraph marks that had vanished with the administration of demon blood. They coursed up his neck, shimmering and vibrating under his clothes as each one reappeared. The light burst through each tattoo, and with it, his muscles flexed, each bruise fading.

The pain subsided as he now felt a new energy flow through his body, something that he had lost many months ago. He pushed himself up to his feet and stood, strong and painless. Whatever was in that syringe had restored him, but he had to make sure that everything was the way it should be. He reached behind his shoulder and felt the hilt of his broadsword. The blade slid free, and he held it before him, the blue flames erupting down the length of the sword.

Inject me, and then get out as fast as you can. The words looked up at him from where the paper lay at his feet.

It wouldn't be long before someone came to check on him, and whoever wrote that note was waiting for him. Now he just had to escape a hive of thousands of demons, as well as Lucifer's den, and run to the promenade. Sure. No problem.

He re-sheathed the sword and wrapped his strong fingers around the iron collar. With a single, forceful pull the iron shattered and he dropped the damned thing to the floor with a loud clang. That would probably be enough to force his guards to check. It wouldn't matter, though. He stepped up to the door, braced himself, and landed a power kick to the gate of his cell. The door crashed outward, splintering the frame and braces.

The lieutenants down the hall turned at the sound of the crashing door. As soon as they saw him, their eyes burned demon-orange, and they sprinted toward him. He reached behind his shoulder, pulled the blade free and his tattoos undulated with sapphire light as they approached.

They rushed him, screeching and glass-shard fragments of teeth appeared in their mangled jaws. He gripped the sword and ran toward them. As they neared, claws outstretched to him, he dropped to his knees and slid across the floor between them and just under their arms with a swing of his sword. The blade caught them both in the torso as he slid into a somersault and then turned to face them in a crouch. Both demons collapsed to the ground, lifeless. He replaced the sword and stood.

Two lieutenants. Thousands to go.

Unless he could slip out the back door undetected.

CHAPTER 23

JASON

Every time the sound of footsteps echoed down the corridor, Jason pressed against the wall and held his breath. He had made it as far as the lower kitchens, which had been abandoned long ago. But where there was a kitchen in a mega hotel, there had to be a loading bay close by. The sound of his heart thrumming in his ears made it difficult to concentrate on the noise around him. He rounded the stainless-steel tables and headed toward the back of the kitchen when the chaos sounded outside the main doors. The length of the kitchen made it hard to make out what was going on from where he stood, but he was pretty sure he understood what was happening.

Shouting, gunfire and the hammering of boots against concrete meant that someone had discovered that he was gone. The clock began ticking. He clenched his fists and turned away from the doors just as they burst open. Torches and lanterns lit up the doorway, but Jason had bolted toward the rear doors and exited the kitchen. He plunged into the darkened storage rooms, and that was when he noticed the large horizontal sliding doors. This had to be the loading bay, and it could lead to freedom.

The horde of demons that followed him wasn't far away, and it would only take seconds to realize that he had gone this way. There was very little time left. He ran to the first bay and pulled open the sliding door. The desert night air brushed over his skin as he jumped down from the bay, landing on the pavement. He didn't have to look back to see that a swarm of drones had run into the loading bay and saw the open door.

His feet pounded against the concrete as he ran, the fresh warm air filling his lungs with each step. The freedom of movement, away from an iron collar and a heavy chain, fueled his sprint. The street turned westward, flanked by high concrete barriers on either side. Wherever this road went, he had to follow it. There was no climbing over the berms, not without an additional boost. He had to hope that it opened out onto Las Vegas Boulevard.

Without the familiar lights of Vegas, he could barely make out the street ahead of him. It all looked like chunks of dark cement and abandoned cars. The end of the drive loomed in the distance, almost close enough to touch.

Three figures jumped down from the top of the concrete wall, landing and then running at him with the grace of cats. Through the dark, he saw the orange glow in their eyes. Lieutenants. Belphagor didn't send out just the drones to find him. He released the big guns.

The power of the fluid that now flowed through his veins filled his core with a vibrant energy that begged for release. There was never anything this powerful inside of him as the seraph, and it curled through his muscles as though it wanted to take over. With three lieutenants bearing down on him, he had no choice. He planted his feet and hunched forward, letting the energy flow from deep inside of him. The pupils of his eyes illuminated into a blinding blue light and his tattoos shimmered with power.

The demons approached with determined stealth through the dark, and with each step they took, he felt the energy build until it simmered just below the surface of his skin. He knew what the power wanted, what it needed to do. He had seen Nikka do it several times. This must have been how she felt all the time.

He reeled back, stabilizing his frame as the power coursed down his arm and collected in a brilliant blue sphere within the palm of his hand. The energy surged and twitched, begging to be released. The demons approached and just as they neared him, he threw the orb to the ground at their feet. It exploded into a bright flash of white, sending out its impact ring that tore through the demons, turning them to ash before him.

The aftershocks of the power still trembled in his bones as he stood there, gazing at his hand that had held the orb. How did he do that? Whatever was in that syringe must have been the same juice that gave Nikka her power, and now it moved as one with his body as though he could anticipate what it wanted.

The sounds of the approaching drones drew his attention. He would have to wonder about the power later when he wasn't trying to run for his freedom. He pushed forward and sprinted through to the street.

A full moon glazed light over the landscape of dark hotels that stood along the street. His mental map of the boulevard placed each building where he remembered. Just one block south and he would be at the promenade. He turned right and sprinted down the abandoned sidewalk, dodging overturned cars and chunks of cement that had fallen from surrounding buildings. The demons had left the city in ruins, all except the largest hotels and casino where the devil made his nest.

Even through the dark, he could see the wide-open pool of the abandoned fountains. The water no longer moved and danced with light and spray since the electricity had died. The EMP had left it as a wide, festering pool of green algae and garbage that slowly evaporated in the heat of the desert. But this place was the beacon that his mystery savior had chosen, and he would go, no matter what.

As his lungs burned, he sprinted across the empty street and slid over the hood of an abandoned sedan, one of many cars that littered the street and blocked the crosswalk. He landed on the other side and dodged under the trees that lined the path to the promenade.

A flash of violet light blinded him for a moment, and he collided with something huge and solid in his way. He fell back and lost his footing, tumbling to the sidewalk. The light dissipated as soon as it came, but he knew what it was before he even looked up.

"Samael," he said through clenched teeth.

The angel loomed over him, his pale blonde hair cut close to his scalp almost appearing as a halo. Those steal blue eyes glared down at him.

"There is nowhere to run," the angel said to him. "I will find you wherever you go."

Jason smiled as he looked at the angel. That was all he had left as he faced Samael, the one who showed the demons how to subjugate and torture him.

"Find me like you did Nikka?" Jason said, the words as pointed and acidic as he had meant them to be

The angel's eye twitched at the sound of her name.

That had gotten under his skin, just as he had hoped. "I'll never lead you to her."

Samael took a step closer, his pupils flashing into orbs of violet. He raised his hand and formed an orb of violet angel light in his palm. As the purple glow illuminated the tattoos on the angel's bare arms, Jason felt the pull of his own energy in opposition to this power. He knew the anger that burned inside of Samael. This creature had been so desperate to find Nikka that he would do anything to get her, except control his own rage. And now he was ready to strike Jason down with it.

The angel's arm reeled back, gearing back to slam the light into Jason's chest. This is how it would end, he thought. At the hand of one who should have saved us. He held his breath, his throat tightening and a swirl of nausea rising in his gut as he readied himself to face the angel fire.

Another flash of bright violet light illuminated the railings and the trees lining the promenade and left flickers in Jason's vision. He flinched as it appeared and the reflex of it sent his hand to his face to shield his eyes. When his vision cleared, he saw Samael fall to his knees, his eyes bulging in shock and his body surrounded by ribbons of electrical light that bound him in place.

A figure moved just out of the circle of violet and shifted in the shadows, but Jason saw the dark hoodie as it moved. This was the one who had freed him, had given him the blue serum and restored his power and then some. Jason pulled his hand away from his face and scrambled to his feet as the figure stepped toward him, its hand out and directed the energy that bound Samael. It moved toward him, and a hand pulled the hood away to reveal the face of a woman, her brilliant blue eyes illuminated by the flickering violet light. Her long brown hair fell over her shoulders, mussed by the removal of the hood.

She reached her other hand out to him. "Come. We do not have much time."

He wanted so much to trust her; after all, she created his escape. But what if she was just another creature sent to ruin everything, just like Samael or Belphagor? The sound of the coming demon horde stirred him into action.

His eyes fell onto her outstretched hand, and he grasped it. She pulled him in close, holding him against her torso as her wide eyes gazed back into the darkness toward the army of demons that descended on them. Her arm wrapped around his waist, taking no time to become familiar with him before she pressed her body tight against his.

Then her pupils flashed bright violet. A light arose from somewhere between them, the warmth of it filling his abdomen as it enveloped him. He still felt her arm around him and her body against his even though he could no longer see through the blinding light. He closed his eyes and tucked his head down. The woman that held him pulled him even closer, enough so that he could smell the lavender fragrance in her hair.

His feet left the ground, and a sudden jolt took his breath away.

Chapter 24

Jason

When the light enveloped him, Jason still held his breath, afraid to let go of her. But the woman released her grip on him, and he fell into the permeating white glow that surrounded them. The light burned brighter as it almost blinded him even with his eyes closed. Every tattoo etched into his skin sizzled and stung deep into his limbs. And then the pain came again, familiar and instant. There was so much about the light and the burning, searing pain that he recognized from a past that was not too distant. The last time he faced something like this, he awoke as the seraph and Nikka was gone.

And now it had come to take him again.

The breath he held rushed out in a pained scream as the light torched against his skin, feeling the white-hot brand of something move from his shoulders to his neck. His back arched as he tried to fight against it, but his limbs wouldn't move.

The ground had disappeared under his feet, but now it formed, and he fell hard as the light that had held him now released its grip. His body slammed into solid earth and grass, the air rushing from his lungs as he fell face-down to the ground.

His limbs trembled with the aftershocks of what had just happened. A glaze of cold sweat beaded against his skin and he didn't want to move. Every muscle ached when he tried, so there was no use fighting it, and he just stayed there, his face turned toward the ground as he tried to open his eyes.

"It is over," a woman's voice sounded out to him as though she spoke through a long tunnel.

A warm blanket touched his back, the skin there still sensitive, and that was the moment he realized he was naked. The light had taken every piece of clothing that had covered his body, just like it did when it made him the seraph. It had stolen from him yet again. A hand touched his back through the blanket, and the warmth of it penetrated into his flesh.

"You are free," she said, and this time her voice sounded much closer.

He forced his eyes open and turned to see her, the same blue-eyed woman with dark hair that had found him at the promenade. Her piercing stare watched him without blinking as the moonlight shone behind her.

"What happened?" he said as he tried to pull himself up to his elbows, but his muscles only trembled.

The woman's hand wrapped around his upper arm, and she helped to pull him to his feet while she wrapped the blanket around his body. His legs wobbled, but she steadied him. For such a petite thing, she was stronger than she looked.

"We have saved you from Lucifer's hold," she said.

We? There were more of her?

He blinked his eyes clear and looked beyond her into the dark. Moonlight shone down onto a grove of trees that surrounded the grassy spot where he had landed, and the two of them weren't alone. At least a dozen other men and women stood around the glen and watched him with silent interest. Each of them was beautiful and young and perfect. And each of them probably had the same penetrating stare and power that this woman held.

Angels.

The woman stepped back from him. "Are you well?"

His knees wobbled again, but he caught himself this time and held the blanket close. "Am I well?" The question had caught him off guard. "I—I guess so."

She turned and signaled to one of the others, who reacted and carried something to her. The woman turned and reached out a stack of folded clothes to him. "I believe these will fit you."

He accepted them but raised his eyebrow as he glanced at the group. "Who are you guys? I mean, I know that you're angels, but who are you? Why did you save me?"

"We are the guardians," she said. "We protect the gateway to Heaven and monitor the affairs of all angels. I am Zumiel."

"All right," he said and turned away from her with the blanket tucked around his torso. "Zumiel, so why me?" He unfolded the jeans that she had given him and slipped into them while struggling to keep the blanket around him. The angels probably didn't care if he dropped his concealment, but he cared.

"You are the seraph, and you have been recruited for a higher purpose," she said.

He turned back toward her as he buttoned the jeans and then slipped the dark gray T-shirt over his head.

"What does that mean?"

A smile appeared on her lips, and a faint dot of violet light appeared in her pupils. She stepped toward him and held out her hand. As she neared him, he took a step back and almost flinched when her fingers moved upward to his neck. The moment she made contact with his skin, a zing of power surged through his body and coursed upward to his chest. The energy shot through his neck, into his skull, and it burned through his eyes in a shot of purple light.

Even in the dark of the glen, he could now see each of the angels that surrounded him with perfect clarity, and not only the people that stood there. The violet power that surrounded each of them like an aura shimmered at the edges, just above the skin. The energy now pumped in his veins and drew away the trembling and weakness in his body. This was so much more than seraph power.

He glanced down at his arms, the tattoos decorating his skin illuminated in purple light, to the new marks like three parallel lines that arced up both sides of his neck from his shoulders. These tattoos energized something inside of him, and if he didn't know any better, he would have thought that he was a god.

"What have you done to me?" he said, turning his hands over as he inspected the tattoos.

"You are no longer a seraph." She backed away from him, the smile still on her lips. "You are an archangel. A guardian. You are the executioner."

His brow furrowed as he looked up at her. "The what?"

"The executioner. A destroyer of angels."

This power was more than he had ever felt before, but he had never heard of such a thing. Something completely new and the strength of it flowed from the earth under his feet without him even trying to manipulate it. He had no doubt he could destroy an angel, but why would they give him such power?

Zumiel stepped around him and held her arm out in the direction she wanted him to follow. "Come. I have something for you."

He followed her but glanced at the others that stepped in line with her. He padded over the dew-damp grass from the glen and into the dark of the trees. The light that shimmered from his tattoos lit their small space and sparkled in the reflection of the angel's eyes as she glanced back at him. Despite her beautiful eyes and calm demeanor, he wasn't about to trust her just yet.

They moved down a gentle slope and then emerged into another clearing, where a figure kneeled in the center of the glen. The angels moved from behind him and surrounded the person, opening the way for Jason and Zumiel to approach. As he neared the shape in the center, his footsteps slowed. This was an angel, tied down in a kneeling position and chained with tethers staked to the ground. The light of his tattoos cast down on this man, and he immediately recognized his short, pale hair. The man's icy blue eyes turned up to him and narrowed as he looked up at him. Samael didn't struggle against his bonds but only glared at Jason as he neared him.

"What is this? Why is he here?" Jason said, glancing at each of the angels that surrounded them.

"Samael has fallen," Zumiel said as she took slow steps around him. "He has been in league with Lucifer. It is because of him that the world is dying. He created Nikka and turned her into something she was never meant to be, all because of his selfishness. Millions have died because of him."

The moment she mentioned Nikka's name, the surge of anger sparked in his gut which only made his tattoos glow brighter. This angel power wanted to take over, and he almost let it. The flow of energy pulsated in his chest, boiling to the point of consuming his only thought: I want to destroy Samael. This rage came from somewhere so primal, so distant to his own thoughts that no matter how much he tried to pull away from it, the ferocity of it still simmered just under his skin. This is what it meant to be an executioner: to hold the rage close and use it as fuel for his power. Zumiel turned her gaze up to him.

"He is to be executed," she said. "It is in your power now."

Jason kept his gaze down to Samael, who still stared at him with such hatred. This was the angel that took Nikka from him and stole her memories. He was the one that orchestrated the events that led to the EMP detonation. He had wanted all of this to happen to the world.

He reached behind his shoulder and grasped the hilt of his sword. The blade pulled free, and violet flames danced around the length of the weapon as he moved it to his side. The glow settled across Samael's face.

"You will provide justice," Zumiel said.

Samael's lips parted in a crooked grin. "Take your revenge."

The angel knew exactly what Jason wanted, and that made his calm even more unnerving. Of course, he wanted revenge for every injection of demon blood, for every time he thought of Nikka and how she had suffered because of Samael. His fingers tightened on the sword. He was meant for this. An angel of justice. An executioner.

"Do it," Samael said. "Strike true. But know this: they are using you as much as I used your precious Nikka."

The power burned like a hot furnace in his chest now, and he clenched his teeth. The muscles in his shoulders tensed at the sound of her name on his lips.

"It is time," Zumiel said, stirring Jason from his thoughts.

"Nikka will burn with you all," Samael said and braced himself, for he knew that it was coming.

The angel fire coursed in Jason's muscles, forcing them into action. He raised the sword and his ribs contracted in a shout as he swung his weapon in an arc of purple light and metal. The blade met the angel's neck, and there was no resistance as it sliced cleanly through his flesh. The power moved up his arm from the hilt of the sword as he stepped to the side, letting the angel's head fall to the ground. The body slumped forward and then morphed into a statue of black ash that crumbled under its own weight.

He had done it, executed an angel because the others had told him to. No. Because he wanted to.

Jason backed away from the pile of ashes and replaced the sword. The moment the light of the blade disappeared, his tattoos blinked into dark ink and the violet light faded from his eyes.

"Well done," Zumiel said and smiled as she looked at him.

Her matter-of-fact demeanor still itched at him. Samael was probably right, there was something more here.

"I know you didn't spring me from Satan's dungeon just to kill him," he said, pointing to the ashes in the center of the glen.

"You are correct." Zumiel stepped up to him, and he could see her face in the moonlight. "You are needed for something so much more important. As guardians, it is our duty to protect this world. This is not how it was supposed to be, but Samael triggered this. The end of days is coming, and it will come down to a war with Lucifer. He wants this world for himself, he always has. And it is because of Samael that we are losing."

"You're all angels," he said, the volume of his voice raising more than he had expected, but he couldn't contain it. "You've been fighting the devil since the beginning of time."

"And, yet, he now has the upper hand," she said. "His legions have been loosed onto this world. They have brought humankind to the brink of extinction, and now he has the final weapon in his war."

"Nikka's baby," Jason muttered as the realization hit him.

"The child will be the anti-Christ. The last remaining humans will follow him into oblivion. And now the final seals have been broken, and Armageddon is at hand."

"The seals? You mean like the last day kind of seals from the Bible?"

"The Harbingers have been loosed onto this world, and they are the final key."

"What do you mean by Harbingers?"

"You would know them as the Four Horsemen," Zumiel said, a slight flash of violet in her pupils.

Shit. The Four Horsemen of the Apocalypse. He wanted to sit down and stop the dizziness that started in his head.

"It is the Four Horsemen that will herald the end of days. They will pave the way for Lucifer to reign, and the one who controls them will be the devil's right hand. Then he will never be stopped, and the world will be lost. That archangel and the child must be destroyed, or all will die."

He swallowed hard against a dry throat. All of this end-of-the-world stuff made him sick, and he wanted to throw up, but he was sure there was nothing in his stomach but acid. This is not what he had been born for, a soldier at the end of time. But it was the entire world at stake. These angels—the guardians—freed him from Lucifer's grasp for this singular purpose. This was a Biblical terror. Hell, the anti-Christ? How could Nikka's baby become so evil?

"You know why," Zumiel said and leaned toward him.

Could she read his thoughts? He looked away from her and hunched over, the breath sucked from his lungs, and his stomach turned.

"Think about it," she whispered and placed a hand on his shoulder. "A child of a seraph and a demon. And not just any demon. Pazuzu, the devil's prince. Conceived in evil, born as a result of a horrific act. And now he is in Lucifer's possession, contained to be molded into the devil's perfect son."

Everything she said made him sick. He couldn't deny it. Jason had been there the moment Belphagor handed over the baby to Lucifer, and he saw the way the devil handled him. With such care and affection. Zumiel spoke the truth, and he knew it. No matter how hard he tried to push the thoughts aside. The baby would become everything Zumiel said he would.

The angels brought him here and created him into the executioner. That's what he had to be.

He swallowed the knot of fear and closed his eyes. They didn't have to say it because he already knew. They meant for him to kill the child. And another archangel. If it would save the world and bring humankind from the brink of extinction, he had to do it. Maybe someday Nikka could forgive him, but he had to end this.

Jason looked up at Zumiel. "I'll do it."

The angel stood straighter.

"An archangel broke the seals," he said, and Zumiel nodded. "Where do I find this archangel?"

Zumiel took in a steady breath and tilted her head to the side. "Nikka is the one who broke the seals, she is absorbing the Harbingers' power. She must be stopped before she has taken all four of them."

The ground grew dark as he fell to his knees, his ears ringing. It can't be. Not Nikka. Why would she do this? He had only seen her for a minute when he had to fight her under Belphagor's orders. But in that minute, she had lost her baby because of him. Was she so desperate to get him back that she did something reckless?

"You must not fail in this task. She has already begun the transformation, and Lucifer will use her and her power to end this world," Zumiel said as she stepped toward him. She crouched down with a warm hand on his back. The scent of lavender drifted from her hair and made his head swim. "There is only this task we ask of you. If you fail, another executioner will be called, and you both will be culled."

CHAPTER 25

GIDEON

he sun had already set when the vehicle approached the border. Gideon slowed down as he neared the gate, a volley of abandoned cars, RVs and trucks stopped in lines that approached the gates. No armed guards. No manned posts behind the booths. The vehicles left behind had been looted of anything valuable, windows smashed, and some of them burned until there was nothing left to take. His fingers tightened on the steering wheel, and Nikka sat up from where she rested her head against the seat. He followed her gaze out to across the rows of empty cars as they drove through the only open gate that had not been blocked.

Blues and greens of the coming twilight fell on the desert landscape that opened beyond the checkpoint and into the southernmost reaches of Texas. The heat of the day still radiated from the sand as they rolled along the desolate road until it poured into the outskirts of a small border town, but this one was just as empty as the dozen others they had seen since leaving Tampico.

As Nikka leaned her head against the door frame, the wind drifting into her hair through the open window, he glanced at her. "Shall we stop for the evening?"

She looked back at him, the glint of the dashboard lights reflecting in her tired eyes.

"We should stop," Jadriel's voice interjected from the back seat.

The muscles along Gideon's spine tightened and his teeth clenched. The sound of the angel's voice grated on his nerves tonight.

"It's a good idea," Nikka said as she shifted back to speak to the angel.

Gideon watched the angel in his rear-view mirror, at the way he gazed at Nikka when she spoke, but it only made his stiff neck hurt even more.

"I'm exhausted, and I'm sure that you need some rest too," Nikka said, placing her hand on Gideon's forearm. Her touch eased the tension in his shoulders, and she was right. He had been driving for hours. They all needed some time away from the road.

"I do," he said with a nod and slowed the vehicle as he turned into the residential streets of the town.

Everything here remained dark. No candlelight in the windows. Cars and trucks looted. Most of the homes had broken windows and gaping doors, but the town had now gone silent. Gideon stepped from the Jeep and glanced through their surroundings. Each of them had their own routine down by now: search the area until one of them finds the safest place.

Amy called out to them, and Gideon found Nikka as they walked together to find what she had discovered.

Nikka hugged her arms around her torso, her head down. Gideon stepped beside her and placed his arm around her shoulder, pulling her close to him.

"You need rest," he said. She nestled her head against his shoulder.

"More than you know. Ever since I got this thing," she said as she held her forearm up to the moonlight and Gideon saw the new tattoo on her skin, "I just don't feel right."

"How do you mean?"

"I don't know how to describe it," she said. "Everything feels off. Jad said it might be the power in it, waiting to be released."

His hand tightened on her shoulder, and this made her lean away from him. "You spoke to Jadriel about this?" he asked.

"Well, yeah," she said, her brow wrinkled as she looked at him. "He knows a lot about this stuff."

Speaking about the angel created a gnawing pain in the center of his gut. "We do not need him here. He cannot help us any longer, you should just get rid of him."

Nikka stopped, her mouth agape as she watched him. Gideon's arm slipped from her shoulder, and he halted.

"You can't be serious," she said.

"About Jadriel? I am very serious. He is only a liability."

"Gideon, he has helped us in so many ways. And he can help us get our son back."

His jaw clenched again, and he tightened his fists. It had been so long since he felt this level of anger, and he did not want to direct it at her. But she continued to defend the angel, as though she had grown fond of him.

"He will do no such thing. The angel would kill us both the moment you remove the binding sigil."

Her eyebrows rose as she looked at him. "So, what are you suggesting? That we kill him? Is that how you want to get rid of him?"

The idea had not occurred to him until she said it, but it had some merit. They could not undo the binding spell for fear that he would retaliate, and that would put Nikka at too much risk. Neither of them could actually kill the angel, but Nikka could exorcise him and leave him without a body long enough for them to escape.

Nikka let out an incredulous laugh and crossed her arms over her chest. "I can't believe it. You're actually considering it. What's wrong with you?"

The sigils etched into the skin of her arms squirmed with fine points of violet light, something that he was sure Nikka hadn't noticed at first. The subject of Jadriel had elicited enough of a reaction from her that he knew where she would stand if something happened to the angel. That was all he needed to know.

Gideon shook his head. "Forget about it. I think I am just tired and need a break from him for a while."

She let her arms slip to her side, and the light faded from her tattoos. "Okay."

Even though she stepped in sync with him again, he noticed the stiffness in her shoulders. But that did not matter to him, as long as she was still by his side. He slipped his fingers through hers, and she hesitated at first but then clasped his hand as they moved through the front porch of the large house that Amy had found for them.

The place had been closed for far too long and smelled of dust. The front windows had been broken, leaving a fine layer of sand that had blown in and covered the main room. As they moved through the place, into each bedroom, Gideon found the six bedrooms mostly untouched. The beds still had linens, although the blankets needed shaking to remove the dust, and mattresses were clean. Good enough to stay in for one night.

Nikka walked with him into the master bedroom, and as he turned to close the door, Jadriel stepped down the hall, and their eyes met. The angel stopped, watching him from the dark of the corridor. Gideon's fingers tightened on the door handle. A small kindling of heat grew in his chest, in the place where he kept his demon half that raged to be set free. That part of him wanted to fill every space of him and lash out at the angel, to tear his throat from his body and leave him on the floor.

Gideon looked away and closed the door, but it took every effort he had to turn from Jadriel at that last second. His fingers still clutched at the handle, leaving his knuckles white. His self-control frayed at the edges, and somewhere in the center of his being, he knew it would only be a matter of days before he would strike at the angel.

Why could he not stop this feeling that welled in him, that threatened to take over his entire body? He had tried too hard to master this, but Jadriel's presence peeled away at his resolve.

He glanced back through the dark to see Nikka pulling back the top blankets of the bed and lay on the white sheets. That was when he knew why he had so little control. She was the reason. From the moment he first saw her, lying in that hospital bed, her frailty at the surface, he knew he had to protect her. Protect her from the evil that would try and destroy her. From the others that threatened to take her away from him.

Her long legs stretched out over the sheets, her feet bare of the shoes that she had worn all day. Gideon crawled across the bed and rested his head on the pillow beside her, his hand snaking over her torso. The heat of her skin through her thin tank top warmed the flesh of his arm. Her hand touched his arm as he pulled her closer. She turned toward him, her face nestling into the curve of his neck as she relaxed into sleep next to him.

She belonged to him, nobody else.

The heat inside his chest pulsed through his veins with each beat of his heart, reaching into his fingertips and strengthening his muscles. It flooded his brain as he thought on every moment he had ever possessed her. The warmth spread into his abdomen and reached lower, growing as he took in her scent. The lavender scent of her that he owned.

He opened his eyes to gaze on her perfect archangel form and saw her through the points of red embers that glowed within his pupils.

CHAPTER 26
NIKKA

The smell of pine surrounded her, a fragrance so familiar that it made her open her eyes to see the log ceiling of Jason's cabin. But that would be impossible. The cabin was gone, swallowed up in the heat of a volcanic explosion over a year ago. She blinked her eyes, but the logs remained, and so did the scent. She sat up with a jolt from the bed and glanced around the room. It was the same small space with a single lantern light on a nightstand and the window that faced to the east. The environment was dark, cast in the black of nighttime except for the light from the lantern that barely illuminated the small bed.

Something moved to her right, and she glanced down to see Gideon's form next to her. She froze for a moment as he opened his eyes and looked at her, two fine points of red light that lingered in his pupils. Looking into the eyes of Pazuzu. He propped himself on his elbow, his muscled torso bare and the rest of him covered by the blankets. His hand reached out to touch hers.

"Is everything okay?" he said.

The warmth of his hand felt real enough, but this was all so impossible. They were somewhere in southern Texas, not the extinct cabin.

"I'm not sure," she said and moved her gaze over the room. The pine scent drifted over her again, mixed with the smell of canvas and old leather. "How did we get here?"

"We have always been here," he said.

"No, we haven't." She bit her lip. A tickle of worry moved up her spine. This was all too familiar.

"This is the place you never left."

Nikka shook her head. "That's not possible."

She moved to stand, to pull her hand out from his grasp, but his fingers tightened like a vice around her wrist. The worry turned into panic, and she held her breath, trying to pull her arm free. The red in his eyes flared as he sprang across the bed, his mouth opened in a wide and wicked grin.

This can't be happening again.

She cried out and shoved her body away from the bed, but he still held onto her with a ferocious grip. He moved so fast that she couldn't see him in the blur of the dark until he had pulled her down to the bed, his weight on top of her as he pinned her arms above her head with a single hand. She fought to worm her hands out of his grip, but the muscles in his arms tightened into cement bulges. Although she tried not to cry, the tears formed at the corners of her eyes and fell down her temples into her hair.

"Why are you doing this?" she cried as she attempted to twist her body away from him.

His free hand moved to the button at the top of her pants, his fingers brushing against the bare flesh of her abdomen.

"Because you belong to me," he said, the demon growl evident just under his breath. "Not Jason. And not the angel. And you will learn that before this is all over."

The rough edges of his finger nails forced the zipper down, and that was enough to ignite the power in the center of her being. It surged into her chest and down her arms with a single pulse of energy. The light erupted from her eyes and the tattoos along her arms flashed into a violet glow. The power flowed into her muscles and gave her the strength to force him off of her, throwing him across the room. The glow of it all illuminated the room into hues of neon purple as she stood to face him, the anger of what he had just done flowing into every cell of her body.

He crouched against the wall, his hand shielding his red eyes from her light.

Now was her chance, to strike him down and punish him for everything that he had done. Her fingers flexed into tight fists at her side and the power amplified down the length of her arms. Only one blow with her power is all that it would take . . .

She bolted up from her pillow and gasped as her eyes opened to the darkness of the room. No scent of pine lingered around the blankets. Only old dust and the dry, hot desert outside the house. The only light came from the single window that allowed the moonlight to shine on the bed. Her heart raced in her chest with the last vestiges of the dream that still danced in her thoughts, the same images that left smoke trails of anger and hate in their wake.

Gideon's form stirred next to her, and he sat up, his hand moving to her back as she breathed fast.

"Is everything okay?" he said.

That's exactly what he had said in her dream, and it made the prickles move across the skin of her arms. She shifted away from him, and his hand fell from the space between her shoulder blades. A tear fell from her eyes; she really had been crying.

He moved across the bed and pressed himself behind her, his arms wrapping around her as he settled his head on her shoulder and spoke in her ear.

"It was only a dream," he whispered.

The feel of his breath in her ear and the pressure of his arms around her had meant to comfort her, but it only agitated the tremors that lingered in her chest. The aftershocks of the dream still danced around the edges of her thoughts, and everything that he had done in it. But it wasn't only the dream. It had actually happened once when she was alone with him, and he took what he wanted from her. There was a time when she had let these fears and anger go, but for some reason, it plagued her thoughts and even her dreams tonight. She grasped his wrist to try and pull him away, but he held her fast.

"I think I just need some fresh air," she said, but she had wanted to yell at him, to tell him how angry she still was about things. She twisted against him, but his grip didn't loosen.

"You do not need to go anywhere," he said as his hand moved up to her throat, his fingers tightening enough for her to know that this was no longer her nightmare.

Nikka grasped his other wrist and tried to force him off of her, but his fingers grasped tighter around her throat as he pressed his face in closer to her ear.

"You cannot go to him," he said, the growl of a demon just under the sound of his voice. "Jadriel will not love you as I do."

Her heart raced faster than it had in her dream as she gasped for air against his grip. What was happening? This can't be real.

The door of the bedroom flew open, and a flash of violet light rushed into the room. In a millisecond, Gideon's grip fell from around her, and she collapsed on the bed as Jadriel pulled Gideon from her and slammed him against the wall. Her throat spasmed as she coughed and crawled to the floor, away from the brawl on the other side of the room. In the moonlight, Jadriel pinned Gideon to the wall, his forearm against his throat. The angel's eyes now glowed a neon purple light to balance the fierce red orbs that resided in Gideon's eyes.

"I will kill you now, demon," Jadriel said through clenched teeth.

Gideon grasped at the angel's shirt, bunching it in his fists. "You will never be a match for me, or for her."

"Stop," Nikka tried to shout, but her throat had tightened enough that it only came out as a raspy squeak.

The angel lifted Gideon into the air and tossed him back through the window. The glass shattered in a shower of glittering fragments that caught the dim light. Jadriel then leaped through the window, jumping down to the dry brown lawn to finish what he had started.

Nikka scrambled to her feet as she fought back the surges of coughing that rumbled in her throat. They were truly going to kill each other, and for what? Something had triggered this, even the nightmare that had brought her fears back to the surface. They were all so angry, and even rumbles of hate still throbbed in her chest. She hadn't been this upset with Gideon for so long. Why had it come back tonight?

This had to stop before it got out of hand.

She ran down the stairs and burst through the open door to find them in a struggle, Gideon on top of Jadriel, their hands clutched at each other's throats.

"Stop," she screamed at them, her voice a little more than a whimper now. Dust kicked up around them as she reached in to pull Gideon from the angel, but he lashed back at her and shoved her back down to the ground.

A gunshot rang out into the night, the sound of it ricocheting around the desolate neighborhood. Nikka looked back to the front porch and Gideon, and Jadriel stopped as they glanced too.

Amy stood in the moonlight, her hand raised into the air with the pistol she had just shot. Her hand still shook as she brought the gun down and trained the barrel to both of the men that crouched on the dusty ground. The whites of her eyes shone through the dark, her face streaked with tears.

Nikka moved to stand on wobbly knees, her eyes focused on Amy as she stood there with the gun shaking at the men. "It's okay, Amy. Just a misunderstanding. That's all."

"Just stop," Amy said to the men.

Gideon moved to his feet, his hands up before him and he stepped away from Jadriel. The ember glow remained in his eyes, however, as he glanced back to the angel. Jadriel rose and dusted himself off before shooting a violet glare at the demon.

"See, it's okay," Nikka said. "They're going to stop fighting now." She took a step toward her.

Amy's wide eyes flashed to her, and the barrel of the gun shifted to face her. Nikka paused, her heart dropping in her chest.

"Don't come any closer," she said.

Nikka's brow furrowed. "Amy, it's me, okay. Everything's going to be fine."

"Not it's not." The gun trembled, and tears glistened in Amy's eyes as she looked at her. "This is all your fault. They're fighting because of you. We are all here because of you."

Nikka's mouth went dry. "Amy, I—"

"Shut up. It's your fault that my son is gone, that the world has died. You did this."

"I didn't mean to," Nikka said, and the shaking started in her hands.

"Leave her alone," Gideon growled at Amy, and she flashed him an angry look.

"Or what? What will you do?" she said to him, the gun still trained on Nikka.

"I will kill you."

Amy clenched her teeth, and Nikka saw it happen before the gun flared. Amy spun the weapon toward Gideon, and her finger tightened on the trigger. The shot rang out as Nikka ran the opposite direction and into the dark alley between houses. In the corner of her eye, she saw Gideon move into the dark as well, taking Amy down before the third shot echoed. Nikka bolted, her feet pounding on the pavement and the air burning into her raw throat. The beat of her heart rattled against her ribs, but she couldn't stop. She dodged into the main street and ran toward the large empty warehouse, where she plunged into the dark shadow at the side of the building. She crouched against the corrugated metal wall and pressed her body into the darkness, her wide eyes searching the street behind her.

The night remained quiet, no more gunshots. But her heartbeat throbbed in her ears, and she tried to hold her breath. There would be no good hiding here if her panic gave her away. Hiding. From her friends. Her friends that had just tried to kill each other and her.

She placed her hand over her mouth to quiet her breathing as she listened into the dark.

Another shot rang out, and a bullet struck the metal wall in a volley of sparks. She flinched at the flash. Burning pain erupted in her arm where the first bullet had grazed her. She pressed her hand to the wound, the warm wet blood soaking her fingers. Nikka got to her feet and ran behind the building until she found a door and pushed through into the warehouse. When it slammed shut, she slid the deadbolt into place and crouched into the shadows as she held her arm.

"Nikka," Amy's voice shouted into the night. From the way the sound echoed through the building, she could tell that Amy was probably across the street somewhere.

She closed her eyes and tried to control her breathing, but between the pain in her throat and her arm, that control began to wane. Little light came through the few windows in this place, and most of it scattered through the rows of shelves that extended across the wide lower floor. The others would have a difficult time finding her in here if she stayed low and among the shelving.

She crawled to the nearest racks and peered through them to the windows on the farthest end of the building. The building was mostly empty, whatever had been in here was taken a long time ago. Nothing to use as a weapon or a shield.

Maybe she would have to rely on her own power. Her power against her friends.

"Hey," a voice whispered behind her.

Her fingers reached behind her and withdrew her sword in a sudden motion when she heard the sound. The violet fire lit up her space in the warehouse, casting light across Jadriel's face from where he stood only five feet away.

He brought his hands up and stayed in a crouch as he looked at her. "It is okay. I am sworn to protect you, remember?"

The sword shook in her hands, and she kept it trained on him. She wanted to believe him, but after everything she had just seen, she wasn't sure anymore.

"How can I trust you?" she whispered.

"The binding sigil can only be broken by your hand, or your death," he said. "Not even the Angel of War can break it."

The tip of her sword faltered, and she let the weapon move to her side. "Angel of War?"

Of course. Such anger and hatred could only be spawned by an other-worldly being. Another Horseman. It had found them and now used them against each other.

Jadriel nodded. "Yes. The angel is close. Otherwise, it would not have such power over us. You must find it before we all kill each other."

Nikka re-sheathed the sword, plunging them into darkness once again. "Where?"

A hand landed on her shoulder from behind, grasping her and lifting her to her feet. The body tossed her into the racks, and she crashed into them, landing hard against the farthest wall. The impact of it knocked the air from her lungs, and she gasped with the spasm in her ribs. As the final shelf fell around her, she lifted her head and gazed across the room, to the looming figure that stepped toward her. The creature was all muscle and bone, a man that looked more like a professional wrestler or an ex-convict than an angel. In the moonlight, the faint outlines of tattoos stretched from his chin to his chest and then painted his body. Yes, more like an ex-con. The flash of his shaved head above angry dark eyes loomed over her.

"I am right here," he said, "and I have been waiting for you."

CHAPTER 27

NIKKA

he Angel of War loomed over Nikka, and his heavy fist came down toward her like a flash in the dark. Before it struck, she channeled her power in a rush of violet light through the palms of her hands and directed it at his chest. The energy drove him backwards, but he planted his feet, leaving a trail of cracked concrete where his feet had skidded. The green glow in his pupils trained toward her like a predator in the dark, unfazed by the power she had just thrown at him.

The moment her violet energy dissipated, the angel pounded his large feet toward her, the impact of each step rumbling through the ground in violent tremors. Although every bone in her body hurt after he had thrown her across the room, she couldn't wait for him to get any closer. She moved to her feet and ran into the dark of the warehouse, between the rows of metal shelving.

"There is no use hiding from me," his booming voice echoed in the great space of the building. "I will find you."

She bolted around the edge of a break in the shelves and crouched down in the shadows. If he was following the sound of her footsteps, this would have to throw him off her trail until she could collect her thoughts and figure out a way to stop him.

The darkness lit up into a bright flash of violet light, and Nikka peered around the corner to see Jadriel step toward the Harbinger, his power directed at full strength from his hands at her attacker. The

Angel of War turned to face Jadriel, throwing his forearm up to shield himself from the onslaught.

What was Jadriel doing? He didn't have the power to defeat War, and he knew it.

War twisted back to face the angel and bounded toward him, the angel power only a small deterrent as he charged at Jadriel.

The Harbinger would be on him in only a second. She had to think of something. This giant of a horseman barely flinched at her power. Maybe she would have to take him down with sheer strength. But as she watched him bear down on Jadriel, the muscles rippling along his bare back like a grizzly on steroids, she knew that she was no match for him either.

While he was distracted with Jadriel, she scrambled further into the darkness and got to her feet. Then she turned to watch War descend on the angel, tossing him across the room as easily as he did to her.

She had to face him—and defeat him—eventually. The Harbinger turned his gaze back to the room and searched for her in the shadows, the ghostly glow in his pupils flashing as his eyes twitched. She steadied her knees, forcing out the shaking that started in her legs, and she reached behind her shoulder to find the hilt of her sword. Once she withdrew it, the purple fire would draw his attention. But that was the only thing she had left. She would have to face him with only her strength and her sword, but there was more than muscle to pure might. Agility might just be on her side.

Her fingers wrapped around the hilt and she pulled the sword free. The metal scrape against the invisible scabbard resonated in the room. War's green eyes stopped as he heard the sound and then he saw the violet fire. A smile spread across his lips as the thick muscles in his shoulders sat like boulders below his neck.

"Little girls should not play with such toys," he said, his voice course like gravel. He moved at her, his feet bounding through the dark.

She forced away the trembling that had started in her core and willed her feet to move against her own will. Sprinting toward him in a dangerous game of chicken, she gripped tight to her sword and held her breath. His face contorted into a twist of anger as he came toward her. A thick, callused hand came down at her, ready to grasp her as she neared him.

At the final second, she arched back and dropped to her knees, gripping the sword with both hands. The blade caught his leg as she slid past him. He cried out, more in rage than anything else, but she didn't wait to see if the Goliath had fallen. She twisted her body in a somersault and leaped back up to her feet.

But the giant spun around, faster than she would have expected and swung his fist in the dark. The impact struck her in the chest, sending her crashing back into another series of shelves that collapsed around her. The sword fell from her hand when she collided into the shelves, clattering somewhere in the darkness and out of her reach.

"You humans are all the same," he said, his voice growing closer as he stepped toward her. "So easy to manipulate."

The ribs along her right side seized when she tried to move, and she clenched her teeth against the pain of fractures sliding against one another. A trickle of blood wet the side of her temple as it flowed from her hairline. The angel's voice came closer, and she couldn't move without pain wracking her entire body. The sword was gone, and her power was all but useless against War.

"You won't stop us," Nikka said between tight breaths. She tried to get to her feet, but she stumbled among the metal pipes and sheeting that had scattered around her.

"Oh, really?" he said. "I can get you every time. Lust. Rage. Jealousy. Hatred. The very foundations of war and you all responded to it. You will react every time. Even the demon bent to my will."

The hulking creature stepped through a sliver of moonlight that cast through a single window. His frame towered over her, green eyes boring into her as she tried to step away from him.

"I will spread across the face of the earth," he said with a crooked smile that formed on his lips.

He was probably right, about everything. War had manipulated each of them. The Harbinger had planted the dreams in her head, stirring up the feelings that she had been too afraid to face. She had always hated what Gideon had done to her, even if it was Pazuzu. War had forced open the thing that kept Pazuzu in control, and Gideon had been powerless. The demon part of him was all lust and jealousy. Jadriel's hatred of Gideon had no boundaries when War was nearby. Even Amy was under the angel's spell. None of them could escape him.

Nikka closed her eyes and steadied her rapid breathing. Even now, the angel tried to use her to attack out of fear and rage. She had to stop him, not out of revenge or anger. This was to get her son back.

The muscles in her back stopped twitching and trembling as she concentrated on the sound of his footsteps. Each one heavy and lumbering. The sound of cement cracking under his feet as he walked rang in her ears. Just like Goliath, he was a towering hulk of a creature, wrapped in thick bulging muscles. Muscle that had limited flexibility.

Her eyes flashed open, and she watched him step from the moonlight and into the darkness where she stood. She had to act now.

Despite the ache in her ribs and blood flowing from a laceration in her head, she readied her mind to react. He took another step and reached toward her, and that was the moment she had to move. She dodged from his grasp and scrambled to the ground between the wide stance of his legs. His reflexes were not as fast, and his hand reached for her, but she was too quick. She turned, feeling the burning shot of pain in her ribs as she sprang to her feet and leaped onto his back. Her agile legs moved fast, climbing up his back until she could wrap her arm around his neck in a choke-hold.

His hands reached behind him, flailing to grasp at her but the muscles in his shoulders and arms were too thick, and he couldn't find her. He spun around and tried to fling her forward, but she wrapped her legs around his waist and locked her ankles together. The angel bucked and twisted like a rodeo bull, and each movement sent a new wave of pain into her lungs.

His meaty fingers grasped at her arm, but she tightened her hold. The choking sound in his throat gurgled as he thrashed.

She only needed a moment, a second when she could grasp at the angel inside of him. Once she had it, the host would fall, and she could defeat him.

She loosened the hold of her left hand, keeping her right arm around his throat and she fixed her gaze on the space between his shoulder blades. Her angel-vision sparked, and she could see the ephemeral swirl of the gossamer light inside the human. The thing resided in his chest, through his ribs and the layers of thick muscle. She only needed to grasp and remove it before he freed himself from her grasp.

Her hand plunged into his back, the layers of human tissue fading into a non-substance through her angelic force that flowed into her arms. She found the angelic being, like a warm mist that swirled around her fingers, and she wrapped her hand around it.

War shouted as soon as it felt her fingers around his center. His entire frame seized as he cried into the night. He spun around, nearly throwing her off balance. Her arm gripped around his neck, but her fingers loosened around the angel soul inside his core. War moved into the dark, and she didn't see the wall that came at her as he slammed her back against it. Her hand slipped from inside of him as she almost fell to the ground.

The painful shot of another crack in her ribs made her cry out as he slammed her again, trying to free himself from her grip. She tightened her arm around his neck as he reeled back for another shot against the wall.

She only had a fraction of a second, and the next slam would probably knock her off his back. There was no way she would ever get another chance.

As he leaned forward, ready to throw his back against the wall again, she plunged her fist into his back and found the filmy center where the angel resided. The hulk angled back, ready to drive the full weight of his body against the wall. Her fingers tightened around the soft, warm center, probably tighter than she had wanted, and she pulled fast until it snapped free. War's trajectory had already started though, and he slammed her back against the wall just as the angel pulled free from his body.

Nikka crashed into the wall with the weight of the man against her, but his body collapsed just after they collided. She fell with him as the breath rushed from her lungs and the stabbing pain plunged into her chest. The warmth of the angel soul in her grasp kept her conscious long enough to fall to the ground.

Everything fell silent, the body of the huge man lying in a pile beside her as she lay against the cold cement, her breathing rapid and short to avoid the pain that now coursed into her spine. The adrenaline of the last few seconds pulsed in her veins and left her shaking. Everything in her brain told her that she just needed to stop, to close her eyes and avoid the pain, but she forced her eyes to stay open as she looked toward the thing she still held in her hand where it rested against the broken cement.

The green hue of it cast like a neon glow stick against her skin as it writhed around her fingers, tendrils of green reaching out to examine her flesh. The warmth of it still lingered just under its undetectable weight, soothing the ache she felt in her joints.

Before she felt the heaviness of her eyelids, the ephemeral creature dissipated into the skin of her hand, leaving pulsating green light threading just under the flesh of her forearm. The warmth turned to white heat, and she clenched her teeth against the pain of the mark than now seared into the skin, just below the tattoo of Pestilence. The pain turned into agony, mixed with the fresh rib fractures, and her brain no longer wanted to feel any of it.

Her world plunged into the dark memories as she watched the last of the tattoo etch into her skin.

Chapter 28
Gideon

The fog of anger and hatred lifted from his chest, and Gideon could finally breathe. The darkness around him no longer hovered like a shroud. But as those few seconds of clarity trickled into his thoughts, he remembered what he had just done to Nikka.

Pazuzu had slipped from his bonds. The demon had let loose, if for only a few minutes, but the damage was done. Not again. Gideon stepped from the shadows and into the moonlight that shone on the empty street that now appeared like a black river disappearing into the horizon. His hands trembled as he clasped them behind his head and his eyes searched the dark landscape of the abandoned town.

"Nikka," he shouted into the night. She was the last thing he had seen before the gunshot rang out, and that was when she had run from him – from Amy.

What had happened to all of them? There had been no control, only fury, and selfish desire, and that was enough to let the chains of control fall from Pazuzu, and the demon took over. These last few months had only been a ruse. Everything he had thought about dominating his alternate half was false. Just one night and feelings of jealousy were enough to show him that he was wrong.

His gaze searched the dark horizon, between the houses and white fences. She had run from him, and now she waited in hiding somewhere nearby, but it might as well be a thousand miles away as far as he knew.

Something moved in the distance, through an open door of a large building at the end of the block.

It had to be her. She must have heard him.

His heart pounded against his ribs when he saw the movement, and he broke into a run, but the shape of the thing in the dark was not right. The quick pace he had first started now slowed as he watched the silhouette move into the moonlight.

Jadriel's face first met the light, and then Gideon saw her in his arms, a quiet body of dangling limbs. A lump formed in his throat, threatening to choke off his air when he saw her. Nikka's head lay back against the angel's arm, but she had not become limp. Her body, though unconscious, now twitched as Jadriel carried her. The angel rushed from the shadows toward Gideon.

He wanted to hurry to her, to collect her in his arms and hold her until she awoke and saw him again. But something was wrong, her face pale as her arms flexed close to her chest and her fingers clenched into tight fists.

Gideon's jaw fell slack as the angel met him and he dropped to his knees, letting her down to the warm ground.

"What happened?" Gideon said, his mouth dry as his hand touched her face. She would not open her eyes but only twitched under his touch.

"She found it," Jadriel said, gasping for breath. "War did this to us, and she stopped it."

Gideon leaned closer to her and touched his fingers to her clenched fists. "This is not right. This never happened with Pestilence."

The angel shook his head and caught his breath. "He almost killed her. I have tried to heal her, there were many broken bones. But I cannot seem to fix this."

Gideon grasped her hand and forced her left arm away from her body, but it was more difficult than he had expected. Her muscles fought against any movement. He extended her arm and the pale silver light cast onto the fresh mark on her forearm. But something was different. The tattoo appeared similar to the mark of Pestilence, but threads of black and green rippled out along the veins just under her skin like streaks of dark lightning. They trailed up her arm from both new tattoos, inching toward her shoulder as he watched.

The ground under his body felt empty, and he wanted to sink away with her. This mark had infected her with something unexpected, and he could not help her. He released her hand and her arm reflexed back against her chest as her body continued to spasm in his arms.

His hand moved to her face, and he felt the unusual heat that emanated from her skin.

"She is extremely warm," he said, his heart rate rising again.

Whatever was happening to her, he had to do something. He collected her in his arms and rushed toward the house where all of this had started. At least in there, he could find a place where she could lie comfortably until this broke. The angel stood and followed him to the threshold of the door.

Gideon plunged into the shadow of the house and moved up the stairs to the room he had shared with her, if only for a short time. He placed her shuddering body on the cool linens of the bed and touched his hand to her clenched fists.

Jadriel appeared at the door, his breath rushing in quick bursts. "What can I do?"

"Water, towels. Anything to cool her off," he said, not taking his eyes off of her.

"Okay." The angel disappeared into the dark, leaving him in silence as he watched her suffer.

There had only been a few times in his life when he had experienced tears, but his vision now flooded as he looked down at her. His fingers grasped hers and willed any strength that he had left into her body. So many times, he had prayed to a father that had abandoned him here in this world and never heard an answer, but that did not stop him from trying again for her. His silent prayers whispered out from under his breath in every language that he had ever learned. After all this, he could not lose her now.

"What have I done?" Amy's voice broke behind him.

He glanced back to where she stood in the doorway, moonlight falling on her red hair. She had tears in her own eyes as well, and she held her shaking hands to her mouth.

"I don't know what came over me," she cried. "And then I think I shot her."

Gideon shook his head. "You did not do this to her. This happened because she saved us yet again."

Amy stepped into the room and stood at the end of the bed, her green eyes looking at Nikka in dread. "I don't understand."

"The Angel of War," he said and looked back at Nikka's silent twitching head against the pillow. "It did those things to us, brought out the things that we try to keep to ourselves. She stopped it."

Jadriel appeared at the door, his arms full of water bottles and a collection of linens. "I found what I could in the car."

"It will have to do," Gideon said.

Amy helped them soak the towels in water and placed them on Nikka's head. The water was not going to be cold, but it was the best they could do at the moment. Gideon kneeled at the bedside and grasped Nikka's hand despite the continued spasms. Amy and Jadriel remained quiet, as though they expected her to awaken at any moment.

The seconds turned into minutes, and nothing changed even though he switched out the warm towels for cooler ones. Her eyes remained closed and unaware of his presence beside her.

Jadriel broke the silence. "We will leave you with her." He nodded to Amy, who still stood at the end of the bed with her hands to her mouth. "If you need anything more, just let us know."

Gideon glanced back at him, the rage no longer clouding his thoughts when he looked at the angel. "Of course."

The others exited the room and closed the door, leaving him alone with her. Without them to watch, he let the tears fall down his cheeks as he looked down at her. His fingers still clutched around her hand. He swallowed the dryness that had formed in his throat. This could not be the end of everything that they had done. Not like this. Not when the last thing she saw of him was Pazuzu.

"Please forgive me," he whispered as he looked at her silent face. "I know that there is so much that I beg of you to forgive."

Still, nothing, as though she was no longer in her body.

"I cannot – I will not —live in this world without you."

He wiped the back of his hand against his cheek and moved beside her in the bed, gathering her in his arms despite the stiff twitching of her muscles.

"Please come back to me," he whispered and touched his lips to her warm forehead.

At that moment her body relaxed, the endless spasm dissipating through every muscle. He held his breath and looked at her face, at her still eyelids, waiting for them to open. He held her close to his chest, her face resting against his shoulder, but she would not move. The only thing that fueled his hope was the shallow rise and fall of her chest with each breath she now took.

"Nikka? Wake up."

He shook his arm, hoping to stir her senses. Her head fell back against his upper arm, and her mouth gaped open. The motion made his heart race again, and he stilled as her eyelids slid open. An absent sigh escaped her lips, and he gazed at her face, a reflection of spectral green light emanating from her pupils as she gazed toward nothing. The center of his gut pulled as though he had fallen from the edge of a cliff when he looked down on her. That green glow, just like the Harbingers . . .

Then, her face pulled in with a wince of pain. Her eyes clenched closed, hiding the light that should never have been there in the first place. Her lips thinned against her teeth in a grimace for only a second before she went limp in his arms again.

Gideon pulled her close to him, holding her head against his chest. If she had been conscious, he was sure that she would hear his heart pounding through his ribs and feel the shaking in his arms. The longer he held her, the more her body temperature dropped until she began to feel normal again. No more convulsions. Now she only lay in his arms as though she were asleep, but he knew better. These new marks, the Horsemen sigils, were changing her. Pestilence might have been subtle, but War was different. And there were two more to go. If the others were even close to this, she would never make it.

He placed her down on the bed and lay beside her for the rest of the night if only to convince himself that he could protect her from what was to come.

The morning light shone through the shattered window with the warm air of the south Texas desert. Gideon took in a deep breath and opened his eyes. The ache in his muscles told him that he had not slept for long after he had settled in beside Nikka. When the light met his eyes, the coming dawn did little to ward off the fatigue that still settled around him. He sat up on his elbow, and his gaze drifted to the empty space beside him in the bed.

The first shudders of panic shot through his chest as he got to his feet and glanced around the room, but Nikka was gone. The depression in the mattress and linens was the only thing that bore evidence that she had been there. He stepped into the darkened hallway, but it remained as quiet as it had all night. The thrum of his heart raced into his veins, and he stepped to the window, the jagged fragments of glass still lingering in the frame of the window, a brief reminder of Jadriel throwing him through it last night.

In the pale twilight, he saw her standing on the dead brown lawn of the house, her form just a silhouette in the twilight. She stood rigid, facing toward the east as she gazed out to the mountain ridge in the distance. The tight fists he had held now loosened as he pushed away from the window and rushed downstairs to her.

She stood silent as she watched the coming dawn and never moved to acknowledge that she heard him approach. Her stance remained firm, feet planted solid and at shoulder-width, arms at her side. The only movement that surrounded her was the steady rhythm of her breathing. Gideon slowed as he neared her, and his eyes fell on her face.

Unblinking eyes stared toward the sunrise, her head slightly down-turned like a predator watching a herd. A lump formed in Gideon's throat as he watched her for a moment, unmoving and unnerving.

"Nikka," he said, the tremor evident in his voice, but she never moved or even looked at him.

He reached to touch her forearm, and she still stared forward. The spasms had stopped, hopefully for good, but something had changed.

"Nikka, are you all right?" he whispered to her.

"I can hear everything," she said, the words falling from her lips like an exhale. "I can feel the movement of the earth, the pull of the moon. Everything spinning in the universe."

It sounded the like the rantings of a mad person. His fingers moved to her hand, and he grasped onto her, but she still did not move.

"Come inside. You need to lie down. You were very sick last night."

She jerked her hand away from him, and she finally turned her eyes toward him, but he saw the glint of green light like a reflection in her pupils for only a second, those same predator eyes watching in the dark. Her gaze had grown wide, a mix of thrill and fear residing there.

"It's inside me," she said, her hand moving to her chest and her fingers clutched at her shirt. "It's waiting, growing. I know you understand this."

Of course, he understood it, and far too well. Trying to control his demon half felt the same way, like a caged creature that will spring forth and bite if given the opportunity.

"This sounds crazy," she said, "but it's like the werewolf movies. There's something hiding in me, and when the full moon comes out, the creature will be free. Not literally the moon, but you know what I mean."

He squeezed her hand again, and this time her fingers wrapped around his. That was when Nikka's rigid body loosened. He pulled her toward him and wrapped his arms around her. She molded against his chest and rested her head on his shoulder. With each breath she took, he sensed the subtle quaking in her body as though the tremors from last night had never really subsided. Her hair brushed against his chin, and for the first time in months, the lavender fragrance that followed her had diminished.

Gideon did not know what to tell her; all of this was new territory for him. He had never faced the Harbingers before. There were only stories passed among the angels and the demons like cautionary tales. Nothing he told her could bring either of them peace.

"Whatever is inside me wants to explode," she whispered. "What if I don't make it?"

"Do not speak of such things," he said and pressed her closer to him.

"If I die, you have to find Adam. You have to save him."

His heart sank at the way she sounded right now, so fragile and human. The morning light did little to warm him. What scared him the most was that she might be right.

CHAPTER 29

NIKKA

He last memory of that day was at sunrise as Gideon embraced her. Nikka remembered following him to the house, but that was it until she awoke in the back seat of the Jeep, her head resting on Gideon's lap with his hand on her back. The sky had grown dark again, and if it weren't for the bumps in the road, she probably would have slept even longer.

She sat up, her eyes flashing to Gideon who now looked at her with that worried gaze and the furrow between his brows.

"Where are we?" she muttered as she rubbed her eyes and turned her gaze out the window.

"New Mexico," Amy said and looked back at her.

Everyone had that same concerned stare at her. She could even feel it in Jadriel's glance at her through the rear-view mirror.

"Are you okay?" Gideon said, his voice low and meant only for her.

Other than the stiff neck and the sore spots on her arm and back, she felt fine. "Yeah," she said with a nod.

"What happened? Did I sleep all day?"

"Yes," Gideon said, his hand still on her back. The heat of his skin made her uncomfortable, and she pulled away. He turned his eyes away from her, but the concern still hung around him.

"We should stop soon," Gideon said, his voice carrying to the front seat.

The dark of the night pressed in around them while the vehicle eased into the parking lot of an empty gas station. The minimal starlight barely illuminated the peeling white paint of an automotive shop behind the small convenience store. The moon had long since fallen behind the mountain range, leaving the desert in inky blackness.

Everyone stepped out of the Jeep, and Nikka's back felt stiff and achy as she slid across the seat and arched her neck back to work out the kinks. Her lungs filled with the warm, dry air as the distant sound of a coyote bellowing in the night caught her ear. The sounds around her had dampened since she first awoke with her spirit buzzing like a live wire. At first, things were sharp and too loud, but now she could tolerate the sounds of the bats flitting around the cactus or the scurry of an insect across the sand. The aches still throbbed in her bones every time she moved, although that had improved as well.

"How are you feeling?" Jadriel's voice spoke from behind her.

Nikka turned to see him in the dark. Amy and Gideon had wandered away from the vehicle.

"Good, I think," she said and stretched her neck again.

"I must tell you something," he said, his voice dropping low enough so the others could not hear. "Things are beginning to change."

Her brow furrowed. "What do you mean?"

"After you defeated War, the angel infiltrated your body."

She glanced down at her hands, which now appeared so pale in the starlight. "I know. I can feel it riding along my nerves, in my brain, looking through my eyes. But not possessing me."

"It is affecting you in other ways. There was a lot of damage to your body after your battle with War. Your back was broken in four places, your left arm in two."

The news hit her in the gut like a stone. She raised her arm to the faint light, turning her hand back and forth as she examined her forearm. Maybe that's why it hurt so much tonight. It appeared to be fine, but something deep inside was all wrong.

"I healed you to the best of my ability, but it is merely like duct tape and super glue," he continued. "I'm afraid it is only a temporary measure."

"What do you mean temporary?"

"Whatever power is now circulating inside you is blocking what I can do. It could shatter if strained hard enough."

The nagging ache in her back now made more sense. She clenched her fingers into a fist and felt the sharp pain begin midway down her arm, right beneath the bruise that had begun to fade just under the skin. Somewhere under there a thin fracture still lingered across the bone, bridged by only filaments of tissue placed there by an angel.

"So, what do we do about this?" she said, lifting her gaze to see him through the darkness.

"I am not sure that there is anything that can be done," he said. "This is something I have never seen before."

"Well," she said and cleared her throat. "Then we'll just play it by ear."

Jadriel nodded as he turned away from her. "Very well, but you must be careful." He walked toward the empty gas station, its windows barren and staring blankly into the night.

As the angel walked away, his feet crunching against the gravel in a sound that grated in her ears, the empty space that he had just left grew darker with each second. Perhaps it was the revelation of what he had told her, but she could feel the pain up and down her spine now throbbing as she stood still in the night. The whirr of crickets buzzed against her skin enough to make her uncomfortable, and this spurred her to follow the others into the dark of the building.

At first, she thought it was a dream, the rough jostling of the fight with War still fresh just under her skin. But the voice grew louder and more familiar. Jadriel. His hands touched her shoulders and shook her until she opened her eyes and peered at his face in the dark.

"Get up," he said, an edge of panic lacing his voice. "They're coming."

Her head still swam with the last vestiges of a dream and her heart raced, but she rolled to her side and pushed herself up to her feet.

"What's going on?" Amy said, her voice cracking. She sat up in the dark across the room.

"They are almost here," Jadriel said again and grasped Nikka's wrist, trying to tug at her to follow him.

Gideon paced to the dirty windows that looked out across the barren parking lot. The faint starlight danced in his eyes as he searched the darkness around the abandoned gas station.

"We don't have much time." The angel pulled on her arm again, and she let him lead her toward the door. Amy and Gideon followed as they emerged into the night of the desert, where the air still held onto the heat that radiated off the sand.

As soon as he released her arm, Jadriel moved around the Jeep and Nikka grabbed the passenger side door.

A burst of violet light came from the darkness, and Nikka never saw it coming. It struck her in the chest, sending her careening across the gravel parking lot. The swirl of light and dark made her dizzy and then her body struck the ground, skidding over the layer of rocks and dirt. She felt every pebble that scratched her skin as she landed on her back and slid to a stop.

The light vanished as quick as it had arrived, leaving her out of breath as she rolled to her side. Pain exploded in her back as she moved. She remembered Jadriel's warning that she was held together by only the weakest of elements. Every fracture in her back threatened to shift and split as she moved. She pressed her hand against the ground and steadied the dizziness that had started in her head. The horizon straightened, and she gazed across the lot. In the faint light, the silhouettes of dozens of people walked along the edge of the road, pacing toward her and the Jeep where her friends now stood shouting at her. The hushed tones of their voices met her ringing ears.

Sparkles still interrupted the edges of her vision, the last vestiges of the violet energy that had struck her. The purple and white light dissipated, but she knew what it meant. Angels. She and her companions were too late.

Nikka pushed herself up to her feet despite the pain of the thinly healed fractures that argued with her. Gideon rushed toward her, his voice still a muffled noise in her ears. As he reached his hand out to her, another burst of light exploded around her. The blinding light and the impact of it made her arms move up to cover her head in a reflexive maneuver, but it also knocked Gideon off his feet and sent him crashing into an abandoned truck across the lot.

Her vision cleared from the flash of light as she brought her arms down. Her gaze fell on the group of angels that approached her, their eyes now illuminated in pin-points of violet light. The silhouette of a man neared her, walking ahead of the others, his eyes dark and his face cast in shadows.

The tremblings of her racing heart shuddered in her chest, but she willed her body to work. She reached behind her shoulder and withdrew her sword. The violet fire flared along the edge of the blade, casting a neon purple light across her body and toward the man that now approached her.

As soon as the firelight fell on his face, she almost choked, and the sword quaked in her hand.

The tousled blonde hair that framed his face and covered his neck was unmistakable, although he looked healthier than the last time she had seen him. But their previous encounter, as cruel and awful as it had been, Jason had been in the company of demons. Now he walked toward her surrounded by angels. The purple light illuminated against the black parallel lines now tattooed along the front and sides of his neck, plunging below the neckline of his dark T-shirt.

"Jason?" she said, her voice shaking more than she had expected. She knew it was him; at least it looked like him.

The other angels stopped as he continued to approach her, his shoulders broad and his gaze fixed on her. Then he halted as he came to the edge of her circle of firelight.

"Nikka," he said, his voice steady but cold. He watched her without faltering.

So many questions swam through her brain as she looked at him and then to the angels in the dark. In her periphery, she knew that Gideon, Jadriel, and Amy approached her with caution, keeping their distance from the angels that now faced them.

"What happened to you?" Nikka said to him.

That was the first time his gaze shifted away from her, and he looked down to the ground. "I was their prisoner, in Lucifer's lair. Tortured and forced to do their bidding. They have the ability to control us, make us do anything they want."

"They made you take my baby?" she said, trying to force back the lump that had formed in her throat. "Where is he? Where's Adam?"

"Lucifer has him."

The sword shook in her hand, and she felt her grip loosening on the hilt. She wanted to cry, to scream at him, but there was some other purpose to this group now. They had come for her, and everything about this cadre of angels told her there was something sinister in their intentions.

Her fingers tightened on the sword again, and she raised the tip toward him. "You handed him over to Lucifer?"

Jason's gaze rose toward her again. "I had no choice."

Nikka's teeth clenched as she fought against the anger that welled in her chest. "Then help me get him back."

"I can't do that. There's no way that it can be done."

"Yes, there is. I found a way."

"I know you believe that," he said, tilting his head as his gaze fell on the fresh tattoos on her forearms. "And that's why I'm here."

"Nikka," Jadriel's voice broke between them, but she didn't shift her eyes away from Jason. "Don't trust him."

The angel's warning pierced into her heart. He didn't have to say it, she already suspected. Jason didn't just happen upon them, not with a group of angels that Jadriel had tried to warn them about.

"He's an executioner," Jadriel said, his voice low and right behind her. "The killer of archangels."

Just as he said it, the dark of Jason's pupils flashed into fine points of violet light. It was true. He was no longer a seraph, and she should have suspected it when she realized that his tattoos were different. The violet light meant he was now powered by angels, just like her.

"I've come to make you stop this mission you're on," Jason said. "You must contain the Harbingers before it's too late."

The surge of anger welled in her throat now. "You don't understand."

"No, you don't." He stepped toward her again, and she raised the sword, strengthening her arm as she took a step beck. "Think about it. Whose idea was it, to raise the Horsemen. A rogue angel and a demon? Am I right?"

The niggle of worry worked its way into her brain, but she held her stance. He was trying to confuse her, to cast doubt. That's why he came for her now.

"Stop," she said as he stepped toward her again.

"This quest will only end in the death of the world," he said. "And I can't allow that. Nikka, you know I love you, but I have to stop you."

The glow in his eyes intensified. Whatever the angels had told him, he now believed them, and he had the full power of an army of archangels to back it. The air between them zapped and buzzed with the energy that flowed around them, and she knew that the talking was over. He now pulled the power of the earth into himself, and if she was going to survive this, she had to do the same. And do it quickly.

CHAPTER 30

NIKKA

The power flowed into Nikka's free arm, but as she collected it into her hand, she saw the violet light flowing into his hand as well. He pitched back as the light intensified. Nikka willed the energy faster, and she lurched forward, sending the energy toward him just as he did the same. The violet light crashed together in a chaotic meld of electrical energy and vortices that disrupted the air around them. The impact of it nearly knocked her off her feet, but she steadied her stance and faced him.

Then he turned, something she hadn't expected, and swung his sword across his body. The edge of the blade caught the full force of her energy, but it acted like a mirror, and it rebounded toward her. She dropped to the ground just as the light collided past her and exploded into the pile of scrap metal behind her.

A flash of violet light moved through the dark, and she rolled to the side as the broad sword crashed down onto the gravel where she had just been lying. She scrambled to her feet and swung her katana toward his midsection, but he met her with the edge of his sword.

His reflexes now matched hers, blow for blow. But she held back. This was Jason, and she really didn't want to hurt him. She only hoped he felt the same.

She couldn't see his face in the dark except the few glimpses that the firelight allowed as she defended another swing of his sword. Then, something she didn't expect.

His foot moved through the dark, just under the edge of her sword, and his boot landed in her midsection. The impact of his sent her falling back and sprawling across the gravel again, the air in her lungs gone. She fell back, her head striking the ground. The spasm in her abdomen sent her ribs into a powerful cough that made her almost throw up. Her fingers still felt the heat of the sword in her palm, though, as she forced out another choking cough.

Jason's boots crunched on the gravel as he neared her. "Stop this. I don't want to kill you."

"You can't kill me," she said, her throat tightening before she coughed again. "I won't let you."

The violet light of his sword moved through the dark again, but she countered with a pull of energy from under her body. With so much of her torso pressed against the earth, she willed it faster into her hand, sending out a pulse of energy into Jason's dark figure that loomed over her. The force of it threw him from his feet and colliding back into the side of the Jeep.

As she moved to her feet, the painful spots along her spine screaming at her again. A gust of cool air drifted over the desert and skimmed over her face, the chill so profound that it caught her attention. In all the scuffle with Jason, she hadn't seen them coming in the dark, and neither had the angels. Something evil lurked at the very edge of their battle ground, and it had snuck up on them in the middle of this terrible fight.

She turned her gaze away from where Jason had crashed and now moved to his feet. The shadows behind the gas station moved, shifting and warping into bodies that sprang from the dark. Jadriel and Gideon followed her gaze just in time to see inky black turn into a swarm of bodies that emerged from the dark, eyes a collection of black, red and orange. Demons of all kind now descended into the fray, surrounding them.

Nikka scrambled to her feet as she felt Gideon's hands on her. He helped her up and held her close to his body as the swarm of violent beings came toward them, rushing at the angels. As Gideon pulled her away, shielding her with his body, she peered over her shoulder toward Jason. He moved to his feet, watching her as the demons descended toward him. His sword sliced through the air, catching three of them before he backed toward the army of angels that all had swords drawn.

Nikka turned away from him and watched Jadriel pull Amy into the protection of the gas station. The fray of demon bodies crashed toward them from all sides, screeching and screaming with horrific wails that only demons could create. A cold claw wrapped around her wrist, yanking her from Gideon's grasp.

In the dark, she watched Gideon's face fall away from her but not before his eyes erupted into points of red coal. His arm reached back just as a cord of fire drew from his palm and snaked out into a long thread of a whip. The lash curled like a cobra around his body and over his head before it cracked down on the creature that had her in its cold grasp. The demon screamed—a sound that pierced her ears, as it fell away with the fire lash.

Another creature reached toward her as Gideon reeled back for another attack, but she gripped her sword with both hands, and the katana swung with angel fire through the demon's torso, leaving it a wisp of black smoke as she took a step back. Another fray of drones, some inhabiting bodies and others as black spirits, fell between her and Gideon. She pulled her sword up for another attack when she felt the instant pierce of pain in her back just below her right shoulder blade.

The bite of it sent shockwaves through her body, tightening all her muscles into a rigid spasm. Nothing would respond to her bidding but only remained as an unyielding mass of muscle and bone. She couldn't even breathe in the seconds that the wracking pain took over her body. At the moment the bite stopped, her muscles went slack, and she collapsed, but not before an arm caught her and wrapped about her torso. It pulled her in toward another cold body and then her vision distorted in a whorl of color and darkness.

The spasms had stopped, at least for now, and she could finally breathe. The dizzying swirl of light and dark had now just become shadows, with the earliest signs of morning beginning to break somewhere in the east. She blinked her eyes again where she lay and noticed the fading light of the stars overhead as the dark began to recede to the dawn.

That was when she knew she was lying on rocky sand surrounded by low Joshua trees. The crunch of sand under a boot caught her attention, and she tried to sit up, but every muscle and joint hurt and she collapsed back down on the sand.

"Don't try to fight it." The voice spoke nearby in the dark, but the sound was familiar and made her stomach turn. "Getting Tazed is a bitch."

She forced herself up onto her elbows as her eyes adjusted to the faint light. The sand shifted under her, and her eye caught the glint of her sword lying next to her, silent without the fire of her touch. A dark form moved just beyond her peripheral vision. When she saw him, she understood why she felt sick. Just as she had suspected: the familiar black and red hair formed into the faintest hint of a Mohawk, open leather jacket and the crooked smile on his evil lips.

"Belphagor," she muttered and finally moved to sit upright.

He moved toward her and crouched over her legs, his pupils glowing with red-orange light. His fingers grasped at her jaw and forced her to look at him. "Are you completely awake now, because we gotta get going."

"Go where?" she said and pulled her face from his grasp.

"Back to my master," he said with a smile. "Had to get you away from those angels, so I transported us here, far away from all those awful creatures. I didn't know where you were until they showed up. All that power in one place tends to light the map up if you know what I mean."

"I'm not going anywhere with you."

"Oh really?" he said, the wicked smile spreading over his lips again. His eyes, lined in black, peered at her. "I can take you to Adam."

Her heart sank into her stomach as he said the name.

"You can be reunited with your child, never to be separated again."

The trembling began in her fingers, matching the quivering that now settled in her chest. Waves of nausea spilled over her as she fought against the desire to find her baby.

She turned her gaze toward him again. "And what's the catch?"

"Catch?" he said, his brows rising as he leaned back on one knee. "No catch. You can be with him, protected from the angels that want you both dead."

His voice took on an air of smooth silk as he spoke, losing the cocky rock star attitude that he usually carried.

"We can keep you both safe," he said, his finger tracing along her jawline as though she were his lover. "Forever. The world will be yours, just as it was meant to be."

As much as she tried to avoid it, the tears welled in her eyes as he spoke. She knew there was always a catch, especially when it came to Belphagor. "You mean forever with Lucifer."

"He is the father of light," the demon said. "And he can be your protector. He only wants the best for you and Adam."

The fury rose in her chest, and she shoved him away from her as she rose to her feet. Belphagor scrambled back through the sand, but his red eyes still fixed on her through the dark. "I will never join you, and I will get my baby back."

The demon rushed at her and grasped her wrist. She tried to pull away from him, and she saw his brow furrow as he pulled her closer, peering into her eyes. His eyes went dark and bored into her soul.

"Something is different," he said and sniffed the air around her. "You've changed."

You can't let him know what you've done. He can't know about the Harbingers, she thought.

His eyebrow cocked with suspicious concern, the wheels of thought spinning out of control in his brain. He was right to be worried: she had ungodly powers coursing through her veins. She had no idea that anyone else could discern it, but it didn't surprise her. The power of it constantly thrummed just under her skin. A creature sensitive enough would have to pick up on it sometime.

Belphagor's free hand moved to his back pocket, and he produced a taser, the thing sparking between the prongs as he pressed the button and swung it at her. Before he could make contact with her skin, she pulled in energy through her feet where she stood and powered it into her hand before she released it with a quick shot toward his chest. The light raced through his body and sent him sprawling into the sand before he knew what had happened. His hand released its grip on her wrist, and she lunged for her sword. The moment her hand met the hilt, it burst into violet fire. She quickly sheathed it and turned, running into the dark of the desert.

Her feet slipped in the soft sand, and she stumbled as she dashed into the dark. Somewhere behind her, the cold breeze drifted off of Belphagor's body as he stood and shouted her name into the coming morning. The brush grew thick around her as she plunged through the desert, the thorns scratching at her arms and clothes. The ground below her tilted into a slope and her ankle rolled. She collapsed into the slope of rock and salt brush, slipping down in a cascade of broken shale and twigs. The slope increased, and she couldn't stop her fall, her body rolling over the rocks. Every impact pounded against the fragile breaks in her spine and arm, sending lightning bolts of pain throughout her body.

Everything became a kaleidoscope of dark and light as the ground gave way below her and there was nothing but air. The seconds that passed filled her mind with the terrors of what lay below: sharp boulders, deep crevasses, and gardens of cacti that would all leave her broken and dying. And Jadriel, Gideon or Amy would never know what had become of her.

When her feet first plunged into the water, her brain couldn't interpret what she felt. Then the remainder of her body fell into the rushing river, swirling over her head and pulling her deeper into the undercurrents that rolled and tumbled over her. The water pushed her forward, and her head emerged above the rapids for a millisecond before it yanked her down. But she pulled in a short breath before she plunged into the dark rapids again. Her arms flailed, trying to paddle toward the surface, but each stroke sent pain into her forearm and back.

The water shifted and rolled, drawing her to the surface, and she gasped for another breath, ready for the next current to pull her under again. But this time it only shoved her further downstream with a softer flow that finally eased into the rest of the river.

She rested her head back and let the current take her where it wanted. There was no use fighting it anymore, and she had no more energy left to struggle. Then her eyes grew heavy, and she swallowed, the throbbing pain growing along her spine.

CHAPTER 31

NIKKA

C old, rushing water had numbed Nikka's feet and hands, surrounding every cell of her body and seeping under her clothes. When warm arms wrapped around her and pulled her from the water, she opened her eyes for a moment, but she could only see dark shapes with a background of light from the morning sun. Voices—women's voices—echoed in her water-soaked ears.

"I think she's still alive."

"Help me get her out," one woman shouted to someone further up the bank.

Several hands drew her out of the cold water and then the morning went dark again, the pain disappearing for a brief respite.

What seemed like only seconds later, she felt a stab of pain move from the center of her back and into her chest as she sucked in a quick breath. Her eyelids flew open and then she shut them just as fast as the bright, harsh light entered her pupils. First, there had been the cold water, but now her body no longer shivered. As she blinked her eyes several times until they adjusted to the light, she moved her legs against the warm blankets that lay over her.

She glanced up to see white canvas walls around and above her, the walls of a large four-post tent whose fabric undulated in a gentle morning breeze. White light filtered through the canvas and onto the army-green fabric flooring stretched out over the length of the entire tent. Nikka lifted herself up to her elbows, a motion that made her bones creak and create more pain down her spine, but it let her see the pile of blankets that covered her body where she lay on a raised cot. She also realized that she had no clothing on under those blankets.

The flap of the front entrance pulled back, and a woman filled the space, her long white and gray hair braided down her back. Her brown eyes looked at her with surprise for a moment, and a gentle smile creased the corners of her mouth. She halted as she saw Nikka upright and looking at her.

"I'm sorry dear," she said. "I thought you were still asleep. I didn't mean to surprise you."

"It's okay," Nikka said, but her voice croaked, still graveled with sleep.

The woman entered the tent, her arms carrying the clean and folded stack of Nikka's clothes that she had been wearing. She approached the cot and kneeled beside her, placing the laundry on the ground.

"These are finally dry," she said. "And so are you, by the looks of it."

Nikka sat up despite the shot of pain in her forearm that she used to push herself up. She held the blankets close to her chest, trying not to expose too much to the woman, although she was now sure that the woman had already seen enough. Strands of her blonde hair fell around her face, tangled but dry.

"I guess so," she said, running her fingers through her hair.

"Are you feeling okay?" the woman said. As she leaned in, her head tilted to the side, she reminded Nikka of her grandmother.

"Not sure. But I think I'll live."

The woman reached a hand out to her. "Well, I'm Helen."

"Nikka." She shook her hand.

"Nikka," she said, nodding as though it was her own way of remembering things. "You were in pretty bad shape when I found you. You looked like a drowned kitten. Wasn't sure you were still alive. Are you out here all by yourself, sweetie?"

Nikka swung her legs over the edge of the cot, her bare feet resting on the green fabric floor and let the dizziness in her head subside. As she listened to the woman and her questions, she knew that the sweet old lady routine was probably an act. Helen was pumping her for information. In this new world, it was hard to trust anybody, and Helen was not alone out here. She heard more than one person as they pulled her from the water. They were good enough to rescue and dry her, but they were just as leery as she was.

"Yeah," Nikka said, and she would have to keep her own secrets until she knew more about this place. "It was too dark, and I got lost. I'm trying to find my way back to Phoenix."

Helen sat back on her heels, the smile still on her face. Her hand patted the stack of clothes at her side. "Well, I'll let you get dressed and come on out when you're ready, okay?"

Nikka nodded as Helen stood and walked out of the tent, letting the front flap close behind her.

The effort to get to her feet and put her clothes on was much more than she had expected. The water – or the taser that Belphagor had used on her – had weakened her more than she had originally thought. Even her pants seemed to hang on her hips as though she had lost weight in the hours that she lay here. After she pulled her shirt over her head, she glanced at her hand in the filtered light of the tent. Her skin had shrunk over the back of her hand, revealing the thin tendons just below the surface. Pale and sallow. A shudder ran along her spine as the memory of the effects of her chemotherapy flooded her thoughts. Losing her hair. Skin tight on her bones. All things that had been memories that she wanted to forget.

Maybe it wasn't the effects of the taser, or almost drowning in the river. What if it was the Harbinger's power that flowed in her veins? Perhaps it was draining her life, little bits at a time. Drop by drop in a never-ending bucket.

She clenched her fist and brought her thoughts back to the present. Just have to keep going, gotta get back to Amy and Gideon and Jadriel. She slid her feet into her boots and took a few steps forward, the pain of it making her limp with cautious steps. Helen stood just outside the tent when she emerged into the bright daylight. Beyond the threshold of her shelter, a large camp of people had settled around her. Numerous other tents and lean-tos dotted the desert landscape. Heads turned toward her: men, women and many children scattered throughout the camp.

Nikka walked beside Helen, although the limping made it difficult to keep up. The older women slowed her steps and shot a glance at her.

"Are you sure you're okay?" Helen asked.

"I'll be fine. Just a little bruised up, that's all." Nikka's gaze darted to the faces of those that looked at her. So many people here, in the middle of Nowhere, New Mexico. They had each other to lean upon. Mothers. Fathers. Friends and family. Such support that Nikka hadn't seen since they were in Mexico. But something nagged at her, tickling the back of her thoughts. As much as these people seemed to have, they all shared one thing. Each of them held a pallor, a blankness about them.

And she realized where she had seen that before. That same look in their glassy, sunken eyes, thin cheeks, and chapped lips. It was in every documentary she had seen from the starving nations of Africa. Some were worse than others, but now that she recognized it, she even saw it in Helen's face and her frail hands.

"I believe we have some pain reliever in the medical tent," Helen said as she led the way. Nikka quickened her step, seeing that she had fallen behind while the camp had distracted her.

They wound through a series of tents, some with people lying in their cots and watching her walk by. Nikka tried not to stare, but that was harder than she had thought. She lifted her eyes to the path before her as they approached a group of large tents, some as big as the one she had awakened in. Each tent was interconnected by side doors and canvas. She followed Helen into the center structure and halted as she gazed over the contents of the shelter.

Boxes and boxes of canned food, bottled water, and other non-perishable food filled the tents. Helen breezed past these things and to a table erected at the far end. Cabinets of medical supplies stood on the table, and Helen searched through bottles until she found one with the pills that she wanted.

Nikka stepped around the boxes of food and water, some wrapped in plastic and others torn open with some of the goods missing. So much food, enough to feed the entire camp for a year.

Helen cleared her throat and drew Nikka's attention. She glanced at the old woman, who held out her palm with two white pills in it. "Ibuprofen okay for you? It will help with the pain."

Nikka accepted the medication and glanced up at Helen. Her eyes betrayed no malicious intent, just fatigue and what appeared to be kindness.

"Can I ask you something?" Nikka said, wary.

"Of course."

"What's wrong with everybody here?"

The smile slipped from Helen's face, but the creases remained around her mouth and eyes. "They're starving."

Nikka shook her head. Impossible. "No way. There's so much food here." The thought then occurred to her that someone was hoarding the food, but there was nobody guarding the place, and the people didn't seem to be clambering to get to the food supply.

"Yes, there is. We were prepared when calamity hit." Helen turned her eyes down to the ground. "But then about a week ago, something changed. Everything we had spoiled. The water became poisoned. We have no idea how it happened. One day there was just no more usable food and water."

Nothing for them to eat. The people were starving despite having so much in front of them.

Nikka's eyes moved over the stacks of pre-packaged food and found a crate of bottled water, wrapped in neat transparent layers of cellophane. She tore at the packaging and fished out a bottle, the lid still sealed from the time before the electricity disappeared. The cap twisted with a snap of the safety tab and she sniffed at the bottle. Nothing. No odor, no color. Sealed for her protection. She lifted the bottle to her lips, but Helen interrupted her.

"I wouldn't do that," she said, her voice shaking.

She eyed the woman with the bottle still at her lips, and the pills clutched in her hand. Despite the warning, Nikka had to check it out herself and confirm if her subtle suspicions were true. The moment she saw these people, a single thought bore into her brain, and she couldn't let it go.

The bottle tipped back, and the water slipped into her mouth, fresh and clear. Tasteless, just as water should be. She swallowed, taking in the liquid against her dry mouth. As she took in another gulp, she let the bottle slip away from her lips, and she waited. The bitter snap of a poison didn't bite back, as she had expected. Nikka glanced at Helen, her previous concern starting to fade and now she began to wonder if the powers-that-be here were only trying to withhold the rations from everyone else.

Then the sudden sting hit her stomach and rushed into her chest. Her fingers tightened around the bottle, crushing it in her grip before it slipped to the ground. She hunched over as the wretch came, violent and quick, water and bile rushing out of her mouth. Her stomach twisted and cramped with one gag after another, her body rejecting everything about the water.

Helen's hand touched her back as she hunched over, her hands on her knees. The warmth of her hand against the sore spots on her spine comforted her, but only a little as the last of the water exited her system.

"I told you," she said. "The water is poisoned. Everything here is damaged."

"I know, but I had to see for myself," Nikka said and wiped the back of her hand against her lips. And now her suspicions were confirmed. This was no coincidence that she had found this place, or rather that this place had found her. "Is there anyone else new here in the camp, I mean besides me?"

"New?" Helen shook her head. "No. Everyone here has been with us from the start."

"Is there anybody who is not affected by the food?"

"No. All of us have gotten sick, I'm sure of it."

"But you don't know?"

"Well," Helen said as she stepped back, wringing her hands. "There are so many people here, it's hard to keep track of everyone."

Nikka stood straighter, every vertebra falling in line along her back and creaking with the effort. She stepped from the tent and scanned the town in front of her, at every face that turned her way and appeared interested in the new member of the camp. Eyes that looked her way were now curious suspects.

She popped the two pills into her mouth and swallowed against her dry tongue. Those were going to come in handy in a short while because someone out there was not who they seemed. There was a Horseman mingled in with these people, and she was pretty sure that it was Famine. Better start dealing with the pain now.

CHAPTER 32
NIKKA

ikka's eyes scanned each face that looked at her, even those peeking through the open flaps of the tents. Helen kept pace with her as she limped along, meeting every eye that watched her.

"What are you looking for?" Helen said, her eyes following Nikka's gaze.

"For the one who caused this."

"You know why this is happening?"

"Yes," Nikka said and continued down a worn path between tents. People moved out of her way, and she watched each of them as they wandered away from her. She knew who was responsible for this, but she wasn't sure how she would identify the angel when she saw it. Famine could be hiding behind any of these gaunt faces.

She met the eyes of a child as the young girl walked across her path, her thin hand in a woman's grip. The girl's gaze lingered far longer than Nikka would have expected, but then she turned away as her mother tugged on her. The woman's eyes also fell on Nikka, but they held more fear than malice. But how would Famine appear?

A cough resounded through the camp from behind the canvas walls of another tent. People walking everywhere, between the shelters, down the paths. Easily over a hundred members of this camp, and those were the ones still in the tent city. There could be even more that have ventured out for the day. She stopped in the path, turning in all directions as she scanned the expanse of the encampment.

But, of course, sometimes the angels want to be found.

She stopped turning as her gaze fell on a woman who stood at the end of the long path, several tents down. People milled back and forth across the bath between them, but the woman fixed her stare on Nikka. She stood a half foot taller and a good fifty pounds lighter than most of the women here. If she had been anywhere else at some other time than this, Nikka would have mistaken her for a runway model, the kind everyone whispers about because she probably has an eating disorder or something. Gaunt and lanky but hauntingly pretty at the same time. Platinum blonde hair fell from her head in thin strands to her waist. Pale blue eyes watched Nikka without blinking, her orbs rimmed with the protruding edges of her eye-sockets. The woman's skin was so white that it must have never seen sunlight before today.

Helen stopped short behind Nikka and glanced down the path. "What is it? Do you see something?"

Nikka didn't turn her gaze away from the ghostly woman ahead of her. "I think so."

"What? Her?" Helen said. "That's Abby. She's Frank Corman's daughter."

As Nikka watched her, Abby shifted to the right, but her gaze never faltered. Just as she disappeared behind a tent, Nikka was sure she saw a brief flash of green light in the woman's pupils.

"That might be true," Nikka said and stepped to the right as well, hurrying down to the next row of tents to catch sight of Abby as she emerged at the end of the path. And she was there, as though she played a game of catch-me-if-you-can. "But Abby is not who she seems to be."

"What are you talking about? You think she poisoned the food and water? That's ridiculous."

"Helen," Nikka said with a controlled sigh, keeping her eye on Abby as the girl shifted behind the next row of tents. "I need you to clear out these people as quickly and quietly as you can."

"I can't do that—"

"Just listen to me," Nikka said and glanced at the old woman. "Something really bad is about to happen."

The woman swallowed as Nikka stared her down and grasped her hand. "Please don't hurt her. She's a good girl."

"I'm sure she is; that's why I need to help her," Nikka said and turned her gaze back down the path, but the girl was gone. She stepped quickly down to the next row and the next, but Abby had hidden somewhere while she had her attention on Helen. Nikka turned to the old woman once more. "Go, now."

Helen clutched her hands together and hurried away as Nikka ducked around the edge of the next row. In the tents behind her, she heard the hushed murmurs of people as Helen's voice whispered to them. She could only hope that she got enough people clear before the fight with Famine became too severe. Nikka stalked along the edge of the shelters, heading northward to where she last saw the girl. People's frantic eyes turned to her and back to Helen, who now motioned for anyone listening to follow her to the edge of the camp.

Before long, the north side of the tent city was quiet and empty. Nikka stepped with caution over the gravel and came around the furthest edge of the encampment, but there wasn't anybody left around here. She peered into the open flap of the tent, but it was also deserted. She straightened her stiff spine and walked back to the next row, gazing down the empty aisle.

"I know you're here," she spoke to the gentle breeze that drifted against the canvas walls.

Her boots crunched over the gravel as she moved down the next row, peering into each tent as she went. She pulled open the next flap, but the last tent in the row was as empty as the next. Nikka bit her lip in frustration. She was sure of what she had seen. Abby had the green eyes; she had been right there in front of her, and somehow the girl had just disappeared.

She stood straighter as she stepped away from the tent door. As swift as the wind, a flash of green light almost blinded her. Abby stood mere inches from her, how she got there without Nikka seeing her, she would never know.

"I hoped you would find me," she said, her hands now moving with such speed that Nikka didn't see them until it was too late. Her palms were at Nikka's temples, and the green light flashed again.

Nikka couldn't move, she couldn't think or breathe. The light infused into her eyesight, blinding everything around her. Her muscles locked as quickly as they had when the demon tazed her. Then the light was gone as fast as it had arrived, but her knees gave out. Nikka collapsed to the sand and gravel ground with the last embers of green still flashing in her eyes. Abby stood beside her and crouched down to meet her eyes, but Nikka couldn't move.

Something inside her gut swirled and pulsed, and with each beat it drained her power, sucking it deeper and deeper. Her hand moved out to try and push herself upright, but as she watched it, the skin sank around her tendons as the thing inside her leeched her body away from her. Within seconds, her hands looked the way they had when she was in her last hours in the hospital before Gideon had come. The hands of a girl dying of cancer.

Her fingers trembled as they moved to her face, feeling the tissue under her cheeks slink away. They moved to her head, and large wads of her hair fell to the ground. Hollow pits formed in her chest where her lungs should be and she gasped for air. All of this was too familiar.

"What have you done to me?" Nikka rasped with a weak breath.

Famine placed a thin, boney finger along Nikka's cheek and up through her scalp, tearing more of her long hair away with it. "I am Famine. I bring starvation in all its forms."

Nikka watched her, helpless and trembling while she kneeled on her fragile knees. It was as though the angel had known everything about her former state: the girl who once lay dying of leukemia. Everything was exact, down to the way it hurt to take a breath. Yes, she had been starving at that time, every small calorie taken by the cancer that had ravaged her body.

"I know who you are, archangel," Famine said, her voice so feminine and small. "But this is one battle you will not win."

Nikka turned her gaze away from the Harbinger, feeling more of her strength ebbing away. Her bones creaked, and her thinning muscles trembled at every effort to hold herself upright. This is how she thought she would die, starting at the small age of seventeen when she was first diagnosed. With just a touch, this small woman had brought it all back.

There had to be a way to fight this because if she failed then her baby would be lost forever. Her eyes focused on the pebbles below her hands, to every grain of sand between her fingers. This was just another display of power by an angel who didn't want to lose. Just like the others. Walking corpses or a really pissed off ex-con angel. They were no different than this waif of a girl next to her.

She closed her eyes and concentrated on the power below her body, the energy that surrounded the earth. Even in the desert, there was life that had power. The weakness in her body threatened to consume her, but she pulled her thoughts away from that and felt the vibration of life that surrounded everything, drawing it in through her hands as she sunk her fingers into the sand. Anything to get close to the source of the power she needed.

The girl placed a finger on Nikka's neck, and it interrupted the flow of energy through her hands. It zapped right out of her and into Famine. She fed on it just like she did the life force of everyone in the camp. Nikka's arm's trembled, and she collapsed to the ground, every breath rasping in her throat.

"This is my mission," Famine said, her beautiful voice ringing like a crystal bell in Nikka's ear. "I will not fail."

Her fingers shook as they clutched into the sand. Not like this, she thought. I won't die like this.

The desert stretched around her, behind the Angel of Famine. It's life force throbbed in the daylight like emanations of heat off the pavement. If she couldn't channel her power through her body, maybe she could bring it to her from the environment. Nikka closed her eyes and reached her thoughts beyond the encampment. Just like the moment she awoke with War's power, she could hear the sounds of the desert: the insects clicking across the sand, the whistle of a breeze through the thorns of a cactus, a bird lighting on a branch. The energy of all this pulsed, building into something more powerful than the Harbinger at her side.

The weakness in her limbs subsided as the energy rushed toward her. Famine took in a breath and stood just before Nikka turned her gaze toward her again. The violet light of the archangel power shone through her pupils. The Harbinger's face turned into a sneer, and she tried to jump away, but Nikka released the energy from her hands.

The power struck Famine, and she crashed back into the wall of a tent, collapsing it under her small frame.

Nikka grasped the pole of the tent next to her and pulled herself up, but it was much harder than she had expected. Famine's powers still held onto her with a death grasp. The Harbinger scrambled to her feet from the mess of the shelter and faced Nikka with the green glow fully alight in her eyes.

"Impossible," she screeched with clenched fists. Her fingers splayed toward Nikka once again, sending tendrils of green energy flooding over Nikka.

The power drained her further as Famine sucked at her with everything she had. Her knees wanted to fold, but she forced them to stay strong. Under her trousers, she could feel the muscles thinning and the bones protruding just under her skin. It wouldn't be long before she was at her dying weight. More of her hair fell out around her shoulders, drifting like angel feathers to the sand. The pain in her spine now shot through her chest as something cracked in her back. Nikka gasped at the pain, but even the air moving in and out of her chest made things hurt more.

She only had seconds left before she could no longer harness the earth's energy. Famine would kill her as soon as she could no longer control it. One last surge, and there would be nothing left. She pulled in a final flow of power from under her feet. The energy pulsed into her body and traveled to her fingers with every beat of her heart. She faced the Harbinger and took another step toward her despite the intense flow of power that the angel forced on her.

Nikka raised her palm to the Harbinger and released the power in a single strike, the strongest she had left. Famine screamed as it struck her in the chest, holding her in place as Nikka stumbled toward her and plunged her hand into the girl's chest.

"If you had found anyone else, you might have won," Nikka said, out of breath. "I've been here before, and it didn't stop me then. You won't stop me now."

Her fingers became ephemeral, piercing through the tissue and bone as though it had no substance. The angel shimmered around her grasp, and she held onto the warm creature of light as she pulled it from the girl's chest. The wispy thing in her hand slipped free of

Abby's body, and the girl collapsed to the ground. The green energy that had pierced into Nikka's torso vanished as soon as the girl fell.

Nikka could no longer stand and fell to her knees. The rocky ground bit into the flesh of her legs. She gasped as the shimmering light in her hand seeped into the flesh of her palm. Threads of green light moved just under her skin, up her forearm and settled into a dark tattoo that formed on her flesh. As the mark burned into her skin, a rushing sensation started in her chest and expanded in her torso as though it filled a void that had once formed there. In a single breath, the muscles in her arms and legs swelled again, back from the shriveled and thin strands that Famine had left. The sensation of it was almost painful as her shoulders broadened and the hollows of her cheeks vanished. She finally sat back on her heels as the last of her muscles found its strength. Her head fell to her clenched fists where they lay in the sand as she took in quick, slow breaths. Her fingers opened to touch the top of her head, where she felt thousands of strands of healthy hair still attached to her head.

She didn't dare move for a few seconds, waiting for the pain in her back to start again. Maybe it would when she stood up, but at least for now she was healthy and alive, even though the power of a new Harbinger coursed along her nerves, firing up all her senses at once.

Three Horseman. Only one left.

CHAPTER 33

GIDEON

The pounding of the veins in Gideon's temples caused his head to ache ever since the scout arrived to tell them of Nikka. He had not heard much of what the young man said after he described how they had found her and that she was at their camp right now. Gideon insisted upon driving as the scout led the way through the desert back roads, but he focused only on finding her.

Last night had been a chaotic blur, with the arrival of the angels and Jason at their helm. Then, the demons had ambushed them and Belphagor arrived. Before he could stop him, the demon had taken Nikka and vanished in the dark. Gideon couldn't protect her or even stop him from leaving with her. Shortly after, the angels scattered outnumbered and outmatched. They must have been coming just to find Nikka because as soon as Belphagor had grabbed her, the rest of them slunk back into the darkness.

Gideon's fingers clenched tight to the wheel as he accelerated over the bumpy desert road, the late afternoon sunlight pouring gold into his eyes under the visor. She was okay, at least that's what the kid said. Whatever had happened, she was able to escape from Belphagor, and these people found her. But that also meant the demons would be looking for her again. The vehicle crested over the edge of the hill and he could finally see down into the basin of the desert. A tent city splayed out along the edge of a river, shelters built in neat rows and avenues around a central hub. The shadow of the mountains in the west crept toward the small city with the coming dusk.

With the arrival of a motorized vehicle, several people gathered at the edge of the town as Gideon pulled to a stop. So many faces looked at them, from inside the tents as well as in the avenues, but Gideon could not stop, not now. He just needed to see her.

The scout led them into the center of town, to a large supply tent where an older woman with a long gray and white braid turned toward them with a smile and a greeting.

"I'm Helen," she said and extended her hand as the scout brought Gideon, Jadriel, and Amy to her. "Looks like we were lucky to find you."

"Is she here?" Gideon said, his impatience now creeping into his limbs.

Helen smiled, her eyes betraying her inner kindness. "You must be Gideon. She told me about you." She placed a hand on his upper arm and stepped around him, meeting Jadriel and Amy's eyes as well. "And you are Amy," she said as she extended her hand to her.

Her green eyes met Helen's. "Yes."

The woman then looked up to Jadriel's face as he towered over her. "And you are Jad. An unusual name but she didn't explain it."

She turned back to every one of them and met Gideon's eyes. "Now, I will take you to her. But only you first."

The lump that had formed in Gideon's throat grew thicker. He left the others behind as he followed Helen from the tent. Perhaps he should care more about them, leaving them alone in a new and strange place, but he only worried about one thing right now.

The woman wound through the rows of tents until they approached one on the outer edges of the town. A man stood outside the door flap, possibly as a guard. To keep anyone out or someone in? Gideon was not sure yet. Helen flashed the man a gentle smile as she approached. His shoulders eased, and he stepped aside from the door as soon as he saw her. Helen pulled back the canvas door and ducked into the darker space of the tent. Gideon followed close behind.

As his eyes adjusted, he stepped around Helen to see Nikka lying still on a cot, her body covered with layers of blankets. The breath stopped short in his throat at first as he saw her, her skin pale and darkened circles under her closed eyes. But when he saw the rhythmic rise and fall of her chest, he relaxed and hurried to her side where she slept.

Helen stepped behind him before he could touch Nikka and laid a hand on his shoulder. "She's been sleeping for a while now. There was an incident shortly after we found her."

"An incident?" he said, scanning her blonde hair splayed over the pillow.

The woman described the conditions of the camp before Nikka had arrived, the starvation and despair. Then she talked about what happened when Nikka awoke and discovered the cause of their sorrows. Helen did not know exactly what she talked about, but Gideon deciphered the meaning of it in her description. Nikka had encountered a Horseman here.

As Helen spoke about what she had seen, as unbelievable as it was, Gideon pulled back the covers to reveal Nikka's arms. His fingers traced along her forearm and he turned her palm out, revealing the new mark etched into her skin. It was true. She had faced and defeated Famine.

"She saved us all," Helen finished, and then the smile faded. "But I don't think she's well. It took a lot out of her, and she's been sleeping ever since."

As Gideon held Nikka's hand while he inspected her forearm, her fingers flexed around his. He glanced up to see that she had opened her eyes.

"You found me," she said, and her lips parted in a smile.

Helen leaned down to whisper in his ear. "I'll leave you two alone for a while. But don't be long, we've got quite a feast planned tonight." She turned away and stepped from the tent.

"They found us," Gideon said. He tried to force a smile, but he knew it would only be fake, something to mask his concern. "Belphagor took you, and I did not know how to find you. But they sent someone and said that you were here."

"Are you all right?" she said and placed a hand on his face. Her touch was so warm, almost hot.

He closed his eyes and placed a hand over hers where she touched him. Then he looked at her again. "You defeated Famine."

She nodded her head, but even that motion made her look even weaker.

"I do not like what this is doing to you," he said and grasped her hand, pulling it away from his face. "This needs to stop."

The circles under her eyes seemed to grow darker. "I can't. I have to finish this. It's the only way to get our son back."

"There must be another way, and we will find it."

"No. I only have one more to go −"

"Yes. One more and that one is Death, the worst of them all."

She took in a steady breath and clenched her fingers around his. "We have come this far. It's too late to stop now."

"It is never too late."

Nikka pushed herself up with her elbows and winced as she forced her body into a sitting position. Her legs swung over the edge of the cot as Gideon kneeled in front of her. She leaned toward him, placed her arms around the back of his neck and her forehead pressed against his. "Only one more, and then we have our son back."

"One more, and then you must face Lucifer himself to get our son back."

"Yes," she said and forced another smile. "I will fight the Devil himself."

"And an army of angels who want to stop you as well."

"Yes. Them too."

"And Jason, the Executioner."

The smile faded, and she closed her eyes. "Nobody will stop me. Not even Jason."

He tilted his head toward her and kissed her. The feel of her fingers curling behind his neck sent shivers down his spine, and he pulled her in closer. She might be confident about her ability to do this, but the doubt still wormed its way into his thoughts. Especially after Jadriel had confided in him that he no longer had the ability to heal her. Even now, as they held each other, he felt the heat of the Harbinger's power just under her skin, a fault line of energy just waiting to erupt.

He spent the remainder of the evening at her side, watching her limp around and take caution with the pain in her back. They sat together before the large fire as everyone in the camp ate the best feast they had in months. Nikka leaned on his shoulder and only nibbled at the meal on her plate despite his urgings. Gideon tried to distract his own thoughts as he turned his gaze toward Amy, who smiled and laughed with the people as she had not done in so long. And then there was Jadriel, standing at the edge of the camp and keeping watch. The firelight barely touched him where he waited.

Somewhere out there, two opposing armies waited and hoped to have the upper hand. And they both wanted one thing.

CHAPTER 34

NIKKA

The morning came too quickly, or the night was too full of shadows and dreams of war. Either way, Nikka hurt all over and walking didn't seem to take the edge away. She plodded away from her cot and the tent long before the sun rose and found a spot on an outcropping of rocks that overlooked the river. From here, she could see the best view of the sunrise.

It had been a while since she remembered seeing the dawn without the threat of something bearing down on her. The constant buzz and hum inside her chest made it hard to sleep anymore; that, and the ache in her spine. So, why not just get up and watch the sunrise where nobody else could feel her worry or ask if she was okay.

Of course, she wasn't okay, but she couldn't let Gideon know that. She suspected that Jadriel knew that she felt . . . off. And more than her simple aches and pain, which were not that simple when she thought about it. He was keenly aware that she had started to change. That hum in her chest, she knew it wasn't coming from inside of her body. No, it came from her soul. Something in there gestated, waiting for release, and there was only one more piece of the puzzle to make it whole.

Soft hues of pink and orange edged the black silhouette of the mountain range in the distance. She pulled her knees to her chest and hugged her arms around them. It occurred to her that the last time she might have had this kind of quiet in the mornings was when she held Adam to get him back to sleep. The thought made her eyes wet, and she blinked them clear.

This was all for him. A final and desperate effort to save him.

Final.

In the few quiet hours she had had since leaving Belize, she knew well that this could be final. So many things up to this point had felt like it would be the end: losing Gideon to the hell pit, the flaying torture she had endured, the battle of the demons and angels at the cemetery. But this was so much more than any of those. With the collective power of the Harbingers boiling inside of her, she knew that something big was going to come out of this and there was the distinct possibility she may not survive to see the end of it.

Maybe none of them would see it to the final outcome.

"You left," Gideon's voice sounded behind her.

Startled, she swallowed the lump that had formed in her throat and wiped the tears from her eyes with the back of her hand before she turned back to face him.

"Yeah. Couldn't sleep."

He climbed up the edge of the rock outcropping and sat beside her. "I was worried."

"Sorry. I didn't want to wake you."

Settling down next to her, he faced the oncoming sunrise. The light made his skin look bronze, and she watched him as he gazed at the light with fascination. He didn't say anything else but only looked forward with his legs dangling off the edge of the rocks.

There was no asking if she was okay.

Just quiet reflection on the light at the horizon.

And she smiled because of it. She leaned against him, and he clasped her hand as they watched the intensifying light to the east.

The constant thrumming inside her chest kept Nikka awake, more alert than she had ever been. While the remainder of the tent city began to stir and mill about the camp, she watched from her place on the rock outcropping. Gideon had left her there to her own thoughts while he descended down to the camp. He didn't have to say anything; she already knew they would need to leave this place today. There was no settling down here, not in this new world with her child still too far away. At least he was kind enough to keep the words to himself, the knowledge that one more horseman awaited her before she could find her son.

But the hour soon approached for them to leave, and she came down from her place to walk among the people that still watched her as she moved through the camp. A crowd had begun to gather about the Jeep at the edge of the tent city, where Jadriel and Gideon loaded provisions into the rear of the vehicle. Nikka's brow furrowed in curiosity to see the cases of food and water that some of the men from the village carried toward the vehicle.

Helen stood at the side of the Jeep and turned as she approached.

"What is all of this?" Nikka asked as she shaded her eyes from the morning sun with her hand.

Helen smiled. "A simple gesture of thanks."

"But these are your supplies—"

"And this is not enough for what you did." Helen stepped toward her and embraced her the same way her grandmother used to. "I know you must leave us, but please consider staying."

Nikka melted into the woman's warm arms as she smelled the scent of brown sugar on her clothes. "I wish I could."

"I understand," she said and released her. "Gideon didn't tell me everything, but he told me enough."

Nikka stepped back and glanced at Gideon and Jadriel as they loaded the final box of supplies and closed the hatch of the Jeep. They were ready to leave, and she felt the pangs of abandoning home again, something that she had not experienced for so long. She looked at their expectant faces, back to Helen, and then to the watching eyes of the men that helped them.

But something wasn't right.

"Where's Amy?" she said and took another step back, looking through the crowd that had begun to gather around them.

A shift of the crowd drew her attention, and Amy's red hair first caught her attention. She stepped into the group but then hung at the edge, not getting any nearer to the vehicle.

"I'm not coming," she said, her toe of her shoe digging into the ground as she clasped her hands in front of her.

Nikka approached her. "Are you sure?" She understood what was happening here, but it still left a hollow pit in her gut.

"Yes," she said. "This is where I need to be right now. A group of us are planning on travelling up north. Maybe I can make it Oregon."

Her green eyes dropped to the ground as she bit her lip. Nikka wrapped her arms around her and pulled her in, feeling Amy's arms hold her tight as well.

"I hope you make it," Nikka whispered. Amy had suffered so much since the beginning, since long before she had even met her. Maybe this place could finally bring her peace. And it was destined to be much safer than going further with them.

Nikka pulled away and felt the sting of tears in her eyes. Amy must have too because she looked to the side and brushed her index finger under her eyelashes.

"Good luck," Amy said and smiled, but it wasn't a hopeful look. Nikka could see the pity written on her face.

"Thanks." Nikka turned away from her and stepped up to the Jeep. She climbed into the front passenger seat as Gideon moved behind the wheel and Jadriel slid into the back seat. The sound of the doors shutting unnerved her as she watched Amy step back among the people of the tent village. Leaving her here felt like she was abandoning a sister, and deep in her heart, she knew that she would never see her again. Helen stepped beside Amy and placed an arm around her shoulders as she smiled at Nikka.

All of these people depended on her still, but they didn't know it. Going to Las Vegas to do what she had to do could save or destroy all of them, and they had no idea. Except for Amy. And that must be why she looked so sad. There was nothing she could do to help them anymore.

Nikka turned away from them and placed her head back on the seat, the thrum of Harbinger power still gyrating in her chest. She closed her eyes to the sound of the engine starting. The vehicle moved forward, forever leaving the tent village behind them.

CHAPTER 35
GIDEON

A dark mood had descended over her since she awoke that morning, long before she had to leave Amy behind at the tent village. The smile that she sometimes forced when she looked at Gideon held the shadow of worry, but she would never talk to him about it. Maybe saying it would make it too real: the possibility that they were driving to the end of the world. He had as much concern about the final horseman as she did and watching her now sitting in the passenger seat and gazing out the window as she bit her nails, he did not want her to find the last Harbinger.

The desert landscape changed as the sun moved across the sky. The empty freeway wound through the hills and then across an open plain. According to the map, the Las Vegas valley would be just over the mountain range, only a couple-hour's drive from where they now stopped.

The sky had been clear blue all day, but as they neared the Nevada border, a darkness loomed to the north as though a storm cloud gathered in the distance.

Jadriel leaned against the side of the vehicle as he poured gas from the red container into the tank. Even the angel eyed the dark weather ahead.

"I suppose it won't be too hard to find," he said and ticked his head to the clouds.

Gideon squinted against the stark gold light of the setting sun that crossed his vision. He watched Nikka wander along the side of the road, her eyes fixed to the north as well.

"Can you feel it as we get closer?" Gideon said. The last hour had been unusual, and at first, he had thought it was just from driving too long. But he now began to wonder if the subtle jitters he felt along his spine now came as a result of the immense power that they neared with every mile they drove. His demon core knew that a kindred spirit waited in the valley just ahead, and Pazuzu twitched with anticipation.

"Yes, but I have tried to ignore it."

The angel would have felt it too. He was the embodiment of a polar opposition to that dark energy in Vegas, the fallen archangel that Jadriel was born to fight. And now as Gideon glanced to Nikka, who walked among the dry, brown weeds with her hair drifting in the desert breeze, he knew she had to feel it too. The Harbinger power that grew inside her reacted, perhaps even stronger than his own, to Lucifer's energy. Inside of her was the primeval force that created the universe, the hand of God himself.

"Nikka," he called out to her. She turned to him, strands of her flaxen hair falling across her eyes, and for only a moment he swore he could see a flash of green deep in her pupils. "Are you okay?"

She turned away from him without saying a word. He was not sure what made him ask, but he was certainly thinking it all the time. She was not okay.

With the Jeep fueled, they collected together and started on the road again, driving toward the darkness that loomed ahead of them as the sun began to set.

The drive through the desert remained silent between them. The sun set into darkness, leaving only the double headlights of the vehicle ahead of them. An abandoned town came into view, more desolate than the others they had seen in the last hour. Not even a coyote or a rabbit dared to dwell this close to Vegas. Jadriel stopped the car in the center of town.

When Gideon stepped from the Jeep, even through the dark he could see that Nikka moved slow, her hands shaking and the breath catching in her throat. But his lingering stares in her direction would only make her uncomfortable. He slipped from the passenger seat and closed the door as he waited for her to walk around the front of the vehicle. The dark here was so much thicker the closer they got to Vegas and he could barely see her as she stepped toward him.

He reached his hand out to her, but her arms clutched around her torso as though she were cold despite the desert heat that still emanated from the ground. Trembling fingers reached for his hand but stopped short as though she had hit a wall, a barrier that now shimmered with faint ripples of silver light.

Nikka's eyes widened, and she halted as both of her hands reached to find the barrier between her and Gideon. The faintest hint of lavender danced over the salt brush, and Gideon knew what was coming. Jadriel's heavy hand landed on his shoulder before he could rush toward Nikka.

"You can't hide from me," a voice came from the darkened desert behind Nikka.

The color drained from her face and Gideon watched her jaw slacken as she heard the voice too.

Pinpoints of violet light appeared in the shadows, a pack of angelic wolves surrounding the perimeter. A single figure stepped from the dark, only feet behind Nikka. The angel runes tattooed on his arms and up his neck illuminated in a white-purple light, casting a ghost glow around their small circle where the executioner held Nikka in his shield.

Nikka's eyes focused on Gideon as she held her palm up to the invisible shield that separated them. Her lips parted in a whisper. "Run."

"I will not leave you," Gideon said, trying to pull away from Jadriel's grasp.

"You have to go," she said, her eyes glistening. "Find our son and get him out of there."

Jadriel pulled him back. "You cannot stop them," he said.

"Protect him, Jad," Nikka said as her gaze sharpened to Jadriel.

The angel's jaw tightened, and he nodded.

Gideon pulled free from Jadriel's grasp and he rushed to meet Nikka's touch, but the barrier held firm between them. A glance over her shoulder told him that Jason approached, his tattoos glowing and his gaze firm toward Nikka.

"You have to kill him," Gideon whispered to her, "or he will kill you."

The white-violet angel glow that surrounded them shimmered in her eyes. "I'm not sure that I can do that."

"Enough of this," Jason's voice boomed over the sand. "You stand accused, Nikka, an abomination that must be ended for the sake of the world."

Jadriel's grasp on Gideon's shoulder tightened and he pulled him away from her. As he slipped back, Nikka turned to face Jason, her arm out before her and a light erupting from her palm, sending a shield of her own around them. The violet light flashed as quick as lightning and settled in a barrier that surrounded only her and Jason, keeping out even the other angels that had come to witness the execution.

CHAPTER 36

NIKKA

The moment Nikka looked into his eyes, she no longer saw Jason. The body before her, fierce and intimidating, was now only a vengeful archangel sent to destroy her. Lucifer and his demons had taken the world, but Heaven's angels had taken Jason from her now too.

"Nikka Connors," he spoke, his voice resonating like a judgement from above, "you have been deemed unworthy and have put this world at risk."

"Jason, they've clouded your thoughts—"

"Silence," he shouted to her, a ripple of light coursing from his marks and threading across the sand in strands of purple electricity. He stepped closer and she planted her feet into a battle stance, her hand up and ready to send energy his way if he were to strike at her. The lines on his forehead creased. "What you've done has started the clock to the end of the world."

Her voice caught in her throat as she looked at him and she tried to keep it steady. "I'm trying to save it."

"You have allied yourself with Harbingers," he said. His head tilted to the side, just like he used to when they argued, and he had tried to convince her about his version of things. "The Horsemen. Nikka, they are the Harbingers of the Apocalypse."

"Whatever they have told you," she said, ticking her head toward the army of angels hiding in the dark outside of the barrier, "is a lie. They're using you, Jason."

A woman stepped up behind Jason and stopped at the shield, her face alight in the glow from Jason's tattoos, the same woman Nikka had seen the last time Jason had attacked them. "The time for judgement has ended. The execution is to begin."

Jason glanced back at her and nodded. As he turned back to Nikka, his hand reached behind his shoulder and withdrew a heavy sword that erupted in violet flames as he held it at his side. The tattoo lines along his neck glowed brighter.

Whatever fragment of Jason that had remained in his body diminished as the purple light glowed in his pupils. The shudder started in Nikka's chest first, a fracture of the smallest hope that Jason was going to be okay. Her lungs hurt as she tried to breathe and look at him.

"Don't do this," she said, trying to force back the tears that started.

"Judgement has been rendered," he said, his grip tightening on the hilt of his sword. "And the sentence will be carried out."

The muscles in her arms fought against her will, but she reached behind her back and withdrew her own katana. The flames danced along the blade as she held it out before her and steadied her stance. She blinked the tears away and gazed into his eyes, hoping to see something there that would stop him. But there was only hot violet light.

"Jason," she said, and her voice quivered despite her best effort to stop it. "I still love you, no matter what happens."

The muscles in his shoulders tightened and his feet burst forward as his broad sword flashed through the air. Before she knew what he was doing, he lunged at her. The friction wave coming off his sword brushed against the skin of her arm as she dodged out of the way. She collapsed into a somersault and rolled away from him. The movement at her periphery caught her attention and she pulled her sword up just as his weapon came down on her again where she crouched. The blades met in an explosion of violet electricity that shuddered outward in a tremor that shook the earth. The violence of it made her pause, but only long enough to notice his proximity to her and his left flank was exposed.

With both hands on her blade, she shoved his sword to the side and released her left hand to lash out at him, filling her arm with the energy that flowed through her body. Her fist met his side with a powerful strike that caught him off guard. As he howled in pain, he jumped away from her which gave her a quick second to shift to her feet and step back from him.

The ache of her heart pounding against her ribs made her breathe faster as she looked at him. The grimace across his lips told her that she had hurt him, but it wasn't enough to stop him. He paced around the edge of their joined barriers, a tiger stalking his prey as he walked off the throbbing pain of the jab she had given him. But even she had held back. That strike could have been worse; she could have gone in for far more damage, but she only wanted to stop him for now, to show him that this was wrong.

But seeing the rage in his eyes made everything too clear. He wasn't going to hold back for her, not with his thoughts clouded by what the angels had told him.

"Jason," she said, the breath rushing in and out of her lungs now, "don't make me hurt you."

A smile formed on his lips. "That's nice of you to think that you can defeat me, but it's not possible." His pace changed direction, but his gaze stayed fixed on her. "I will stop you before this night is through."

He lunged at her again, his movement so quick that it caught her off guard. She brought her sword up to meet his, but the power behind his strike drove her down to her knees again. The motion of it threw off her balance and it exposed her torso. Before she could recover, his boot landed on her ribs, driving her to the ground. Then another blow pounded into her back. Her ribs spasmed in pain, forcing a cough laced with the copper hint of blood. Her sword clattered to the ground and the panic of the loss kept her thoughts clear. She made her muscles move against their will and she scrambled to her hands and knees, her fingers grasping at the hilt of her sword.

The crunch of his boots in the sand behind her echoed loud in her ears. She twisted into a crouch, bringing the sword in an arc with her. Her eyes only saw alternating dark and light, but the edge of her blade caught something, and she heard Jason howl again. The blur in her vision cleared and she dodged to the right as Jason leaned to grasp his fingers around the slice in his thigh. The tip of her sword dripped wet with fresh blood.

As she watched him limp to the edge of the barrier and his fierce gaze turn toward her, she realized that he wouldn't stop. Not now. Each of them had now drawn blood, and this was for real. He planned to kill her.

The ache still throbbed in her back and she knew it was more than just the kick that he had landed. Her bones slipped and ground on one another, a loose network of angel duct-tape that began to fray. Somewhere behind her, on the other side of the barrier, she still heard Gideon's voice as he shouted into the night, but it blended with the ringing in her ears into a cacophony of sound.

Please, Jadriel. Get him out of here.

Jason straightened and the sword in his hand pointed toward her. "This will stop tonight."

She knew it was coming, but she had hoped that it was all a nightmare. He lunged at her again, his sword a blur of light and metal. The katana took the first few blows, each one with a tremor of fury that shuddered down to the hilt. Her limbs moved languid with each strike, meeting them in a clang of sparks. She saw the glow in his eyes as he shifted before her, she knew that this was the moment that would change everything. That violet light in his pupils burned supernova now.

The next strike came down harder than anything she had ever felt before, the tremor of it rattling deep in her spine. It must have shaken the fragile seams in her bones because it came with a shot of pain into her arms and legs. The impact forced her to step back, once and then again when the next blow came. Nikka held her breath when the sword flashed again. The grimace in his face deepened, the shadows accented against the violet light in his eyes.

Another step back unbalanced her when his sword came down at her again, clanging with a shower of sparks against her katana. The horizon tilted, and she stumbled backward, catching herself with her free hand just in time to meet another blow with her sword.

For only a second, she heard Gideon shouting from beyond the invisible shield that held him and Jadriel away from them. The sound came as a muffled cry in the dark, beyond that thin veil between them. If only that second could have lasted a bit longer.

The sound of Gideon's voice faded into nothing when Jason lunged at her, the broadsword clasped in both of his hands. The determined glare in his eyes bore down on her the same time she saw the tip of his weapon flash in the purple light. The angel light around him zapped with ribbons of electricity as he moved in the dark, his boot striking down in the gravel next to her just as his sword struck true.

With a gasp and the white-hot surge of pain in her chest, she knew it was too late.

CHAPTER 37

GIDEON

So many times in the past, Gideon had prayed to God for a chance to relive a single moment, to correct a single mistake but that prayer had never been answered. And now God had let this happen to Nikka.

The world disappeared into a vacuum at the moment Jason lunged at her. Gideon's hands tightened into fists as he pounded against the shield that kept him at bay. The shouts that bellowed from his chest left his throat raw, but it did no good.

Jason leaped across the short distance to where Nikka fell. Her hand gripped the hilt of the katana and brought it up to defend herself again, but it was too late. Jason landed in a crouch over her. A pulse of violet light as blinding as lightning flashed across the desert, and for a moment Gideon saw only sparkles of light shimmering in his retina. At the moment his vision returned, the blade had already struck home.

Everything stilled as his cries stagnated in his chest, caught in the shock of the moment. This cannot be happening.

Nikka lay on the ground, her eyes wide as she stared at Jason who still hovered over her with his hands on the hilt of his blade that now plunged into her chest. Her mouth opened with quivering lips as she tried to speak but no sound emerged.

Gideon found his voice when the noises of the world returned to his ears. "How could you?" he shouted and pounded his fists against the shield. Halos of faint violet light emanated around the impact of his fists. "She loved you. How could you?"

Tears burned in his eyes and sizzled as they flowed down Gideon's cheeks. There was no stopping the demon as it burst from its locked hideaway in his soul. His eyes flashed into a deep red ember glow as he pounded on the shield again, anything to tear Jason away from her. Pazuzu broke free, rippling in his muscles and bones. Another strike against the shield made it tremble under his fists.

Jason never turned toward him, though, despite the low growl that rumbled in his chest. Instead, he released a shaking hand from his sword and touched Nikka's cheek as she still struggled to speak. Her head dropped back against the gravel and the quivering in her lips stilled as her body grew limp under him.

Jadriel reached for Gideon's shoulder, but the demon shoved him away, keeping his gaze on Nikka's body.

"We have to go, now," the archangel warned.

"I do not care," Gideon said, the low growl heavy behind his voice.

He did not turn away from her as Jason's visage softened and his head dropped. Beyond Gideon's shouts and pounding, he could see that Jason now cried, his shoulders trembling as his hand touched her face. With his right hand still on his sword, he pulled it free and let it fall to the ground beside Nikka's body. He leaned over and wrapped her still form in both of his arms, holding her close to him as he cried into her neck.

The archangel grasped Gideon's shoulder again and pulled him back from the shield, but he could not tear away his gaze from Jason as he held Nikka's lifeless body against his own.

"We must leave this place," Jadriel said, his eyes with a faint shimmer of violet residing in his pupils. "Something is not right."

The army of archangels that had followed Jason now gathered around the shield that had kept everyone out of the battle circle.

"You have succeeded," Zumiel spoke as she approached the shield. "We will take her body with us now."

Jason stiffened and raised his head, his face red with tears as he grasped his sword and faced the angel with the flaming blade directed toward her. "You won't touch her," he shouted to her.

Jadriel leaned closer to Gideon as he watched the angels circling the shield. "There is nothing you can do for her now," he whispered.

The demon raged inside him and everything in his sight burned red, but he knew the archangel was right. The angels had them both outnumbered. Nikka was gone now, and he was the only one left that could find his son. He would have to deal with Jason some other time than now.

He backed away with Jadriel's hand still on his shoulder, but his gaze never left Nikka's pale and limp body as Jason held her close to his chest.

"This is over," Zumiel said, her voice raising to intimidate him.

"I've done what you asked," Jason cried, the sword pointed to the angel. "It's done, now leave her body to me."

"That is not part of the deal," Zumiel said.

Jason shifted and sheathed his sword onto his back, where it vanished when his hand left the hilt. He pulled her body close to his as he turned to glance back to Gideon. For only a second, their eyes met, violet angel to red demon, before a pulse of violet light burst from between Jason and Nikka's body. The light erupted in a brilliant flash and the force of it rushed outward in an impact tremor. It struck Gideon in the chest and knocked him to the ground. The army of angels fell backward with the pulse wave and a wave of dust rushed outward over the sand.

The light vanished in an instant, leaving the desert in darkness. When Gideon scrambled to his feet again, the shield had disappeared and so had Nikka and Jason. Only the footprints left in the sand remained to tell of the epic battle that had taken place there.

Jadriel nudged him and Gideon glanced to the archangel. Yes, they had to leave. They were no match for an army of angels that could decide to turn on them at any second. The archangel's hand fell on his shoulder and they were surrounded by violet angel light as Jadriel transported him away from that dark area of the desert.

CHAPTER 38

NIKKA

L ight and shadow fell around Nikka and only the smallest sounds, like birds in the distance, hung over the space where she lay. Flashes of memory stung just behind her eyes, tiny barbs of pain and screaming, but the sound hadn't come from her throat. Someone just outside of that light made those sounds and they were for her.

Gideon. It was Gideon's voice.

There should have been more pain, though. This wasn't right.

She blinked open her eyes to the blurred golden shafts of light around her. The heavy scent of leather filled the air with hay and dust sprinkled over the firm surface under her body. Her vision cleared to see that same dust shimmering in the beams of sunlight that cast through slats of wood to her left. She lifted up on her elbows, feeling the shifting of her sore bones in her spine, as she looked down at the thick wool blanket that separated her body from the layer of straw on the ground.

The pain. The light and the smell of hay. There was no way she was dead, and this definitely wasn't Heaven.

The last images of violet light mixed with dark played in her head. The quick flash of a sword. Jason's angry face.

Her hands moved to her chest, half-expecting to feel a gaping wound there, but even her shirt remained untainted. Only the beat of her heart under her warm fingertips lingered there.

"I'm sorry," Jason's voice rose from the corner.

That same heartbeat fluttered as her eyes darted across the shafts of sunlight, to the corner of the hayloft that still rested in shadows beyond the morning light. She could barely make out his form from where she lay. Her hand darted behind her shoulder, but the hilt of her sword wasn't there. The panic surged in her chest and she scrambled into a crouch, ready to run.

"No," he said, his hand moving out into the light. "It's okay." His other hand emerged into the sunbeams, her katana held in his palm. He tossed it toward her and it landed with a skid over the carpet of straw. "You dropped it, so I grabbed it before we got out of there."

She leaned over the blanket but kept her eyes sharpened toward the corner. Small glints of light caught the edge of his shoulder-length blonde hair and the goatee around his mouth. He stood, taking more of the light against his face. Her hand grasped onto the sword and she held it out before her.

Of course, she could only posture for now. He had already bested her, and in the fragile broken state she was in, he could probably do it again. But she wouldn't go down without a fight.

"I won't hurt you," he said and stepped toward her. The sunlight fell on his broad shoulders that now looked hunched as he kept his hands stuffed into the pockets of his jeans.

"A bold choice of words," she said and stood straighter, the katana held firm in her hands.

"I had to make it look convincing." His blue eyes caught the light, and he looked just as he had back in this grandfather's cabin, handsome and innocent of this world of angels and demons before she lost him to Lucifer's army.

"What did you do to me?"

"Zumiel recruited me to be an Executioner," he said, his gaze falling away from her. "I knew she only used me to find you. They told me what you've been up to, the thing with the Four Horsemen. But I knew there was something they weren't telling me. The angels want you dead. They don't want you to succeed."

Nikka felt her throat go dry. "They're afraid of me, I think. They worry that Lucifer will turn me to his side."

"That, and the fact that without mankind in the way, it's only a battle between angels and demons to have rule over the earth."

"The Harbingers were the fail-safe to keep that from happening," she said, her voice falling as she realized the weight of the things she said. "That's how God planned on keeping the balance."

He stepped closer to her and the sword faltered in her hand. "I couldn't kill you, but they would only keep hunting you until an Executioner eventually did the job for me. I had to buy you more time."

As she looked at him, to the face of the man she had loved, she let the sword drop to her side. It felt too heavy, as everything did with the thrum of the Harbinger bomb just waiting inside of her. She approached him and reached a hand to touch his arm. The breath hitched in his throat as she touched him, but he finally pulled his hand from his pocket and wrapped an arm around her shoulders.

The familiar scent of his clothes surrounded her as she took in his warmth. It had been almost a year since she had held him like this, back in a time when she thought that exorcising a demon was as bad as things could get.

"I'm sorry I had to do it," he said, his breath warm on her ear. "I wasn't sure if I could beat you."

The Harbinger energy quivered in her chest, always reminding her that it still waited to be freed.

"It's getting easier and easier to beat me these days," she said and pulled away from him. "I have to tell you something."

His face grew pale as she explained the new power that she had acquired, and the damage it had done to her body. When he glanced over the fresh tattoos on her forearms, his hands shook as he held her arms out before him.

"How will this defeat Lucifer if it destroys you before you even get there?" he said.

"I'm not sure. I've just got to have faith that it will work."

"But there is still one more out there."

"Correct." She nodded her head. "Death."

"So how do you find the Angel of Death?"

"He will find me."

He let out a frustrated sigh and ran his fingers through his hair. "I don't like the sound of that."

"Don't really have a choice anymore."

"I know," he said and stuffed his hands into his pockets again. "But you have me now. Let me help you with this."

A thin smile spread on her lips. There he was, the same Jason that always wanted to take away her pain and suffering, no matter what it meant.

"I know you want to help, but when the time comes, I'll have to do it myself."

She approached him and wrapped her arms around his torso. She relaxed a little bit and let his hands touch her again. "At least I can walk you to the brink of Death if needed."

He leaned down and kissed her, something she had only experienced in her memories of him when she thought he had died at Lucifer's hand. His hands wandered to her back and he pulled her closer, bending her spine in just the wrong way.

She flinched, and he immediately froze, his eyes opening to look down at her.

"What did I do?"

As the pain subsided to a dull ebb, she forced a smile up to him. "Nothing. It's okay."

"No, it's not," he said and pulled his hands away from her. "This thing with the Harbinger's power. It's worse than you're telling me, isn't it."

The dryness in her throat returned as she looked at him. "Jadriel, the archangel that is with us, he told me I won't be able to heal the way I used to. He patched me up the best he could but it's not quite enough."

Furrows formed on his brow. "Are you dying?"

That was something that had drifted in and out of her thoughts since she first faced Pestilence, but she had always pushed it aside. Now she heard the words out loud, from someone who could not help her.

"I don't know," she said. "But it doesn't change anything. I still have to do this. It's the only way to get to Lucifer, to find my son."

He grew quiet and withdrawn again like he often did when he worried about something that he had no control over. His boots crunched over the layer of straw as he paced, his hands balling into fists in front of his chest.

"Maybe there is something I can do," he finally said.

The pit of anguish started in her gut. "I appreciate it, but I can't lose you again."

"No, you don't understand." He turned toward her, his eyes now alive. "I know where Lucifer is keeping your son."

The familiar sinking started in her gut as Jason detailed where Lucifer kept Adam in the vast outstretches of Las Vegas. Even as he described the armies of demons that surrounded the city and the enormous ruins of the casino where she would have to go, nausea welled in the back of her throat.

She placed a hand on her knee and eased back down to the ground before her legs wobbled beneath her. Jason crouched down beside her.

"It sounds impossible," she muttered.

"I can get you in there." His hand rested on her shoulder. "And if we can find Gideon and this other angel of yours, that's even more strength on our side."

That's what worried her: all of them rushing in to the Devil's lair, all to help her. It was a suicide mission. But she had known that all along.

"I don't even know how to find Gideon," she said, shaking her head. "Not without using my power and alerting the angels."

"We will find him." He settled into the carpet of straw next to her. "I figure we can just start heading toward Vegas. Gideon would go that way too. He thinks you're dead and he still needs to find his son."

She looked up at him, at the way the sunlight fell on the half-smile and optimistic glint in his eye. "I wish I could have as much hope as you do in this."

"Somebody's gotta do it." He nudged her with his shoulder. "So are you up for some walking? Let's just head toward Vegas and we don't use any of our abilities until we get there. Stay under angel radar."

"I think so," she said, but the twinge in her back nagged at her again. I didn't matter how much it hurt, though. She had to get to her son, and this was the only way now.

Jason stood and held out his hand to help her up. She accepted it and followed him from the dust of the barn and out into the open world again.

CHAPTER 39

NIKKA

---

espite the heat rippling off the desert, they walked down the deserted highway that drifted north toward Las Vegas. She walked at his side, trying to keep pace with him, but she noticed when he slowed down to accommodate her at the point where the pain in her back became too much. The temperature didn't dip much as the sun began to creep westward, tipping the edges of the mountain range in the distance.

She pushed through the raw burning of new blisters that started in her feet, a small inconvenience if it meant that she could make it to the edge of Vegas before dark.

The road curved around the edge of a butte with the approaching twilight. The dark green and blue hues of night fell on the expanse of desert that surrounded the city. At one time, it sparkled with neon lights and the worming motion of cars down the freeway that split the city in two. Now, only the skeletal remains of hotels and broken casinos lay scattered among a field of dead vehicles that clogged the roads. They were still several miles away, but from this vantage point, Nikka could see to the far north side of the darkening city.

Dark and dead, except for a single glint of firelight in the center, the highest remaining building in Vegas.

"You can see it," Jason said as he watched her line of sight toward the city. "That's where he is. Lucifer stays in the top penthouse."

"And Adam is up there?"

He nodded. "The last time I saw him, he was."

Nikka started down the road again, but Jason placed a hand on her shoulder. "Wait." She stopped and turned back to him, the fading light casting shadows of worry over his face. "Are you fully prepared to face him like this? I mean, you have no idea what he has done to your son. This is the Devil we're talking about. I didn't spend a lot of time around him, but the little I did made me not want to do it again. That is the purest evil I've ever felt."

"It doesn't matter," she said, the words feeling like dust in her mouth. "I have to go. I can't just leave Adam behind in his hands."

"I understand that," he said. "But I just want you to think about what you might see when you try to get him back. Do you have any idea why Lucifer wanted him to begin with?"

"Some," she said. The child of a demon and a seraph was the lure for the demons. Even when she had come face to face with Lucifer in his incorporeal form, he had spoken about wanting the child of Gideon. "Adam bridges Heaven and Hell. I think with whatever power Adam holds, Lucifer can use it against the angels and take over this world."

"But what power is that?"

The thought settled like a stone in her stomach. "I have no idea." She turned back to face the glimmer of firelight in the middle of the city. "But I can't let Lucifer find out."

She started forward, Jason's hand slipping from her shoulder. Those horrible little thoughts had plagued her ever since she had been pregnant and pursued by the armies of Heaven and Hell. So many unanswered questions about what resided inside Adam, and nobody but the Devil to answer them.

The distance grew between her and Jason with each quickened step she took down the highway with the dark silhouettes of broken buildings ahead of her. At this pace, she would tire too quickly, but she had to keep moving.

A spark of pain bloomed in her stomach, just a flare at first. She winced and slowed her pace as it ebbed away with each beat of her heart. Another step forward and another. Then a stab shot through her core. She gasped and fell to her knees as she placed a hand on her stomach. The ache pulsated, growing stronger as she struggled to breathe. Jason rushed to her side, placing a hand on her back but the heat of it only made her skin burn.

"What is it?" he said, but the words echoed hollow in her ears.

She had no voice, the last of it taken away by the throbbing pain in her body that now welled in her arms and legs. It drained her lungs of any air, and she couldn't even cry. Her hand moved to the pavement at her feet to support her body, and the new sigils etched into her forearms flickered with points of green light, the glow intensifying as the pain worsened. Any other tattoo that she had on her arms now faded into her skin until they had disappeared, leaving only the three Harbinger marks.

Ghostly green light erupted in her eyes, casting its glow over the road and against her arms. Jason stood and stepped back from her.

"What's happening?" he said.

The cringe in her throat loosened enough for her to speak. "I don't know."

As soon as it had started, the pain in her gut released like a fist that had wound through her body and now let its fingers open. She took in a quick breath and collapsed to the ground, shuddering with the aftershocks of what had just happened. The light faded from her eyes and the marks on her arms. Tears trickled from her eyes and fell on the warm pavement where she lay as Jason knelt beside her and placed his hand on her face.

"Has this happened before?" he asked.

She shook her head, the motion small and careful. "No."

"Whatever the Harbingers have put inside you is fighting to get out." His fingers found hers.

Nikka lifted her head, but her arms trembled with the effort. Something had changed in the last few minutes, the result of it still strumming in her bones. The ache in her spine was now a stabbing prickle that worsened with every movement. A panicked thought raced through her head as she gazed down at the bare expanse of skin on her arms where angel tattoos had once resided. She pulled her hand free of Jason's grasp and reached behind her shoulder where her katana always waited.

Nothing. No sword. No hilt.

"It's gone," she whispered, her voice shaking.

"That can't be."

Her fingers searched along the upper edge of her shoulder blade, but she knew what had happened before she even tried to find the sword.

"It's all gone." Her wet eyes looked up at him the dying light. "I have no power anymore."

CHAPTER 40

JASON

———————————————————————————————

*T*he weight of her in Jason's arms worried him the most. She had grown thinner, fatigued and frail in the many months since she and the others had vanished from the cemetery. Whatever power the Harbingers had put in her had taken a significant piece of her life, and now it had stolen whatever power she had left, leaving a withering shell.

Her arm curved around the back of his neck and she rested her head against his chest as he carried her to the outskirts of the city. Black and gray husks of buildings, homes, and warehouses lay scattered in various degrees of ruin. As his eyes darted into the shadows for anything that may lurk there, he pulled her closer to him. At some point, she must have fallen asleep because her even breathing never faltered despite his hesitation to continue in the dark.

The ache in his arms grew with each passing minute, and he knew they would have to stop for the night. Vegas was right here, but neither of them was in any shape to face a demon army. Not without just a little rest.

And then there was the fact that Nikka was no longer an archangel, powerless and maybe less than human right now. But if she wasn't human, what was she? Something else lurked inside her, like a parasite waiting to emerge. Images of the creature from the Alien movies continued to play in his brain along with the recurring thought of the thing bursting out of someone's chest. He forced those thoughts to the side as he carried her through the threshold of an abandoned grocery store, the sliding glass doors cracked and sitting askew on their railings.

After arranging a make-shift bed of anything that might be a cushion (table cloths, dishtowels, a puffy and intact bag of marshmallows) from broken shelves, he placed Nikka down and she stirred. Her eyes opened when he settled down next to her, sitting back against an empty row of shelves. Through the dim moonlight that shone through the broken windows of the store front, he watched her eyes in the dark for any sign of the green light that might make its presence known.

"Where are we?" she asked, her voice cracking.

"Outskirts of town." He glanced down at his own hands, hoping she wouldn't see him probing for the light in her eyes. "You doing okay?"

"I feel like I have the flu. Everything hurts, and I can't stop shaking."

"You just need some rest."

A small laugh broke through her lips. "You and I both know that's not true."

He forced a smile and fished in his pocket for the wrapped granola bar that he had found on one of the shelves. The wrapper crinkled as he held it out for her. "You just need to eat something."

She shook her head. "I'm not hungry. Just tired." Her hand reached out to him and grasped his forearm. "Stay with me."

The trembling in her fingers vibrated against his skin, but he pushed that aside and curled down beside her. Her hands wrapped around his and she just looked at him through the dark.

"I'm not going anywhere."

"If I can't make it to the lair, please help Gideon get there," she said, her voice a whisper.

"Don't say that. You'll get there. You'll get your son back and you will stop Lucifer."

The moonlight played at the edges of her mouth with her smile. Her eyes glistened in only faint sparkles, but no green light flickered in her pupils.

"Hey," he said and grasped her hand tighter. Maybe that would help the shaking, but nothing seemed to change. "You have this new power for a reason. The Harbingers have a plan, I have to believe that it's true. Only one more to go and then everything could change."

"Only one more," she said. "Death."

The word created a ripple of chills down his forearms like spiders tickling his skin. "But it's the last one."

Her head nodded, the curl of her fingers in his hand weakening. The shadows fell deeper on her face when her eyes closed, and she drifted to sleep. It was just the two of them now, like in the days they spent in his grandfather's cabin. He once thought that was as bad as things could get while the two of them had stayed in hiding deep in the woods. If only they could go back to that now. He would give anything to have those days again.

The trembling in her hand eased as she slept with her fingers intertwined in his. He allowed his eyes to close, even if it could only be for a few hours.

The sound of breaking glass blended into the fevered dream that flashed behind his eyelids, and at first, he only tossed his head back until the crash came again, stirring him awake. It happened only moments before he saw the violet light burst into the abandoned grocery store like a flash of lightning. He jerked upright at the same time that Nikka did, but not before the light came again.

In a blur of motion, Nikka's eyes grew wide and glanced at him. Her fingers were still in his grasp, but a second later something pulled her away from him, her body sliding into the flashing shadows. The scream that came from her mouth was the only thing that told him where she had gone.

The sound of another shattered window echoed into the store and Jason moved to his feet, darting through the strobe of light and shadow as he followed the trail where he last saw Nikka before she vanished into the dark. He sprinted down the trashed aisles and to a set of double doors toward the back of the store. Blood pulsed with each hard pound of his heart. He burst through the doors, plunging into the dark space of a storage area. Another rupture of violet light flashed through the dark, guiding him to the open loading bay door in the back. His feet pounded against the pavement, eyes trained to the faint moonlight now pouring down through the opening in the dark.

The air burned in his throat with each breath. Archangels had descended on them, and he knew exactly why they were here. He burst through the loading bay when another flash of light almost blinded him, but in that light, he could make out the silhouette of a figure in the open lot behind the store.

A man, broad shoulders muscled to perfection underneath a thin white T-shirt, held Nikka by the back of the neck and forced her to the ground. She cried out against his grasp and struggled to fight him off but he towered over her. The tendons along his arms rippled in the moonlight and a shimmer of violet light flowed along tattoos that decorated his skin up to his neck. Jason sprinted faster as the light moved along the rows of straight sigils along his neck up to his jaw line, the same marks that adorned his own skin now.

This was no ordinary archangel. The man that held Nikka down was an Executioner, just like him. Jason had been replaced by an effective killer that could put an end to them both.

The angel reached behind his shoulder and withdrew a saber from behind his back, the sword appearing in a flash of violet flames as he grasped its hilt and pulled it forward. The light flickered over Nikka as she looked up at him, her hands grasping at his while she struggled to get free.

It can't happen. Not here. Not like this. Jason pulled every last bit of energy he could find around him, in the ground and in the air, until it pulsated under his own marks. The tattoos on his arms and neck erupted into violet light as he leaped toward the Executioner. He struck him in the hardest tackle he could manage, driving the massive angel down to the ground. The sword clattered against the pavement and the angel's hand lost its grip on Nikka's neck. Jason rolled with him, his fingers clutched as tight as he could hold to the angel as they both rolled to the ground.

The Executioner twisted in his grasp and Jason scrambled away into a crouch before the angel could right himself.

He glanced back to Nikka, who now pulled herself up from the pavement. "Run," he called to her. To his relief, she didn't hesitate.

She darted into the darkness, disappearing between two dumpsters at the far end of the lot.

The archangel turned to face him, his massive form rising upright with light emanating from his pupils.

"Looks like they replaced me," Jason said, his lungs aching for breath. Maybe he could buy himself and Nikka a few seconds before the angel struck at them again.

The archangel's shoulders tightened. "You never belonged. They used you to get what they needed, and we just found her."

We. Shit. That meant the Executioner wasn't the only one here. As though they could hear his thoughts, flashes of violet erupted from around the lot. Shadowy forms emerged from the lights as more archangels appeared.

Jason reached behind his shoulder and withdrew his long-sword, the violet firelight of it warming his hand as he situated it before him. The glow cast against the Executioner's face, leaving behind a ghostly purple tinge to his skin.

"I won't let you take her," he said to the angel.

"You do not have a choice."

The Executioner stooped and hefted his saber, the fire emerging along the blade as he straightened and stepped toward Jason.

CHAPTER 41
NIKKA

***

Nikka couldn't look back, not now. Not when Jason did what he could to free her from the archangel's grasp. He needed her to run, so that's what she did.

The power that it took to sprint into the dark drained her faster than she had expected. Not only had her angel powers vanished, but her own physical energy had sapped away with it as well. Her lungs fought for air, feet stumbling over the uneven grass behind the lot. The large expanse of lawn was shrouded in trees and outbuildings, leaving long drags of shadows in the moonlight.

A flash of violet light almost blinded her, and she staggered back. A hand emerged from the light and tightened around her throat, stopping her advance like a freight train. The vice-grip lifted her off her feet, squeezing the blood flow in her neck.

Nikka gasped for air, but her throat only squeaked with the effort. Her fingers tightened around the wrist that held her. Two violet pin-points of light glowed before her in the dark, and in her dizzying state, she saw the face of a woman. The angel that had arrived with Jason when he had first come to collect her. The archangel that had made him into an executioner.

The angel's eyes bored into hers, cold and without emotion. They simply stared at her as she squeezed the life from Nikka.

She kicked at the angel and clawed her fingers against her wrist, but the grip held her so tight that she knew there were only seconds left.

"You look at me as though I want you to die," the angel said, her voice even and stale. "I do not want to take a human life, but you have left me without a choice. And the Executioner will finish the job."

Nikka kicked at her again, anything to get air.

"This world must belong to either Heaven or Hell, and I cannot allow you to make that choice for us."

The angel's grip tightened, something Nikka didn't think was possible. Ringing started in her ears and the darkness around her somehow grew blacker. Her nails raked against the angel's skin, breaking on the stone-like composition of her flesh.

A slit of red light broke through the dark and a shriek sounded above the ringing that deafened her. The iron grip on her throat loosened and she collapsed to the ground. Her lungs gasped for a breath and she coughed against the violent inhale. Another flash of red light illuminated the pavement, followed by a blitz of red and violet sparks. A warm hand grasped her arm, jolting her as she coughed again. Her eyes darted into the darkness and settled on the face of an angel that she recognized.

"Jad," she wheezed. His arms wrapped around her and he lifted her to her feet, holding her against his lavender-scented chest. The angel turned with her, and she knew what he was trying to do. It wasn't his fault; it was exactly what she had ordered him to do. To protect her. He prepared to take her away from all of this, away from Jason and Gideon.

"No," she said and wriggled from his grasp.

The warfare of violet and red light across the space from where she stood caught her eye. Gideon had the archangel pinned against the ground, his demonic red whips extended from both of his fists and curling around to strike at the angel. Her face had twisted into a grimace of anger, the purple light in her eyes intensifying. Lights erupted along her tattoos in a brilliant flash and a rupture of her power threw him off of her in blinding glow. Gideon tumbled to the ground in a roll, but he landed on his feet and faced her just as she threw a surge of energy at him.

Nikka freed herself from Jadriel's grasp, but more bursts of light broke the darkness all around them. Dozens more archangels now appeared, the expanse of lawn and parking lot now a vast battlefield that had them outnumbered.

Gideon dodged the energy thrown at him and moved his whip toward the archangel that had stopped Nikka. It caught her shoulder and that archangel howled, the sound a pealing cry like a Valkyrie. The rush of angels bore down on him, and Gideon turned away from them and sprinted back to where Jadriel and Nikka stood.

The angel grasped her hand and the three of them darted behind the closest outbuilding.

Gideon breathed hard and fast beside her, the red demon-light in his eyes illuminated their dark space.

"How did you find me?" she said, feeling him press back against the shed door.

"All this angel fire power in one place could only mean it was you. Jadriel homed in on it and brought us here."

"Pazuzu," the woman archangel called out to them. A steady violet light now emanated from the other side of the shed. There had to be a hundred angels out there to give off that much light.

Gideon stiffened next to her, his red lights looking at Nikka in the shadow of the outbuilding.

"Bring us the human."

Jadriel's grasp on her hand had never loosened, but the warmth of it heated in her fingers. Gideon twisted to glance around the side of the shed for only a second and then he pressed back against the wall.

"Get her out of here," Gideon whispered, his gaze darting to Jadriel.

"No," she said and pulled her hand away from the angel. "Jason is out there right now. He saved me. We can't let him just stay here to fight them."

The archangel called out to them again. "Bring her to us, or he will die."

Her throat tightened, the words falling like a stone. They had Jason. The executioner had taken him. She knew Jad and Gideon would try to stop her, but she scrambled to her feet anyway and shuffled around the side of the building to face the angels.

So many of them stood on the open ground, pinpoints of violet light staring out of darkened eye sockets looking right at her. The executioner stood in the center of them and Jason was among them as well, his sword in his hand as the executioner circled him. Blood trickled from his forehead and looked black in the purple angel light.

Jadriel's arms wrapped around her, strong and warm as he pulled her back into the shadows. This time he wouldn't allow her to wriggle free, and Gideon welcomed it.

"You need to get her out of here now," Gideon said.

He spoke to the angel as though she wasn't there, ordering him to do with her what he wanted. And she understood what was happening. The angels out there were going to kill Jason, and probably the rest of them, whether or not they had her in their grasp.

The shudders started down her spine and wormed into her chest, pulling the air from her lungs. Everything was so cold despite the warm angel that held her. She had no more energy to fight any of them: angels, Gideon, Jad. If she still had her angel power, she might have been able to do something, but now she was unable to save them. Any of them.

Gideon shifted in the dark again and peered around the corner. Jadriel kept his stance, his arms wrapped like a snake around her. Gideon's red pupils looked back at her through the shadows. Even in the dark, she could read his face and the hopelessness that resided there. Everything in her chest emptied into a black hole, falling through her legs and into the earth. Hot tears filled her eyes, blurring the red eyes that stared at her. A demon's face that gazed at her with pity, for there was nothing he could do.

"Take her away from here, Gideon," Jason's voice shouted out from the field of archangels, a sound tinged with a slight tremble.

The sound of it hurt even more than looking at Gideon. From their shared place in the shadows, she felt the edge of fear in Jason's voice. But there was also the sound of determination, and that scared her even more.

Gideon nodded, those two points of red light moving in the shadows. Jadriel's grip tightened and the warmth coming from his chest rose. She knew what he was trying to do: to transport her away from all of this, somewhere safe from harm and away from what was about to happen.

There had to be something she could do. The angels would let him go if they had her in their grasp. Maybe they would let all of them go and just take her. She knew all too well what they would do to her, but she couldn't just stand here and let this happen to Jason. To all of them.

"No," she cried out and used the last of her strength to break free of his grasp. She almost stumbled as the force of it surprised her, but she caught her footing and lunged around the side of the shed.

She broke into a sprint to the shadows, rounding the edge of the shed as she saw the army of angels that gazed back to the executioner. Those few seconds seemed like minutes, everything appearing slow and deliberate. Something that would never leave her memory. Her legs burned with the effort, each step heavy and painful.

The executioner turned away from the angels, his saber drawn, and he lunged toward Jason. The swiftness of it took Jason off guard and he stumbled as he blocked with his own sword. The force of it drove him to the ground. The executioner came around him again, his saber flashing with angel fire, and the sword falling toward Jason. He blocked it again, but he had no leverage and his own sword fell to the ground.

Nikka ran, every beat of her heart pounding so loud in her ears that she could hear nothing else. She knew that Jadriel would be right behind her, but she had to get to Jason, whatever it took. Before the archangel could get to her.

The executioner took another deliberate step, so slow in Nikka's vision, and the saber in his hand rose again. Her foot struck the soft earth again and again, trying to get to him. The sword, swathed in violet fire, rose above where Jason crouched, blood dripping from his head and each drop like dew hitting the grass. He looked up only once, his brilliant blue eyes catching her gaze as she ran to him.

Jadriel's iron grasp wrapped around her again, stopping her with a jolt and lifting her off her feet. Only a fraction of a second ticked onward as his angel light surrounded her, ready to pull her away to another location and far away from the army of angels. Away from this eventual pain and suffering

But in that time, the executioner's saber fell through the dark, a swath of violet fire. In that brief moment that lasted forever, the sword sliced against Jason's neck and his body collapsed to the grass, his head rolling away into the shadows.

A scream echoed through the night, and only when Jadriel's light abducted her did she realize it was her own scream that deafened her.

Part Ten

And I looked, and behold a pale horse: and his name that sat on him was Death, and Hell followed with him.

Revelations 6:8

CHAPTER 42

NIKKA

The scream left Nikka's throat raw enough that she tasted blood. It made her cough and choke and she couldn't catch her breath. With Jadriel's grip around her chest, pinning her arms to her body, and the whorl of light and rush of air, sickness welled in her stomach.

And then the last thing she saw flooded her thoughts, sucking the last bit of air from her lungs. It couldn't be real. He's not dead; it was only an illusion. It had to be. The Executioner didn't just behead him.

No. She had to go back. She had to find him and get him out of there.

But the tears burning in her eyes made it all too real.

Although she held her eyelids closed, the light and motion around her changed. Something jerked her forward and her body plunged down, like a sudden fall from a roller coaster. The flashing violet light around her dimmed and the air stilled. Solid ground coalesced underneath her and her hands and knees pressed into granular sand. The sudden lack of rushing air made her gasp and she coughed against the spasm in her throat.

The tight clenching in her chest wouldn't let up, though. That same gripping horror that started the moment the Executioner's blade fell through the night.

Despite the movement in her diaphragm, she couldn't catch her breath. Especially not with the sobs that wracked her body, shaking along her spine as she bent over the sand that she had yet to see.

The bitter and pointed odor of ash first seeped into her nose and she finally forced her eyes to open. No more angel light. The vast expanse of desert around her opened into a metallic gray light, like the sky just before a vicious thunderstorm. Daylight surrounded this barren spot of earth, not the black of night where she had just been hiding with Jadriel and Gideon.

A tickle brushed the back of her hand that pressed with clenched fingers into the dull sand. At first, she thought it was a snowflake, small and intricate against the fine hairs on her skin. But as she raised her hand closer to her eyes, she saw that it was a papery wisp of ash. Another lilted down before her eyes, falling to the barren desert in absolute silence.

She sat back on her heels and gazed out to the dark gray skies, to the flakes of ash falling all around her. The dread quiet stilled the sobbing in her throat. The air caught in her lungs and she held her breath.

Nothing stood around her or made a noise. It was only her. No Jadriel. No Gideon. Something had gone wrong. At some point, when Jadriel had tried to take her elsewhere, she had gotten lost. She wasn't sure if she kneeled on the sands of Earth, or if something took her away from the world as she knew it.

The tingle of fear like insects crawled along her back. Her eyes darted over the barren landscape with rolling dark clouds and falling ash. This was no place on earth that she had ever seen before. Maybe, this was no place on earth.

Through the still silence and bleak gray desert, something moved on the horizon. Dark and light at the same time, the form shifted through the ashen desert, growing as it neared where she knelt. Moving closer, the shape of an ornate carriage led by a team of four horses coalesced. But even with the pounding of each hoofbeat in the sand, this oddity in the desert still made no sound, as though nothing in this existence could.

Nikka clenched her fingers into white-knuckle fists and rose to her feet, ready to run at any second. The carriage neared her, the horses a white gray against the odd light from the desert. This was in stark contrast to the black carriage, stylized and ornate like something she had seen in a movie set in the Victorian era. Windows blocked with black velvet curtains. Twisting artwork decorated the four corners of the carriage, and as it neared her, Nikka saw that the curling forms were carved skeletons reaching up to four spires on the roof.

She stepped back from the approaching silent carriage but the sand softened under her feet with each step. The air around her thickened as though it was a fog she couldn't see. The team of horses neared, each of the animals' eyes a milky cataract white that searched the vast desert. The team slowed, coached by some unseen force at the driver's seat. Although the white horses shuffled in the sand, heads bobbing against the bridles and leads, they still made no sound.

Her hands shook against her will, but her feet wouldn't move any more. This force, dark and silent, intended to keep her here. If it wanted to fight, she had no more reserve to defend herself. And she didn't want to anymore. The weakness in her body brought on by the power of the three Harbingers still sucked away her life. And after what she had just witnessed with the angels – and Jason – she had nothing left.

The carriage door swung open, an intricately designed panel in the wall of the carriage also decorated in skulls with silver eyes. Nikka held her breath again, waiting for the thing that would emerge.

At first, a foot stepped out onto the iron pedal below the door. A woman's black high boot with leather laces and a high heel. A lacey black dress flowed down around the boot, falling as the figure stepped out onto the sand. A woman stood there, adorned in a high hat with a black gauzy veil cascading down the wide brim, falling over the narrow black corset and wide skirt. Long, black lace gloves covered her narrow fingers and inched up to her concealed elbows.

The figure stepped forward, each footfall silent in the sand.

Like a wraith.

No. Like Death.

This was the last Harbinger. It had to be.

Nikka tried to step back again but the sand held her in place now as the ash fell around her. The pounding in her chest hurt against the grip of fear and grief that still resided there.

As the figure approached, what had appeared to be black lace trickled away from the woman's arms like blood in water. Maybe smoke. The woman tilted her head to the side, moving the entire headdress with the movement. The black veil shifted, and the tendrils of dark lace rose in thin swirls from her body.

A lace-covered hand reached to the veil and thin fingers pulled it to the side. The woman stopped before her, revealing a face that could have been whole and beautiful if it were not for the flashes of the bleached skull beneath her skin like an optical illusion.

Nikka steeled her muscles, tightening her shoulders and spine, ready to defend herself when the wraith decided to strike. But it simply stood before her, the face gazing forward with empty eye sockets when Nikka looked at her in the right light.

Her dry tongue froze and stuck in her mouth. "Death, right?"

The figure stared at her, the serpentine wisps of lace still rising into the air like smoke. The horses continued to paw at the ground, their ghostly eyes looking across the desert for nothing.

The woman raised her gloved hand, reaching to touch Nikka's cheek. Her throat tightened, and she leaned away, but the sand that held her in place wouldn't let her get far. The lace-covered fingers approached her skin and she clenched her eyes closed.

But the cadaver-cold touch that she had expected never came. Instead, warm fingers touched her cheek, devoid of the scratch of lace.

Nikka opened her eyes and she looked into the face of a woman she hadn't seen for so long. Someone she was sure that she would never see again. The black lace and bleached bones had vanished, leaving somebody else standing there. Familiar brown eyes with that tiny mole that she always had under her left eye. Soft light brown hair cascaded in natural curls to her shoulders. Even the desert light had changed, bringing a soft orange yellow glow of a sunrise into her hair.

And the hand caressed her cheek, just like she had always done since she was a small child.

She would never forget her mother's touch.

"Mom?" Nikka said as tears flooded her vision.

The woman smiled and nodded. "I can be what you need me to be."

Nikka grasped her hand that still touched her cheek. Warm and soft. She even had the light pink nail polish on her manicured nails that she wore the day they sat together in the doctor's office to hear the bad news.

"I don't understand?" She tried to keep her voice from breaking, but it was too late.

"I am Death, and I can be whoever you need to get you through this."

Nikka wanted to let go of her hand. After all, this was only an illusion, but it wasn't enough just to look at her mom's face one more time. But her heart sank a little. How was she supposed to defeat Death when she looked like this?

"Fear not, for you have already bested me," her mother said, tilting her head to the side with a small smile that made the little wrinkles form around her eyes.

Death knew her thoughts already.

"But I've just met you," Nikka said.

"No. You have known me most of your life. And you have already defeated me." Death reached her other hand to cover the back of Nikka's hand that still held onto her. Images flashed in her memory, quick and pointed.

The night that Gideon came to the hospital and took her to the morgue when he injected the glowing substance into her IV and she awoke as a seraph. She was supposed to die that night; Gideon had told her that. An image of her lying on the ground at the army base right after the EMP detonated. She had been dying that night, bleeding into the pavement, when a cherub pulled her into the void. And then she heard the baby cry, and there was so much blood when Adam was born. She had closed her eyes, ready to sleep but it never came. She awoke to more bloodshed, gifted with the powers of an archangel.

The images evaporated, and she looked into the face of her mother again. Her fingers still held onto her hand, not ready to ever let go.

"Thrice have you lived when you should have come with me," she said. "Now, you are worthy to carry the powers of the Harbinger."

Both of her hands moved to Nikka's chest. She knew what was coming. It had already happened three other times, but she knew she would never be able to prepare for it. Pin-points of green light appeared in the pupils of her mother's eyes. A green glow came from under her chin, where Death pressed against Nikka's chest, and the burning sear of the marks etching into her skin made her cringe against the pain. Nikka closed her eyes, holding back the cry that wanted to erupt.

Thankfully it was quick, and the hands moved away from her chest. The power of it ebbed and flowed through her muscles, the fatigue and weakness now vanished and replaced with a power stronger than she had ever felt. Stronger than the seraph or even the archangel. Each breath she took in filled her muscles with strength that buzzed with power. Nikka opened her eyes again and gazed down to the tingling flow of energy in her forearms. Four circular tattoos now decorated her skin, two on each forearm, and they undulated with green light that waited to be released. She smiled and glanced back up to Death, but the air caught in her throat.

Her mother no longer stood before her, but Death had changed again, morphing into someone she needed to see one last time.

The fire of the sunlight behind him made his blonde hair glow like a halo. Jason's brilliant blue eyes looked down at her and he smiled, his goatee framing his jaw and highlighting the dimples in his cheeks. Nikka grasped his hands, solid and warm, as though it was really him.

"This next part is not gonna be easy," he said, speaking in the same way Jason did when he wanted to convince her of something.

Tears trickled down her cheeks as she held onto his hands.

"God has saved you just for this," he spoke, his head turning down so his blue eyes could look deep into her soul. "Nobody else can do what you have to do now. He was the one that gave you the powers of the archangel. The events set in motion when Gideon found you placed you here at this moment to accept this power. Within you lives the power of the Angels of Pestilence, War, Famine, and Death. You are now the Angel of Apocalypse, God's messenger and one who can end this war."

Nikka's shoulders fell, and she shook her head. "I can't do all that—"

"You must, or else this world will fall into carnage and war." He pulled her closer, his hands cupped around her face, and she smelled the familiar scent of his hair, woodsy mixed with a hint of motor oil.

"The Angel of Apocalypse is more powerful than the angels, more powerful than Lucifer. You have the power to change a single decision that has been made, the power to change the future. You are destiny."

A quiver of fear nestled in her chest. "A decision? You mean one that has already been made?"

He nodded. "A choice that has set this future as you know it. You can change it and remove Lucifer's power in an instant."

"How am I to decide which one? Of a hundred – a thousand – choices, how am I to know the right one?"

"You will know what to do when the time is right."

When her head fell, and her shoulders slumped, he pulled her in and wrapped his arms around her. His strong frame belonged to Jason, even though she knew it was Death showing her what she needed to see.

"This next part will be the hardest thing you have ever had to do," he said.

Her arms moved around his torso and held him close for the few moments she knew she had left.

"I don't want to do it anymore."

Jason pulled her back so he could look into her eyes, but she could barely see him through the tears. "Lucifer and the angels must be stopped."

"I know," she said. "I'm so tired. I just want this to end."

"It will, and you will get your rest. Just a little longer." His fingers moved to her hands and held them open to see her new marks. "You must listen, now. This is important: your power will not be full until you partake of the blood of an archangel and Lucifer. When you do this, you will be able to stop them. Remember: all you have to do is change a single choice and you will change the future."

He released her and placed his warm hands on her face. In a quick second, he pulled her in and kissed her. She closed her eyes and grasped his wrists, hoping he would never let go, even though she knew it was a lie. But it was a beautiful lie.

A rush of air swirled around her and the warmth of his touch disappeared. The ground shuddered under her feet and when she opened her eyes, the steel gray desert had vanished. She stood alone on edge of an empty and abandoned neighborhood, the night sky still cast over the edge of Las Vegas, with her new tattoos tingling just under her skin.

CHAPTER 43

NIKKA

---

*T*he ground still quivered under Nikka's feet, or maybe that was still the after-effects of transporting to this abandoned place. A rim of morning light began in the horizon, just barely enough to see the broken pavement where she stood, and enough for someone to see her standing there.

"Nikka?" a voice came from behind a shut door in the house across the street. The door opened with a creak.

Gideon stood there for only a second and then rushed toward her. He didn't wait to speak to her anymore but wrapped his strong arms around her frame that shook under his touch. Of course, she was relieved to see him, but no words would come out of her mouth. Anything that she could say would only make her cry again because he was there when the angels had attacked. It was his idea to have Jadriel take her away from all of it.

And he was right to have done that.

When he pulled her into his chest, she wrapped her arms around his torso and let her head rest on his shoulder.

"I did not know what had happened to you," he whispered as he held her.

"I'm okay."

"It is all right if you are not," he said, his arms still around her.

She pulled back and felt the reluctant give of his embrace. "I found Death."

Even in the faint twilight, she saw the ghost of fear move through his gaze. He glanced down at her forearms, undoubtedly seeing the fourth mark etched with the others.

He grasped her hand. "Come inside." His gaze burned onto her, searching for the trauma that resided inside her soul.

She walked with him into the abandoned house, its windows shattered long ago. The dusty closed-up smell of musty old furniture filled her senses. Jadriel stood in the corner of the living room, watching her as she entered the house. Gideon walked her to the sofa and settled next to her.

"I don't know what happened," Jadriel said and crouched before her, looking at her the same way Gideon did. "I had you one second, and then you were gone."

Nikka didn't want to meet their gazes and feel the pity that hung there. "It wasn't your fault." As she stared into the darkest corner of the room, she told them about the desolate expanse of desert and the arrival of Death. But she would never tell them how Death appeared to her, the illusions it presented. That was only for her. Maybe someday she would tell Gideon, but not now.

"Death said I needed to taste the blood of Lucifer and an archangel, and then I would be able to stop this war." She finally looked up and met Gideon's gaze. "It will be the only way to activate my power."

Furrows formed on Gideon's brow. "That means you will have to get terribly close to Lucifer."

Jadriel stood, towering over her and reached out his forearm toward her. He pulled back the sleeve of his black jacket and pressed his nails to his wrist. A trickle of blood formed around his fingertips.

The sight of it made her stomach turn, but she knew what he was doing.

"The blood of an archangel," he said.

She looked up to his face, which remained emotionless as he held out his arm to her. "I don't think I can."

"It is half of what you need," he said. "And I give it freely."

The blood welling at the site of the nail lacerations on his wrist looked like oil in the dark. Death had told her what she needed to do but faced with the reality of it she now felt the shudder start in her gut. She reached a shaking hand to the thin trickle of blood and touched it, the sticky fluid warm against her skin. She drew it toward her lips and hesitated. With the blood on her fingertip, she closed her eyes, remembering Jason's face as he told her what she needed to do.

She touched her fingertip to her tongue and tasted the blood. To her surprise, it was sweet, and the cringe that had developed in her chest eased. For the first few seconds, the taste dissipated, and she let out the breath that she had held. Then the zap of energy surged through her veins like a live wire coming to life. Her eyes flashed open with a flicker of green light emanating from her pupils. Jadriel stepped back when she gasped at the wave of power pulsing in her veins.

The flow of energy subsided as quickly as it had started and the muscles in her shoulders relaxed again, but it still burned like a furnace deep inside her body. She stood to ease the twitch and ache in her legs, pulling her hand free of Gideon's grasp.

"Are you okay?" Gideon said as he watched her.

There was no way to answer that question. Her senses revved on overload now, with the aftershocks of Harbinger power zapping in her nerves and the ghost memory of seeing Jason lying on the ground with the Executioner hovering over him. She diverted her gaze away from him and held out her hand. "I just . . . just need to lie down or something."

She moved across the living room and into the darkened corridor that moved deeper into the house. Her hand stayed along the wall, feeling for a door or anything to get out of the living room. The wall gave way to crown molding, and her fingers fumbled with a door knob. She turned it, opening to a bedroom with gaping windows that looked to the southern sky. The same closed-up smell greeted her as she stumbled into the room, the tightness of anxiety gripping in her chest again.

Why couldn't she get it out of her head? The same few seconds replaying in terrible detail: Jason on his hands and knees, the flash of the Executioner's sword, and then seeing his head separate from his body. Over and over again until the pain grew sharp in her heart and she fell onto the bed. Her fingers gripped onto the blankets, something to hold onto before she fell into oblivious darkness. Her chest tightened, and the wheeze of air whistled in her throat.

Hands gripped her arms, and her eyes flew open. Gideon turned her to face him and pulled her against his chest. The fingers that had gripped so tight to the blanket now grasped at his shirt. His hand touched the back of her neck, trying to ease the shaking.

"I am here," he whispered to her. "This is a panic attack, and it will pass."

She shook her head. This will never pass. How could she ever get that memory out of her brain?

"I will not leave you."

He moved down with her to the floor beside the bed as she shook in his arms. The thoughts still tormented her, but at least she could hold onto him while the pain ebbed in her chest. Her breath slowed, and she settled against him, but her fingers remained clamped onto his shirt.

If she could have fallen asleep, the feel of his breathing against her might have lulled her. But the hum of the Harbinger power kept her alert like she would never sleep again. She closed her eyes despite the shaking in her arms. They stayed intertwined that way until the sun rose high, leaving the desert hot.

CHAPTER 44

NIKKA

---

*T*he light of a setting sun burned against the skin of Nikka's bare arms, but it left little heat to warm her core. It cast deepening and ever elongating shadows along the cracked pavement and broken houses. From the balcony of the house where she stood, she faced the tall buildings of the Vegas strip, the remaining windows catching the dying sunlight in prisms of gold, a bright contrast to the dark clouds that swirled over the highest points of the city.

She had never been this close to Las Vegas, and she knew the thrum of anxiety that pulsed through her veins wasn't from seeing the casinos up close. The city was dead, in every way possible, inhabited only by demons and the humans they farmed. The buzz that originated from deep inside her bones came from the power that sensed Lucifer within the heart of the city. He waited for her, beckoning her to come to him and take her boy.

And she was about to walk right into that. She had no other choice.

The air behind her shifted, but she didn't have to look back to know it was Gideon. His demon energy preceded him, something that she hadn't been able to sense before. The same was true of Jadriel. Each of them gave off an aura that tingled on her skin and made her new marks spark inside her muscles. One, light and feathery. The other, dark and heavy. Each of them the opposite sides of the same entity.

"Are you ready?" Gideon spoke as he stepped up next to her, gazing out at the darkening city.

"Does it matter?" She looked at him, catching the faintest hint of red light in his pupils. "We are about to go into a literal devil's pit to get our son. I don't think there is any way to prepare for that."

His fingers brushed hers and then grasped her hand. The skin of his palm had become roughened in the last several months while in Belize. "We will do what we have to do."

The lavender angel scent drifted across the balcony, and she sensed an aura of peace settle around her. She glanced back to the doorway where Jadriel rested against the frame. His handsome face caught the last of the sunset. The angel looked at her, anticipating what was coming for all of them.

And this made her chest ache again. The thing she had done to him made her cringe a little inside, and she could no longer keep him prisoner, forced to dive into the sea of demons and risk his life as a slave to her.

"Jad," she said and turned fully toward him. "I can't make you come with us anymore. I'm sorry that I had to do that, to begin with, but I had to keep my friends safe."

He smiled. "If I had to be bound to someone, I am glad it was you."

She bit the inside of her lip just enough to keep tears from coming. This had to be done, even if it meant that they had a new enemy on their hands.

"It's time to release you," she said and stepped forward, but Gideon grasped her forearm and stopped her.

"Are you sure?" he said and stood between them. "Once he is released, he can turn on us."

"I can't make him risk his life for me. He could die in there," she said, pointing back to the heart of the city. "We all could, and I can't force him to do that."

Gideon's grip relaxed. "Do what you must."

He stepped aside, and Nikka faced Jadriel again. The angel stepped away from the door frame and stood tall as she approached him. She splayed her fingers and placed them on his chest, over his shirt that covered the binding sigil. Her eyes focused on her hand, but then Jadriel grasped her wrist and turned his head down to her.

"I had to see what you would do," he said, his grip soft and his face blank. "The binding vanished after you lost your power. I have been free since that time."

Nikka stepped back, and Jadriel released his grasp. For a moment, the flutters of nerves started in her gut, ready to see the archangel reach for his weapons and strike. But he stood there and looked at her. No violet angel light. No swords drawn.

"You have demonstrated what this world needs. Compassion. It is what the other angels do not see when they come here." He stepped toward her and removed his jacket, handing it out to her. "I will fight with you. Now take this; you need to cover your marks. The element of surprise is the only thing you will have when you face Lucifer."

The angel stood there, as still and beautiful as a Grecian statue but deadly as a snake. Anxiety coursed in her nerves as she looked at him. With a shaking hand, she reached for the jacket and grasped it.

He stepped to the balcony edge and gazed out to the city. "There will be a legion of angels at the perimeter. They will not want to you go inside, for they fear your allegiance to Lucifer. And there will be a force of demons at the gates. You must get in there under the guise of allying yourself to him. That is the only way you will be able to find your son. And then, you must face Lucifer and unleash your power."

"A Trojan horse," she said and followed his gaze.

"Exactly," Gideon muttered. "Only this will be far grander."

She took in a deep breath, hoping to settle the flutters that had now moved to her chest. "Okay. Let's do this."

But do what? She still had no idea how she was supposed to defeat Lucifer. Death said she could change a single choice and affect the future. But how could she pick the right one out of a lifetime of decisions?

CHAPTER 45

GIDEON

ightfall had settled over the remains of the city, and Gideon led the way across the sun-scorched and broken bones of Las Vegas. They ran in silence down a street littered with dead cars coated in layers of dust and sand. His eyes darted into the shadows around buildings, just waiting for an ambush of angels at any moment.

Nikka ran at his side, her breath light with her quick pace, a significant change in her energy since before she had met Death. Prior to her meeting, there was no way she could have made it this far. Her eyes caught the ruins of a fallen sign at the end of The Strip, once made famous in movies and TV, but now it lay broken and spray-painted to read Welcome to Hell.

Jadriel paced in front of him but stopped near the end of an abandoned tour bus left in the middle of the street. Gideon's muscles tightened, and the bristling power of the demon inside him rose to the surface. His pupils flashed a deep coal-red and glanced into the shadows of the casinos that surrounded them. The angel stood still, his eyes focusing on the dark.

"What do you see?" Gideon spoke, feeling Nikka close behind him, her breath held in silence.

He turned his head to the east, and violet light flashed under his feet. The ground heaved, a split forming across the street. The bus tilted and creaked with the violent shaking. Jadriel fell back as another flash of light burst through the crack in the earth. The lights appeared all around them now, each rupture of light bringing an angel onto the street.

Gideon grasped Nikka's hand. "Run," he called out to her, and she never hesitated. He sprinted around the bus as Jadriel scrambled to his feet. The angel pulled the rounded sabers from behind his back, and the violet fire ignited along his blades. Just as they ran behind the bus, Jadriel faced the army of angels that charged at him.

"We can't leave him," she said, her breath quick as she ran with Gideon.

"He will be fine, but we need to keep going." He ran along the side walk, the flashes of light behind them like lightning.

The shadows darkened along the alley ways as they ran, the looming skyscrapers of the old casinos looming over them, and only one of them lit with fire in the windows. It towered at the end of The Strip, still an obstacle course away.

A quick burst of light almost blinded him, the force of it striking him in the chest like a semi-truck. He fell back hard, his hand losing his grip on Nikka. He hit the pavement, knocking the breath from his lungs just in time for him to see the face of Zumiel.

The angel turned to Nikka and wrapped her fingers around her neck before Nikka could run. The violet light glowed in her pupils, two pin points of angel light in otherwise dark eyes.

"I will not let you destroy this," the archangel growled, slamming Nikka back down to the pavement. The ground shuddered with the impact of it, sending cracks ripping through the cement. "This world is ours."

Gideon's head cleared and the ache in his ribs ebbed into a dull pain enough for him to pull himself to his feet. The demon residing in him stirred in a sudden and violent pull down his arms. The fire whips burned into long lashes down from his wrists. He planted his feet and struck both whips out toward the angel, but Zumiel's glance shot up toward him just before they landed. Her free hand reached out, allowing the whips to tangle around her wrist and then she grabbed them in a spark of angel light and devil fire. She yanked at them, pulling him off balance toward her.

But he stopped his forward momentum with a single step down. The fire whips went taught, to the angel's surprise. Gideon pulled her off Nikka as soon as the whips tightened. Zumiel fell to the ground in a harpy squeal of anger.

His glance moved to Nikka, who now scrambled to her feet from the crater in the pavement. "Keep going," he shouted, feeling the angel free herself from his whips.

Nikka bolted down the side walk, with only a single glance back to him.

Zumiel sprang to her feet again and dodged at him in a rush of brilliant light, tackling him to the ground. A burst of energy rose in her arms when he fell back, and he braced an equally powerful shield against her attack. When her energy hit him, the ricochet of it forced her back. This disoriented her enough for him strike at her again. She fell back, her weight lighting off him enough for him to scramble to his feet.

She wheeled around again, a ball of violet energy forming in her palm. She reeled back to toss at him when another flash of light threw her off balance.

Jadriel appeared between them, brilliant fire coursing along his half-moon swords. He landed in a crouch and faced her just as Zumiel released the energy. His swords crossed before him and blocked the power in a shower of purple sparks. She screamed into the night, the violet light in her eyes intensifying. Jadriel lunged toward her with swords slicing through the air. The blades caught her neck, beheading her and strangling the sound in her throat

Gideon pulled his whips back, and they disappeared into his hands as Jadriel turned back to face him. The angel nodded and broke into a run with Gideon, bolting into the dark and down the side walk where Nikka had disappeared.

CHAPTER 46
NIKKA

ikka ran down the empty street, the flashes of light and the cry of the angel behind her. Staying there would only have put her in the way of the angel, and Gideon was the only one who could face her. It wouldn't help if the angel discovered that she was a full Harbinger now. So, she had no choice but to keep running.

But then the lights stopped flashing behind her, and the city went silent. Nikka held her breath and turned around. Maybe Gideon would be back there. Or Jadriel.

The city remained quiet and dark, though. No angels coming for her. And that was the most suspicious thing of all.

Through the jacket that covered her arms, the cold air seeped through the leather and settled against her skin. It was a chill that she had felt dozens of times, and it only meant one thing.

"Ring around the rosie," a voice echoed into the dark, feminine and ghastly. "A pocket full of poseys."

Chills sprinkled goosebumps over her arms. Nikka turned toward the sound of the voice. A figure moved through the darkened alley, the faint starlight sparkling like two reflective mirrors in the demon's eyes. It tottered toward her, a teenaged girl in a thin and flimsy white dress. But she was not what she seemed. The girl was only a shell that contained the rotting drone inside of her. Its head twitched to the side, and she smiled as she came out of the deepest shadows.

"Ashes, ashes," she spoke as black fluid dripped from the corners of her mouth. "We all fall down."

When she was a seraph, Nikka could have dispatched this creature with a quick swipe of her sword or an exorcism, but she no longer had the power to do that. She wasn't even sure what power she had at this moment or if the demon would even respond. But she felt the chill and smelled the brimstone emanating from this beast.

"Little Bo Peep has come to the place where angels fear to tread," the drone said with a girlish giggle.

It stepped closer to her and reached her pale, wooden fingers toward her. Nikka swallowed the frozen lump that had formed in her throat. "Take me to Belphagor."

The drone stopped and smiled wide, her fingers twitching where they hung. "And why should I?"

"Because he has been waiting for me," Nikka said.

The demon's twitching stopped, and her eyes squinted as if really seeing her for the first time. Then it reeled back with a gasp. "You are the mother of Adam. The creation of Samael, the Fallen."

Footsteps sounded behind her, and she didn't have to turn to sense Jadriel and Gideon appear from the shadows. The drone's black eyes glanced to the others and skittered backwards a few steps.

"Pazuzu," she hissed, the twitching starting up again in her head. She turned back toward Nikka. "And why should I take you to him?"

Nikka's throat had gone dry. This was her only shot to get past the gates. "Lucifer has sent for me, and you don't want to disappoint him. Not with the archangels at your doorstep."

The drone froze, her eyes glancing back to the shadows behind them. The violet light started up again in rapid bursts all around the city. They knew that Nikka and Gideon were there, and it would only be seconds before the angel army would fall down on them.

"They're coming," Nikka said, watching the drone squirm at each flash of light. "What's it gonna be?"

The drone's black eyes darted back to Nikka, her cracked lips peeling back from yellowed teeth. "Follow me."

In a blur of motion, the demon darted back into the shadows. Nikka glanced at Gideon, his eyes still red with demon energy. Gideon and Jadriel moved with her, plunging into darkness with only the faintest hint of a figure in a white dress that ran ahead of them.

The demon darted right, turning around the end of the alley and then plunged down a stairwell at the back of a towering casino. Everything here was so dark that only the smell of the drone before her told her the path to follow. The creature shoved through a heavy metal door, and they emerged into a blackened tunnel. The white of the demon's gown faded into the darkness, lit only by the faint moonlight that fell through the open stairwell door. Thick, closed air filled her lungs as they plunged down the stairs, Gideon close behind her. But the door stayed open, allowing in the slightest of fresh air. Only one set of footsteps sounded behind her, and the pull of anxiety tugged at her chest.

Nikka stopped, and Gideon almost ran into her when she turned around to glance back to the stairwell door.

Jadriel's form stood at the door, unmoving and dark with the light behind him.

"Jad," she called to him, hearing the footsteps of the demon continue into the dark of the tunnel. "Come on."

His silence unnerved her as she waited for him, but the angel didn't move. "I cannot go down there."

"Don't be foolish," she said. "You can't stay out there."

Flashes of violet light exploded around the city, casting bursts of light behind his silhouette. "This is where I must leave you, Nikka."

"Jad—" She tried to step past Gideon, but he stopped her. "Don't do this. Just come with us."

"I am not welcome down there," he said.

"You will die out here." She tried to force herself past Gideon, but his grip remained firm on her shoulder.

"He cannot come further. Angels are unable to remain in the presence of Lucifer, not without the power of an angel army with him," Gideon said, his voice almost a whisper.

The sound of that name caused the shivers to bloom on her arms again. Everything that she needed to do now, it would all end with her facing the Devil himself. And now she would have to do it without one of her strongest allies.

"I am sorry, Nikka," Jadriel said as the flashes of light intensified. "But I will guard the door."

"Thank you," she said and swallowed back the lump that had formed in her throat. The archangel nodded his head, and his pupils lit into pinpoints of violet light.

Gideon's grip loosened as Nikka stepped down again and turned away from the angel. The door behind them closed with a heavy click, plunging them into a dark tunnel. Nikka quickened her step, following the scampering sounds of the demon that had run far ahead of them.

A deep red glow emanated from beside her. Gideon strode at her side now, his eyes a fire red and the whips forming in his fists that lit the tunnel ahead of them in a strobe of firelight. The muscles along his arms had grown taught, the light dancing over his form like a dread god. Hopefully, it was enough to distract whatever might be down here from attacking. Trusting the drone that moved ahead of them made her nervous enough.

And then there was the fact that the air had grown significantly colder the further they ran.

Her attention had been distracted enough that she hadn't seen the shift in the shadows. A burst of red light erupted from the darkness and zipped past her shoulder to strike Gideon square in the chest. He fell back, his fire whips dancing into the dark. Before she could run, a cold shadow rushed at her, its icy hand around her neck. It lifted her off her feet and thrust her against the concrete wall of the tunnel. The chill froze against her skin, but its grip took her breath away as it held her fast. Then its eyes opened into two red orbs, lighting their small area of the tunnel.

"You are awfully brave, just the two of you coming here," Belphagor said, his lips gaping in a wicked smile. Red wisps of hair fell over his right eye as he held her above his head.

The shadows around them moved and then hundreds of red, orange and black eyes opened to surround them, demons of all legions filling the corridor, arms dragging Gideon to his feet and pinning him against the wall. The icy grip on her neck tightened and Belphagor pulled her away from the wall, throwing her to the ground.

The impact against the ground took the air from her lungs once again, and she gasped.

Belphagor stepped toward her, straddling over her as he gazed down at her with all his power. "But I knew if I waited long enough, you would come to us."

Nikka coughed, trying to catch her breath. The demon crouched down, and his cold hand touched her cheek, forcing her to look at him.

"Is this finally checkmate?" he whispered to her. "Have you come to submit yourself to Him?"

The spasm in her throat finally abated. "We've come for our son."

Belphagor glanced up to Gideon, who glared at him with reddened pupils. "I see. Well, in order to even see him, you must be audience to Lucifer." He turned his gaze back down to Nikka. "Do you agree to this?"

A deal with a devil. But there was no other way. "Yes."

The demon's grin slipped, and he leaned down to her, his eyes only inches from her as though he scanned her thoughts. He craned his neck and leaned in toward her shoulder. The chill drifted from his skin and threaded against her neck as he moved to the other side.

"You've changed," he whispered, his eyes looking at every inch of her shoulder. "I know something has changed about you, even more so than the last time we met. What have you done?"

This made her heart almost stop. He couldn't know that she was a Harbinger. The demon had come close to sensing it in her when he had her in his grasp in the desert. She hadn't shown her tattoos, and she kept any sign of her power hidden. How could he possibly know her secret?

The demon pulled back to look into her eyes again. "Time with archangels has done something to you." Deep furrows formed on his forehead.

His long fingers moved along her neck and danced across her collarbone, a simple gesture, but she knew that he scanned for the slightest information in the form of her bones. She held her breath and clenched her fists, ready to fight him off the moment he became aware of her secret.

The darkness behind them ruptured into a burst of white and violet light. Brick and cement fell in the thunderous chunks as the tunnel collapsed and creatures of light flowed into the shadowy space. Cherubim clawed over the mounds of brick, their white skin glowing with ethereal bright light. Their manes flowed back from gaping mouths of bone-white teeth, deep howls surging from their throats and causing the walls of the tunnel to quake. Archangels appeared in flashes of violet light, hundreds filling the corridor and chasing away the darkness.

Belphagor growled, grabbing Nikka and lifting her to her feet. The horde of demons charged toward the gap in the tunnel filled with their enemies, leaving Gideon against the wall.

The demon grasped her wrist. "Come with me," he hissed at her and pulled her deeper into the tunnel, with Gideon following closely.

The battle raged behind them as they ran into the dark, the light of the angels fading the further they ran.

Belphagor's cold hand released her as they plunged down the corridor and then he slowed. The darkness chilled, as frozen as the deepest part of winter. Her breath rushed in white puffs from her lips. The cold seeped through her clothes and brushed against her skin. She had felt this freeze only once before when she had been held in the abandoned power plant to face the thing that moved in the dark. The thing that had wanted her baby even then.

The demon slowed his pace to his usual rock star swagger until he stopped. As Nikka approached him, Gideon's hand slipped into hers. She glanced at him, his eyes still red and focused forward, but his face had hardened. His gaze trained on the space in the tunnel before them.

Nikka and Gideon stepped beside the demon, who now faced a shimmering curtain of liquid darkness before them, like a sheet of glittering black water that lay in a vertical plane and obscuring the tunnel. This was the source of the extreme cold, dead and black and empty of anything worldly. The great power that now thrummed in her bones didn't come from inside of her, but from the dreadful thing that lived beyond this gate.

"You will have to go in there if you want to see your son," Belphagor said. He ticked his head to the tunnel behind them, to the battle that still raged back there. "The archangels won't be able to save you in there, not where He dwells."

"I don't want them to save me," she muttered, staring at the undulating surface of the gate.

Belphagor smiled. "That's a good starting place because you will never make it out of there unchanged. You will belong to him before the day is through."

Gideon's hand tightened in hers. She wasn't sure at first, but she could swear that she felt him trembling in her grasp.

The demon stepped up to the gate and opened his arm out toward the surface. "After you," he said with a wide grin.

Nikka held her breath. Of course, she knew that this would be a one-way ticket. After everything Death had told her, that was the only conclusion. But she still had no idea how she was supposed to defeat the Devil, how she would draw his blood and then change a single choice that would alter the course of history and the future. The only thing she knew was that she had to face him to do it, and this was the only way.

CHAPTER 47

NIKKA

Nikka stepped through the gate, Gideon's hand still in hers. The liquid surface of it smoothed over her flesh just like the undulating surface of a polar lake. She gasped at the chill of it as she emerged on the other side, the air so cold that it burned in her lungs with every rapid breath. The sound of angels and demons battling silenced the moment she crossed the threshold, plunged into absolute stillness.

Belphagor walked ahead of them, down the corridor that opened into a wide chamber and a stairway ascending into the base of what had once been Las Vegas' biggest casino. Two great doors gaped open, and they emerged into a vast atrium. But there were no flashing neon signs and the glitz of the former hotel. Now, the walls crawled with slithering black creatures with oily dark eyes that watched them. She had seen these things before, the same monsters that had infected the monastery after Abaddon had breached the threshold and had come to face her. They must have followed in the path of the darkest evils, and this was home to the worst of them. And just like they had back then, the creatures urged them forward. There would be no going back now.

She tried to slow her racing heart, but that was futile as they followed Belphagor deeper into the Devil's lair. Gideon remained silent at her side, but his grip in her hand reassured her that she was not alone. Belphagor led them through the dim chambers and into a vast auditorium that had once hosted musicians and performers in the active days of Las Vegas. The black monsters had even infected this place, slithering over the rows of seating. Most of the front rows had been removed, opening wide to the stage where the only light illuminated in this entire place. Spot lights glowed with harsh intensity onto a platform raised in the center of the stage.

The shoddy platform appeared uneven and crude at first, but as Nikka neared it, she realized that it was irregular for a reason. The boards weren't wood but formed of human bones linked end to end, with joints tied by knots of hair. The center of the platform rose into a gruesome throne, the back peaked with skulls that stared with hollow eyes into the empty auditorium.

Air caught in her throat, and her feet stopped the moment she knew what she saw up there. Gideon glanced back to her, his pupils still burning red but the furrows of concern now deep in his forehead.

"We must keep going," he whispered to her. "For Adam."

The trembling in her hand might have been caused by her, but it could have been Gideon too. She tightened her fingers in his grip and forced her legs to move again.

"My Lord," Belphagor called out to the emptiness of the auditorium, his voice echoed against the crumbling facades and up to the balconies. "We request an audience."

The demon continued to swagger forward, as though his words only a formality and he had no intention of not meeting with the thing that lingered somewhere in this place. Nikka knew that Lucifer was here, dwelling in the deepest shadows that hung behind the stage or among the slithering creatures in the seating. Although unseen, his eyes burned on her and his fingers played at her in the chill of the room.

Belphagor moved up the stairs ascending along the side of the stage, taking them two at a time like an eager child waiting to show his parent what he had brought home. The demon flashed a glance and a broad smile back to them, and he moved along the stage and to the grisly platform, leaning against it and waiting for what would come next.

Invisible but powerful, it swam through the dark corners of the rafters, jumping in and out of the shadows along the facades as though it had always been here in one form or another. Nothing gave it away, but she felt it move, lithe and black and wicked. The tightness in Gideon's grip told her that he could feel it too.

Of course, he knew it was here. This was the thing that he had run from thousands of years ago, trying to escape from Hell. And he had been successful until he met her and then his world began to crumble. That thing in the shadows had taken him back into the pit and turned him into a puppet. Lucifer had tormented him into doing the things he did, but she had saved him. She finally had given him redemption, and the symbol of it still lingered on his chest after she had touched him. He was no longer subject to the Devil, even if the demon inside him still lusted after the power.

The chill wasn't the only thing that raised the little hairs on her arms. The evil that now lurked in the dark behind the stage, looking at both of them, left an electric charge in the air that buzzed deep into her bones. The light that shone over the stage and the platform dimmed, taking on a ghostly yellow hue that flickered as it tried to fight the draw of power flowing out of it.

A heavy boot fall struck the wooden planks of the stage. Then another. The shadows coalesced, swirling in a fog of shimmering dust in the faint yellow light until a form stepped out of the dark. At first, it was only a silhouette, tall but with few distinctions. But the black fog thickened, and its legs took shape, then the torso and the shoulders. The man that stepped from the shadows appeared as any other, and Nikka wouldn't have thought anything by just looking at him.

But she would have known something was different. Evil. Maybe it was the look in his eyes, with dark lashes over lids that closed half-way across his eyes. Not to keep the light out, but to gaze into the souls of others. A simple tie held back his long black hair, but this just accentuated the black eyebrows and black goatee that framed his handsome face. Yes, she would have suspected he was evil if she had just come across him, but there was something strangely alluring about him, and that's what worried her the most. Even in this dead world filled with the scraps of humanity, he stepped out onto the stage in a tailored black suite and white silk shirt and pocket square.

The moment his form took shape in the light, his dark brown eyes fell on her from under those half-closed lids. Like a wolf, he searched for her weakness, and she prayed that he couldn't sense her new power. This was Lucifer, in the flesh. The creature she was supposed to defeat, and what had Death called her? Angel of Apocalypse? What would that even mean to a creature like this?

"Welcome, Nikka," he spoke, his voice booming across the emptiness of the auditorium. The sound made her shudder. "I have been expecting you."

Lucifer stepped across the stage, his shoulders broad and his spine straight as a half-smile formed on his face. He ascended the ramp of bone and hair to the throne, making him look even taller than he was before as he towered over them and gazed down to where she stood.

"And my prodigal child has returned." His eyes shifted toward Gideon.

His hand trembled in hers. Nikka glanced at Gideon, who had averted his gaze away from her and from Lucifer. The tendons in his neck bulged and his chest rose and fell in rapid succession.

Lucifer settled down on the throne with his hands spread out over the arms of the chair made of long femurs and ribs. His legs crossed as his foot tapped a deaf rhythm, his glossy black leather shoes catching the yellow light that shone down on him.

"Nothing?" he said, his eyebrow raised. "Pazuzu has nothing to say for his absence?"

Gideon waited in stony silence, and Nikka now understood the gravity of him coming down here with her. He risked everything to be at her side.

She swallowed against a dry throat and released his hand. With weak knees, she forced her feet to step forward.

"I've come for my son," she said, trying to keep her voice from shaking.

Lucifer's eyes shifted back to her. That's what she had hoped for. Anything to keep him distracted from Gideon.

"Of course, you have." He smiled at her again, those eyes searching her soul. "A mother without her child. A father," he said, and his glance drifted back to Gideon "without his family. It is painful when a child is lost."

"Please," she said, but this time the quiver sounded in her voice.

Lucifer's smile widened, and he turned his gaze down to his suit jacket, as though he inspected it for cleanliness. "And let me guess: you would do anything to have him back."

She had a hard time catching her breath with the chill that pulsed over her. "What do you want from me?"

"I'm so glad you asked." He lost the smile that had been painted over his face, and those dark eyes flashed up to her. His legs uncrossed, and he leaned forward, his elbows resting on his knees. "That child is a special one, but I don't have to tell you that, do I?" His voice rose, and the timber of it shook the foundation of the theater. "He is kindred, a child of all worlds. Born of seraph and demon, Pazuzu, a Prince of Hell."

The angry fluttering of moths in her gut made her dizzy, or maybe it was the evil that flowed from him. So much wickedness concentrated in one place, a power unlike she had ever felt.

"Adam will be the ruler of this world when we have defeated the angels," he said, the smile appearing again.

Nikka cleared her throat, hoping that would be enough to catch her breath. "You're evading the question."

"You are a smart one. I see where he gets it from," he said and stood, his form towering above the stage again. "What I desire, over all else, is that when we rule this world, I wish to have you with us. At my side. An archangel with me in the final battle of Armageddon. The most powerful angel of man, beside the Bringer of Light, the son of the Morning Star."

His dark brown eyes flashed into a brilliant light, a mix of red, orange and violet that chased away any shadows that still lingered in the auditorium. Nikka shielded her eyes with her hand, unsure that the light only came from his eyes. It bled from everywhere on the platform, pouring out of Lucifer and burning against her skin. The cold chill that had been there now vanished, replaced by the heat of his light.

In all of this, she had forgotten that he was also an archangel, the most powerful save only God. And he was as awful and unfeeling as the archangels that battled just outside the walls of the casino. They all came from the same origin, before the great war that created the rift between them. And mankind had been stuck in the middle of it all.

The light dimmed until only the last flickers of it remained in his eyes, but he still looked at her, awaiting her answer.

She knew that this was his goal all along. Taking Adam was the easiest way to bring her right to him, and it worked. Looking at the course of the last couple of years, it had always pointed in this way. The angel Samael had set it in motion and Lucifer took advantage, knowing that it would end just like this.

And she still had no idea how to stop the inevitable from happening. There was no way out of here. Not on their own. Belphagor had warned them of that.

She clenched her fists. There has to be something. "I want my son."

"Come," he said and raised his hands, his fingers waving both of them to the stage. "You will see him."

Belphagor moved away from the platform, descended the steps into the auditorium and approached Nikka. She stepped forward, mostly hoping to avoid the touch of the demon that neared her. Gideon moved with her and grasped at her hand again. Although they stepped closer to the Devil, his hand in hers gave her legs strength to keep moving.

The chill had returned to the air, like a frost that drifted from the platform. Nikka moved up the steps and to the stage. Belphagor glided around her, his neck craning to look at her, examining every inch of her face with such curiosity, while he smiled as though he awaited something grand.

"Bring Adam to me," Lucifer called out to the shadows behind him.

Nikka held her breath when she heard footsteps coming from the curtains behind the stage. Three figures emerged from the darkness. Two men flanked another on both sides. The men on the outside were obvious drones, black oily eyes and cracked peeling skin. But the person in the center held none of these characteristics.

She first thought he looked young, but as he entered the light, he appeared to be about her same age. His hair caught the light in golden curls that seemed to glow like a halo. Dressed in a white T-shirt and white pants, his skin hinted of darker tones, she could have mistaken him for an angel. His hazel eyes looked out at her with recognition.

"Come, boy," Lucifer spoke as he turned to them.

The drones stepped aside and allowed the young man to approach the platform. The man's eyes turned to Lucifer, innocent and curious as he looked upon him.

"Adam, these are your parents," Lucifer said with a nod to them.

CHAPTER 48
NIKKA

The spasm started in Nikka's throat, and she thought she would choke. This young man, no older than her, he couldn't possibly be Adam.

Gideon released her hand and stepped forward. The red light burning in his eyes frightened her. "What have you done to him?" he growled.

Lucifer glanced at Gideon, the smile slipping from his lips. Those dark lids closed half-way again as he glared. "The child had too much ability that needed to be gilded to keep him as an infant. There was no need."

The flutters moved to Nikka's chest, and her knees shook. Staring at him, at the man who was supposed to be her son, made her want to collapse. Her child was gone forever.

"Adam, boy," Lucifer said as he leaned toward him. "This is your mother."

The man's beautiful, bright eyes turned to her, and a faint smile appeared on his lips. He stepped, at first hesitant with his fingers wringing before him. But his gaze didn't falter. The cold never preceded him, and she couldn't smell the brimstone on his skin like with most of the demons. The spotlight still caught his hair in angel light as he neared her.

Gideon watched him approach her, his shoulders tensed and his fists clenched, but he stood his ground.

Adam's eyes searched her face, his gaze clear and innocent. Trembling fingers reached out to touch her cheek, but the flutters intensified as they rose into her throat. She grasped his hand to stop him, but his flesh was warm and smooth. Nothing like the hard and cold touch of the demons that surrounded them.

Just like the baby she had held in her arms only weeks ago.

"Mother?" he said, his voice cracking.

His hand quaked in her grasp. This man, who appeared so different than she had expected, was as human as she was. Or used to be, anyway. His eyes watched her as his eyebrows knit together in wonder.

She released his hand, and his fingers lighted onto her cheek. "I remember you," he said.

Warmth flooded from his fingertips, flowing into the flesh of her cheek and pulsing into her mind. Flashes of memories blinded her to this moment, and she knew that his touch triggered them, but they weren't her memories.

She saw herself through small eyes, her face smiling down at him and singing with the soft crash of waves behind her. Sunlight poured through her pale blonde hair while small fingers grasped at her strands. A breeze played against the palm trees, soft and sprinkled with the faintest hint of salt spray.

He remembered her, and he carried that memory even into this form despite what Lucifer had done to him.

And not only did she see his memories, his touch kindled that draw she had for him. The same pull that brought her from the deserts of Central America to find him.

She opened her eyes, and her fingers met his, tears filling her eyes. He smiled at her, his fingers still against her cheek and warm. "I know you, mother."

With those memories came a flood of emotions that soaked into her skin from his hand. Love. Wonder. Curiosity. Everything that he felt at that moment warmed through her blood with every beat of her heart.

He withdrew his hand, but she still grasped his fingers as the images and feelings dissipated. His eyes remained wide, and he smiled at her through her tears.

Adam turned those beautiful eyes toward Gideon, who gazed at him below a furrowed brow.

"This is Pazuzu," Lucifer spoke.

The Devil's voice did little to break the calm that had settled in Nikka's chest as she watched him turn toward Gideon. The warmth of this touch still lingered on her cheek, and she couldn't turn her eyes away from him. He had become so beautiful, and she still loved him like the first day she saw him.

Adam reached his hand toward Gideon's cheek as well, but he flinched back from him. If he could only see what Adam saw, Nikka knew he would understand. He didn't need to fear him.

"You are my father?" Adam asked, advancing toward him.

"Gideon," Nikka spoke. "It's okay. It's really him."

But Gideon didn't look at her, his gaze focused on the young man before him, the one who carried the color of his own eyes and skin. Adam's fingers brushed against Gideon's cheek, and he froze, the muscles in his shoulders tight.

"Yes," Gideon whispered, his breath quickening.

Adam tilted his head, his fingers still placed against Gideon's cheek, and he turned back to glance at Lucifer.

The blooms of warmth that she had felt on her cheek vanished in that moment of a single glance. Her eyes followed Adam's as he looked back to the creature on the throne of bones. Lucifer grinned, his eyes widening only a little, and he nodded. Adam turned back in all his angelic beauty and faced Gideon.

"I have a new father now," he whispered. "I no longer need you."

The next few seconds ticked by so slowly. Nikka's knees weakened when she heard him speak. The unspoken glance between Adam and Lucifer told her everything that she knew to be true, and what would happen next.

The rhythm of her heart faltered in that glance. Before she could move, Belphagor's iron grip wrapped around her in anticipation, and all she could do was flail against him. When it happened, she screamed, but it only sounded muffled in her ears, the pain of it stuck in her throat.

Adam's face remained calm and beautiful, without emotion, when he faced Gideon. In those slow seconds, his fist reeled back and then plunged into Gideon's chest with terrifying ease. The young man stood firm, his stone fingers gripping his father's demon heart while he stared him down with those beautiful and calm hazel eyes.

Gideon gasped, a sound that never struck Nikka's ears beyond her scream. His hands grasped at Adam's wrist, unable to take purchase as his eyes widened. Adam held fast despite Gideon's futile struggle. The gaping wound in Gideon's chest shuddered, the edges flickering into blackened flakes rimmed with the red of hot coals. The black spread across his chest in a rapid growth of ash and cinder. His fingers spasmed against Adam's wrist again before the ash expanded, consuming his body. Gideon's head flailed back in a silent scream just before the threads of coal and fire engulfed the whole of his body. And within only a few seconds, the ashen body collapsed in a heap of swirling gray dust, just as the hundreds of demons had done when she had dispatched them as the seraph.

The only sound left was Belphagor's laugh as he held her. Even the scream that she still forced from her throat wasn't enough to make her ears hear.

Hot tears flooded her eyes, making the dim light and shape of the figures around her swirl into dizzying shape. It was either the tears, or she was about to faint. The firm grip around her torso loosened and her legs wouldn't hold her upright any longer. She collapsed to the hard wood floor of the stage, her body wracked with despair as she cried. The smell of the ash filled her nose, making her want to gag. With her head pressed against the ground, her fingers trembled and reached out to the warm ash that coated the floor around her. The only thing that remained of Gideon.

Alone. Gideon was gone. Just vanished in a heap of ash that still swirled around her head. Maybe it was the coal-smell of it, but she couldn't catch her breath. Or perhaps it was the vast emptiness that now grew in her chest with each breath. And her ears still couldn't hear anything but her cries.

Her fingers grasped a handful of ash and clenched tight until her nails dug into her palm. She raised her head, but the tears flooded her vision, and all she saw was gray and black and the cold still pressed against her skin.

Everything was gone. Gideon had stayed with her to the last, and now she knew that he had planned to die in here. There was no getting out. He had been with her at the beginning, and now he left her at the end. Lucifer had taken everything from her now, and she still had no way of stopping him.

With the ash in her hand and the blood that trickled from her nail lacerations, her vision cleared. The thought came lightning fast, just a single memory. Gideon had been with her in the beginning . . .

"Mother," Adam's voice echoed in the theater.

Her hearing sharpened, more pronounced than ever.

The voice of Death whispered in her memory, and she remembered the ash falling all around her when she had been stuck in that vast desert with the Harbinger: the events set in motion when Gideon found you placed you here at this moment.

It all became painfully clear now.

"Come with me, mother," Adam spoke, his hand settling on her shoulder. "Join my new father and me."

The trembling stopped in her arms and legs as she opened her hand and watched the wells of blood form on her palm.

You will know what to do when the time is right.

And Death was correct. The course had been set long ago, and she needed to alter a single choice, one that would change the course of the future. And she needed Lucifer's blood to charge her new power.

Nikka closed her eyes, blocking out the carnage and light and death around her. Her heart beat slowed, and only her whisper echoed in her head. "Yea, though I walk through the valley of the shadow of death, I will fear no evil," she muttered to herself, the words steeling the muscles in her legs and arms.

She pushed herself up and opened her eyes. The buzz of her power now sparked to life inside her gut, setting off a series of flares along her nerves like a fuse. Adam stood before her, his face still framed in light from the spotlights above them. His hand grasped hers, and he pulled her close, placing a warm kiss on her forehead, just as a loving son would do. Despite the warmth of his lips, her spine went rigid. When he pulled away from her, his eyes met hers.

The tears still felt wet and hot on her cheeks, but she could see him more clearly now. A beautiful lie sent to destroy everything. Starting with his father.

"We will be a family forever now," he said, the calm lilt of his voice now hollow.

He turned and stepped toward the platform, pulling her with him. Her limbs felt like wood, but she forced each step forward. Lucifer gazed down at her and stepped down the ramp of bones to meet her. Belphagor stepped with them, keeping at her side. She didn't have to see his face to know that he smiled with self-satisfied malice.

Adam stopped and sidled beside Lucifer, an obedient child and released her hand into Lucifer's icy cold grip. His penetrating gaze burned down on her now, but that evil couldn't stop the electrical hum from the marks along her arms still concealed by Jadriel's jacket.

It was almost time, and she knew what she had to do.

"We will be gods, and we will create our own world on this Earth. We will purge the angels from this realm. Together," Lucifer spoke.

"Together," Adam echoed him. "All of us."

She wasn't sure if it was anger or the Harbinger power building and writhing on itself, but her heart burned in her chest. Nikka lifted her eyes, forcing herself to look at him.

"Together," she said, the word like poison on her tongue, the same word spoken by the man who was once an innocent child. Now, he stood with the Devil, his hand still covered in the ash of his patricide.

"A promise," Lucifer said with a smile. "Sealed with a kiss."

He leaned in toward her, his massive and dark form nearly consuming her where she stood. She held her breath and tried not to lean away from him. This was the only way.

His lips touched hers. The cold frost of his kiss turned into something dreadful and wicked, the taste of death and hatred filling her mouth. She froze when his hands moved to her face. Ribbons of cold evil flooded from his grasp and his kiss, trying to steal away every last bit of humanity that she had left. It searched for the vestiges of seraph and angel that might still lay hidden within her. That single kiss had enough power to consume the last of her soul.

But she had one mission, and she couldn't fail.

His grasp held her against him tight enough that she could do one last thing and he wouldn't be able to react fast enough. And that's when she bit him.

He flinched a fraction of a second later, and he reacted faster than she had expected. His hands pushed her away and shoved her to the ground, back to the pile of ash still in a heap on the stage. She gasped, catching her breath again. The thrum of her power ebbed stronger, chasing away any remnants of the darkness that Lucifer had tried to infect into her.

"Father?" Adam said with a spark of concern.

A growl started deep in his chest. His hand rose to his lip and wiped away the faint smear of blood. "I see that I will still have to break you. And I look forward to doing just that."

She heard the grin in his voice when she ran her tongue over her lip, tasting the sharp copper tang of blood. Lucifer's blood.

That single motion set a spark along the fuse that linked her marks. Something moved and buzzed just under her skin, like a powder keg ready to blow. It energized every muscle in her body, powering her with heat that rose with every beat of her heart. This was the power of God, so much more than the archangels or the seraph. And she knew exactly what she had to do with it.

Nikka pushed herself up to her feet, her spine clicking into place as she straightened her shoulders and faced Lucifer. The smell of the ash had vanished. The Devil's icy chill no longer plagued her flesh. Nothing could penetrate the shield of power that now flowed over her body. Even her sadness and despair had been replaced with hope that she could change all of this.

Belphagor turned to her, his brow creased as he looked at her. "Master—" he said, half turning to Lucifer.

The Harbinger power overflowed into a green light that appeared in her pupils.

Lucifer glanced to Belphagor and then to Nikka. She took in a deep breath and unzipped the jacket, letting it fall to the ground. The circled tattoos on her forearms glowed a brilliant green, the marks spinning in clockwise turns. The shimmers of light glittered from them as she held out her arms.

"Mother?" Adam spoke and stepped toward her. "What is happening to you?"

A flash of a protective shield expanded around her body, emanating from the marks on her arms. The power now calmed her soul even though Lucifer's lips peeled back into a grimace of terror and anger. His once calm and sophisticated demeanor turned into desperation, but this did nothing to stir the peace in her soul.

The human mask that the Devil wore burned away as the beast inside of him tore free. "Harbinger! Impossible." Large black spiraled horns rose from his black and oily flesh. Great orbs of red, orange and violet light swirled in his eyes above a gaping mouth of glassy teeth. He roared and lunged at her, but she remained protected behind her shield. No amount of Hell-rage could break through it now. Not through a guard created by the Angel of Apocalypse. Belphagor even changed into a monstrous form she had seen from him before, and he pounced at her, clawing and gnawing at her shield.

The power burned through her and inside of her, sending out swirls of green and white light that surrounded all of them. She urged her will into it, and it obeyed with ease. Nikka had no idea how it would happen, but the power flowed through her and followed her urge to comply. She was the Angel of Apocalypse, and this is how everything would change.

She knew she could stop the Devil himself or stop the end of creation.

The light grew into a blinding force that filled the theater. She no longer saw with her human eyes but with the sight of a god. It burned through everything that stood in the casino, expanding out in a rapid burst of power. The screams of everything that it consumed fell silent into her perfect ears. Her chest stopped moving; there was no need to breathe any longer.

This was the place of light and peace, this brief time of silence and hope. The time before she could right what had gone wrong.

She found the moment that needed to be changed. With one sigh, she pulled the energy to her core and twisted the fabric of time.

CHAPTER 49

NIKKA

---

*T*he white, warm light cradled Nikka's body, hanging in suspension within the silence, but she knew this would only be temporary, for she had set the powers in motion to change the course of time. This was but a reprieve before the real test began.

The pain came first, a lance of stabbing and aching that started in her spine. Her lungs burned for air, and she fought to take a breath, but her ribs wouldn't move. The spasm followed in her chest and the air finally moved into her throat. She had tried to prepare for this in the few seconds she had in the light.

Nikka's eyes flashed open with the first gasp of air. This must be how a newborn feels when it first enters the world. Her back arched with the painful breath and she lifted her head from where she lay.

Dull gray light shone down on her through rain-spattered windows behind her head. The room where she lay was otherwise dark except for the light of the oncoming storm just outside the window. But it still hurt her eyes, and she squinted against it. The blur of waking up after what just happened left the room spinning, and she couldn't stop it.

"It's okay," a woman's voice spoke, and a hand grasped hers as she reached out for something—anything—to stop the spinning. "It was just a bad dream."

A figure moved in front of her, a blur of pink and yellow that formed a pattern of flowers as the woman stepped closer. The scent of sterilizing hand wash wafted over her, a smell with which she had become too familiar not long ago. The hand squeezed her palm, and the figure leaned next to Nikka, easing her head down on something soft. A pillow.

She blinked her eyes, hoping to clear the blur and it started to work. Nikka took in another breath, but it made her sternum ache. That's when she noticed the puffs of air that streamed into her nostrils from something pressed against her face.

The fingers of her free hand fumbled toward the thing under her nose. A thin line, cold and firm, trailed behind her ears and to her nostrils. Puff. Puff.

"There we go," the woman spoke again, her hand still holding Nikka's. "We'll increase the oxygen just a little. That might help."

Nikka blinked her eyes again, and the room came into view. Layers of sterile white blankets covered her where she lay. Everything was far too familiar, though. Dark blue walls dotted with pictures of far-away landscapes. A door opened to a hallway painted in murals of children's fables and lit with bright fluorescent lights. Beeping machines just behind her head that would sometimes sound an alarm if needed. She turned her head despite the ache it caused in her neck. The woman beside her leaned over the white plastic railing and fumbled with the oxygen lines that snaked toward Nikka's nose.

Her face, her eyes and long dark hair. A person she hadn't seen in almost two years. Someone she never thought she would see again.

"Caroline?" she said, but the sound came out choked.

"Yeah, sweetie," the nurse said. "I'm here. Like I said, it was just a nightmare. Your oxygen levels are coming up just fine now."

It was true. She pulled her hand free of the nurse's grip and held it up to the dull light of the window. Bone and sinew protruded just under the thin layer of pale skin. Her fingers trembled as she placed her fingertips on her face, trailing up toward her temple. Just cold, empty skin. No hair.

"Are you cold?" Caroline asked. "I can get a stocking hat for you."

"No," she said, more urgent than she had meant it. "Don't bother."

The Harbinger power had worked, but she knew there was no way that she could have prepared for it. But this was the only thing that could work. This was where it all started, and where it all went wrong.

"Is everything okay?" another voice came from the doorway.

That voice. Yes, she would be here. Just like she was on that day originally.

"Mom?" Nikka said when she saw her standing there, her shawl over her shoulders and a paper cup of coffee in one hand. Tears flooded her eyes, and she could no longer see her.

"Oh, honey," she said, and her mother approached, but all she saw was a blur of color. "Did you just wake up?"

Her hand slipped into Nikka's. Her mother settled into the chair next to the bed.

"Yeah," Nikka said and cleared her throat. "I guess I did. Crazy dreams."

"The pain medications can do that," the nurse said and stepped away from the bed. "Mrs. Connors, just let me know if you need anything else. I'll be down the hall."

Her mother nodded and then glanced back. Nikka couldn't stop staring. This wasn't Death masquerading as her mother. No. She was the real deal, the smell of her orange blossom hand lotion and everything.

"I just went to the cafeteria to get a coffee. I promise I wasn't gone long," her mother said with a smile.

Nikka pulled in a ragged breath. "Oh, but I was."

She forced a laugh. "I'm sure it felt that way. You know what the medications do to you."

"I know, but it was so long, you don't even know."

Fatigue settled into her bones, something that she had forgotten. It didn't take much activity to weaken her system when she had been like this. Even just a conversation could drain her, and this was all certainly enough activity to do it.

Her eyelids grew heavy, probably from the medication dripping into the IV. But she didn't want to fall asleep now. There wasn't much time left, because this was the day that everything changed. This was the day that she was supposed to die.

"Well, your dad is coming after work," her mother said and placed Nikka's hand over her abdomen. "So, try and get some rest, okay?"

Nikka's weak fingers felt along her torso, and she glanced down. Her bony hands and arms looked so foreign, and no marks adorned her skin. No tattoos. They had all disappeared into the light. Her fingers twitched as she felt along the concave structure of her abdomen. Empty. Devoid of any further sign of life. This body had never been pregnant, and never would.

She tried to hold back the tears again and turned her head away from her mother. Maybe she wouldn't see it. Her mother couldn't understand, and if she tried to explain, it would just be another hallucination brought on by chemo and pain meds. Adam was gone and would never exist.

Nikka closed her eyes as tears flowed down her cheek and wet the linen of the pillow. The puffs of oxygen blowing into her nose lulled her enough, and mixed with the drugs, her mind settled into darkness, but it wasn't frightening. Behind her eyelids, she saw Jason and Gideon, and they were happy. Amy was there with her own son, Dylan, and they greeted her like old friends. And in her arms, she carried her beautiful baby, just as he was on those warm, sunny days on the shores of Belize. Innocent and wonderful.

A sound stirred her awake, and she blinked open her eyes, but the room had grown darker. The sky outside had turned to evening, but the rain pounded harder on the window behind her bed. Muffled voices cleared as she forced herself against the will of the drugs and tried to wake up.

"Mrs. Connors," a man's voice came from somewhere in the room. "I am Dr. Smith, and I was sent to consult on your daughter."

Nikka would know that voice anywhere, with his thinly veiled accent. She craned around and pulled herself onto her back from where she lay on her side. The small floodlights around the room illuminated his form from where he stood in the doorway.

Smooth, dark skin. Those hazel eyes that could see into a soul. His shaved head. And everything camouflaged in scrubs and a white coat and fake glasses.

The racing of her heart registered on the monitor. When he looked at her, he did so for the first time in his life. He had no idea who she was, or who he was to her.

"Well, I guess I wasn't expecting anybody else to see her," her mother said. "We spoke with hospice this morning, and they're arranging a transfer to home tomorrow. Dr. Taylor said there was nothing left to do."

Nikka tried to lift herself up, to see him better in the low light of the room, but her arms had grown too weak.

"I came as a treatment consultant. I spoke with Dr. Taylor last night and provided him with some new information that has recently been released. This is a breakthrough treatment with remarkable success." Gideon sounded so official. He had tried hard to convince her mother even then to take her daughter.

"It's okay, mom," Nikka said. Her finger found the button on the railing to lift the head of the bed. As it moved her upright, she couldn't take her eyes off of him. "I need to talk to him."

Gideon looked at her with surprise and stuffed his hands into the pockets of his white coat. She had forgotten the gold-rimmed glasses he wore when they first met, and how ridiculous they looked on him now.

"Okay," her mother said and stepped with Gideon into the room.

"Alone," Nikka said with a weak smile, "if it's okay."

Her mother lost her smile. "All right. I'll be back in five minutes, though. Okay?"

"Sure." Nikka nodded and watched her turn and walk out the door.

Gideon stepped up to the side of the bed and looked down on her. She could get lost in those eyes if she watched him for too long, and she might not have the strength to do what she had to do. Already, she had changed things from the way they went that night.

"I have a cure," he said, leaning down. The smell of the soap on his skin flooded her senses, and she wanted to bathe in it for as long as she could. And every second that ticked by made it so much harder. "I can take away your illness forever."

She licked her dry lips and lifted her hand, placing it on his cheek. He flinched at first, surprised at her forwardness.

"I know you can," she said, even that statement enough to make her out of breath. "And I wish I could accept it."

A knot formed in her chest and tears flooded her eyes again. His brow furrowed with the same look of concern he always got when he worried about her.

"But I'm not the one you're looking for."

His hand touched hers, and he leaned closer. "You do not understand. You will die tonight if you do not accept this cure."

"I know," she said, each word getting harder to say. "At 10:37 pm."

He took in a quick breath and leaned back again. "How do you know—"

"It's not important. Just know that there is someone else out there who is more deserving of this. I can't do what you want of me. I was never supposed to be the one. You must find the right one, and his name is Jason."

He tried to step back but her bony fingers clasped on his hand. She would never see him again after this, and it was too hard to let go.

"But I thank you for everything. I want to be there with you for everything that happens. To both of you. Just know that I will do everything that I can to watch over you. Forever."

The tears burned in her eyes. She pulled him closer, and he leaned down to allow her to whisper to him. "Thank you."

Fatigue overtook her again, and she could no longer hold onto him. Gideon pulled away, his eyes glistening as he stared at her.

Sleep grew closer, taking away any energy she had left. She forced her eyes open one more time. Just to see him once before he left. He stood at her bedside, his hand trembling and pulling the glasses from his face.

"Have we met before, Miss?" he asked, a spark of recognition in his eyes.

"Not before today," she said and swallowed the lump that had formed in her throat. "But the adventures we would have had." Her lids grew heavy and the drug pulsed through her veins again. His form blurred in her eyes just before the last words left her lips. "The monsters we would have seen."

CHAPTER 50

GIDEON

---

*T*he girl closed her eyes, this young woman he had been sent to collect. Nikola Connors. Nikka, to her friends and family. A young woman dying of leukemia and would surely not live to see the sunrise.

Never had a candidate refused the offer that he would have proposed to her. And yet, this woman staring down death gave up her option to live.

A throat cleared at the doorway, catching his attention. Although his heart raced as he looked at the girl, he put his glasses back on his face and turned to see the mother standing there.

"Everything okay?" she asked as she approached the bedside.

His thoughts were flustered, jumbled in a mess of confusion. "Uh, yes. It seems your daughter is not a candidate. I am truly sorry."

The woman's hopeful gaze fell, and she settled into the chair beside the bed.

"Well," she said with a sniff, bringing a wrinkled tissue to her nose, "I guess we are getting used to the bad news."

She averted his gaze, but he could not make his legs move. Something still drew him to this girl, now sleeping in the bed. The woman cried over her dying daughter, and it pulled at whatever humanity he still had left inside of him.

"I am sorry, ma'am," he said, "but have I met you or your daughter before?"

She looked back up at him, her eyes glistening. "I don't remember you, I'm sorry."

Gideon nodded, but it still nagged at him. He forced his feet to move and pull away from the room. The woman never looked back at him, but he watched the sleeping girl as he backed out of the doorway. So frail and weak. It was a miracle she had made it this far.

He had met enough of the sick and dying to know that they would often ramble about hallucinations and false memories, but her words still haunted him. This young woman had a spiritual insight he had never experienced, as though she knew so much more than she said. Every step he took away from her room and toward the elevator bank pained him. She was the next seraph; he was sure of it. He had never made a mistake in his whole of existence. The message was not garbled. Nikka Connors was the next chosen one.

How could she have refused?

He stepped into the elevator, and the doors closed, leaving him in solitude. He pulled the glasses from his face and stuffed them into the pocket of his fake lab coat.

But she knew far too much. She knew the exact time of her death. And she spoke of monsters.

The ding of the button panel caught his attention, and the doors opened. The sounds of people shuffling in the evening hours at the hospital lobby did little to distract him. He drifted through the lobby and out into the damp night, his thoughts still pulled to the woman in the cancer ward.

A hollow formed in his chest the further he walked away from the hospital, as though he left behind something that belonged to him. Something that he loved more than anything. And it was going to be taken away from him forever. But how could that be? He did not know that girl or her family, so why did it hurt so much to walk away?

Gideon wandered as the night wore on and he settled into the park bench, the bright sodium lamps shining down on him. Maybe it would just take time to ease the difficulty of a candidate who had refused. He had never experienced something like this before, but he felt physical pain in his chest that only worsened as the hours ticked further on.

His fists clenched tight, and he forced himself to his feet. No. He could not let himself fall into this spiral of thoughts and emotions. That was never his job. He was only to seek the next seraph, and that is just what he would do. Gideon stood and took in a deep breath, the damp air filling his lungs. Maybe that would be enough to fill the hollow in his chest. Maybe it would ease the pain.

He pulled the coat from his shoulders and wadded it into his hands before he dumped it into the trash can at the edge of the park. No more of this charade. It was no longer needed, after all. He squared his shoulders and moved through the dark toward the bright streets of the downtown. Cars still buzzed by on the weekend night, filling the city with life and light even if he could not feel it. Just get back in the car and make it to the monastery, he thought. Tomorrow will bring a new candidate. Hopefully.

He stepped to the curb of the crosswalk with a host of other people waiting for the signal to walk, but his thoughts still drifted back to the girl in the hospital. Her touch lingered on his fingers, something that felt so familiar.

The beep of the signal sounded, and the crowd moved into the crosswalk. He almost did not hear it, but the brush of someone's shoulder stirred him from his thoughts. Gideon stepped off the curb behind the crowd.

A bright flash of a light almost blinded him, and then the bumper of a car smashed into him, sending him tumbling into the street. The pavement struck the back of his head as he landed, and the rain-soaked street bled through the back of his shirt where he lay.

Voices sounded hollow in his ears. So many people milling about him and his head swirled in dizziness and pain.

"Mister," a woman's voice called out to him, but she sounded so far away. "Hey, are you okay?"

"Damn, dude." A man's voice spoke as he approached. "I'm sorry. I didn't see you there."

Gideon opened his eyes, but the lights above him blurred in and out. Voices spilled all around him now.

"Someone call an ambulance."

"Don't move him."

"Hey buddy," another man said, his voice close and his hand pressed to Gideon's shoulder. "You doing okay?"

Gideon forced his eyes to focus, and he saw the man kneeling beside him. His blonde hair fell long along his shoulders. Poignant blue eyes stared down at him, and he smiled below a blonde goatee that accented dimples in his cheeks.

"What happened?" Gideon said and tried to sit up, but the man pressed on his shoulder.

"Whoa there," he said. "Just take it easy. You were just hit by a car."

Pain throbbed from the back of his head, but it was nothing that would not heal in a day's time. He sat up despite the man's urges. People milled around him now, voices chattering and trying to talk to him and each other all at once. Everyone but this man, who focused on him.

"Think you can walk?" he said to Gideon.

Gideon nodded, and the man held out his hand to help him to his feet. The man kept a grip on Gideon's arm, however, as he walked him to the benches under the bus stop awning. He knelt in front of Gideon, looking him over.

Rain had spattered on the man's leather jacket and the motorcycle helmet he held in his hand.

"I guess someone called 911," he said to Gideon with a smile. "An ambulance will be here soon."

The way he talked, the lilt of his voice and the slightest hint of a grumble in his voice from a history of tobacco use, it too sounded familiar.

"Do I know you?" Gideon said, rubbing the back of his head.

"I don't think so," the man said but his brow furrowed. "But you look familiar to me, too. I work in the college library. Maybe I've seen you there."

Gideon introduced himself, his hand held out to him.

"Jason," he said and shook his hand.

The name echoed in his ringing ears. The chance that he would be hit in a crosswalk and a bystander there that he recognized was too much to ignore. This made his head hurt even more. Nikka. Jason. Why did this stir memories he could not possibly remember?

"You okay?" Jason said. "You look like you're ready to throw up."

"No, I am not okay," Gideon said and stood.

"Take it, easy man. You could have a head injury."

"None of this is okay." Gideon paced under the awning while Jason watched him. He stopped and looked up at Jason. "Do you know what déjà vu is?"

Jason raised a curious eyebrow. "Yeah. Like when you are sure you have lived something before? Have you been hit by a car before? That's just really bad luck—"

"That is not what I mean." He moved toward Jason and placed his hands on his shoulders. "I mean that I know you. You know me, but we do not remember how. I have met someone else tonight that I know, too. That cannot just be a coincidence."

Déjà vu. A phenomenon that was all too real, even if humans had no idea what it meant. Usually, it did not affect him because it was a result of something done by the angels, and a human would not be able to know the difference. But it could never happen to him. He knew what the angels did behind the scenes. They never altered him.

But this was unmistakable déjà vu. Someone had changed it enough, could they have even altered time? Did someone change the natural course of things, beyond what the archangels could do?

A well of nausea started in his gut. "Does the name Nikka mean anything to you?"

Jason's brow furrowed, and a spark of recognition bloomed in his eyes. "Sounds familiar, but I'm sure I don't know anyone by that name."

His knees grew weak. That girl had done something. She knew far more about her fate than she should have, and now time was trying to correct what had been done. She had even told him the name of the next seraph. Jason.

Could this be the man she meant? How would she have known, unless she was the architect of it all?

His heart raced, and he looked down at his watch. 10:17 pm. Twenty minutes and she would be lost, and then he could never save her. The same fire in his chest that urged him to find her blossomed again. That was his destiny. He had to save her before she was lost forever.

"What is it?" Jason said. "You look like you've seen a ghost."

"I may have," he said and looked up to him. "And I may have left her. She's dying, and I am the only one who can stop it."

"Who's dying?"

"I have to stop it from happening. She knows. She knows about all of us. I have to get to her." He glanced around for his car, but he had no idea where he even was anymore.

"Okay, dude," Jason said and patted his arm. "I have a bike. I can take you where you need to go."

Maybe he had sensed Gideon's desperation, but Jason showed him to his motorcycle. Despite the urges from the people that still milled around the crosswalk, they rode away as the distant sirens of an ambulance neared the accident site.

Gideon rode behind him, his hands clasped to Jason's jacket as they approached the hospital across the park. He did not have time to explain what was going on, but Jason followed anyway. They ran to the elevator bank and stepped out onto the cancer ward. He remembered the room number, his breath catching in his throat as he tried to think of what to say to her.

They approached the room, and he stopped short when he gazed at the empty bed in the center of the room. A pile of blankets and linens were bunched on the mattress. Abandoned.

The hollow started in his chest again, and he looked at his watch. 10:21. No. It was too soon. She cannot be gone yet.

A nurse passed by them, and Jason got her attention. "Hey, my friend is looking for someone who was in here earlier."

The nurse looked at Gideon. "Dr. Smith? Yes, I remember you."

Gideon tried to slow his heart rate, and he turned to her, his clothes still wet from lying in the street. "Where is she? The patient that was here."

"Connors," she said, and the ghost of sadness passed over her face. "They arranged for hospice to take her home tonight."

"But that was not supposed to happen until tomorrow."

"I know. But Nikka insisted that she wanted to go home tonight."

Gideon felt his legs weaken and he leaned back against the door frame.

Jason glanced at Gideon and the nurse. "Could he get an address, maybe?"

The nurse gave him a stern look. "I can only give it to the doctor."

"That's all he needs."

She turned away from him but not before looking back at Gideon. She returned with a slip of paper with an address scrawled in her handwriting.

"Thank you," Jason said, but she walked away without a word to him. He read the address and looked up at Gideon. "It's not far. We could get there in about ten minutes. I'll drive you 'cause you got me intrigued now."

With Jason's urging, they rushed back out of the hospital and onto his motorcycle. The air had grown cold with the falling rain, and it stung his face as they rode through the night, winding through city streets. Jason tried to avoid the traffic lights, but one light stopped them. The pounding of his heart in his chest gave Gideon pain as he watched that red light, but Jason throttled the bike as soon as it turned.

They rode to the outskirts of the city and into a suburb where the porch lights still shone into the night. Rain glistened on the freshly mowed grass that carpeted manicured lawns and gardens.

Jason stopped the bike before a house where lights shone through the front windows. Gideon stepped from the motorcycle before it completely stopped, and he rushed through the front gate and down the walk.

He did not care what he would say when they would open the door. It did not matter. She was dying, and he could save her. They could not stop him.

Gideon ran up the steps to the porch and pounded his fist on the door. He pounded, again and again, harder each time. There was not time for formalities.

A footstep sounded on the floor beyond the door. The lock latch clicked. The door creaked open, and Gideon stood straight, ready to force his way into this house and save the dying girl within its walls. And then he would find out what she had done with time, and why she ever did it at all.

Soft golden light poured from a lamp in the atrium, illuminating the form of the woman he had met at the hospital. Her mother.

But she could barely stand, her hand trembling and clutched to her mouth. Tears streamed down her face from red-streaked eyes. Her shoulders shuddered with her sobs, and Gideon's gaze drifted to the grandfather clock in the room behind her, the minute hand ticking past 10:38.

About the Author

When she isn't delivering babies, **Carrie Merrill** is a prolific writer who has put pen to paper since the age of 8, when she wrote her first story about a dragon that lived in a cave across the river from her house in Idaho. A day has not gone by since that time when she didn't have a story floating around in her head. Her widely-read and praised series, Her 4 volume Angel Blade Series received great praise. Her other book, *The Key, The Outlaw and The Treasure*, is an exciting YA novel that takes place in the old West and is filled with adventure and anger. She is currently a full-time OB/GYN in Wyoming with her six rescue cats when she isn't writing about the things that lurk in the dark.